Each Time We Love

SHIRLEE BUSBEE

Each Time We Love

AVON BOOKS ◆ NEW YORK

They say that all things come to those who wait, and while I don't know for sure that these dear ones have been waiting for this, it's high time that they finally got their very own dedication. And so, this book is affectionately dedicated to the following:

Our very dear friends and neighbors for nearly thirty years, Henry and Lillie Thiessen. Yes, Lillie, the horse babies are doing just fine; and, Henry, Howard is waiting impatiently for you to come up so he can show his latest junk—er, treasures!

And one of our favorites pairs of in-laws, William and Martha Busbee. Bill, God still loves you best; and, Marty, keep weaving those blankets!

And, of course, who else, Howard, *still* the very best friend and husband a woman could have!

Prologue

False Fortune

Spanish Texas, Fall, 1804

Oh, breathe not his name! let it sleep in the shade,
Where cold and unhonour'd his relics are laid.

IRISH MELODIES
Thomas Moore

THIS HAD NOT BEEN A GOOD TRADING EXPEDITION FOR Jeremy Childers—his partner was dead, and instead of the riches they'd planned on reaping this trip, Jeremy's reward for nearly a year's efforts was one old wind-broken horse. Considering the past few weeks, Jeremy guessed he was damned lucky to have that!

Giving up any further pretense of sleep on the hard ground, he scratched for the ever-present fleas and lice; after squashing a particularly persistent flea between his dirty fingers, he sat up, cursing the day he had ever crossed the Sabine River into Spanish Texas. Resentfully he stared at the scarlet dawn beginning to break over the canyon rim, his moody thoughts on just how *very* bad the scheme to trade with the Indians had been. He should have listened to Yates and not that fool Haley!

It had seemed such an excellent idea when he and his partner, Orval Haley, had first discussed it in the winter of 1803. They had been sitting in a darkened corner in one of the many dens of vice with which

Natchez-under-the-Hill abounded, and both of them had been more than half drunk. But in the morning, despite their aching heads, the scheme to slip undetected into Spanish Texas to trade with the Indians for horses had seemed like a sure way to enhance their meager finances. And an unexpected stroke of luck had settled the matter: not two nights later, they had stumbled over a drunken riverboat captain and, not a pair to overlook opportunity, a swift rifling of the man's pockets had brought into their possession a tidy sum.

With never a backward look, they had used their stolen gains to purchase the supplies and horses and mules needed for their venture. Very early in 1804, the pack animals loaded down with all sorts of brightly colored cloth and trinkets with which to tempt the Indians, the partners had slipped across the border into the jealously guarded Spanish territory and headed west. West to make their fortunes!

Luck appeared to be with them in the beginning, and by early fall they were happily congratulating themselves on the large herd of horses that they had amassed to sell at exorbitant prices in Louisiana. They expected no trouble smuggling the animals safely across the Mississippi River and were already discussing the riotous time they would have in New Orleans, spending their money on liquor and fancy women.

Unfortunately, it was then that they had allowed their innate greed to overcome what common sense they possessed. Word of a band of Comanches, the Kwerhar-rehnuh, or the "Antelopes," who were rumored to be the possessors of unlimited herds of horses, reached the two traders. The fact that these Indians were known to be the wildest and fiercest of all the bands of the Comanches did not deter the two men, nor did the fact that the Antelopes were situated deep in the remote windswept ranges of the

Llano Estacado. The only thing that Jeremy and Orval could think about was all those horses. . . .

Finding a secluded canyon with plenty of grass and water in which to corral their herd of horses until they returned from the Comanches with more horses was simple enough to do, and it was then that things started to go wrong for them. They were busily erecting a barrier across the only entrance into the canyon when a Spanish patrol stumbled across them. Since they were caught by surprise, there was never any question of the outcome. All their possessions were promptly confiscated and a Spanish jail looked to be their residence for quite some time. But their luck seemed to hold. As the group came closer to the small settlement of Nacogdoches, the Spaniards grew careless and Jeremy and Orval were able to slip away one night with a pair of horses and a couple of mules still laden with the remainder of their trading supplies. The next morning they watched glumly from the concealment of a canebrake as, after a cursory search for the escaped prisoners, the Spaniards shrugged and rode away, driving in front of them the horse herd that Jeremy and Orval had spent months acquiring.

Their fortune disappearing in a cloud of dust, Jeremy and Orval decided to waste little time in finding the Kwerhar-rehnuh. Which turned out to be the very worst idea they had ever had, Jeremy thought resentfully now as he bit into a hard biscuit. Again Yates's words came back to haunt him: "Are you crazy?" Yates had demanded in Natchez when he and Haley had originally thought to cut him in on their scheme. "You think you're going to get rich, but I'll tell you what's really going to happen—you'll both end up dead and your bones will lie bleaching on the plains! Trading horses with Comanches! Fool notion if I ever heard one!"

Yates was right, Jeremy thought dejectedly, and Orval should have listened to me after we lost our

horses, when I told him that we should go back to
Natchez! But no, Jeremy mused with a bitter twist to
his mouth, he said we could recoup everything if
we'd just show a little grit! Well, that "grit" had
served Orval precious little when that Comanche
buck lifted his hair! Jeremy decided spitefully.

Swallowing the last of his stale biscuit, he kicked
his bedroll together and methodically saddled his
horse. It didn't do any good ruminating about what
they *should* have done, but as he swung up onto his
horse, he couldn't help but think that Orval had been
a damn fool for trying to cheat those Comanches at
dice. Which, of course, had precipitated Orval's
scalping and his own frantic escape from camp.

Remembering Orval's dying scream, Jeremy shuddered and glanced nervously over his shoulder, fearing to see a bloodthirsty band of warriors bearing
down on him. He'd seen no sign of them for two
days now, and thankfully, all that met his gaze were
the soaring walls and rock-strewn floor of the canyon. Which didn't exactly reassure him—he was lost
in the seemingly impenetrable maze of cottonwood-
dotted arroyos and jagged walled canyons.

Doggedly he urged his horse into a trot. Keep
moving, he told himself grimly; keep moving, and
sooner or later you'll find a place that looks familiar!

The sun was blazing over the rim of the canyon by
now, and to his growing excitement, Jeremy saw that
just ahead of him the canyon appeared to open onto
a rocky, brush-spotted plain. Jubilant that he had finally found his way out of the aimlessly wandering
canyons, he was on the point of kicking his plodding
horse into a swifter pace when the stillness was broken by the chilling, agonized scream of a man in
mortal pain. Jerking his horse to a standstill, Jeremy
first thought his imagination was playing tricks on
him—that it was the memory of Orval's final shriek
that rang so terrifyingly in his ears. And yet . . .

Face white, he reached with trembling fingers for

the battered old rifle secured on the cantle of his saddle. Swinging down from his horse, he swiftly tied
the animal and stealthily crept near the mouth of the
canyon. Concealed by a jumble of tumbled rocks, he
cautiously peered around one of the big boulders.

His breath stopped and his heart banged painfully
at the sight that met his eyes. Not a hundred feet in
front of him, a naked man lay spread-eagled on the
plain, and standing over him with a bloodstained
knife was the most magnificent and frightening savage Jeremy Childers had ever seen. Tall and powerfully built, with bronzed hawklike features, the
Indian wore his lustrous black hair, which shone with
blue lights in thick braids—but it was the sunlight
glinting on the bloodied knife that held Jeremy's
fearfully fascinated gaze. He couldn't tear his eyes
away from the knife, so shocked was he by the sight
before him that it never occurred to him to lift his rifle and fire.

In stunned terror, Jeremy watched as the Indian,
with never a backward glance at his victim, effortlessly leaped onto his horse and rode away. Even after the Indian had disappeared, Jeremy remained
frozen in his hiding place, his heart pumping at a
frantic rate, his mouth dry with fear.

Eventually Jeremy gathered his shattered courage,
and after a thorough scrutiny of the area, retrieved
his horse and walked over to where the man lay.
Staring down at the pitiful wreck that remained,
Jeremy blanched.

Jesus Christ! he thought sickly as his gaze moved
over the mutilated body. It was obvious that the man
had been staked here for a while, and equally obvious that he had suffered greatly before the Indian
had inflicted the final terrible wound—castration.

I wonder what the poor devil did to deserve such
a fate, Jeremy wondered, his curiosity stirring. From
the signs, it was apparent that the Indian had deliberately waited and watched for some days before de-

ciding to strike the final blow. Again Jeremy's gaze briefly touched the naked man. A Spaniard, he decided, noting the black hair and swarthy skin. The ruined features still showed a faint vestige of a once-handsome face, but even in death there was a disagreeable air of arrogance about the man. No peon, Jeremy thought as he stood there considering the dead man. Some fancy hidalgo must have crossed the wrong Indian.

His courage returning, Jeremy glanced around again. In front of him, nothing but the vastness of the plains met his gaze, and behind him, he knew, lay the twisting canyons with their incredible spires and pinnacles. A fine-looking horse wearing a saddle lavishly inlaid with silver was loosely tethered nearby, and Jeremy guessed it had belonged to the Spaniard. He sighed. Except for the corpse at his feet and the two horses, he was alone.

There wasn't anything that he could do for the man, and he decided that since the Spaniard's horse and saddle looked a damn sight better than his own, there was nothing to stop him from improving his lot. He turned away, his boot heel crunching on the uneven ground.

"Blood Drinker?" croaked a voice behind him. His eyes widening in disbelief, Jeremy spun around to stare at what he had thought was a dead man.

Incredibly, the poor wretch was still alive! Dropping down beside him, Jeremy quickly cut loose the rawhide that bound the man. "What did you say?" he asked.

The Spaniard stiffened. "Who are you?" he gasped.

Jeremy hesitated, not trusting even a dying Spaniard, but it was obvious that the man would not live more than a few moments longer. "Jeremy Childers," he answered. "Who are you?"

"Blas Davalos!"

The effort to say even his name exhausted the man,

and Jeremy waited a second before asking, "Who did this to you? I saw that big Indian buck ride away."

The blackened lips twisted into a snarl and Davalos muttered painfully, "Jason Savage . . . Blood Drinker murdered . . . me!"

The names meant nothing to Jeremy, and swiftly reaching for his canteen, he poured a little water onto the man's lips. Greedily Davalos drank the precious moisture. The water appeared to momentarily revive him, for his voice grew stronger and he said, "Savage must be punished!" Weakening again, he added feebly, "Find him . . . New Orleans or . . . plantation, Terre du Coeur."

Having no intention of involving himself in Davalos's vendetta, but knowing that time was running out for the man, Jeremy said soothingly, "I'll do what I can." Bluntly he added, "Is there anyone you want me to tell of your death?"

Davalos nodded faintly. "Daughter . . . bastard," he gasped. "Savanna O'Rourke. Crow's Nest. Stack Island."

Jeremy's eyebrows raised. He was familiar with Crow's Nest and he was surprised that this Spaniard's daughter lived there. Situated fifty miles north of Walnut Hills, it was well known as a hideout and gathering place for all sorts of unsavory men.

Davalos seemed to lose consciousness, and Jeremy, oddly loath to leave the dying man, hunkered down beside him to wait uneasily for the end. But the Spaniard was not done yet, and he suddenly thrashed about and muttered fiercely, "I must find the gold! The map! Jason knows!"

It was obvious that Davalos was raving, but at the word "gold," Jeremy's interest became acute. Avarice gleaming in his blue eyes, he leaned nearer the dying man. "Gold?" he questioned softly. "What gold?"

"Nolan's golden armband . . . I killed him . . . hid it! Savanna will have it. . . ."

Jeremy's eyes widened. A golden armband! His interest fully whetted, and impatient with the man's ramblings, Jeremy murmured eagerly into Davalos's ear, "Tell me about the gold."

"It's here! It's mine!" Davalos panted feverishly. "Mine! Aztec treasure! They found it, but it's mine— all *mine!*" He had barely stopped speaking when there was a funny little rattle deep in his throat and he lay very still.

"Here?" Jeremy yelped, glancing around at the bleak landscape. "What do you mean it's here? Where?"

There was no answer from Davalos, and reaching out to touch him, to shake him, Jeremy knew the instant his fingers had touched him that Davalos was dead. Disgustedly Jeremy stared at the dead man. Now, why couldn't he have lived just a few minutes longer? Now I have to go find that daughter of his to figure out what she knows, and then I'm going to have to find this Jason Savage! As for the Indian, Blood Drinker . . . Remembering the tall savage as he had stood over Davalos's naked body with the bloodied knife in his hand, Jeremy shuddered. No. He wouldn't go looking for Blood Drinker. Savanna O'Rourke or Jason Savage should be able to tell him what he wanted to know.

Already speculating on ways to make Savanna tell him about the treasure, Jeremy walked over to Davalos's horse. Deciding that the obviously well-bred animal was a vast improvement over his own sorry mount, he quickly transferred his rifle and bedroll to the dead man's horse. Whistling tunelessly, he swung up into the saddle. Taking one last look at Davalos's corpse, he concluded gleefully that maybe this hadn't been such a bad trading trip after all. Wait until he told Yates! He glanced around the vast landscape. An Aztec treasure, huh? A treasure just waiting for someone to find it. . . .

Leading his old wind-broken horse, he kicked the Spaniard's mount into a swift trot, his thoughts busy on how he was going to find Savanna O'Rourke and, er, *convince* her to tell him all she knew about the Aztec gold. And then there was always Jason Savage.... Confident that his luck had finally changed for the better, he was eager to leave the Spanish territory and begin his search for the golden treasure.

But fickle fate wasn't quite through with Jeremy Childers; three days later he rode smack into another Spanish patrol. Worse, this particular patrol had been led by a lieutenant named Blas Davalos—a lieutenant who had mysteriously disappeared with a Cherokee named Blood Drinker....

Davalos's men had been searching for their vanished commander for nearly a week, and though Jeremy vociferously protested his innocence of any wrongdoing, the fact that he was in Spanish Texas illegally and was riding Davalos's horse, with the lieutenant's prized silver inlaid saddle still on the animal, was damning evidence against him. Feeling the noose tightening around his neck, he frantically told them how he had come to possess Davalos's belongings. Sullenly they listened to his story, but it was obvious they did not fully believe him.

Even his eager, desperate cooperation in leading them to Davalos's body did not help him—it only seemed to increase their certainty that he had killed the lieutenant. As far as the temporary leader of the patrol was concerned, there was nothing to do but bury Davalos and leave for San Antonio with their prisoner. The officials there would decide what to do with the gringo.

All too soon Jeremy found himself locked in the adobe-walled jail in San Antonio, fearing that every day might be his last. For months he languished in his small cell while the Spanish officials argued and waited for word from Mexico City about what to do with him. And when word did finally arrive, Jeremy's heart sank—he was to be taken to Mexico City to be tried for the murder of Blas Davalos.

In Mexico City, his plight did not improve dramatically even though he was found innocent of killing the Spaniard. He was still a gringo and viewed with great suspicion by the Spanish. To his horror, he found himself sentenced to ten years in prison simply for having been in the country without permission and, of course, for stealing Davalos's horse and saddle.

Nearly a year later from the day he had first laid eyes on Davalos, as Jeremy stared morosely out of the barred window of his tiny cell, a cell that would be his home for ten long years, he viciously cursed a fate that had shown him the way to great riches and then had cruelly prevented him from seeking it.

But time will pass, he told himself grimly as he began to mark off with a pebble the days of his confinement on the walls of his prison. Time will pass and when it does ... A crafty smile curved his mouth. When it does, I'll be paying a visit to Savanna O'Rourke. . . .

Part 1

Fortune's Daughter

Spring, 1815

Come, send round the wine, and leave
points of belief
To simpleton sages, and reasoning fools.

IRISH MELODIES
Thomas Moore

Chapter 1

"SAVANNA, PUT THE DAMN RIFLE DOWN! YOU KNOW you're not going to shoot me!" The voice was huskily masculine and decidedly exasperated; the gleam in the dark eyes, however, was exceedingly warm. But then the sight of Savanna O'Rourke often brought a warm gleam to the eyes of most men, and Bodene Sullivan was no different—even if he was her cousin.

Standing merely an inch under six feet, endowed with the face and form of some ancient goddess, Savanna O'Rourke was undeniably a pulse-stirring sight as she stood there tall and proud in the late afternoon light of the Louisiana sun, the fading rays turning her glorious mane of waist-length, wavy redgold hair into a halo of fire that danced around her bewitchingly lovely features. Even the plain gown of brown homespun couldn't disguise the exquisitely formed body it clothed, her temptingly full breasts straining above the modest bodice, her narrow waist and womanly hips clearly defined under the coarse material. She was barefoot, her slender feet balancing easily on the old log on which she stood, strands of ghostly gray-green Spanish moss, hanging from a swamp cypress behind her, framing her head and shoulders. Few men remained *un*interested in her presence, but this morning, despite her sensual appeal, it was the long black rifle held so menacingly in her slim hands that was the object of Bodene's rapt attention.

When Savanna remained unmoved by his words, Bodene held out his arms placatingly and in his most coaxing tone, one that seldom failed him, said, "I promise, I haven't come to play any more tricks on you."

"*That's* what you said the last time!" Savanna O'Rourke snapped, the rifle holding steady. Not the least bit intimidated when confronted by a charming, powerfully built rascal who stood five inches over six feet, she threatened darkly, "I warned you, Bodene, that if you dared show your face around here again, I'd shoot you on sight!"

Bodene's handsome mouth quirked into a grin. "But you know you didn't mean it, sweetheart—you wouldn't shoot your only cousin, now would you!"

Savanna tried hard to resist that devilishly attractive grin and the wheedling note in his voice, but despite her avowed determination not to let Sullivan inveigle his way into her life again, she could feel herself weakening. Her aquamarine eyes narrowed. Sullivan was *not* going to slip under her guard this time! "Go away! Go back to New Orleans and your gaming house and fancy women! There is nothing here for you!"

"You're here," he growled unhappily, his glance taking in the dismal surroundings. His tall, broad-shouldered body garbed in form-fitting buckskin breeches, an elegantly cut dark blue jacket and an embroidered waistcoat, Bodene stood on a small landing with a roiling, muddy Mississippi River to his back; in front of him, behind Savanna, lay the dark, mysterious swamps; to his right, a pitiful cluster of dilapidated buildings was the only sign of human habitation. A few scrawny chickens scratched hopefully around the sagging porch of one of the dwellings, and a pristine sign declaring proudly "O'Rourke's Tavern," hung from the edge of a roof badly in need of repair. Behind the buildings Sullivan knew that there were more chickens, as well as some pigs and a skinny cow. His mouth twisted.

He *almost* wished the damned British had been able to penetrate this far north of New Orleans before the Americans had driven them back—he'd now be looking at a pile of burned rubble and Savanna wouldn't have any excuse to remain here. The only problem with that scenario, he admitted ruefully, was the fact that if the British *had* gotten this far inland, the Americans wouldn't have been the undisputed victors of the Battle of New Orleans and the War of 1812 wouldn't have ended on such a resoundingly triumphant note for the United States. But fortunately, in January of this year of 1815, the Americans *had* won the Battle of New Orleans, for which Bodene was inordinately thankful. He smiled grimly. He'd be even *more* thankful if he could now just convince Savanna to give up the ridiculous notion of eking out a living in this godforsaken stretch of no-man's land! If only she weren't so damned stubborn!

Distractedly running a hand through his rebellious black hair, he muttered, "I heard you had some trouble. A gambler came into my place recently and said he'd stopped by here on his way downriver and that some of Hare's old gang—Micajah Yates, to be exact—had paid you a visit and damn near wrecked the place."

"*Por Dios!* That has *nothing* to do with you!" she flashed back, outraged that he had assumed that she couldn't take care of herself, yet touched at the same time. But then that was typical of the feelings Bodene Sullivan aroused within her—nearly all her life she had been alternately torn between wanting to wring his neck and adoring him!

There were only six years between the cousins— Bodene was twenty-eight and Savanna had just turned twenty-two in February—and while their resemblance to each other was not marked, their kinship was apparent to most people in their impressive height, the stubborn curve of their jaws and the utterly mesmerizing charm of their flashing smiles. Their personalities were more alike than either would have been pleased to admit—both were hot-tempered, unbelievably obstinate and proud almost to the point of being arrogant, yet they were generous, quick to laugh and fiercely loyal. They had been raised together and they shared something more than just having grown up together—both were the children of men who had not seen fit to marry their mothers, and both had suffered because of it.

The bond between them was exceptionally strong, despite their frequent, loud and vociferous disagreements, and Bodene's eyes took on that bitter gleam Savanna knew of old as he said grimly, "It has *everything* to do with me and you damn well know it! How do you think it makes me feel to hear that a band of outlaws have been harassing you? *Especially* "Murdering" Micajah! You're up here all alone, miles from anywhere or anyone, and you just can't seem to understand that you might be in danger!"

Savanna's full mouth curved into a faint smile. "I'm not alone. Sam's with me."

"*Sam!*" Bodene bit out explosively. "What the hell good is Sam?"

"I'se a lot more good than I look, Mister Bo," claimed a soft voice, and an old, grizzle-haired black man stepped out from between the buildings, a rifle that could have been the twin of Savanna's held competently in his bony hands. In his youth Sam Bracken had been a magnificent specimen of manhood, tall and deep-chested, but now, at almost seventy-five years old, after a hard life spent working in the cane and cotton fields, he had an obvious frailty about him.

Bodene looked discomforted. When he was a child, Sam had outfoxed him and tanned his backside more times than he cared to think about. And despite his age, the old man would prove to be a surprisingly tough and tricky opponent if the need arose.

"Sorry, Sam—I didn't mean to belittle your abilities," Bodene apologized wryly. "It's just that I go half mad when I think of her up here, living God knows how! When she could be safe in New Orleans or with Elizabeth."

Savanna snorted. "Live with my mother? She might yearn for respectability, but it doesn't interest me—*especially* not if it involves marriage to that earnest young shopkeeper she's been wishing on me since I was eighteen!"

Bodene grimaced. Elizabeth O'Rourke, Savanna's mother, was undoubtedly one of the sweetest, gentlest women alive, but having turned her back on the genteel world of her birth, she craved respectability for her daughter. Heedless of Savanna's outraged arguments, Elizabeth just couldn't get it through her head that her daughter *really* didn't want to marry and didn't give a damn about respectability.

"Look," he began placatingly, "could we please go inside and talk?" His eyes hardened and he muttered, "And would you please put that damn rifle down before we both do something we're going to regret?"

An impish grin suddenly curved Savanna's full mouth. "Such as you forcing me to shoot you!"

Bodene grinned back. *"Exactly!"*

She stared at him for a long moment, then carelessly swung the rifle over her slim shoulder. "You can come inside, but I'm warning you—no tricks! I'm not going to let you try to cheat me out of the tavern, like you tried to do the last time you were here!"

Turning away, she strode rapidly over to the building with the sign and mounted the steps, then crossed the rickety porch and disappeared inside.

The inside of the building belied its shabby exterior, although it certainly was not elegantly appointed. Some effort, however, had gone into making it not only habitable, but comfortable as well. It was astoundingly clean; the wooden floors were scrubbed and had been painstakingly bleached to a soft white patina; a colorful quilt adorned one rough wall, and the few pine tables and chairs which were scattered about gleamed from frequent polishing. Against the back wall there was a long oak counter and behind it, neatly arranged, stood several gleaming bottles of liquor and various glasses and mugs. The scent of a spicy venison stew simmering in the kitchen behind the tavern, which was attached to the main building by a dogtrot, wafted tantalizingly in the air.

The aromatic smell of the stew reminded Bodene that he hadn't eaten since very early that morning, and shrugging out of his jacket, he murmured, "Is there any chance that you will feed me before we start arguing again?"

Standing behind the counter and deftly pouring a glass of whiskey, Savanna felt her lips twitch. Covertly she studied her cousin as he pulled out a chair and made himself comfortable, his long legs stretched negligently in front of him, his wide shoulders resting easily against the back of the chair. He looked supremely confident, very sure of himself, and Savanna toyed idly with the notion of throwing the whiskey in his handsome face, but promptly discarded it—Bodene's vengeance was always swift and exceedingly uncomfortable!

Thinking of the devilish revenges they had wreaked on each other through the years, Savanna finally let the grin that had been tugging at her lips have its way. *Dios!* How she had missed him and his infuriatingly overbearing ways!

Placing the whiskey beside him on the table, she asked curiously, "Did it ever even occur to you that I might really shoot you?"

Bodene took a long, appreciative sip of the liquor before he answered. His dark eyes full of laughter, he looked up at her and murmured, "In a rage, without a doubt! But not in cold blood. And since it's been some months since the last time I, er, annoyed you, I figured you've had plenty of time to get your temper under control."

Savanna sent him an exasperated look. "Someday, Bodene, you are going to push your luck too far, and I only hope that I'm around to see you get your comeuppance!" She walked over to the small doorway that led to the dogtrot and, opening the door and sticking her head through, she called out, "Sam, we might as well feed him! Bring some of the stew and bread when you can, *por favor.*"

While they waited for the food, Bodene savored his drink and looked around, smiling as he caught sight of a beautiful silver bell hanging over the doorway of the dogtrot—trust Savanna to instill a touch of elegance even here! he thought. Savanna busied herself behind the counter, absently fiddling with the glasses and bottles, studiously ignoring her cousin. There was, however, a not *un*companionable silence between them, each one busy with his own thoughts.

Not even aware that she was doing it, Savanna sighed, wishing that Bodene's unexpected appearance hadn't aroused such a storm of ambivalence within her. Part of her always yearned impatiently for the next time he would breeze into her life; part of her was certain she never wanted to lay eyes on him again. I'm happy with my life, she told herself stubbornly; yet when she listened wide-eyed to Bodene's enthralling tales of New Orleans, when he described in vivid detail the sights and the smells of the city, the houses, the people ... the stunning gowns worn by the women, Savanna was increasingly aware of a dangerous longing deep within her.

Giving herself an angry shake, she asked abruptly, "How's Mother? Did she know you were coming to see me?"

"She's fine, relieved that the war is finally over," Bodene answered easily. "And yes, she knows I'm here to see you—she gave me her blessings."

"Naturally," Savanna returned dryly. "Although why, since she can't convince me to marry that fool Henry Greenwood, she would want to see me established in your gaming house is beyond me!"

Bodene's lips thinned. "You know damn well that I would not allow you to work there!"

"And how else would I earn my living?" she asked sweetly. "As a charwoman? Or perhaps a rich man's toy? Or do you think I'd make a good whore?"

Forcing himself not to rise to her baiting, Bodene settled back in the chair. "You know, someone ought to have strangled you at birth—you certainly are the most infuriating woman I have ever known!"

Having ruffled his feathers, Savanna laughed delightedly, an infectious sound that caused Bodene's own mouth to soften into a smile. Sam entered just then with a tray of food, and the next several minutes were spent in eating.

During the meal, the cousins put aside their differences and concentrated on exchanging current news. Savanna did not have a great deal to contribute. O'Rourke's Tavern was situated in one of the many uninhabited and largely unexplored wilderness stretches along the Mississippi River between Natchez and New Orleans, and consequently it was not a hub of activity. The fact that the site of the tavern was on the opposite side of the Mississippi River from the bustling, more well-known river towns also added to its isolation, and the few visitors eager to partake of its modest amenities were mostly men on the run from the law, although there was the occasional brave settler who stopped for the night. The isolation, however, suited Savanna perfectly—she had grown up in such surroundings and the wild, trackless wilderness called to something deep within her and gave her a sense of peace and satisfaction she had never experienced at her father's home, Campo de Verde. Even the lawless men who crossed her path were more like old acquaintances, which in truth they often were, than like outlaws to be feared, and—except for a few such as "Murdering" Micajah— having known her as child, for the most part they treated her with a rough sort of respect and admiration. Savanna felt *comfortable* here, this way of life was familiar to her, whereas life at Campo de Verde had seemed stultifying and unnatural. Although the tavern was often a lonely place to reside, Savanna loved it, and since Bodene lived in the glamorous and sinfully exciting city of New Orleans, it wasn't surprising that Savanna and Sam were listening with bemused attention to his every word.

"You actually saw the pirate Lafitte *and* General Jackson?" Savanna asked breathlessly, her food momentarily forgotten.

"Mmm, that I did, sweetheart," Bodene murmured as he soaked up the last bit of gravy with his bread and popped it into his mouth. "The Battle of New Orleans made some very strange bedfellows, I can tell you!"

Her elbows resting on the table, her hands propping up her chin, she stared with dazzled eyes at her cousin. "What did they look like? Oh, tell us more, Bodene!"

Bodene complied with alacrity and they spent a very enjoyable hour together as he related the exciting events that had taken place so recently in New Orleans. But eventually the conversation drifted onto dangerous ground.

"And Mother—was she frightened when the British attacked? Did she come into the city or stay at Campo de Verde?"

"She came into the city—there was concern that the plantations south of New Orleans might fall into British hands. She wasn't frightened in the least—thought it most exciting, even when the artillery was at its most thunderous." Bodene sent Savanna a long look. "There is only one thing that frightens your mother," he said deliberately, "and that's the thought of you up here at the mercy of whichever murderous bandit happens to be in the area."

Savanna's face tightened and, dropping her hands, she pushed herself away from the table. "It didn't seem to frighten her when we lived—if you can call it that—at Crow's Nest!" she snapped.

"Davalos was still alive then, and that's where he wanted her to be, you know that," Bodene answered reasonably, his expression revealing none of his own emotions.

A silence suddenly fell as they both were lost in remembrances of the unpleasant days of their youth.

Bodene had been three years old when his mother, Ann Sullivan, had died and his father, Innis O'Rourke, a wealthy planter in Tennessee, had reluctantly taken in the motherless boy. His parents had not been married, and, unwanted and unloved, Bodene had endured a miserable existence until Savanna's mother, Innis's gentle sixteen-year-old sister, had arrived two years later from Ireland for an extended visit. Elizabeth O'Rourke had taken one look at the black-haired, dark-eyed, unhappy little boy and had instantly opened her generous heart to him. Life suddenly became idyllic to the unwanted child, and Elizabeth became his shining angel. But those days at his father's plantation, Sweet Meadows, had not lasted long—Innis and Elizabeth eventually had gone on a long trip to New Orleans, and within weeks of their return, Elizabeth seemed to cry all the time and Innis was in a black, violent mood.

Then the Spaniard had arrived. Bodene had not trusted Blas Davalos from the very first second he had laid eyes on the slim, arrogant man, and his mistrust had turned to white-hot hatred when it gradually dawned on him that this man was the cause of his adored Elizabeth's tears and Innis's rages and her eventual banishment from Sweet Meadows. He still vividly remembered being awakened in the middle of the night by a sobbing Elizabeth and hurried into his clothes and hustled down the wide, curving staircase into the small gig driven by Davalos. He had never seen his father or Sweet Meadows again.

Bodene didn't remember a lot of those first days after he and Elizabeth had gone away with Davalos, and it was years before he realized that Savanna's birth, in one of those dreary little settlements along the Mississippi, had brought great shame and disgrace upon Elizabeth and had made her an outcast from her own family. And that by neglecting to marry Elizabeth, Davalos had branded his own child a bastard.

If Bodene had not trusted Davalos on sight, Savanna's earliest memories of her father were somewhat hazy. She was nearly six years old before she fully understood that Davalos was actually her father—which wasn't surprising, since Davalos would conveniently abandon them for months, sometimes even years on end. Life was hard for them during those times, but when he would unexpectedly appear, for a while everything was very different: there were sudden luxuries—extra money, a silk gown for her mother, a fine knife for Bodene, a china doll and sweets for her. As a very young child, she had equated Davalos's infrequent appearances with mostly pleasant things—her mother's delight, the dazzling gifts he lavished upon them and the general air of gaiety that seemed to abound while he was with them. In those days, Davalos was a wondrous figure to her, someone whose presence made every day happy and exciting. But he stayed only a week or two, never more than a month, and then one morning he would simply mount his horse, leave her mother in tears and disappear . . . back to his *real* life, back to the life that did not include the gentle woman he had disgraced or the child she had borne him. Only as she grew older did Savanna come to bitterly understand that she and her mother had played a very small part in Davalos's life; that while he had been alive he had deliberately hidden their existence from the other world in which he had lived.

It had taken her a long time to piece together the puzzle that had been Davalos, but from things her mother had said or *not* said, and from Bodene's recounting of his early memories, Savanna had finally come to several unpleasant conclusions about her father: he had seduced Elizabeth because he had assumed that Innis would settle a fortune on her, and when that had failed, he had kept their very existence a secret because he didn't want to lessen his chances of perhaps making a wealthy match for himself. Savanna had wondered grimly for many years why he had even bothered with them at all, and it was only recently that she had concluded that, in his fashion, he *had* loved Elizabeth, and perhaps even herself. . . .

Bodene glanced across at Savanna's set face, knowing that as hard as it had been for him to deal with his illegitimacy, to ignore the taunts and sly jeers, the contemptuous looks and scandalized glances, it had been a hundred times harder for her.

Savanna suddenly gave an uncomfortable laugh and flashed him a wry look. "Sorry," she muttered, "but every time I think about those days, I'm afraid I live up to my red hair!"

Bodene smiled faintly, but there was a thoughtful expression in his dark eyes. "Savanna, someday you're going to have to forgive him. . . . What he did may be incomprehensible to us, and how Elizabeth could have gone on loving him may always mystify us, but you're going to have to accept it. As long as you hold the past against him, it's going to eat you alive."

Her features instantly closed down and Bodene bit back a curse. "You have every reason to be angry with Davalos—he should have married your mother, I don't deny it. But he didn't, and the man is *dead!*" he said urgently. "Has been for over ten years! He can't change anything now, so give him credit for trying to rectify some of the wrong he'd done to you—didn't he leave you everything he owned?"

Savanna snorted. "Do you think *money* is going to make any difference to me? Besides, as you well know, it was no fortune I inherited from him—only a ramshackle house and a hundred and fifty arpents of land with broken levees south of New Orleans, all that remained of his family's plantation." Her face softened and she smiled warmly at Sam, who, oblivious of the argument raging around his grizzled head, was busily gathering up the dishes. "Oh, and Sam. He gave me Sam and his family."

Sam grinned at her. "That he did, missy, and it was right wonderful of you to have given us our papers! Fine thing you did setting us free!"

Bodene looked impatient. "Yes, it was a fine thing she did, fine, too, that she used what money there was to make the house livable and insisted Elizabeth live there, but it is not fine that she persists in living in this godforsaken hellhole or that you're abetting her pure bloody cussedness!" Bodene was fairly shouting by the time he came to the end of his words, his hold on his temper extremely light. The look of amused tolerance that passed between Savanna and Sam was his undoing, and smashing his fist against the table, he snarled, "Jesus Christ! You're *both* crazy! Don't you realize that one of these days Micajah, or someone like him, is going to catch you by surprise, and if you survive—which isn't damn likely, knowing *him*—you'll have been raped and abused, possibly left pregnant with his child—or won't even know the father if his whole gang takes their pleasures, too!"

Savanna's face went white at his harsh words and Bodene was satisfied to see a flicker of unease in her beautiful eyes. Good! At least she hadn't totally lost all sense of self-preservation. His rage dissipating at the strained expression on her face, he said in a softer tone, "I love you—it would damn near kill me if something happened to you. Won't you let me help you?" When she didn't respond, he took heart and added, "I know you've worked hard to reestablish yourself since Stack Island sank in the earthquake four years ago, and I know you're proud that what you've accomplished you've done on your own. But this is no life for you. You're young! You're beautiful! You shouldn't be wasting away here in a damned swamp!" He took a deep breath. "Pride is a fine thing, just don't let it kill you."

Bodene's words bit deep and Savanna was painfully aware of the truth in everything that he had said. She had always understood the risks she ran, and while Bodene might think to the contrary, she wasn't a fool! It was just that she felt more comfortable living in the familiar surroundings and circumstances she had known from earliest childhood. New Orleans with all its exciting pleasures fascinated her, but it also made her uneasy and vaguely frightened. Campo de Verde was certainly not a grand plantation—too few acres remained of the once-vast Davalos estate—but with Bodene's help and money, the house and outbuildings had been repaired and refurbished and the levees rebuilt. With Sam's children, Isaac and Moses, and their families to work the remaining land, her mother had a life of reasonable comfort and semi-gentility. Savanna had felt constricted and smothered during the five years that she had lived there with her mother, and at eighteen she had stunned both Elizabeth and Bodene when, taking only Sam with her, she had struck out on her own, returning to the small tavern that Elizabeth had run on Crow's Nest while Davalos had been alive.

Elizabeth had been devastated by the news of Davalos's death, but to this day Savanna was still confused about her feelings for her father. She didn't think that she had ever *truly* loved the dark stranger whom she had seen so seldom over the years, but she had never forgotten those early days when he had been a source of laughter and delight to both herself and her mother. It had been to please him that she had learned to speak Spanish, hoping it would make him proud of her—and it had. Even now, knowing what she did about him, she remembered the pleased glow that had suffused her features when, the last time she had ever seen him, she had shyly welcomed him in Spanish and he had praised her accomplishment. But if she remembered the good times, and there had been a few, she also remembered her mother's tears and desolation when Davalos would once again desert them. . . .

Pushing aside her unpleasant thoughts with an effort, she smiled at Bodene and replied with forced lightness to his earlier comment. "You worry too much, Bodene—you just can't face it that I've grown up and don't need you to fight my battles anymore."

Bodene snorted and was on the point of replying scathingly when the silver bell tinkled—once. The intent expression that suddenly came into Savanna's eyes stopped him, and as the seconds passed, her face paled, but her gaze remained locked anxiously on that silver bell, almost as if she were willing it to ring again. "What is it?" Bodene asked sharply, instinctively reaching for the short-barreled pistol he kept handy at all times.

Tearing her eyes away from the bell, she swiftly reached for the rifle she had held earlier, as well as another one she kept behind the oak counter. Deftly tossing the second rifle to Bodene, she said urgently, "The bell is our signal—Sam's in trouble! Bad trouble!"

Chapter 2

"WHAT THE HELL DO YOU MEAN, SIGNAL?" BODENE rasped as he caught the rifle and instantly crowded against the wall, the rifle held ready.

Impatiently Savanna hissed, "The damn bell! We have them scattered throughout all the buildings with pull-ropes in handy places. One ring means desperate situation; two, that someone looking like or for trouble is approaching; and three, that strangers are nearing and to be on the alert. Either Sam has somehow hurt himself or—"

"Or Murdering Micajah has returned," Bodene drawled coolly.

Savanna gave a sharp nod of her red-gold head and muttered, "My, my, how clever you have become these days!"

A scuffling sound from the dogtrot caused both of them to freeze. They exchanged a tense look and then Bodene melted into the shadows and Savanna dashed behind the counter, hastily concealing the rifle, but ready to snatch it up in an instant.

Twilight had fallen, and since they had been so

busy conversing, the candles and lamps had not yet been lit and the inside of the small tavern was filled with murky shadows. Savanna could hardly make out Bodene's large form in the corner, but simply knowing he was there helped to calm the nervous tension that coiled in her belly.

Sam was suddenly shoved violently through the doorway of the dogtrot, his face contorted by the pain in his right arm, which was twisted cruelly behind him. A wicked knife blade was held menacingly against his throat. Over Sam's shoulder, Savanna saw Micajah Yates's stubble-covered face, his lank brown hair hanging almost to his shoulders and a smug smile curving his too-full lips.

Micajah Yates was not precisely an ugly man, his eyes were very blue and his coarsely handsome features seemed appropriate for his big, burly build; but unfortunately, soap and water were not often employed by him, and he had the most *un*appealing habit of indiscriminately killing anyone who annoyed him or had the unfortunate bad luck to cross his path when he was in a bad mood. At thirty-six years of age, he was a well-known robber and murderer, and Savanna and Bodene had been acquainted with him from the early days at Crow's Nest.

Unaware of Bodene lurking in the darkness behind him, Micajah pushed Sam farther into the room and drawled, "Surprised to see me again so soon, Savanna?"

Savanna's eyes narrowed, and leaning her elbows on the counter, fervently grateful for the nearness of the concealed rifle, she shrugged carelessly. "Should I be?"

"Now that depends," Micajah said easily, "on whether you really thought you had bested me the last time I was here."

"Why don't you let Sam go and we can discuss it?" she replied levelly, her slim fingers cautiously inching toward the rifle as her eyes met Sam's.

Micajah smiled nastily. "Now, I don't believe we can do that, sweetheart. If I let Sam here go, you'll try to shoot me with that rifle you think you're hiding from me. Think I didn't learn anything from our last encounter?"

Savanna took a deep breath and forced a smile, neither stopping her movement toward the rifle nor admitting the truth of his statement. "So what do we do now?"

Micajah's blue eyes roved hotly over her face and full bosom, and at the hungry expression that leaped in their depths, Savanna's mouth went dry with fear. It was with an effort that she kept her gaze from straying betrayingly to Bodene, poised just behind the unsuspecting Micajah.

"What you do now," Yates said, "is very slowly put the rifle on the counter in front of you and come out from behind it, and if you don't—why, I'm afraid I'll just have to cut this here nigger's throat, and you wouldn't want that, now would you?"

Despite the tenseness of the situation, Savanna felt rage billowing up, and her eyes flashed angrily. "And then?" she demanded tightly.

He stripped her with his eyes. "And then," he said bluntly, "you tie up Sam for me and we go upstairs for a few hours." He smiled meaningfully. "If you're *real* nice to me, I might not kill him when I'm through with you."

Rage got the better of her, and forgetting all about Bodene, she suddenly swung the rifle up and into position, the long barrel pointed at Micajah's head. Her voice thick with fear and loathing, she snarled, "Go ahead, kill him—but be aware that before his body hits the floor, I'll shoot you between the eyes!"

"No," Bodene said softly from behind Yates. "I insist, little cousin, that you allow me that pleasure!" Brutally shoving the rifle barrel into the middle of Micajah's back, Bodene drawled dangerously, "And now what are you going to do, my dirty friend?"

His confident air having vanished and his expression decidedly chagrined, Micajah laughed nervously. "Sullivan! I should have knowed you'd be around somewhere!" Obviously hoping to escape with his hide intact, and never one to argue when the odds were against him, Micajah very carefully released Sam's arm and with equal caution moved the blade away from Sam's throat. An impudent smile on his face, he declared heartily, "Seems like you bested me again, Savanna!" Apparently undaunted by his dangerous position, he added brazenly, "Now how about we all put away our weapons and sit down and have a whiskey together—just to show that there are no hard feelings."

Sam staggered away from Micajah and sank down onto one of the chairs, cradling the arm that had been so viciously held behind his back. Savanna's rifle never wavered and she asked anxiously, "Sam? How bad is it?"

Sam grinned, albeit painfully, and murmured, "Not so bad, missy! He surprised me when I went back into the kitchen—was all over me before I even knew what happened. I'se be all right directly. Don't you worry none about ole Sam."

Savanna exchanged a look with Bodene, who grimaced and shrugged his broad shoulders. His own rifle still shoved between Micajah's shoulder blades, he said thoughtfully, "I've never killed a man in cold blood before, but I suppose there's always a first time."

"Now look here!" Micajah bit out half angrily, half fearfully. "I've done right by you—didn't I let Sam go?"

Bodene smiled grimly. "Only because you didn't want to get a hole blown through you." He shoved the rifle deeper into Micajah's back and continued acidly. "And if I hadn't been here, God knows what you might have done. . . . I've a good mind to shoot you anyway."

"Now, Bodene, you know you don't want to do that," the outlaw replied quickly. "Why, we've known each other since you were just a boy—I didn't mean no *real* harm." An uneasy smile crossed his face. "And Savanna's such a tempting baggage, you can't honestly blame me for losing my head a little."

Savanna snorted and said through gritted teeth, "Try something like this again and you *will* lose your head—I'll put a bullet through it!"

"And if, just by chance, she were to miss," Bodene added with soft menace, "you can be sure I would hunt you down like the dog you are and I *wouldn't* miss! Do you understand?"

"'Course I understand!" Micajah replied testily. "Think I'm a fool? I just don't understand why you all are going on about it! Nothing happened!"

Disgustedly Savanna said, "Oh, shut up, Micajah! Drop the knife and get the hell out of here before I change my mind!"

The knife clattered to the floor and Micajah was out the door in an instant. Picking up the fallen weapon, Bodene said quietly, "He'll be back, you know that, don't you?"

"Yes, and I'll say it for you—next time I might not be so lucky," Savanna muttered, not meeting his eyes. She wasn't about to admit it, but this recent attack by Micajah had scared her. If she'd had any doubts about the extent of his mulish infatuation, it was now glaringly obvious that he just wasn't going to give up; he was going to keep trying, and one of these days . . . Savanna shivered. If Bodene hadn't been there, it might have ended very differently than it had, and she was miserably aware of that unpleasant fact. Because of her own stubbornness, Sam might have died, and it didn't bear thinking about what she would have suffered at Micajah's hands. Bodene was right—there was no use letting her pride destroy her.

She glanced resolutely over at her cousin. "How long do you intend to stay?" she asked reluctantly.

"As long as it takes to convince you to stop being a muleheaded little fool!" he snapped, the obstinate thrust of his jaw very apparent.

Her eyes traveled over to Sam, and meeting his dark, compassionate gaze, she knew the decision that she had to make.

Savanna couldn't remember a time when Sam and his two sons hadn't been part of the household. While Elizabeth had been busy tending the tavern, since his wife had died years before, it had been Sam, in between helping Elizabeth, who had watched over all the children and seen to their needs.

Savanna and Bodene had grown up playing with Isaac and Moses, who were just a few years older than Bodene. Elizabeth had been there for soft hugs and gentle kisses, but Sam had been their main parental figure. He'd been a kind tyrant, fair but implacable about what he expected from them, and his hand had warmed their bottoms on more than one occasion. As Savanna had gotten older, her mother had explained that Sam and his children were actually *owned* by Davalos; that since he was gone so often and he didn't want them lazing around, he had ordered them to stay with her and earn their keep. Savanna had been appalled, and when Davalos had died, giving Sam his freedom papers had been one of the most satisfying acts of her life. In the intervening years he had repaid her a thousand times with his unstinting loyalty.

A tender expression suddenly crossed her face. If it hadn't been for Sam's volunteering to accompany her when she had decided to leave Campo de Verde, she doubted that she would ever have been able to accomplish all that she had—or that Elizabeth and Bodene wouldn't have forcibly restrained her from setting off totally on her own. Neither Elizabeth nor Bodene had been happy about the situation, but with

Sam willing to go with her, most of their arguments had evaporated. While she had been recklessly determined to make O'Rourke's Tavern a success all on her own, there had been many a time that she had been grateful for Sam's solid, reassuring presence, and there had been times without number when Sam had come up to her while she had been intent upon some backbreaking task and said softly, "Well, now, missy! It looks as if you could use some help. There is no cause for you to be working yoreself into the ground when I'se around. Didn't I tell yore mama that I'd look after you just as I alwus done?"

There were many desperate situations that Savanna could have endured, but she wouldn't be able to live with herself if Sam were badly hurt or killed because of her. Straightening her slim shoulders, she flashed a rueful look at Bodene. "I'll need a few days to get things organized. There's an old trapper friend of Sam's who might be willing to move in and take over everything until I decide what to do with the place, but he has to be found and that might take a while."

Bodene relaxed for the first time since he'd left New Orleans. Smiling warmly at her, he said softly, "It doesn't matter how long it takes, just as long as you and Sam come with me."

Savanna's decision to leave O'Rourke's Tavern was not quite the instant capitulation that it appeared—she had always feared that one day she would come up against a situation over which she had no control, and Micajah's unwanted attentions certainly were that! She'd known when she'd struck out on her own that she was attempting the impossible; that it would not be the life her mother wanted for her, nor would it be a comfortable life, free from danger and brutal difficulties, but she'd been prepared for that. After all, hadn't she grown up watching her mother struggle desperately to keep all of them in the bare necessities? Surely she could do better unencumbered by two children. Savanna had also been grimly confident that no man would ever hold her in the same demoralizing enchantment that Davalos had wielded over her mother.

With little more than sheer nerve, some desperately needed luck and a lot of obstinate determination, she'd headed back for the only home she had known—Crow's Nest—only to discover that Crow's Nest and Stack Island no longer existed. The island and the small tavern, which Elizabeth had sold for a meager sum when the news of Davalos's death had reached them, had disappeared beneath the Mississippi River in a tremendous earthquake that same year. A resolute tilt to her chin, Savanna had turned her back on the past and crossed the river, searching for somewhere else to start up another tavern. She'd found what she was looking for in this deserted old homestead and, by sheer grit and guts and with Sam's help, had turned it into a passable business. It was not an easy life she had chosen, perhaps not even the life she wanted, yet she took a stubborn pride in it. But life on the wilderness frontier of Louisiana was relentlessly hard for everyone—especially for a woman alone and for a young woman who looked like Savanna. . . .

Studying her features in a small spotted mirror that night, Savanna sighed. *She* didn't think there was anything remarkable about the stunning clarity of her aquamarine eyes, or the elegant shape of her high cheekbones, or even the lush fullness of her provocatively curved mouth. As for the luxuriousness of her wavy red-gold hair, which only emphasized the milky fairness of her skin and the darkness of her brows and long lashes, well, she didn't think very much of it either! Actually, she hated the color of her hair, wishing instead that she had been endowed with hair as black as Bodene's and eyes that were a plain, unremarkable blue. And what there was about her shape that roused the unwanted interest and pur-

suit of men like Micajah Yates utterly baffled her—
after all, she was formed just like any other woman,
she had exactly the same parts and they were precisely in the same places!

Impatiently putting down the mirror, Savanna
turned away and walked toward her bed. If Yates
and others like him would only leave her alone, she
and Sam would do just fine. But no! There was something about her, something about the tall body that
she took for granted, something about the voluptuous curves that she secretly despised that made her
the angry, unwilling target of the lusts of so many
men who crossed her path.

It wasn't, Savanna argued with herself as she slid
into bed, as if she ever *encouraged* any of their advances! Painfully aware of what a man had cost her
mother, she had sworn never to let that happen to
her. Savanna didn't like men very much, all they represented to her was heartache, trouble and tears, and
she'd never met one who had stirred the least little
tremor of excitement within her breast. Not one.

In the darkness she smiled—not so surprising
when she lived in a society where someone like Murdering Micajah was considered quite a catch! Unfortunately, she didn't expect that the men around New
Orleans were any different, except for being cleaner
and richer and perhaps better-mannered. Tears and
trouble, every last one of them! And she'd happily
die a spinster before she'd let even one of them
breach the defensive wall she kept around her
emotions—which was going to make living with her
mother exceedingly difficult.

She grimaced. It wasn't surprising that, considering the disaster of her own life, Elizabeth was firmly
convinced that Savanna's happiness could only be at-
tained by marriage. Of course, even Elizabeth would
admit that not just *any* man would do for her daughter, but one of the reasons, once she'd gotten over her
grief over his death, that Elizabeth had been so de-

lighted with the contents of Davalos's will had been
because it allowed them to live, as she had said,
"with a much better class of people, dear. Respectable people, *honest* people!" Smiling mistily at a highly
indifferent Savanna, Elizabeth had trilled on, "I know
that because of our unfortunate circumstances you
won't have the marriage opportunities that should
have been your right, but, darling, there are all sorts
of very nice men—shopkeepers and even some hard-
working farmers—who would deem themselves *very*
lucky to have a wife like you!" It had been shortly after this conversation that Savanna had left home.

Fidgeting restlessly under the light covers, Savanna twisted and turned, wishing violently for
sleep. She was not looking forward to returning to
Campo de Verde—not that she didn't love her
mother. It was just that the thought of Elizabeth's
gentle scheming to find her a respectable husband
made Savanna squirm with dread. That, and all the
boring, dull, ladylike occupations that Elizabeth
seemed to feel were required of women. Incredible as
it seemed, Savanna much preferred the desperate
struggle to keep the tavern going and the occasional
facing down of dangerous rogues like Micajah to the
stultifying domesticity that her mother embraced
with such unbridled enthusiasm. It was only the
growing fear of *not* being able to win against men
like Murdering Micajah that was driving her back to
Campo de Verde and a fate she viewed with deep
misgivings and despair.

It was odd, Savanna mused wearily, that her
mother, who had lived such an *un*conventional life,
should now yearn so hungrily for all the trappings of
respectability. Imagining the dull, stupefying *same-
ness* of the days that stretched before her, for just a
second she considered telling Bodene in the morning
that she had changed her mind, that she couldn't
possibly return to Campo de Verde. Suddenly,
though, Sam's pain-filled face flashed before her eyes

and she sighed. No. She'd have to go; it was the only way to make certain that Sam came to no harm, and that was the most important thing—that and keeping out of the clutches of Murdering Micajah! She grinned slightly as she recalled Micajah's chagrined expression when Bodene had shoved the rifle into his back. After today, it was highly unlikely that Yates would continue his unwanted pursuit of her, and, certain she had seen the last of him for a very long time, Savanna didn't waste any more time speculating on the outlaw. Which was most unfortunate!

Smarting from having been humiliatingly bested by Savanna twice in less than a month, Micajah put several hasty miles between himself and O'Rourke's Tavern before he deemed it safe to stop. The notion of doubling back and trying his luck again did cross his mind, but the memory of Savanna's deadly expression above that long black rifle made him think better of it—that and the knowledge that Sullivan was also there. If it hadn't been for Sullivan . . . A vicious look crossed his face. One of these days he was going to have to teach that interfering bastard a lesson, and when he was done, he'd teach Savanna what a *real* man was like!

Thoughts of vengeance, along with an unpleasant spell of bad weather, kept him company during the three-day journey up to Natchez, and by the time he had sighted the majestic bluffs overlooking the Mississippi River which signaled the end of his journey, Micajah was wet, hungry, uncomfortable and in a decidedly foul mood. Leaving his exhausted horse at the livery stable, he immediately set out in search of some liquid comfort.

Natchez was actually two cities. On a high, tree-covered bluff towering above the river was situated the elegant town inhabited by the wealthy planters and respectable merchants and their families. There, along the jessamine-shaded streets, was to be found a charming mixture of Spanish and American architecture, iron grillwork and vaulted corridors mingling with arcades of slender columns and wide galleries. But on the narrow clay shelf nearly two hundred feet below the bluff near the river lay the "other" city—Natchez-under-the-Hill. And if the town above was noted for its wealth and elegance, Natchez-under-the-Hill had gained fame as a haven for every kind of vice imaginable.

Quite familiar with all the dens of iniquity that comprised Natchez-under-the-Hill, Micajah quickly made his way to his favorite haunt. It proved to be a shabby little dram shop named The White Cock, on the notorious Silver Street, and mostly frequented by corrupt men like himself. Sidling into a darkened corner, he seated himself at a small, rickety table and glanced cautiously around the smoked-filled, dimly lit room. Seeing nothing to alarm him, he settled back to enjoy the first shot of throat-burning whiskey from the bottle that he had ordered from the hard-faced slattern who worked as the barmaid.

The White Cock was only half full, and when the doors flew open a few minutes later, Micajah had a clear view of the two men who entered. The shorter one in the ragged blue coat and stained leggings he recognized as a sometime partner-in-crime of his, Jem Elliot, but the other was obviously a stranger. His clothing alone—elegant, form-fitting russet jacket, starched cravat and pristine nankeen breeches— proclaimed him a man of wealth and style, and Micajah's interest was instantly whetted. Now what the hell is Jem up to with a gent like that? Micajah wondered as he covertly studied the two men. Is Jem thinking to cheat him in a card game? Rob him after he gets him drunk? Or something more interesting?

Elliot, his narrowed hazel eyes missing nothing, gave the room the same careful scrutiny that Micajah had earlier and saw him in the corner. He nodded and with the "gent" in tow quickly made his way to

Micajah's table. A toothy grin breaking across his forgettable features, Jem exclaimed affably, "Micajah! What the hell are you doing here? Heard you'd gone to try your luck once more with that red-haired vixen, Savanna." His grin became sly. "Since you're back so soon, figure she must have thrown you out—again!"

Micajah grunted some reply and motioned Jem and his companion to join him. Despite the expression of distaste on the face of the gentleman, both men seated themselves at the table.

Silence reigned until glasses arrived for the two newcomers and Micajah poured both of them a generous shot from his bottle. The stranger, his aquiline nose fairly quivering with displeasure, stared at the dirty glass filled with the amber liquor and snapped under his breath, "I thought we came here to be private! I told you this was a *delicate* matter."

Elliot flashed a wink at Micajah as he sipped his whiskey. "Calm down, mister! There ain't no secrets between Micajah and me and there ain't nothing *delicate* about murder! As a matter of fact, Micajah here might be just the fellow you're looking for—has a lot more experience taking care of fellows like your Adam St. Clair than I have."

Obviously not liking this turn of events, the stranger glared at the unperturbed Elliot, his supercilious features tightened. Elliot smiled serenely back, his shaggy brown hair and stubble-covered jaws making him look even more disreputable than usual. "Ever heard of *Murdering* Micajah?" Elliot asked softly.

The gentleman's green eyes widened and he glanced over at Micajah, a question in his gaze.

Not without a little pride, Micajah smiled faintly and dipped his head.

The stranger reached for his glass and in one swift gulp swallowed the contents. A shudder went through his slim frame as the fiery whiskey seared its way down his throat. Carefully setting the glass down, he looked at Micajah and said bluntly, "There is a man I wish you to, er, remove from my path. He is a wealthy man, well-thought-of in Natchez and not without powerful connections."

"Adam St. Clair?" Micajah asked, already calculating how much he could squeeze out of the man for the deed. Afterward, he might even be able to make the pigeon pay a tidy sum to keep the secret between them.

The man nodded, his fair hair gleaming faintly in the flickering light. He glanced around nervously, and seeing that no one was nearby, he leaned forward and said intently, "I will be willing to pay you four thousand dollars in gold. Two thousand now and the remainder when the job is done."

Micajah took a long, slow sip of his whiskey, never revealing that he was impressed by the sum. "Why do you want him killed?" he inquired thoughtfully. "Murder's a drastic solution. What'd he do to you?"

The man's lips thinned. "I don't think that it is any of your business."

A cold expression in his pale blue eyes, Micajah said flatly, "Then find someone else to do your killing for you."

The stranger sighed. "There is a woman involved. He has her, but I don't want him to keep her. It is that simple."

Satisfied with the answer, Micajah poured himself and the others another whiskey. Raising his glass, he muttered, "Here's to the demise of Adam St. Clair!"

All three men drank to Micajah's deadly toast. Putting his glass down on the rough pine table, Yates asked bluntly, "How soon do I get the money?"

"Don't you want to know anything about him? Where he lives?" the stranger asked uneasily, suddenly wondering if his money wasn't simply going to disappear the instant it reached Micajah's grubby hands.

Micajah smiled coldly. "You can tell me all about

him once you tell me how soon I get that two thousand."

"I can arrange for you to have it tomorrow morning," the man admitted, uncertainty clear in his eyes.

"Good! Meet me at Spanish Lick tomorrow morning at eleven with the money . . . and before another week has gone by, your Mr. St. Clair will be singing with the angels!" Micajah grinned darkly. "Or dancing with the devil!"

After the stranger departed, Micajah and Elliot sat there discussing their new employer. Elliot admitted he had never seen him before, nor did he know his name, but he had the impression that the man was a stranger to these parts. They speculated on that for a bit longer, but decided it didn't matter—as long as he paid them the money, they didn't care who he was! With hardly a pause, they switched the conversation to the more enjoyable subject of how they would split the money.

"Fifty-fifty, as usual?" Elliot asked eagerly.

Micajah flashed him an astounded look. "When I have to do all the work?" he demanded scathingly. "All you did was steer the pigeon to me!"

Elliot grinned. "Can't blame a man for trying! Seventy-five/twenty-five?"

"That's better," Micajah said, nodding his unkempt head. "Now tell me what's been happening while I've been gone."

The two men talked for some time, finishing off the bottle of whiskey. Eventually they parted, and with a slightly unsteady step, Micajah began to make his way toward the boardinghouse that he used whenever he was in the area.

Natchez-under-the-Hill was a dangerous, deadly place, even for rogues like Micajah and as he half stumbled, half walked down one of the twisting, narrow alleys, he gradually became aware that someone was furtively dogging his footsteps. At once he fumbled for his knife and cursed violently under his breath when he remembered that he had dropped it at O'Rourke's Tavern. His pistol was in his saddlebag back at the livery stable, and a film of sweat broke out on his brow as he realized that he was unarmed and being carefully stalked by someone in the darkness. . . .

The threat of danger cleared his head instantly and an ugly light entered his eyes as he clenched his big fists. So someone thought to take on Murdering Micajah, did he? Well, it wouldn't be the first time Yates had killed a man with his bare hands.

Craftily deciding to use the element of surprise against the man who followed him, Micajah spun on his heels and with fists flying lunged at the slight figure behind him. His massive fists viciously pummeled the stalker, hitting the smaller man relentlessly in the stomach and the face.

Caught totally by surprise, the stalker gave a frightened, pain-filled squawk as those first powerful jabs caught him. Bent nearly double from the force of the blows that Micajah was raining upon him, he stumbled backward into the wall of one of the buildings which formed the narrow alley. Half beseechingly, half protectively, he held his hands out, but Micajah swept them aside, and grasping the man by the throat, lifted him upright, then slammed him savagely against the wall.

Fingers digging into the scrawny throat of his one-time stalker, Micajah breathed malevolently, "Thought to rob me, did you?"

"No! No!" the helpless figure gasped, clawing ineffectually at the fingers that threatened to close off his breathing. "Jesus Christ, don't kill me!" he gabbled fearfully. "It's me, Micajah! It's Jeremy Childers!"

Chapter 3

"*JEREMY CHILDERS!*" MICAJAH EXCLAIMED IN STUNNED disbelief. "I thought your bones were bleaching on some godforsaken plain in Texas!" Loosening his stranglehold on the other man's throat, he muttered disgustedly, "What the hell do you want?"

This wasn't precisely how Jeremy had envisioned his meeting with Micajah, but, exceedingly thankful that he wasn't dead, he coughed painfully a few times and rubbed his bruised neck. "Need to talk to you," he said hoarsely. "Private-like."

Considering how he earned his money, Jeremy's request didn't rouse any great interest within Micajah—there were always men needing to talk to him "private-like," men like the stranger tonight. And since his immediate need for money was going to be met by that same stranger, Jeremy's words didn't exactly fill him with excitement.

Shrugging his burly shoulders, Micajah turned away and continued toward the boardinghouse. "Where the devil have you been these past years?" he finally asked when Jeremy followed him, half running to keep up with his longer stride. "Thought you and Orval were going to make your fortune trading horses with the Comanches."

Jeremy grimaced in the darkness. "We were . . . only Orval got scalped by the Comanches and I ran into a Spanish patrol and spent my time since then in a prison down in Mexico."

Micajah glanced back at him. "Talk about bad luck," he commented unsympathetically. "Told you it was a fool notion at the time."

They reached the boardinghouse, a small, ramshackle wooden building which was situated near the river and the livery stable where Micajah's horse was stabled, but a little distance from the main cluster of equally shabby buildings that comprised the lower town. Micajah liked the location since it would allow him a quick exit, and he had a nice little understanding with both the widow who ran the boardinghouse and the owner of the stable; they treated him well and he was willing to pay them equally well for their services or . . .

The widow Blackstone kept a fairly decent room at the back of the house, away from the other boarders, ready for him at all times. Silently Micajah and Jeremy entered the darkened building and made their way to Micajah's room. The candle that Micajah quickly lit once they were inside revealed the meager furnishings—a pine chair and bureau and a bed with a threadbare quilt on it which did little to disguise the lumpy mattress. A washstand with a tiny cracked mirror above it and a few hooks on the wall completed the contents of the room.

The widow Blackstone kept a bottle of whiskey and several glasses atop the pine bureau for Micajah's pleasure, and after shrugging out of his jacket and throwing the garment on the bed, he poured himself and Jeremy a generous slug of the liquor. Motioning for Jeremy to take the chair, he flung himself down

on the bed and, half lying, half sitting, he took a sip
of his drink.

In the flickering light of the candle, he studied the
doleful features of the man across from him. It was
obvious that the past years had not been kind to
Jeremy Childers. His face was creased and lined well
beyond his years, his ragged, light brown hair hung
dull and limp around his unhealthy pale skin and his
eyes were deeply sunken, dark circles emphasizing
their queer glitter. Never a big man, Jeremy looked
smaller and thinner than Micajah remembered, and
there was an obviously nervous air about him: he
constantly fidgeted as he sat in the chair across from
Micajah, starting at the faintest sound, his hazel eyes
never still, always darting around the room as if he
expected someone to leap out at him.

Micajah had been pretty good friends with Jeremy
and Orval before they had disappeared on that trip
to trade horses—they'd run a few rigs together and
Jeremy had been his partner in a couple of robberies.
In fact, Orval, Jeremy, Jem and Micajah had made up
a rather dangerous quartet of rogues in those days,
but mostly they ran their own separate, nefarious
schemes, only joining together when it proved necessary or profitable.

Micajah had been their natural leader; not only
was his personality the most dominant, but he was
four or five years older than the others and was the
more experienced scoundrel . . . and he didn't blink if
there was violence to be done. Jeremy had always
been a follower, following either his or Orval's lead,
and so with Orval dead, Micajah wasn't the least surprised that the first thing Jeremy had done after more
than ten years in a Spanish prison was to come looking for him.

Nursing his whiskey, Micajah said idly, "Since
you've been in a Spanish jail all this time, I can hazard a guess as to why you were looking for me—you
want some money and need a place to stay for a

while." With the prospect of making a large amount of easy money before him and feeling unusually generous, Micajah went on expansively. "You're welcome to bed down here for as long as you like, and as for the other . . ." He smiled darkly. "As for the other—I just took on a job for a tidy sum and I might be willing to let you in on it. Would put a little money in your pocket."

A funny little smile curved Jeremy's pale lips and the queer glitter in his hazel eyes increased. Taking a nervous gulp of the whiskey, he inhaled deeply and blurted out, "And I might be willing to cut you in on a fortune in Aztec gold!"

Jeremy's words did not have the effect that he had expected. Micajah remained unmoved, merely sending him a highly skeptical glance and replying coolly, "You know what I think? I think those years in a Spanish jail have addled your wits!"

"No! No! It's true!" Jeremy said in agitation, never having considered that Micajah wouldn't believe him. "It's *true*, I tell you!"

There was such intense conviction in Jeremy's tone that a faint flicker of interest showed in Micajah's cold blue eyes. "Tell me about it," he said finally.

Nothing loath, Jeremy almost slid across the room in his haste to kneel by the bed, and with the words tumbling frantically from his lips, he told Micajah about the fateful trip to Spanish Texas that he and Orval had undertaken in 1804, and the dying man he had found just before he'd fallen into the hands of the Spanish patrol. For eleven years Jeremy had kept the dazzling secret of the gold bottled up inside him and to finally tell the tale gave him almost a feeling of relief. The candle was sputtering in its pottery holder and the whiskey had been diminished considerably when Jeremy finished speaking.

Micajah stared at him for several long, nerveracking moments. Ordinarily he didn't have any time for tales of hidden treasure, much less of Aztec gold or the men who chased after such nonsense. He knew about all sorts of fools who had wasted years trying to find the notorious outlaw Sam Mason's supposedly hidden fortune near Cave-in-Rock. Having only contempt for men dim-witted enough to believe in such fairy-tale foolishness, Micajah had always turned a deaf ear to stories of hidden treasure, but Jeremy's tale had caught his interest the moment Blas Davalos's name had been mentioned, and when Savanna's name had come up, he'd been fairly riveted by Jeremy's words. He wasn't exactly certain that he believed everything Jeremy had told him—he did believe that *Jeremy* believed it, but what interested him more was the possibility of somehow using this knowledge to get Savanna into his bed.

Taking a reflective sip of his whiskey, Micajah murmured, more to himself than to Jeremy, "So Savanna O'Rourke has a golden armband and a map leading to Aztec gold, does she?"

His expression intense, Jeremy nodded eagerly. "That's what he said just before he died—'Savanna will have it." For a second Jeremy looked confused. "Or was it Jason Savage who has the map . . . ?"

Micajah wasn't concerned about Jason Savage, at least not at present; it was solely Savanna's part in this mesmerizing story that had roused his attention. Tossing off the remainder of his whiskey and sitting up abruptly, he said, "It doesn't matter. I know where Savanna O'Rourke is, and that's all we have to bother ourselves with for the time being."

Jeremy appeared thunderstruck, his belief in Micajah's omniscience sealed. "You know where she is?" he asked dazedly.

Micajah nodded. "Yep, you could say that! After we take care of this little job like I promised, we'll go see her and have a friendly talk with her about that daddy of hers."

"Forget the job!" Jeremy burst out impatiently, his

blue eyes glittering with a zealot's light. "It's the gold we're after! And Savanna can tell us how to find it!"

"And without money, we're not going to get very far!" Micajah returned coldly. "We'll kill this St. Clair fellow and then, with enough money to keep us comfortable and see us outfitted for a trip to Texas, we'll go after your gold."

The implacable jut to Micajah's chin told Jeremy that further argument was useless. "How're you going to kill St. Clair?" Jeremy demanded sullenly.

"Don't know," Micajah returned cheerfully. "But I'm certain before too long I'll think of something very deadly for our poor not-long-for-this-earth Adam St. Clair!"

Oblivious of the unpleasant plans being discussed for his untimely demise, Adam St. Clair was doing what after thirty-four years of perfecting his technique he did with great aplomb and style—infuriating, beguiling and effortlessly seducing a woman all at the same time! Not that the lady in question needed to be seduced!

Upon her arrival in Natchez six months ago from Charleston with her brother, Charles, to visit with their older married sister, Susan Jeffries, Betsey Asher had taken one look at Adam St. Clair's long-limbed elegant length, mocking sapphire eyes and curly black hair and had decided then and there she *must* have him! That he came with a fortune, well-bred connections and a renowned plantation, Belle Vista, was certainly all in his favor, but it was *Adam* who fascinated Betsey and made her chase after him with shameless abandon—despite Charles's displeasure with her choice. Her brother had made it clear that he wanted her to marry a much more malleable gentleman, but Betsey had turned a deaf ear. She wanted Adam! And she intended to have him!

Standing an impressive six feet four inches tall in his bare feet, Adam was definitely a noticeable young man under any circumstances. When that height was coupled with a smoothly muscular build, broad shoulders, rakishly handsome features and a devilish charm, Betsey's pursuit of him was perfectly understandable. But Betsey was after more than a delightful flirtation or even a passionate affair; by choice she was unmarried at the advanced age of twenty-six and now that it was imperative that she marry a *rich* man, she was becoming increasingly wrathful that a man who was not only rich but one she desperately wanted was proving to be singularly elusive when it came to proposing marriage to her.

Unfortunately, while Adam was entirely willing to bed her and have her sobbing with gratification at his incomparable sexual prowess, he had no intention of asking for her hand in marriage! Which was one of the things, besides getting him out of his clothes and into her bed, that Betsey had been angling for since the moment her wide green eyes had met Adam's dancing dark blue gaze at the soiree her sister had held to introduce Betsey to all the eligible young men in the neighborhood.

The darling of her doting wealthy family, born several years after her sister and brother, Betsey had been spoiled and indulged since birth and she was not used to being denied . . . *anything!* As she had grown older, the pattern of being granted her every whim had continued—the fact that she had been generously endowed with a head of wavy blond hair, thickly lashed, mysterious green eyes set in an undeniably lovely face, and possessed an alluringly curved little body had not escaped the attention of the gentlemen. From the age of sixteen she had capriciously kept a string of helplessly ensnared suitors dangling eagerly after her and once she had discovered that there were ways to enjoy the pleasures to be found in the arms of a lover without the confines of marriage, she had blithely refused to even consider the most passionate appeals from the most eligible bachelors for her hand in wedlock. At least that had been the case until the disaster her brother, Charles, had created of their fortune had been revealed to her, and until she had set her fickle heart on Adam St. Clair!

"But why *won't* you marry me?" she demanded with a petulant curve to her pouting rosy mouth.

Sprawled lithely on the tumbled bed that bore witness to their recent lovemaking, Adam regarded her with an amused glance from beneath his thick black lashes. She was sitting in naked splendor at the edge of the mattress and Adam's gaze was decidedly appreciative as well as amused as he looked at her. The dark blue gleam of his eyes was barely discernible, but Betsey caught the faint beginnings of a mocking smile at the corners of his full-lipped mouth and said resentfully, "My question wasn't meant to make you laugh!"

"I'm not laughing," Adam said lightly. "It is just that I find it hard to concentrate on anything but that delectable little body of yours when you are sitting in all your tempting nakedness not two feet away from me."

They were in the bedroom of a surprisingly luxurious cabin that was tucked into a secluded corner of Adam's vast estate, Belle Vista, situated some miles north of Natchez. The onetime hunting cabin had been turned into a discreet trysting place many years ago when Adam had been deeply embroiled in a delicate affair with a married woman. Having gone to great lengths to prepare suitable quarters in which to, er, entertain the lady, he had seen no reason to abandon the place when the affair ended—especially not when there were other ladies, like Betsey Asher, who did not want their sexual liaisons with him to be public fodder. . . .

Adam continued to appreciatively eye Betsey's naked form as she preened at his words, her full, pink-tipped breasts jutting enticingly forward, but there was a part of him that was wondering if he hadn't made a mistake in bringing her to the cabin in the first place. Not that he didn't enjoy all that yielding white flesh brazenly displayed for his gaze or the astonishing things she could do with that pouting mouth of hers, but he'd made it clear from the onset of their affair that marriage was not a state he had ever contemplated. Ever. While Betsey had assured him most blithely some weeks ago when their affair began that marriage was the last thing on her mind, regrettably it would appear that the lady had changed her mind. Adam sighed. God, how he hated scenes!

Encouraged by his remarks about her body, Betsey stretched languidly and, looking coyly over at him, murmured throatily, "If we were to be married, we wouldn't have to meet secretly anymore. This 'delectable little body' of mine that you enjoy so much would be in your bed every night. . . ."

"And whose bed would it grace during the afternoons?" Adam asked sardonically, having no illusions about the young lady.

A gasp of outrage came from Betsey and she glared at him, leaving off her sensuous posturings. Did he really know about her other lovers? she wondered warily. She was certain she had been exceedingly discreet. He couldn't possibly know that when he wasn't available she appeased her appetites with a few other accommodating gentlemen in the area, could he? Not that any of them was as skilled in bed as Adam St. Clair! It was just too bad that he had to be the most desirable, infuriatingly arrogant, utterly charming rogue she had ever met! she thought resentfully.

Adam was undeniably all of those things as he lounged carelessly against a pile of white pillows on the bed. A snowy cambric sheet covered the lower half of his tall body, leaving bare the broad shoulders, wide chest, narrow waist, and part of his upper

abdomen. The fabric lovingly outlined his lean hips
and long legs, and almost seemed to caress his blatant manhood as he relaxed there like a sultan surveying his harem, his virility almost tangible. His
skin appeared very dark against the pristine whiteness of the sheet and pillows, the lavish sprinkling of
black hair which covered his chest and arrowed
down to disappear tantalizingly beneath the sheet intensifying his darkness. A lock of curly black hair
persisted in falling across his broad forehead, and
with those gleaming sapphire-blue eyes, deep-set below thick, boldly arching black brows, those hard-
angled cheekbones, that formidable chin and the
most sensually chiseled mouth Betsey had ever encountered in her life, it wasn't surprising that he had
been the object of more than one woman's fantasy all
of his adult life.

He was also, Betsey reflected bitterly as she sat on
the side of the bed amid the rumpled sheets, undoubtedly the most enraging, the most horrid, the
most fascinating, the most irresistible male she had
ever met in all her years! And it was palpably the
unfairest thing in nature that even as furious as she
was with him, she couldn't help but respond to his
flagrant masculinity.

Her eyes glistening with sudden hunger, she
leaned forward and said with a calculatingly win-
some smile, "Oh, Adam! Let's not fight!" Her eyes
caressing him, she breathed huskily, "Not now. Not
when we have so little time together . . ."

A frankly carnal smile tugged at his lips. "Is that a
hint, my dear?"

A shiver of anticipation ran down Betsey's spine at
the explicit promise in his deep voice. No matter
how many times he made love to her, no matter how
limp and satiated she lay in his arms afterward, she
never seemed to get enough of Adam's addicting
lovemaking. She hungered for him as she had hungered for nothing else in her life and as she stared

fixedly at the growing bulge beneath the sheets at the apex of his lean thighs, her breath caught in her throat. A catlike smile of satisfaction on her full pink mouth, she reached over and, pulling the sheet down to where it rested across his thighs, lasciviously caressed the burgeoning flesh she had exposed, her fingers marveling at his size. "Is *this* a hint?" she asked demurely.

Adam's hands closed around her slim shoulders and with tormenting languidness he pulled her slowly up his long body. His mouth sliding warmly down her cheek to nibble at her lips, he muttered, "Now what do you think?"

His mouth found hers and he kissed her with such blunt passion that she couldn't think at all, not when his lips were pressing demandingly against hers, not when her breasts were crushed against his chest, nor when her soft body was so aware of the warm, hard flesh beneath hers. Her arms closed around his neck and hungrily she met the teasing thrust of his tongue as he deepened the kiss, her senses spinning out of control.

Deftly sliding her off him and onto the mattress beside him, Adam let his mouth travel down to her breasts, one hand expertly seeking the moist heat between her legs. Betsey moaned when he parted the soft flesh that ached for his touch and as he suckled at her breast and his knowing fingers brought her effortlessly to the brink of ecstasy, she was convinced that she had never had another lover as sinfully exciting as Adam St. Clair.

Only when she was writhing wildly beneath his caresses did Adam lean back against the pillows and lift her up over him. Smoothly he positioned her willing body above him, his rigid shaft protruding aggressively upward. With one swift, sure thrust, he impaled her, and his mouth finding hers, his hands on her hips guiding her frantic movements, they both soon found the scalding pleasure they sought.

Collapsed against him, her body still tingling from the feverish delight he had given her, she murmured, "Wouldn't this be wonderful to share every night? If we were married, instead of having to meet only when I can sneak away from Susan and Charles, we could indulge our pleasures whenever we wanted."

Adam groaned and, almost dumping her off him, sat up and swung his legs over the side of the bed. Running a hand through his tousled black hair, he glanced back at her and muttered, "Betsey, I don't mean to be ungentlemanly, but I did warn you— quite candidly, if I remember correctly—that even if we became lovers, I had no intention of marrying you! I told you emphatically that I was not, nor have I ever been, in the market for a wife! Now, if you can't accept that fact, I suggest we stop meeting each other."

Swallowing back the black rage that surged through her, Betsey composed her features into a look of utter woe. Forcing tears to her eyes, she sobbed pathetically, "Oh, Adam! How can you be so heartless? I know you love me! Why *won't* you marry me?"

"What you don't understand or will *not* understand is that I don't love you! I've never said I love you or any other woman and I've *never* given you any cause to believe that there is anything between us but the pleasure our bodies give each other! I won't marry you," Adam enunciated carefully, barely holding onto his formidable temper, "because I goddamn well don't want to, and if I ever were to be mad enough *to* marry, I would want to know that I was the only man in my wife's bed!"

Ignoring Betsey's enraged shriek, he sprang up from the bed, stalked across the room and swiftly pulled on a pair of buckskin breeches. Finding a white cotton shirt, he jerked it over his head. His handsome face hard, he turned to face the woman on the bed. "I don't want us to end this way, but if marriage is what you're after, I suggest that we don't see each other anymore. As a matter of fact, I think it would be wise if we didn't see each other for a while anyway."

Fearful that she had pushed him too far, frantically wondering how he had learned about her other lovers, she made a desperate attempt to regain lost ground. "Oh, Adam!" she wailed mournfully. "What are you talking about? You know that you are the only man I love!" And gambling that he didn't really know anything, she added with commendable innocence, "I just don't understand what you're talking about! Other men in my bed! Why, the very idea!"

His sapphire-blue eyes cold, Adam bit out acidly, "Betsey, that horse won't run! I know about Reginald and Matthew and even poor, silly Edward. I've known about them for weeks, and while it doesn't bother me if you feel the need for other lovers, it *does* bother me when you try to pretend that I am the only man in your life and that my bed is the only one in which you have gamboled!"

Incensed that she had been found out, Betsey surged up from the bed, and forgetting the urgent necessity to find a wealthy husband, she angrily grabbed up her gown and hissed, "Why, you damned gypsy bastard! Who the hell do you think you are?"

Adam froze and something dangerous entered his hard blue eyes. In one swift stride he reached the bed, and grasping her upper arm, he shook her urgently. "Just remember," he snarled softly, "that I am the same gypsy bastard who only moments ago you were professing to love and pleading with so sweetly to marry! And I think you should get the tale correct—I was kidnapped by the gypsies, not sired by one, and as for being a bastard ..." A thought struck him, such as the knowledge that, through a trick of fate, he really was the bastard son of Guy Savage and not the legitimate issue of a man long-dead, as was commonly believed. Suddenly realizing that Betsey's remark hadn't been *entirely* untrue, he dropped her arm and grinned. "You may be right about my being a bastard," he said lightly, "but that fact certainly doesn't speak well for your taste in men, sweetheart!"

"How dare you!" Betsey breathed furiously, her cheeks unbecomingly flushed from the force of her anger.

Blue eyes gleaming now with mocking laughter, Adam drawled coolly, "My dear, there isn't much that I *wouldn't* dare! So you shouldn't be surprised at what I may or may not do!"

Deliberately working herself into one of her tantrums of magnificent proportions, Betsey fumbled angrily with her pale green gown of fine India muslin. "You are rude, arrogant and vile! I never want to lay eyes on you again as long as I live! Get out of my sight!" she spat wrathfully.

"Well, I'd like to indulge you," Adam said dryly, "but unless you plan on walking the five miles to your sister's home, I'm afraid you'll have to put up with my vile presence a little while longer!"

There was a silence fraught with tension and rage on Betsey's part during most of the time it took Adam to escort her in his gig to the garden gate through which she had slipped out several hours ago. It was only as they were traveling over the last quarter mile before they would reach her sister's house, Magnolia Hills, that it occurred to Betsey that Adam really was going to take her at her word and never see her again.

The notion of a man finishing with *her* was appalling, but almost worse was the growing notion that never again would she know the pleasure of his masterful lovemaking, and *that* simply was not to be contemplated! She wanted Adam St. Clair and she was going to have him and *nothing* was going to stop her! Peeping over at the remote expression on his face, she nibbled at her lips nervously, her mind racing for a way to retrieve the ground that she had so foolishly lost.

Reaching the wrought-iron gate which opened onto the extensive gardens of her sister's home, Adam pulled his horse to a stop. Leaping down from the gig, he walked around it and silently lifted down Betsey's slight form.

Shrouded in a black silk cape, with the hood shadowing her small face and concealing the fairness of her hair, Betsey was nearly unrecognizable. Standing there at the side of the road, she glanced up at him, and frantically trying her last trick, one that had never failed her before, she let her eyes fill with tears. "Oh, Adam!" she breathed in low, not-entirely-mendacious tones of heartbreak. "I can't believe that we are actually parting this way!"

Taking her arm politely but guiding her inexorably toward the gate, he said coolly, "We agreed in the beginning that it would happen someday. It just happened perhaps sooner than either of us intended." Quietly opening the gate and thrusting her through it before she had time to prevent him, he added dryly, "You made your feelings quite clear and I don't believe that there is anything to be gained by discussing it further. I never argue with a lady."

"Oh, but, Adam, you don't understand," Betsey murmured softly, not quite able to believe that this was really happening to her. "You made me so angry and I just lost my temper. I didn't *mean* what I said."

Adam glanced down at her, his face shadowed in the darkness. "It doesn't matter, Betsey," he said wearily. "It's over. You want marriage and I don't; there is no middle ground for us, and since I am unlikely to change my mind about that fact, I think it would be wise if we use this opportunity to part as amicably as possible. Good night!"

Spinning on his heel, he swiftly crossed the short distance to his gig and, before Betsey's stunned gaze, leaped into the vehicle and began urging the horse in the direction of Belle Vista. He's actually leaving me! she thought incredulously. Stamping her foot with rage, forgetting the need for silence, she called sharply, "Adam St. Clair, don't you dare do this to me! Come back here this instant or I'll make you sorry."

"I already am, sweetheart!" Adam threw over his shoulder with a mocking laugh.

An instant later the horse picked up speed. Her bosom heaving with baffled fury, she watched in chagrined wrath as the gig slowly became swallowed up in darkness. That Adam St. Clair! He was a devil!

Chapter 4

ADAM MIGHT HAVE LAUGHED, ALBEIT IRONICALLY, AS HE drove away from Betsey Asher, but his laughter faded immediately when he considered all the snares that a woman with marriage on her mind could devise to trap the unwary male. He'd been adroitly eluding them for years, but it didn't mean that he underestimated the danger. Softly he swore under his breath. Women were necessary, but Jesus! They could be the very devil, too!

Returning to his home, he retreated to the quiet elegance of the very masculine study at Belle Vista, but the persistent restlessness that seemed to dog his every step these days returned with a vengeance. By rights he should have been exhausted—he had been up since dawn the previous day and it was now going on four o'clock in the morning. He grinned. And he had just spent several, ah, *strenuous* hours in Betsey's arms! But seeking his bed did not appeal to him, and pouring himself a liberal amount of brandy into a snifter, he wandered about the mahogany pan-eled room with its blue-and-scarlet-hued Turkey rug, sipping his brandy.

He supposed it was Betsey's angry remark about his being a gypsy bastard that was at the root of his sleeplessness. Not that the remark itself bothered him, but it brought to mind those ten years that he and his half sister, Catherine Tremayne, had lived with the gypsies. He had been five years old when they had been kidnapped from Mountacre, his stepfather's estate in England, and once he had stopped missing their mother, Rachael, he had adapted quite well to the nomadic, adventuresome life of the gypsies. He had grown up unfettered by conventional demands—while other boys had been learning their letters, Adam had been increasing his skill with the knife and discovering the bounty that deft fingers could snatch from the unwary. His life had been one of untrammeled freedom as they had constantly traveled throughout the land. The stunning return to Mountacre when he had been fifteen had been traumatic and had left Adam feeling lost in a world that should have been his natural milieu.

Under any circumstances a young man raised like a wild wolf cub as he had been would have had trouble adjusting to finding himself suddenly plunged into the stiffly punctilious world of a wealthy lord of the realm, but there had been an obvious dislike between Lord Tremayne, the Earl of Mount, and his stepson and it had caused endless friction and dissension. Upon his eighteenth birthday, Adam had been thrilled when it was revealed that his real father, an American, had willed him a rich inheritance near the city of Natchez in the Mississippi area. The parting from his sister had been difficult—they had shared so much together during those gypsy years—and while Adam would miss his mother, she was in many ways a stranger to him and so he had been able to leave England with only a little heartache.

Finding himself a rich young man in a land as wild

and lawless as the New World had been a heady experience at eighteen. With no mentor to guide or restrain him, he'd found no dare too reckless, no wager too high, no duel too dangerous, and in a relatively short time he had gained the reputation of being a mercurial daredevil. And yet those very attributes that might have been frowned upon elsewhere were the very things that the wealthy planter society of Natchez admired—hard drinking, hard riding, a quick temper, and a cool head and a steady arm on the dueling field. Adam excelled at all of those activities and he was rapturously absorbed into the aristocractic society of Natchez.

The years had dociled him somewhat, however, and he supposed that Catherine's fleeing from her very new husband, Jason Savage, and arriving pregnant on his doorstep nearly twelve years ago had been the beginning of his attempts to live a more conventional life. Catherine and Jason had settled their differences and were now happily married, but Adam was still plagued with restlessness and the wild recklessness that burned within him sometimes lured him willy-nilly into situations that were filled with peril and danger.

Like spying on the British during the past war for Jason, he thought with a wry twist to his mobile mouth. Adam firmly believed that Jason had made a point to come up with hazardous antics to keep him diverted.

Taking an appreciative sip of the brandy, Adam continued to wander idly about the study, recalling the first time he had met Jason Savage. It had been at Jason's plantation, Terre du Coeur, when having escorted Rachael upon her sudden arrival from England to Terre du Coeur, Adam had discovered that not only was his beloved sister in the hands of Jason's greatest enemy, Blas Davalos, but that Jason's father, Guy Savage, was also *his* father! It had been a stunning shock. Even when Guy and Rachael had painfully explained to him and Jason the bare facts, Adam could hardly take in the enormity of it all— how years before, Guy had gone to England to obtain a divorce from Jason's mother, Antonia, and sincerely believing that he was a free man while visiting in the country, he had met, fallen deeply in love with and married Rachael. Rachael was already pregnant with Adam when the horrifying truth was discovered— Antonia had changed her mind, refusing to countenance the divorce. Legally, Guy was still married to Antonia, his runaway marriage to Rachael invalid. Fearing the gossip and scandal that would accompany the truth, Guy, after bestowing his own mother's maiden name, St. Clair, on the unborn child and having made the proper arrangements for the child's future, had been hurriedly shipped back to America and a conveniently deceased husband had been erected to be the father of Rachael's child.

No one had ever considered that, years later, Guy's legitimate son, Jason, might come to England and fall in love with Catherine, Rachael's daughter by the earl, thereby inadvertently setting into motion the events that would force revelation of the truth. Even though those shattering events had taken place over twelve years ago, sometimes it all still amazed Adam. Guy and Rachael had been married nearly ten years now and to no one's surprise, nine months from the day of their wedding vows, Rachael had presented Guy with another child, a daughter, Heather and barely a year after that had given birth to a son, Benedict. The secret of Adam's birth, however, remained just that—as far as the world knew, Adam was merely Guy's stepson.

Sighing, Adam stared moodily out of the long windows that graced one of the outside walls of the room. Daylight was still a way off, but already the darkness seemed less dense. Another day was upon him and he wondered cynically how he was going to spend it. A competent overseer and staff freed him

from the day-to-day mechanics of running a plantation the size of Belle Vista, and his well-trained house
servants and stablemen stood ready to receive his every command. It was a lowering thought, but Adam
was very aware that he had precious little to do with
the excellent management and wise business decisions that characterized the running of Belle Vista
and the continued growth of his personal fortune. He
had reached that point in life where, unless he
wanted to discharge his excellent overseer, lawyer
and business agent and take over the running of his
vast holdings himself, his presence was almost super-
fluous. Which left him with a hell of a lot of time on
his hands. . . .

God! He was so bloody bored with the amusements to be found in Natchez! Not for the first time
Adam seriously considered leaving the area for several months in search of *some* way to banish his increasing restlessness.

He needed to clear his head of too many nights of
heavy drinking in smoke-filled gaming rooms; he
needed new sights, needed the satisfaction of a body
exhausted from physical exertion and needed to in-
fuse his life with an eagerness to greet each day.
There was only one thing for it—he would go to
Terre du Coeur! A thoughtful expression on his
handsome face, he seriously began to consider the
idea. There was much, he conceded ruefully, to say
for the plan. Jason's plantation was in one of the
wilder, less settled, little-explored sections of northern Louisiana. There were few neighbors and social
affairs were certainly at a minimum, nor were there
any haunts of vice nearby to distract one in a weak
moment from the primeval lure of the land.

Adam grinned, tossing down the remainder of his
brandy. He found the remoteness of Terre du Coeur
utterly appealing. Something about the sheer immen-
sity of the ever-changing panorama, of the raw,
wildly flourishing landscape, called strongly to him.

Setting down his brandy snifter, he decided suddenly that a trip to see Catherine and Jason was precisely what he needed. He would leave today! This very morning! A hasty word with his overseer, a man who knew how to keep his mouth shut should anyone, particularly Betsey Asher, come asking about Adam's whereabouts, and a brief meeting with his equally closemouthed butler would settle the matter.

If there was a flutter in the household at Belle Vista when his staff was informed of his precipitous plans, not by so much as a lifted brow did they reveal it. Despite his sleepless night, by ten o'clock in the morning Adam was on his way to Terre du Coeur. Since he kept several changes of clothing and other personal effects he might need at his sister's home, his requirements for the journey were few, and with little more than a bedroll, weapons and some basic cooking equipment, he rode off astride his favorite black stallion—an impressive son out of the stallion which Jason had bought on that fateful trip to England when a violet-eyed wench, Tamara—which was the name the gypsies had given Adam's sister, Catherine—had caught his fancy.

Adam was an expert woodsman—he had been tutored by Jason's blood brother, the Cherokee brave Blood Drinker—and there was little about taking care of himself in the wild that he hadn't learned. It was with Blood Drinker at his side that Adam had learned to expertly "read" the signs made by man and animal alike and to set effective deadly snares comprised of a bit of vine. With nothing more than the clothes on their backs and knives at their sides, he and Blood Drinker would mysteriously disappear into the vast trackless wilderness for months at a time, living each day as it came, hunting, fishing and exploring land that had never known the footsteps of the white man. Blood Drinker had taught him well, and consequently, when Adam finally arrived at Terre du Coeur nearly three weeks later, he looked fit and vital, his worn buckskins superbly fitting his muscled frame, his eyes bright and clear and his face bronzed by the hot sun. He looked not at all like a man who had spent the past weeks riding along through a feral wilderness, sleeping on the ground and hunting for every morsel he ate.

He arrived around three o'clock in the afternoon in front of the Spanish-style wood-and-brick house that Jason Savage called home. A wide, bow-shaped staircase on the outside of the house formed a graceful arch which led to the vine-draped upper story, and Adam had barely dismounted before Jason strolled into view at the top of the staircase.

"Mon Dieu!" his half brother exclaimed in mock disgust, his emerald eyes glinting with amusement. "Not you! Surely the fast ladies and gaming halls of Natchez are enough to distract you so that I do not have to put up with your less-than-restful presence!"

Adam grinned at him, his teeth gleaming whitely amidst the heavy black stubble that covered his face, a lock of dark hair waving impudently across his brow. "You *did* tell me that I could come to visit whenever the mood struck me, didn't you?"

"Oui! But I didn't think you would actually *do* it!" Jason replied sardonically, his words at variance with the warm smile that curved his mouth. Coming swiftly down the staircase, he approached Adam and pulled the younger man into a crushing embrace. "It is good to see you, little brother," he added.

There were some similarities between the two men, but their resemblance to each other was not marked. Both had thick black hair and both were tall, and while in his youth Adam had been an inch shorter than Jason, now, at thirty-four to Jason's forty-two, he stood as tall as his older brother. Their builds were dissimilar—Adam was a supple rapier to Jason's broadsword. His body, though wide-shouldered, was leaner than Jason's more formidable physique, yet like the lethal rapier, Adam moved with the same deadly speed and purpose, as more than one fool had learned. Jason had inherited his emerald eyes from his Creole mother, whereas Adam's sapphire-blue eyes had come from Rachael, but there was something about the chiseled perfection of their jaws and chins and the faint arrogant flare to their handsome noses that had come to both of them from their father, Guy.

Smiling wryly at Jason's words, Adam murmured, "Not quite so little, I think."

Jason laughed. "Don't take umbrage so quickly, my young firebrand! But enough of this—come, come inside and refresh yourself."

It suddenly dawned on Adam that something was missing—there were not three or four children shouting and racing to meet him, nor was there any sign of Catherine. Normally she would have appeared by now and hurled herself into his arms, an endless stream of excited greetings pouring from her lips.

A question in his eyes, Adam glanced at Jason. Correctly reading his halfbrother's expression, Jason replied easily, "Don't worry! There is nothing wrong. Catherine and the children are in New Orleans at the moment—they have been visiting there for some months. As a matter of fact, if you had arrived a day later, you wouldn't have found me at home either. I leave tomorrow to escort them home."

"Oh!" Adam exclaimed, feeling rather let-down. He hadn't realized until this moment how much he had looked forward to seeing his sister and her pack of rascally brats.

"You could come to New Orleans with me," Jason proposed as they walked up the stairs and entered the coolness of the wide gallery.

Adam grimaced. "It was to escape the, er, amusements of the city that I came here. New Orleans has much the same to offer as Natchez—just more exotic versions of it!"

Jason smiled, but the expression in his emerald

eyes was thoughtful. He made no comment, though, and entering the wide hallway, he led the way into his study.

It was only after Adam was comfortably sprawled across from him in a large russet leather chair, a tall, cool glass of whiskey and mint in his hand, that Jason spoke. Looking affectionately at the younger brother he had come to love deeply, Jason said, "I really do have to leave tomorrow, as your sister will be expecting me in New Orleans. You know that you can stay here as long as you like—in fact, I insist that you remain here while I go to fetch the family home. Catherine would never forgive me if she learned that you had come to visit and I had not done everything within my power to keep you here."

"You're certain you won't mind?" Adam asked politely, although he already knew the answer. He was as much at home at Terre du Coeur as he was at Belle Vista, and while it was not what he had planned, he found the notion of some solitary exploration suddenly very appealing.

Jason shook his dark head. "Don't be ridiculous! Enjoy yourself while I am gone and by the time I return with Catherine and the children you will be sick enough of your own company to view our arrival with joy."

Derisively Adam drawled, "I already am sick of my own company—it is why I came to visit you! But I will accept your invitation to stay and I'll look forward to your return with the family."

Jason shot him a keen look. "Have the pleasures of Natchez palled so soon? I would have thought that after your escapades with the British last year at the capital you would have welcomed a period of time of tranquility."

Adam took a long pull of his drink. "Tranquility," he said scathingly, "can be so bloody boring—you know that."

"Ah, but you forget," Jason replied lightly. "Since

the advent of your sister into my life, I cannot say
that I have known a tranquil moment! If she is not
happily wreaking havoc in my heart and home, then
it seems that our children somehow manage to fill
the void when she is in a sweetly submissive mood.
Something, I can tell you that does not happen often!
Perhaps if you would . . ."

"Find a wife?" Adam asked in a dangerously dul-
cet tone.

Unperturbed to be caught at such blatant match-
making, Jason smiled angelically. "Not just *any* wife,
you understand, *mon ami,* but a wife who will add a
tempestuous element to your life, a wife who will
turn your well-ordered world upside down and keep
you ecstatically employed in her bed. A wife who
will present you with a quiverful of impudent little
scamps similar to my own, and one who will en-
chant, enrage and utterly beguile you. *That's* what
you need, and then perhaps you will not be so intent
upon seeking adventure and risking your life on
whatever dangerous scheme may next occur to you!"

"A wife like yours is what you mean, isn't it?"

"Well, that would be a fair assumption, but since
there is only one Catherine and since she very definitely is *my* wife and your sister, I would suggest
that you look a little farther afield!" Jason answered
with a grin, although his eyes remained serious.

How well did Jason know the devils that drove
Adam! They came from having too much—too much
freedom to do as he willed, too much money, too
much power with no one to gainsay him, too much
pride and temper and far too much attractiveness to
the ladies. Nothing challenged Adam. Everything
was simply too easy, whether it was women or
money or position or even friends. Whatever Adam
wanted . . . Adam got! Jason easily recognized the
reasons behind Adam's constant search for excitement and adventures. Once he had been the same,
and when he was twenty-nine and his father, Guy,

had suggested he marry, he had been outraged. Looking back over the past twelve years, Jason would now readily admit that Guy had been right.

But again, although he believed marriage would do much to alleviate Adam's reckless need for new horizons, Jason was very aware that it would take an exceptional woman to tame his half brother. Marriage to a properly raised, demure young thing was not the answer—such a marriage would be disastrous for Adam—and yet Jason would not like to see him caught in the clutches of a sophisticated, worldly woman either! What Adam needed, Jason conceded slowly, was a woman like Catherine—unconventional, strong-willed, able to hold her own against Adam's forceful personality, hot-tempered, fiercely loyal, yet possessing a heart full of warmth and love.

If he had only known it, Jason had rather aptly described Savanna O'Rourke, but since Adam was at Terre du Coeur in northern Louisiana and Savanna was currently attempting to adjust to living with her mother at Campo de Verde, some miles south of New Orleans, the likelihood of Adam and Savanna crossing paths seemed highly improbable. And as far as Savanna was concerned, the *last* thing she needed at present was a husband—Bodene was proving to be every bit as obnoxiously restrictive and domineering as *any* husband could have hoped to be!

It wasn't, she admitted fairly, as she lay comfortably beneath a weeping willow tree near one of the small bayous that crisscrossed the property, that he meant to be so overbearing, it was simply that Bodene was used to arranging events to suit himself and she was used to doing precisely that same thing! And when they each wanted the opposite . . .

Savanna had known that Bodene would be elated at her apparently easy capitulation to return with him, and since there was no use squabbling over minor things, she had let him arrange their journey to

Campo de Verde without much argument. Their trip downriver had been uneventful and she and Bodene had managed to spend the time together quite pleasurably—no serious disagreements. Until they had reached New Orleans . . .

He had craftily, he thought, suggested that they remain a night or two in New Orleans and then, when she had not objected, had mentioned that she might like to visit the dressmaker who enjoyed her mother's patronage. He'd be very happy, Bodene had continued with suspect indifference, to help her refurbish her wardrobe. After all, she couldn't go around in that same plain brown gown forever, could she? Having seen where he was maneuvering her, she had taxed him with it and they had ended up in one unholy row—Bodene furious that she would not let him deck her out in stylish fashion, Savanna equally furious that he thought she was going to let him start treating her as a poor dependent. They had been skirmishing daily since then, about everything from the way she insisted upon helping with the household chores, despite the adequate staff employed by Bodene, to the fact that she preferred to go barefoot most of the time.

Savanna sighed and, arms behind her head, continued to stare blankly up through the gentle green canopy formed by the branches of the willow tree. The sky was a clear, brilliant blue, but she took no notice of it, her mind on the situation.

She hadn't realized how much she had missed her mother until she had arrived at Campo de Verde and Elizabeth had fairly tumbled down the steps in the excitement of Savanna's arrival. There was little resemblance between the two women as they had stood there in the hot sunlight, embracing each other. Savanna towered inches above Elizabeth's smaller height, and though intermingled in the blond strands of Elizabeth's hair could be seen several glints of red, her hair did not have the flame-red glory of her daughter's. It was only in the brilliant clarity of the aquamarine eyes, which they shared, that their resemblance was obvious, that and perhaps in the full lushness of their shapes, despite the difference in their height.

At thirty-nine, Elizabeth O'Rourke was still a fine figure of a woman, although the signs of her hard life were obvious in the lines and creases that marred her once incredibly lovely features. That she had been born and bred a lady was apparent not only in her speech and manner, but in a certain elegant air about her that she had never lost despite the adversities she had suffered. She possessed a careworn beauty and looked to be the mature woman that she was, a woman who had lived through many difficult years, but had triumphed in the end.

That first evening at Campo de Verde, the two women had sat up until nearly dawn talking about whatever came to their minds, and it had been heartwarmingly wonderful—for the first time it seemed that they met as equals, not just as mother and daughter, and whatever differences they might have had in the past seemed to have disappeared. But there were still delicate areas between them and Savanna had inadvertently touched on one of them when she asked unthinkingly, "Do you ever wonder why he left me his estate when he never publicly acknowledged me as his daughter?"

As the hours had passed, their conversation had touched briefly on Davalos, something it rarely did, and the words had popped out of her mouth before Savanna had considered her mother's feelings. The sad expression that touched Elizabeth's face twisted Savanna's heart, and dropping to her knees beside her mother's chair, she muttered, "I'm sorry. I didn't mean to bring up a painful subject."

Elizabeth smiled wryly. "It's not exactly the subject that I find painful as much as it is your continued bitterness and resentment of him."

Savanna grimaced. "I can't help it. I barely knew the man and I resent what he did to you."

Elizabeth gently clasped Savanna's chin and tilted her head up, then replied deliberately, "Davalos could not have seduced me if I had not been a willing participant—never forget that. I know you and Bodene have never understood, but I *loved* your father. And in the beginning he was everything a young girl dreams of—handsome, witty and charming—and I was swept off my feet. I took one look at him across the Governor's ballroom, saw those dark, gleaming eyes and those arrogant Spanish features and fell madly in love . . . and though I wanted to stop loving him when I discovered precisely what sort of man I had given my heart to, it was far too late. I loved him—even with all his faults." She glanced away, her thoughts deep in the past.

"I know that he was not a good man," she finally said in a low tone. "I know that he treated us disgracefully, shamefully, but while he hurt me dreadfully, I never seemed to be able to stop loving him." She looked unhappily at Savanna. "I know. I should have been stronger. I should have had more pride. I should have hated him for what he did and continued to do, but the *habit* of loving is very hard to break. . . ."

Savanna rested her cheek on her mother's knee. "But didn't you resent what he had done?"

Elizabeth's mouth curved ruefully. "Oh, yes. I resented it bitterly and I can't deny that there were times that I actually felt I hated him. But then he would come to me and woo me and convince me that soon, someday very soon, he would indeed marry me and introduce me to my rightful place at his side . . . and like a fool, I would believe him." She shook her head as if amazed that she had ever been so utterly besotted. "Sometimes," she continued slowly, "you can know that something or someone is bad for you and yet you *cannot* seem to break free of the spell they weave around you—so it was with me and your father." She looked down at Savanna. "I've never pretended that he was a good man, or even an honorable man. I suspect that he may have been a wicked man, but I have to believe that in his *own* fashion he did love us and that perhaps if he had not been killed, he might have one day married me and acknowledged you as his daughter."

She lifted Savanna's head from her lap and smiled. "And in a way, he did acknowledge you, didn't he? In his will he stated clearly that you were his daughter and his heir."

Savanna made a face and attempted to change the subject, even slightly. "What do you think he was doing out there in Spanish Texas when he was killed?"

Elizabeth shrugged. "I have no idea, unless it had to do with some wild scheme of his to find a fortune."

At Savanna's look of curiosity, Elizabeth added reluctantly, "That last time he came to see us he was full of some nonsense about a golden fortune. He kept insisting that this man, I believe his name was Jason, Jason Savage, was his deadliest enemy and that Jason would kill him rather than let him find the fortune first."

"Didn't you believe him? Isn't that what probably happened? That this Jason Savage killed him?"

Elizabeth shook her head vehemently. "I didn't know it at the time, but Jason Savage is very well thought of here in Louisiana. He is, and always has been, very wealthy and moves in the highest circles of society—he would have had no reason to kill your father."

Savanna wasn't as easily convinced as her mother and a faint frown crept between her eyes as she said, "But if there were a fortune involved . . ."

Elizabeth laughed softly, shaking her head again. "No, dear. There was no fortune. It was just a wild-goose chase that your father was running after. He *always* had those sorts of schemes and every time he left me, it was with the promise that it would be the last time, that *this* time he really would have found his fortune."

The explanation didn't exactly satisfy Savanna, but since it had all happened a long time ago, she soon lost interest in it and she and her mother turned to happier topics. And for the first few days in her mother's home, Savanna surprised herself by actually enjoying the quiet, unhurried rhythm of the place.

That feeling hadn't lasted. She had been at Campo de Verde for almost a week now and the place was already beginning to suffocate her. Thinking of how happy her mother was that she was here, Savanna felt guilty for feeling as she did. She loved her mother, and Elizabeth's excitement and open pleasure at having her living at Campo de Verde was deeply touching, but Savanna knew that she didn't belong here.

With the days of Crow's Nest far behind her, Elizabeth had made a totally new and different life for herself, one that Savanna found unbearably restrictive. Here at Campo de Verde, where Elizabeth's former life was unknown, it was assumed that she had been married to Davalos, and so she was viewed as a respectable widow with a circle of equally respectable friends. Those same friends, not unnaturally, expected Savanna to fall into the same mold, but unfortunately, Savanna couldn't see herself joyfully settling down to embroidery work and pleasant little dinner parties at which one chatted about the newest fashions, children and the latest tittle-tattle that filtered down to the delicate ears of the ladies! *Dios!* The future looked bleak indeed to Savanna on this warm April afternoon.

Seeking to escape her unpleasant thoughts, she rolled over onto her stomach, staring darkly across the narrow expanse of lawn to the house that sat at the end of a short oak-studded driveway. The house at Campo de Verde was not impressive, but like its grander neighbors, it faced the mighty Mississippi River. Built over sixty years ago, more as a summer cottage, it was not a large building and it had the raised basement so common to houses in Louisiana, with the family living quarters situated on the second floor. The hip roof extended over the upper gallery that encased the entire second story, and a series of columns, large plastered brick below, delicately turned wood above, gave the house a faint charm, as did the small, curving outside staircase that led to the upper floor. Once the house had been a blinding, glistening white, but now the outside color had faded to a more pleasing, Savanna thought, soft shade of cream that contrasted attractively with the weather-worn cedar shakes of the roof.

Everything had been in a deplorable state of decay when Savanna and the others had arrived from Crow's Nest, but with hard work and as much money as they could afford lavished on the place, Campo de Verde was once again, if not a showplace, a comfortable home. Elizabeth had adored the place on sight, but Savanna had viewed the shuttered, heat-blistered building with its sagging railings with a jaundiced eye.

The surrounding area had been a veritable wilderness, the semitropical climate of lower Louisiana encouraging the rampant growth of every type of plant and tree imaginable. Huge cypress trees and massive oak trees draped with gray-green Spanish moss that drifted eerily in the air at the slightest breeze seemed to close in on the house and outbuildings. Everywhere one looked, palmettos, Spanish dagger, magnolia trees, wild honeysuckle and jasmine all fought for supremacy of the land. The junglelike setting appealed to Savanna, but quite truthfully, it was *all* that found favor with her.

Scowling, she flung herself onto her back and was still seeking a solution to her situation when a small sound made her frown. The next instant, to her horror, she found herself staring up into Micajah's grinning features. . . .

Chapter 5

Micajah HAD WASTED TWO FRUSTRATING DAYS IN Natchez trying to discover the whereabouts of one Adam St. Clair. His inquiries had come to naught and it appeared that for the present, Adam St. Clair had disappeared off the face of the earth. But having received half the money for arranging the death of the elusive St. Clair and with Jeremy whining that it was Savanna O'Rourke they needed to be chasing, *not* Adam St. Clair, Micajah had reluctantly conceded that Jeremy might be right. He could kill St. Clair at any time, but if Jeremy's tale were true, and Micajah had come to believe that it was, a visit with Savanna was definitely in order.

It had been a setback to discover that Savanna had also disappeared. But with only a *little* bloodshed, he had been able to convince the hapless caretaker of the tavern to tell him where Savanna had gone. Swiftly he and Jeremy had scurried downriver to Campo de Verde and for the last day and a half they had been impatiently lurking in the tangled undergrowth, trying to decide on the best way to kidnap Savanna.

Micajah had used the intervening time since Jeremy had first told him the tale of the gold to reflect on what he knew about Savanna and the best way to get her to, er, cooperate with him. He didn't believe that Savanna had any knowledge of the gold—if she did, she sure as hell wouldn't have been running O'Rourke's Tavern! Davalos might have claimed to have left her a golden armband, but it was obvious to him that she hadn't discovered it yet and perhaps never would, if the knowledge of the Aztec treasure still remained hidden over ten years after Davalos's death! He'd already decided that it was Jason Savage who probably knew all the answers about the gold, and Micajah didn't see the need to find the golden armband right away—there'd be plenty of time to leisurely search for it after they had found the main treasure and Savanna had discovered the delights of his lovemaking. Hell, after he found all that gold, he might even marry her if she was real good!

But first Savanna was going to have to be convinced that her father would have come back to her and Elizabeth if Jason Savage hadn't brought about his demise. Jason Savage had to be painted in the blackest light possible while Davalos bathed in a rosy glow.

To this end, Micajah had been ruthlessly drilling Jeremy on precisely what Savanna was to be told about her father's final words. His eyes boring into Jeremy's, Micajah had said grimly, "You don't have to say much—I'll do all the talking, you just nod your head and confirm as the gospel truth whatever I tell her! The important thing is that we get her to go along with us and that she views this Savage fellow as the wickedest villain alive!"

Jeremy didn't quite understand Micajah's reasoning, but he was willing to follow his lead. The gold was all that mattered to him, and if Micajah thought that taking the girl with them would help, well, then . . .

But getting the girl was proving to be difficult and Jeremy had begun to have doubts. That afternoon they hunkered down near a small bayou, hidden by the rampart vines and brush, when suddenly Micajah said with a note of satisfaction, "Well, I'll be damned! There she is, all alone, lying beneath that willow. Looks as if our luck has finally changed!"

Peering through the fanlike leaves of a palmetto, Jeremy caught sight of a tall feminine form not more than ten yards away. His heart leaped. There was no one else in sight and the nearest building was a safe distance away. The sun glinting on the flame-colored hair identified her, and Jeremy was all set to snatch her when Micajah shook his head. "No. We don't want to spook her. I'll take care of it."

After making certain that it was safe, Micajah quickly approached Savanna. She was so lost in her own thoughts, it was only when he was at her side, a smug grin on his face, that she became aware of him.

Instantly she was in motion and before he had time to blink, she was positioned in a low fighting crouch, the sunlight flashing on the blade of the knife she held expertly in her slim hand. Her aquamarine eyes narrowed dangerously, she spat, "*Dios!* What are you doing here?"

Gingerly eyeing the knife, his smile gone, Micajah replied uneasily, "I came to see you. Got something to tell you that you might find interesting."

Not trusting him, she stared contemptuously at him and snapped, "I doubt it!"

"It's about your father, Davalos—he knew of a treasure and he died trying to find it for you."

Savanna was so astonished by his words that she dropped her guard for a moment, and moving with the speed of a striking snake, Micajah's fist caught her viciously on the chin. Savanna gave a soft little sigh and crumpled to the ground.

A swift glance around and then Micajah scooped

her up and hurriedly carried her into the concealing swampy brush. When Savanna stirred sometime later, she found herself propped against a tree, bound and gagged, sitting across from a grinning Micajah and another, weaselly little man she had never seen before. Swallowing the acrid taste of fear that filled her throat, she fought against her bonds, swearing unintelligibly through the gag.

Micajah only smiled and said agreeably, "That's right, honey, curse all you want to. It don't bother me none. Especially since I can't understand you. But if you want to know what this is all about, I suggest you shut up and listen."

Savanna was afraid she already had a very good idea what this was all about, but she ceased her futile struggles to free her hands and glared at him, unaware of how she affected him.

The flame-colored hair framed her lovely features, and with her arms tightly bound behind her, her soft bosom was thrust forward, fairly spilling out of the top of the coarse brown gown. Micajah's fingers itched to touch that pale, warm flesh.

She was helpless, no one to rescue her. . . . He had actually taken a step forward when Jeremy whined, "Let's get out of here! Someone is certain to notice she's missing and come looking for her."

Micajah scowled and sent Jeremy a black look, but he nodded and growled, "You're right! Get the horses."

More terrified than she had ever been in her life, Savanna tried to think coolly. She couldn't let them take her away! She might be bound and gagged, but her feet were free. Scooting upright the second Jeremy disappeared, she bolted in the opposite direction, running and stumbling through the tangled undergrowth as fast as she could.

Micajah gave a startled yelp and was after her in an instant. For one wild moment, Savanna actually thought she might make it, but then Micajah came

charging out of nowhere and with a flying leap managed to knock her to the ground. She fought viciously, her feet and knees flaying desperately, but it
was no use, and horrifyingly, all too soon Micajah
was lying on top of her, his bulky body wedged between her thighs.

Deliberately he ground his hips against her, letting
her know how aroused he was and how very helpless she was against him. A toothy grin on his face,
he muttered, "There isn't time for us to finish this
right now, but don't you worry, I'll take care of you
just as soon as I get rid of Jeremy."

Jerking her to her feet, he half dragged, half carried her back to where Jeremy was now anxiously
waiting with three horses. Roughly throwing her up
onto one of the animals, Micajah tied her feet to the
stirrups. He grabbed the reins of her horse and, keeping a firm grip on them, mounted his own animal.

Savanna remembered little of that terrible ride
through the junglelike growth of the swamps. Her
shoulders ached incessantly from the pain caused by
her arms being tied behind her back, and she was
constantly buffeted by vines and low-growing
branches as they galloped madly through the wilderness.

They rode for hours, and with every passing mile
Savanna's spirits sank lower and lower. She'd never
get out of this alive! The knowledge that she was at
Micajah's mercy made her flesh crawl, and she was
almost certain that death would be preferable to suc-
cumbing to his advances.

But when they did finally stop, miles and hours
away from Campo de Verde, to her relief Micajah
had other things on his mind than taking his pleasure. He dumped her near a half-rotted bald cypress
at the edge of a sluggish bayou and proceeded to
shackle one ankle to the stump with some old slave
irons he kept in his saddlebags. Ignoring her after
that, he and Jeremy swiftly made camp.

It was only after all the most immediate chores had been done and a fire was flickering merrily in the darkness, a pot of cornmeal bubbling in the center of the fire, that Micajah seemed to recall her presence. A menacing knife blade in his hand, he walked over to her and Savanna stared grimly at him, determined not to betray how furious—and frightened—she felt.

Braced for the worst, she was stunned when Micajah grinned and with one quick slash cut the gag and the ropes that bound her arms. He did it quickly and danced out of her range just as soon as he had finished.

The iron shackle around her slender ankle kept her effectively chained to the cypress stump, but after spitting out the gag and shrugging off the ropes, Savanna felt a tiny glimmer of hope—she could at least fight to protect herself now, even if he won in the end. Her hands stung as the blood rushed back to them and she almost groaned with relief when she was finally able to let her arms hang naturally by her sides.

Warily she eyed Micajah and her astonishment only increased when he carefully handed her a tin plate of hot cornmeal and dried beef. Suddenly too hungry to plumb his motives, she took the plate and hastily devoured the food.

Her confidence stirring, Savanna finally set down her empty plate and said tightly, "Don't you think it's time you told me what this is all about?"

Jeremy and Micajah were sitting nearer the small fire, and after stuffing some food into his mouth, Micajah stared thoughtfully at her. "Like I told you earlier," he finally said, "it's about your father."

Her puzzlement clear, she asked blankly, "What about my father? He's dead! Dead for ten years or more—everybody knows that!"

"Yeah," Micajah drawled, "but what you and everybody else don't know is that Jeremy here was at his side when he died. Had a very interesting conversation with yore daddy just before he died, did Jeremy."

Baffled, tired, scared and more than a little impatient, Savanna retorted sharply, "So? Good for Jeremy! But what the hell does it have to do with me?"

"Well, I know you'll have a hard time believing it, but yore daddy was real worried about you just before he died. Seems he'd been searching for an Aztec treasure all those years—wanted that treasure mighty bad to set you and yore mama up real fine. Wanted you and yore mama to have everything you could wish for—money, fancy clothes, servants, a mansion—everything." Warming to his tale, Micajah went on almost dreamily. "That's why he wasn't never around for you when you was young—he was searching for this treasure for you and yore mama. Told Jeremy he was gonna marry yore mama once he found that treasure. Said he didn't feel worthy enough to marry her without it. Said Jason Savage murdered him to keep him from finding the treasure and coming back to you."

If it were possible for someone as naturally lovely as Savanna to gape like a fish, she did so now. Her jaw hanging slack, her eyes slightly glazed, she stared dumbfoundedly at Micajah. Her first instinct was to reject the tale out of hand, but she suddenly remembered that conversation with her mother the first evening she had arrived at Campo de Verde. Elizabeth had stated quite clearly that Davalos had believed a man named Jason Savage was his deadliest enemy and that Davalos had been looking for a golden fortune. Elizabeth had dismissed the idea, but could her mother have been horribly wrong? Savanna shook her head as if to clear her thoughts. Was she going to believe *Micajah* over Elizabeth? She wavered and then her mouth thinned, and with a trifle less vehemence than she would have expressed before she recalled her mother's words, she said,

"That's the craziest story I've ever had! *Dios!* Are you drunk, or just plain crazy?"

Micajah sent Jeremy a mitigating look and Jeremy gulped and rushed into speech. "It's true! I swear it on my mother's breast! Every word! I found him dying near the Palo Duro Canyon area, and he told me about the treasure and about you and that Jason Savage had murdered him."

"I didn't believe him at first either," Micajah chimed in eagerly. "Thought ten years in a Spanish jail had addled his wits, but he's convinced me. Told me yore daddy confessed to killing someone named Nolan and hiding a golden armband—said you had it."

Numbly Savanna stared at Micajah, her thoughts jumbled. The terrible suspicion that her mother had been wrong took hold of her. They were lying ... and yet why would they persist in this wild story? Surely not just to get her to go with them! They *believed* what they were saying. Could there really be a golden armband? But she didn't have it. She'd never heard of it until this very moment! They had to be lying! Fixing them with a look of scorn, she said acidly, "I don't have any damn golden armband! I've never seen it or heard of it!"

Micajah nodded wisely. "Yore daddy told Jeremy that he'd hid it. Told him he hid it so that if something happened to him, you'd find it and you and yore mama would still be taken care of if he wasn't around anymore. Jeremy said all he could talk about as he lay there dying was how much he loved you and yore mama and how much he wanted to set things right."

"It's all true! Nolan. The golden armband. Happened just the way Micajah says," Jeremy averred piously.

With an effort Savanna focused her gaze on Jeremy. He still looked like a weasel to her, but there was such an air of truthfulness about him that she faltered. *Dios!* What if what they said *was* true! She swallowed convulsively and shook her head as if to clear it. "I don't believe you," she muttered unhappily. "You're lying!"

"Now why would he lie?" Micajah asked reasonably. "Don't mean nothing to him."

There was too much to take in, and almost desperately Savanna replied, "All right! Say it's true—what does it have to do with me?"

Micajah took another bite of beef and swallowed it before answering. "Well, since yore daddy was planning on coming back and setting everything to rights for you and yore mama, it seems to me that you'd want revenge on the man that stopped him—the man that murdered him before he could make everything right. Jason Savage."

Helplessly Savanna shook her head again, trying frantically to make some sense of this whole bizarre situation. "Are you telling me," she finally asked, "that you kidnapped me because you want me to take revenge on Jason Savage?"

"Not exactly." Micajah's eyes flickered over her and Savanna was suddenly chilled. "You know the reason why I kidnapped you, so don't play coy, darlin'," he said bluntly. "But since it was yore daddy who was tracing the treasure, by rights it should be yores . . . and yore mama's, too. And for a large share of it, me and Jeremy are willing to help you find it—and help you take revenge on Jason Savage at the same time."

"You're mad if you think I'm going to believe that you've become so noble!" Savanna snarled angrily, her aquamarine eyes gleaming in the dancing firelight, her red-gold hair flaming like a nimbus around her head.

"Don't matter," Micajah said equitably. "All you have to believe is that we're going to help you get the treasure and kill Jason Savage."

"Suppose I don't want to find the treasure or have anything to do with this Jason Savage? What then?"

"Well, then I guess we'll just have to do it without you—which means yore daddy's treasure will be all mine and yore daddy's killer will go free."

Despite not being convinced of the truth of what she'd been told, Savanna didn't like the sound of that at all. If Davalos had found a treasure, by rights she and her mother *should* have some of it, and if Jason Savage had murdered her father to keep the treasure a secret or steal it for himself, then he should be punished. But joining forces with Murdering Micajah! *Dios!* It was unthinkable!

Her chin lifted arrogantly and she said coldly, "You can have the treasure! Do what you want with Jason Savage. Let me go!"

Micajah grinned like a shark and shook his head. "Can't do that, darlin'. I've wanted you for too long and now that I've got you I ain't likely to just set you free, not without having first gotten weary of that tender flesh of yores. Besides, you might know more about the treasure than you're letting on—be stupid to let you go, to follow after us and maybe steal the treasure yoreself."

Savanna's eyes narrowed dangerously. "I'll fight you! I'll make your life so miserable you'll rue the day you ever laid eyes on me! You'll have to watch me every minute, and the moment your back is turned . . ."

Unperturbed by her threats, Micajah slowly shook his shaggy head. "Nope, that's not true. You're going to go along with just about anything I say, because if you don't, I'm going to have to start telling yore mama's neighbors the truth about her 'marriage' to Davalos. Going to have to mention about Crow's Nest and that little tavern she ran. Think all her friends and neighbors would find it interesting?"

Savanna clenched her jaw and stared at him, her mind racing. Would her mother's friends believe him? Wouldn't they just dismiss his words as a malicious tale told by a vicious, disreputable blackguard? Or would they? Some might. Others might not . . . did she dare risk it? If her mother's respectable life was ruined, could she live with herself? Her heart sank. For her mother's sake, she *had* to go along with him! Her mouth set, hatred glittering in the clear aquamarine depths of her eyes, she said coldly, "*If* I go with you, I'm not going unarmed or in chains! You're going to have to free me and give me back my knife . . . *and* you have to swear that you will not lay a finger on me."

Micajah studied her for several long minutes. He didn't like any of her demands, especially the one about not touching her, but he also knew that as long as he kept his distance, she wasn't likely to try to escape, knowing that he would tell of her mother's scandalous past. His gaze moved slowly over her voluptuous form and he sighed regretfully. As much as he wanted her, he did realize that she would be a dangerous liability if he forced himself on her any time *before* they found the treasure. But after the treasure was found . . . Hiding the salacious grin that crossed his face, he looked away and considered her other demands. The removal of the chains didn't bother him as much as giving her back the knife— she was quite capable of killing him and calmly returning to Campo de Verde!

"I swear not to touch you," he said eventually, his dislike of the situation clear. "I'll even take off the irons, but I'm not fool enough to put a weapon in your hand!"

She didn't believe him about not touching her, but she was in no position to argue. She hadn't thought she'd get *any* concessions from him, and hoping to conceal the gleam of fierce satisfaction that leaped to her eyes, she glanced down at the shackle around her slender ankle and demanded gruffly, "Then release me now!"

As careful as if dealing with a savage wildcat, Micajah approached and warily handed her the key to unlock the irons. Keeping out of her reach, he muttered sourly, "Since we're sort of partners, you can clean up the utensils, and yore bedroll is there, where the horses are tethered—being as you're not chained anymore, you can damn well fetch it yourself!"

Meek as a mouse, Savanna did as she was told, but she kept a cautious outlook for any sudden moves from Micajah. She didn't fear Jeremy; instinct told her that his interest lay solely in the gold and that her body held no charms for him. When she walked over to get her bedroll, the temptation to try to escape was almost overpowering—the horses were so near—

"I wouldn't try it, if I was you," Micajah said softly from not six feet away. "You make one attempt to get away and the deal is off!"

The chances of succeeding were slim, and promising herself that there would be better opportunities, she just shrugged. With the bedroll clutched in her hand, she walked slightly beyond the light of the fire and made her bed as far away from Micajah and Jeremy as she could. After the events of the day and all the astonishing things she had learned, Savanna had been certain she would not be able to sleep, but exhaustion claimed her and she fell asleep almost as soon as she lay down.

It was Micajah's hand on her arm that woke her when the first misty light of dawn was gliding through the swampy forest. Like a scalded cat, she was on her feet, her hands curled into claws as she faced him. He smiled nastily and said testily, "We're breaking camp—get your gear together!"

They traveled in silence for hours and it was only when they stopped to eat, around midday, that Savanna found out their destination.

"Jason Savage," Micajah said as he finished off a

cup of strong coffee, "lives several days north of here with his wife and children, on his plantation, Terre du Coeur. We're going there and we intend to kidnap him and head for the Sabine River. I've already made arrangements to have fresh horses and the supplies we'll need waiting for us at Nacogdoches. Once we're safe, I'll force Savage to tell us how to get to the treasure."

Savanna's spirits sank even lower. Micajah had everything planned and it didn't look as if she were going to be able to escape any time soon. She also wasn't so certain that she wanted to—the tale of her father's motives and the Aztec gold made an insane sort of logic, and if she allowed herself to believe it, it explained so much and enabled her to think of Davalos with something other than resentment. Reluctantly she admitted that she *wanted* to believe it.

She glanced at Micajah. It was highly unlikely that he was *really* going to let her share in the gold, but surely, by the time they found it—*if* there was any gold to be found—she would have been able to concoct some sort of plan of escape. A faint smile curved her lips. And if she was escaping, she might as well take some of the gold with her! Besides, if even half of the tale was true, she *was* entitled to a share of it. Thinking how much she could accomplish for her mother with a sizable fortune, she stubbornly closed her mind to further speculation. She would cling to the thought that Davalos *had* loved them and that he had died trying to find a treasure with which to make a better life for all of them. As for Jason Savage having killed her father . . . Her smile faded. Elizabeth had obviously come to the wrong conclusions about the gold and about Jason Savage!

By the time they reached their destination some days later, Savanna had done a very good job of convincing herself that she was doing the right thing. She had even been able to arouse a modicum of hatred for Jason Savage—the bastard who had murdered her father!

Micajah had been true to his word and had made no *overt* moves toward her, but she didn't trust him or the expression that sometimes came into his eyes when he looked at her. She didn't rest well at night, fearful of being attacked by him as she lay asleep, and her lack of a weapon was on her mind constantly. But Savanna was a gambler by nature and she couldn't deny that the prospect of finding a fortune in Aztec gold was a powerful lure. Gold her father had died for, she reminded herself when despair leaked into her thoughts, gold that she was entitled to possess.

The men had decided to wait until after dark before slipping into the house to kidnap Jason Savage. When Micajah refused to let Savanna accompany them and, after an ugly tussle, proceeded to shackle her again to a small oak tree, all her fears and mistrust rushed back.

Glancing down at her from atop his horse, Micajah said bluntly, "I don't trust you and I wouldn't put it past you to queer the deal, so you'll just stay here while Jeremy and I go get Jason Savage. You just wait here quiet-like."

Like a caged tigress, Savanna raged at the length of her chain, cursing Micajah in two languages, as he and Jeremy disappeared into the darkness. More furious than frightened, she waited with growing impatience, every second seeming like an hour, her thoughts on Jason Savage and the unpleasant surprise in store for him. . . .

Safely in New Orleans with his wife and family, Jason Savage was in no danger from Micajah and Jeremy. Unfortunately, the two intruders didn't know that, and so when they slipped silently into the elegant house at Terre du Coeur and discovered a tall, black-haired man drinking brandy in the library, they made the natural assumption that they had found Jason Savage.

Adam had enjoyed the time since Jason had left and was quite at home at Terre du Coeur—there was no reason for him to expect danger. Having already dismissed the servants and having decided to partake of one last brandy before seeking his bed this particular night, he was just lifting the snifter to his lips when his well-honed senses alerted him to menace. He was in the act of spinning around when Micajah viciously clubbed him. Sparks exploded in Adam's head and he knew nothing.

Savanna didn't know whether to be relieved or disappointed when Micajah and Jeremy returned with the limp body of a man thrown across the front of Micajah's saddle. But there was no time to waste—it was imperative that they leave the area before the kidnapping was discovered. If luck was with them, it would be morning before the master's presence was missed, but they were taking no chances.

To Savanna's relief, Micajah immediately released her, and seconds later they were careening through the moonlit darkness. The moon was waxing full and since the swamps had been left behind some days ago, the terrain was fairly level, though heavily forested, but they were able to make good time. Hours later, when Micajah finally decided to call a halt, Savanna could only sink tiredly to the ground, thankful that she could rest at last. Deliberately she did not look at the still body of Jason Savage, his hands and feet now firmly bound, as Micajah threw him callously on the ground.

Thoroughly worn out from the events of the past several days, Savanna fell asleep almost the instant her head hit the ground, and for the first time since she had been captured, she slept deeply. It was the furtive touch of a hand on her breast that woke her hours later and she reacted instinctively, moving like lightning, her teeth sinking deeply into the flesh of the exploring hand.

Micajah let out a pained holler and jerked away as Savanna leaped to her feet in one smooth, dangerous movement. Her red-gold curls bristling like a fiery mane around her lovely face, her aquamarine eyes gleaming fiercely and her fists bunched, she stared furiously at Micajah. "You swore," she enunciated with cold precision, "that you wouldn't touch me."

Nursing his wounded hand, from a safe distance Micajah sent her a sickly smile. "It was an accident. I was just trying to wake you and my hand, er, slipped."

"If you don't want to be permanently maimed, I would suggest that your hand doesn't *slip* again!" she snapped icily.

Micajah shrugged and turned back to the small fire that Jeremy had lit. Certain the threat of danger was over for now, she spun away and stalked over to the narrow, clear stream that bordered the area where they had camped, and proceeded to bathe her face and neck with the cool water. Feeling refreshed, she straightened and with her fingers she halfheartedly tried to bring some order to the tangled curls that fell to her waist.

Later, sipping some coffee from the tin cup handed to her by Jeremy, she stared over at the sprawled lump on the ground that was Jason Savage. "He's not awake yet?" she asked no one in particular.

"Micajah hit him pretty hard," Jeremy replied uneasily, glancing nervously at the man.

"He ain't dead!" Micajah said defensively. "You can see his chest moving up and down. He'll wake up soon enough."

"Well, since we can't hang around here waiting for *Mister* Savage to wake up, I suggest we do something to help speed up his waking process," Savanna remarked grimly. Grabbing an empty pot, she filled it with water from the stream.

As she approached the prone body of Jason Savage, she reminded herself harshly that this was the unprincipled monster who had murdered her father. Hadn't even her mother admitted that Davalos had stated that Savage had sworn to kill him? She glanced down at him, noticing that he was considerably younger than she had expected and astonishingly handsome in spite of the ugly bruise that darkened his temple. Angry that she was even aware of his black, curly hair and the hard beauty of his face, she kicked him ungently in the ribs. When he stirred slightly and groaned, she dumped the pot of water into his face.

Shocked into wakefulness, Adam surged into a sitting position and became aware of several unpleasant things at once. His head ached abominably, his hands and feet were tightly bound and someone had just thrown a great deal of cold water in his face. Ignoring the various pains that were racking his body, he swiftly apprised himself of his situation and surroundings. He did not recognize any landmarks, nor had he ever seen the two surly-looking men by the fire. Memory came flooding back, and he instantly concluded that he had been attacked last night and for some reason kidnapped.

Suddenly aware of a third person nearby, he glanced up and looked at the most gorgeous woman he had ever seen in his life. Unaccountably, his heart gave an unexpected leap as he stared at her tall, magnificent body, the humble brown gown detracting little from the lush curves it covered. Red-gold curls framed the face of an avenging angel and, his gaze mesmerized by the dazzling clarity of her incredible aquamarine eyes, Adam continued to stare in stunned beguilement. The blatant dislike in the depths of her eyes and the unfriendly expression on her face gradually dawned on him, and because he was at a total loss to understand anything that had happened, he began to speak carefully. "I don't know what the hell this is all about, but I think that there is some mistake."

With an effort, Savanna tore her own fascinated gaze away from the brilliance of his blue eyes and ignored a curious curl of excitement deep in her belly. Furious that she was reacting to him at all, she snarled, "There is no mistake! You're the son of a bitch who murdered my father and now you're going to pay for it, Mr. Jason Savage!"

Chapter 6

A DENIAL SPRANG TO ADAM'S LIPS, BUT EVEN AS HE opened his mouth, it occurred to him that telling these people that he wasn't Jason Savage wouldn't solve his problems. From the unsavory looks of the two by the fire, more than likely he'd get his throat slit for his pains and then they would immediately go in search of the *real* Jason Savage! By speaking the truth, he would not only put his life in greater jeopardy, but endanger Jason. . . .

Eyes narrowed in rapid concentration, Adam stared at the flame-haired Amazon before him, wondering with one part of his brain what her position was in the scheme of things. It was obvious she honestly believed that Jason had killed her father, and knowing much of Jason's early wild days, Adam was aware that it was entirely possible that Jason *had* killed her father! To his knowledge, though, his brother hadn't killed anyone in many years, not even in a duel; so was this kidnapping motivated solely by desire for a belated revenge, or was there some other factor involved? And how did the two men by the

fire fit into the situation? Had she hired those two
ruffians to kidnap Jason for her?

Through slitted lashes, his eyes roamed speculatively over her. At first he stared at her trying to figure out her motives, but as the seconds passed, a
decidedly carnal gleam entered into those dark blue
eyes, and his gaze traveled with increasing appreciation from her full, passionate mouth to the lush, firm
breasts that strained against the cheap material of her
gown. Torn between amusement and anger at his unruly flesh, Adam felt his body respond violently to
the captivating sensuality that was revealed in every
provocative curve of her magnificent form.

In growing rage, Savanna watched him blatantly
assess each feminine feature of her body, and her
hands tightened into fists at her sides. "I would
think," she ground out from between clenched teeth,
"that it would be to your benefit to defend yourself
rather than strip me with your eyes!"

Adam was not a bit abashed to have been caught
staring. His chiseled mouth curved into a lopsided
grin. "Well, since you seem to have already convicted
me of the heinous crime of killing your father," he replied smoothly, "I didn't see the point of my trying
to convince you otherwise!" A heavy black eyebrow
arched inquiringly. "Did your father have a name?"

Baffled by his complete disregard of his dangerous
position, Savanna could only stare at him, wishing
savagely that the man who had killed Davalos had
been old and ugly instead of young and outrageously handsome. She'd never seen anyone quite
like him before; she'd never felt this treacherous excitement, this sudden thundering in her blood, and
the fact that the man lying at her feet was the cause
of it terrified her almost as much as it enraged her.

Despite the rigors he had been through, despite the
fact that he had been kidnapped by murderous
rogues, the thoroughly shameless creature lay there
exuding an air of indifferent elegance and an utter

disregard for what might be his fate. The buckskin breeches clung to the long, hard length of his muscled thighs and did nothing to disguise the fact that he was aroused. He was totally uncaring that she knew his state, and Savanna's hand itched to slap that handsome face of his! The fine white cotton shirt fit his broad shoulders admirably, the voluminous sleeves which covered his powerful arms were caught in a narrow band at his wrists and a sprinkle of dark hair showed at the open V of the collar. A lock of blue-black hair fell carelessly across his forehead and the expression in the sapphire eyes made Savanna's pulse behave erratically. He was, she concluded wrathfully, far too sure of himself. Arrogant bastard!

Oblivious of the two by the fire, Savanna glared at him and snapped, "Have you killed so many men that you can't recall all of them?"

Adam shrugged. "I've never killed a man who bore even the faintest resemblance to you, sweetheart."

Savanna ground her teeth audibly at his glib reply, and, unable to prevent herself, she gave him a swift kick in the ribs. "Well, perhaps the name *Davalos* will jog your memory, you murdering bastard!" she snarled.

The kick hurt damnably, but it was the mention of Davalos's name that caused Adam to stiffen and a wary light to leap in his eyes. He was exceedingly familiar with Davalos, and just thinking of the grief the man had brought upon his family made a cold rage slowly seep through Adam's body. Oh yes, Adam knew Blas Davalos—he had met the Spaniard in Natchez when Catherine had been living at Belle Vista, before Jason had spirited her away to Terre du Coeur; had known Davalos before the man had kidnapped his sister, raped her and been the cause of her losing the baby she had carried at the time. . . . From Jason and Blood Drinker, he had learned even more of the details of Davalos's life, including those of his grisly death at Blood Drinker's hands, and if Adam had any regrets, it was that *he* had been denied the pleasure of killing Davalos with his bare hands!

But that this glorious creature in front of him could be the daughter of Blas Davalos was impossible to credit! Davalos had been slim and dark, his Spanish origins obvious, but Adam could not see any sign of Davalos in the furious young woman before him— neither her height, nor the incredible mane of red-gold curls that framed her lovely face, nor the striking aquamarine eyes could have come from Blas Davalos.

"Well, Miss Davalos, you sure as hell don't look like your daddy!" he finally commented coolly.

Savanna's heart had sunk at Adam's revealing reaction to her father's name, and it hadn't been until then that she admitted that she had been hoping that he'd never heard of Blas Davalos. But his actions and words condemned him, and her jaw hardened.

"The name is O'Rourke, and whether I look like Davalos or not doesn't change anything!" she snapped, barely controlling the urge to kick him again. "He was my father and you killed him and now you're going to pay for it!"

Behind his cool blue gaze, Adam's keen brain was working frantically, and he wasn't liking the thoughts that were occurring to him. His position was dangerous enough, but the notion that there was more to this than simple revenge could not be ignored, and as he turned the situation over in his mind, he was aware of an odd certainty growing within him that he wasn't going to like the real reason for his abduction at all!

The hard planes of his face unrevealing, Adam inquired with deceptive indifference, "And precisely how do you intend to go about doing that? If murder was on your mind, you'd have killed me last night, but you didn't. Why not?"

"Because," said the big, burly man who had suddenly loomed up behind the woman, "you're more interesting to us alive at the moment. We can always kill you, but first you're going to tell us about the golden armband and the Aztec treasure you killed Savanna's father for."

Not by so much as a blink of an eyelash did Adam reveal that he had ever heard of any golden armband or Aztec treasure. He was, however, very familiar with the golden armband—he'd seen it often enough on Jason's arm. He was equally familiar with the story of the Aztec treasure that Jason, Blood Drinker and Jason's friend and mentor, Philip Nolan, had blundered across on one of their horse-trading expeditions with the Comanches. What did surprise him was that someone *else* knew about it!

"I don't know what you're talking about," he said flatly, his eyes clashing with the man's pale blue ones.

The big man grinned and pulled out a knife, then lovingly caressed the blade. "Oh, I think you do, and I think that by the time I get done with you, you'll sing your guts out for me!"

"Micajah!" Savanna uttered sharply. "Not *now!* You said we had to cross the Sabine River before we would be safe from pursuit. Shouldn't we be on our way?"

For a tense second, Adam thought that the man called Micajah might defy her, but he finally nodded his unkempt head and muttered, "Mebbe you're right. A few days won't make any difference." He sent Adam a malicious grin. "And he sure as hell ain't going anywhere but with us."

Adam's situation hadn't improved noticeably, but the fact that Micajah intended to keep him alive until they had crossed the Sabine River gave him a much-appreciated respite. By his calculations, they were over three days of hard riding from the river, and who knew what could transpire between now and then. . . .

Speculatively his gaze traveled over the tantalizing young Fury, Savanna O'Rourke, as he still tried to grapple with the news that she was the daughter of Blas Davalos. She called herself O'Rourke, not Davalos. . . . A most unpleasant notion occurred to him, and he was annoyed at precisely *how* unpleasant he found it—surely she wasn't *married* to that hulking bastard Micajah? His mouth twisted derisively. It wasn't any of his business, Adam reminded himself grimly, even if she *was* married to Micajah. Getting out of this predicament alive was the only thing that mattered, and so far, he decided sourly, he had only two advantages: it appeared that he was relatively safe until they reached the Sabine, and Savanna hadn't seemed eager for Micajah to start carving him up. But he acknowledged that looking to Savanna for help didn't seem promising; her actions made it clear she detested him and thought him the lowest sort of vermin. But I have time, he told himself, and I might as well make the most of it.

When the other two turned away and walked over to the fire, Adam tested his bonds, discovering without any surprise that they were effectively secure. Having found that avenue temporarily blocked, he glanced around, coolly sizing up his three captors with an eye to finding their weak spots.

Savanna had a temper, *that* he'd already discovered and his bruised ribs gave testament to it; Micajah had a cruel streak and enjoyed inflicting pain on others, if his obvious pleasure at the prospect of using the knife was any indication. He also was a bully, Adam observed thoughtfully, watching Micajah impatiently cuff the head of the small man by the fire. As for the object of Micajah's displeasure, it was too early for Adam to draw any conclusions about him and his gaze wandered on, only to be drawn back sharply to the trio by the fire as it became obvious that there was an altercation brewing.

Savanna's fists were clenched by her sides and it was apparent that she was holding onto her temper with an effort. "I am *not*," she ground out angrily, "riding on the same horse with *you!*"

"Well, Jesus Christ! How the hell do you expect us to ride?" Micajah snarled. "In case you've forgotten, there's only three horses, and now there's *four* of us!"

"And whose fault is that?" she asked sweetly, not backing down in the least. The thought of being in such proximity to Micajah Yates as riding on the same horse with him made her sick—she'd actually have to touch him, put her arms around him, and she'd walk barefoot over burning lava before she'd submit to *that!*

Micajah eyed her with mingled desire and dislike. He'd been too easy on her so far, he decided. Let her get too uppity, let her think that she still had a choice. It was time that Savanna O'Rourke learned her place.

Swiftly he drew his fist back to strike her, but Savanna, reading his intent, was already in motion. "I think *not!*" she said fiercely and, dropping to the ground, snatched up one of the pieces of wood from the fire and, holding onto the cool end of it, shoved the flaming point at his face.

Micajah yelped and danced quickly away from the fiery tip as Savanna advanced determinedly, poking her weapon forcefully toward his face. "Don't even *think* about trying that sort of thing with me, you bastard!" she said with obvious relish as Micajah, all idea of brutalizing her gone, kept moving uneasily away from her. "And remember this," she muttered tightly. "You may be stronger than me, you *might* be able to overpower me and beat me into submission for a while, but you have to sleep sometime, Micajah." She smiled nastily at him. "And some night when you're sound asleep, some night when you think you've got me broken"—if possible, her smile got nastier—"that's the night I'll cut out your liver and serve it up for breakfast!"

To Adam, riveted by the scene unfolding in front of him, it was obvious that Micajah didn't doubt her words for an instant. His face pasty, the big man laughed nervously and muttered placatingly, "Now, Savanna you know I'd never do anything to hurt you! You just got me riled, honey. Just made me lose my temper for a bit there, that's all!"

Contemptuously Savanna threw down her weapon. "It had better be all! And I'm still not riding on a horse with you!"

"What about Jeremy?" Micajah persisted doggedly, not certain how he had lost the advantage. "Will you ride with him? It's only until we reach the Sabine— you know I've got more horses and supplies waiting for us there." Some of Micajah's bravado was returning with every second, but he wasn't yet ready to make another attempt to bully her into submission. The defeat, however, left a bitter taste in his mouth; she had shamed him, made him lose face in front of Jeremy, but for the present he forced himself to be content with promising himself viciously that his time would come and when it did, Savanna was going to pay and pay dearly for this little scene.

At the mention of his name, Jeremy, who had watched the confrontation with openmouthed astonishment, averted his eyes from Micajah's sullen face and muttered nervously, "I don't want that devil-witch riding with me! Let *them* ride together!"

Savanna's mouth opened to adamantly protest such a solution, but she suddenly realized that she had fought her way into a corner. She'd made it plain she wasn't riding with Micajah; Jeremy had made it equally plain he wasn't riding with her; that left only . . .

She glanced over at the prisoner and felt her temper rise when she caught sight of the cynical smile on his hard mouth.

"Anything to please a lady," Adam murmured sardonically, aware of her predicament.

"Oh, shut up!" she snapped and aimed a half-hearted kick in his direction.

The ugly incident was over, but it had left Savanna shaken and trembling inside, yet she *dared* not reveal how very vulnerable and frightened she felt. It had been a dangerous gamble to confront Micajah, but she hadn't seen that there had been any other choice. Ever since she'd woken up and found herself Micajah's prisoner, Savanna's emotions had been stretched and twisted to their limit. There wasn't a moment that she could relax her guard, not a second that she wasn't aware of the very danger of her position. Fear stalked her every waking and sleeping moment: the fear of Micajah's careless brutality, the unrelenting fear of rape, the gnawing fear that he would expose her mother's life for what it had been and the growing fear of what lay ahead.

By refusing to let him order where or what she would ride, she had reminded him that he wasn't going to find her easy prey. But Savanna wondered sickly how long she could hold him at bay.

Outwardly she might appear calm and unruffled by the confrontation with Micajah, but inwardly she was very subdued as she moved about the camp, packing the meager utensils and supplies they had brought with them. The Sabine River was still a few days off, she thought dispiritedly; perhaps an answer to her dilemma would occur to her before then. Escape, while longed for, wouldn't put an end to her problems—Micajah could still carry out the threat to harm her mother.

Savanna's gaze slid to Micajah as he saddled his horse, and her full mouth tightened. As long as Micajah was alive, neither she nor her mother would ever be truly safe. There was only *one* way to ensure that the outlaw would never bother them again, and her aquamarine eyes darkened as she realized precisely what she had to do . . . she'd have to kill him! That was the only way to be certain that her mother would be safe.

The decision to kill Micajah wasn't an easy one for Savanna to make. In a temper, in a fight, to protect herself from his brutal attentions, she could have killed him without a quiver, but to cold-bloodedly plan his death was difficult. It also occurred to her, unpleasantly, that if she deliberately killed Micajah, she'd be no better than the man who had murdered her father. The motives might be different, but the act would still be the same and she and the prisoner would share a vile bond—they both would have intentionally taken the life of a fellow man.

Grim-faced, she stared at the object of her thoughts, and her heart gave a funny little hop when she discovered that he was watching her, the expression in his hard blue eyes impossible to discern. His life was forfeit, too, she thought. Once he had told them where the gold was, there was no doubt that Micajah would kill him, and despite knowing that he deserved to die for killing Davalos, Savanna was surprised at how depressed she felt at the thought of that long, lean body lying cold and moldering in some forgotten grave, of those fascinating features dull and lifeless, the infuriatingly mocking light gone forever from those glittering sapphire-blue eyes.

Giving herself a shake, she wrenched her gaze away from him. It didn't matter. It was his own damn fault! And she was *not* going to feel sorry for him—why should she? He had killed her father, ruined her life, and she hated him—that was all she needed to remember!

During the next hour, Savanna found it impossible to decide which one she hated the most—Micajah Yates or the black-haired devil with whom she shared a mount. Once she'd gotten in the saddle, the prisoner had mounted behind her, and with ill-concealed malice Micajah had anchored the wretched creature's hands to the saddle horn and Savanna had been effectively encircled by a pair of unyielding, steel-muscled arms. Worse was to follow as she discovered disconcertingly how *very* intimate riding double could be—it was bad enough that his arms embraced her, but the hard wall of his chest was at her back and his warm breath blew softly against the hair near her ear; his long legs brushed continually against hers, and with every passing mile it became apparent that he was doing nothing to prevent their bodies from touching. In fact, she strongly suspected that he was enjoying himself immensely and she wished vexedly that she had thought faster and demanded that he ride with someone else. Staring fixedly at the long-fingered, finely shaped hands secured to the saddle horn, Savanna wondered viciously if perhaps she hadn't made a mistake in not riding with Micajah! She glanced over to where Micajah rode next to her, and just thinking about putting her arms around him made her shiver with distaste. Telling herself savagely that she had chosen the lesser of two evils, she concentrated grimly on Micajah, which wasn't difficult—she might have the reins to her mount these days, but Micajah was taking no chances and had added a lead rope to her horse's bridle and kept it firmly in his grasp as they traveled steadily through the wilderness.

Under different circumstances, Adam *would* have enjoyed himself immensely; after all, his arms were around a beautiful young woman and they were riding through untamed, seldom traveled land. But lessening his pleasure considerably was the disagreeable knowledge that, given the opportunity, the young woman would have cheerfully skewered him, and as for their two other companions ... His eyes hardened. The two men had every intention of torturing and then murdering him—not a pleasant prospect! There was little Adam could do about his hazardous situation at present, but while one part of his brain weighed various methods of escape, the other part took a connoisseur's interest in the tempting body of the lovely, hot-tempered shrew who shared the horse with him.

Under any circumstances, Adam admitted reluctantly, she would be hard to ignore, but since he'd felt her foot in his ribs, she had made a painful impact on him that no other woman could claim, and while he had a sensuous appreciation of the soft curves so near his own, there was an undeniably hostile cast to his thoughts about her. She wasn't at all happy to be partnered with him, and there was a decidedly diabolical twist to his mouth as he deliberately brought their bodies into close contact time and again during the long day. There was, he finally concluded wryly, only one little problem with taunting her that way—he spent the remaining hours in a state of painful arousal, and his thoughts were no kinder toward her when Micajah called a halt and they made camp for the night.

From the way Savanna shot off the horse once Micajah had untied Adam's hands from the saddle horn and she was free of his embrace, it was obvious that she had not found being in such proximity to him all day to her liking, and Adam wondered idly if he was insulted. Probably not, he decided sourly; after all, she did believe that he had killed her father!

Through slitted lids he watched as she moved around the meager camp. After the day they had just spent, he was achingly familiar with every lush curve covered by that ugly brown gown, and there was a speculative gleam in his dark blue eyes as they rested on the tempting thrust of her bosom. He still found it utterly incredible that she was the daughter of Blas Davalos, and it was even more unbelievable to him that he had been kidnapped in order to reveal the location of Jason's Aztec treasure. It was also, he con-

ceded somberly, entirely possible that unless fate
were kind, he was going to be tortured to death in
about forty-eight hours.

It could not be said that Adam slept well, nor
could it be said, when he was awakened the next
morning by the swift, painful prod of Savanna's foot
in his ribs, that any solution had occurred to him.
Nor during the long day that followed were his
thoughts any kinder toward his captors, particularly
the woman who once again shared a horse with him.

Savanna had not slept well that night either—
notwithstanding her ever-present fears about the future, she had been unable to forget how it felt to
have the warm, muscular body of that sapphire-eyed
devil cradled so intimately against hers. Despite telling herself that she hated him, that he was a murdering scoundrel who deserved whatever Micajah gave
him, she still hadn't been able to stop her rebellious
flesh from responding in a thoroughly unnerving
manner to that wretched creature's nearness. Every
time he'd brushed against her, she had felt a giddy
sensation deep in her belly, and when his breath had
caressed her ear, to her horror, her nipples had
swelled and tightened. She couldn't understand why
she was suddenly being beset by reactions she had
never experienced previously, and she was furious
and disgusted that the man who had aroused these
unwanted emotions was her father's killer. She'd
spent a great part of the night twisting restlessly on
the hard ground, considering several exceedingly
painful methods for the demise of the mocking-
mouthed monster who was the cause of all her problems.

The next morning there was no escape from the
previous day's riding arrangements and, stony-faced,
she mounted her horse and waited stoically as
Micajah anchored the prisoner's hands to the saddle
horn. Today, however, she wasn't about to put up
with his provoking antics, and every time he pressed

against her, whether accidentally or not, she gave him a powerful jab in the ribs, putting all her strength behind the movement of her elbow. After she had viciously jabbed him a few times, she noticed with grim satisfaction that he had lost his enthusiasm for that particular game, but she wasn't about to let up. He had made her life miserable yesterday; today he could suffer!

Adam did. By the time they had stopped to make camp the second night, his ribs were aching incessantly and he seriously wondered if she had cracked one. Her tall, supple body no longer held the slightest appeal to him, and if his fingers itched when she came near him, it was to strangle her and nothing more.

His thoughts were very grim that second night as he lay staring at the black sky. Micajah had pushed them at a brutal pace, and sometime tomorrow they would cross the Sabine River. Time was rapidly running out. So far there had been no opportunity to escape. When not riding, Adam was always tightly bound, his feet as well as his hands, and his trio of captors was always present. Micajah, he knew, was the most lethal of the group, and while two against one wasn't a very good wager, he'd be willing to risk it—if the two were Jeremy and Savanna.

In a vile, dangerous frame of mind when dawn finally broke, Adam was in no mood to be a passive victim any longer, and when Savanna approached to wake him in her usual manner, he was ready for her. Her foot swung forward aiming for his ribs, but with incredible speed, even with his hands bound, he caught her foot and twisted it violently, smiling with savage pleasure when with an astonished shriek she tumbled to the ground.

She lay there glaring at him and he glared right back, sapphire eyes hard and cold. He grinned unpleasantly at her and said icily, "I suggest that in the future you think of another way to wake me."

Savanna leaped to her feet, and from the furious expression on her face, Adam suspected that she would like to launch a *very* painful attack on him. But she got control of her temper and, her fists clenched at her sides, scowled blackly at him and muttered fiercely, "Since this is probably the *last* morning you'll ever see, I don't think there's any point!"

She spun on her heels and proudly stalked away. Her shuttered expression did not reveal in the least how depressing she had found her own words. Micajah was certain they would cross the Sabine River sometime today, and Savanna knew that once they had made camp that night, he had every intention of questioning their prisoner . . . and killing him after he had gotten the information he wanted. A lump rose in her throat and she felt a sinking feeling in her stomach. It shouldn't matter to her that Micajah was going to kill her father's killer, but oddly enough it did, terribly, and reminding herself stonily that it was only what the wretched creature deserved didn't help to lessen or change the intensity of her emotions.

An odd truce seemed to exist between Savanna and Adam that day. He made no attempt to taunt her with the closeness of his body, and she left off her tactics of the previous day. There had never been much conversation between them, but they appeared unduly silent as the small cavalcade wound steadily through the pine forests, each mile bringing them nearer to the Sabine River, each mile shortening the brief time that Adam had allotted himself to escape.

Adam's features were etched in harsh lines when they finally crossed the Sabine River late that afternoon, and it occurred darkly to him that Jason and the family would never know what had happened to him. His disappearance would be forever a mystery, and he was saddened to think of the anguish the others would feel, never knowing precisely what had befallen him, always wondering if he were alive somewhere, always hoping that eventually he would return home. He smiled without joy. He knew exactly what was going to happen to him—in a matter of hours he was going to suffer the cruel, barbaric ministrations of Micajah, and he could only hope that he would die well.

Part 2

The Adversaries

Giddy Fortune's furious fickle wheel,
that goddess blind,
That stands upon the rolling restless
stone.

KING HENRY V
Shakespeare

Chapter 7

SAVANNA WAS UNUSUALLY SILENT AND HER FEATURES oddly somber as she moved about the campsite that Micajah had selected for the night. It was late afternoon when they had finally stopped, and under different circumstances she might have found the area delightful—a stream ran nearby and the pungent scent of the towering pine trees mingled with the sweet fragrance of the coral honeysuckle which curled amiably around the trunks of the trees. Dogwood, magnolias and azaleas were interspersed amongst the tall, straight pines, and here and there the brilliant pink blossoms of the trailing phlox could be glimpsed.

But Savanna was barely aware of her surroundings, her thoughts grappling with the knowledge that they had crossed the Sabine River and that later, Micajah would take out that long, lethal blade of his and use it on their prisoner. She swallowed with difficulty.

It wasn't that she was overly squeamish—she could gut a deer, clean a rabbit or expertly dispatch a chicken without even thinking about it—and it wasn't that she wasn't perfectly capable of shooting or even killing a man, but torture . . .

Torture was on Adam's mind, too, and he was icily determined to bear whatever Micajah inflicted upon him without betraying any sign of pain. He would die like a man and *never* give Micajah the satisfaction of breaking him! The prospect for escape did not look any better right now than it had since he had woken up as Micajah's prisoner three days ago, and since time had run out for him, he was prepared to take whatever desperate measures might be necessary—no matter how slim the margin might be for success.

Repeatedly Adam had tested his bonds over the days of his captivity, but they had always seemed as secure as they had in the beginning. Until this evening. . . . Lying at the edge of the camp, his body faintly dappled by the shadows made by the fading sunlight that filtered through the forest, Adam's hands were bound in front of him as tightly as ever, but he experienced a thrill of savage elation when, cautiously testing the bonds on his feet, he felt a slight give in the rawhide that held him captive. Micajah had grown careless.

Carefully keeping his feet in the shadows, Adam lay there, apparently resigned to his fate, but all the while he was continually, with small, barely discernible movements, struggling to free his feet. It was tedious work, and every time Savanna or one of the others glanced in his direction, he froze and his heart seemed to stop beating.

Concentrating fiercely on his task, Adam wasn't aware of the conversation going on around him until Micajah walked over to one of the horses, swung up into the saddle, and said, "I'll be damned if I'm settling for corn mush one more night! We passed some recent deer tracks not far back, and I could have sworn I heard a turkey gobble a bit before that. I'm going to get us some fresh meat!"

Sending a harsh glance at Jeremy, Micajah growled, "Keep your eyes and ears open and don't trust no one! There could be some dangerous renegades in this area—don't be slow in shooting first!" To Savanna, he said sourly, "As for you, stack up plenty of firewood, but don't wander far from camp—the men you might meet up with won't be as tolerant as I have been."

Jerking his horse around, he flashed a look at Adam and with an ugly smile on his face he murmured, "Yeah, find lots of firewood . . . we've got work to do tonight."

As Micajah rode away, it was all Adam could do to suppress the silly smile he knew hovered about his mouth. For the first time ever, Micajah had left him alone in the camp with only Jeremy and Savanna, and Adam was exultant—even more so when Micajah disappeared from view and, with one last, furtive movement, *his feet were free!*

Surreptitiously Adam eyed the other two, noting with interest the taut set of Savanna's shoulders before his gaze slid lower, lingering on the tempting thrust of her buttocks as she bent over to gather up pieces of fallen wood. Angered by both his momentary distraction and his body's instant response, he fixed his gaze on Jeremy, considering his next move.

Jeremy was obviously extremely nervous about the situation. His small eyes constantly darted from Savanna to Adam and back again, as if he could not make up his mind which one of them was the most threatening. Adam smiled unpleasantly. Jeremy was already rattled, and after having observed him these past days, Adam was certain that in a crisis Jeremy would prove to be an unstable link. Which left only Savanna. . . .

Savanna was trouble in more ways than one as far as Adam was concerned, and the thought of extracting more than a little revenge from that tall, provocatively curved body was frequently at the forefront of his mind. Escape was his first object, but having all that supple, pale flesh to torment at his leisure was definitely in Adam's plans.

Knowing that he didn't have a lot of time, he immediately set events into motion. Jeremy was closer to him, which suited Adam just fine. Doubling over as if in great pain, he cried loudly, "Jesus Christ! A snake! It bit me!"

Jeremy, who had been crouched by the feebly burning fire, leaped to his feet, his face paling. Savanna, who was farther away, dropped the load of firewood she was carrying and began to run toward Adam. Jeremy stood there indecisively, clearly not certain what to do.

Adam groaned as loudly and pitifully as he could and heard Savanna say breathlessly, "*Dios!* Help him, you fool!"

Her words prodded Jeremy into motion, and picking up the long black rifle propped against the tree, he uneasily approached Adam's crumpled form. "Where is it?" Jeremy asked warily. "I don't see no snake."

A feral grin on his face, Adam growled softly, "Right *here*, my friend!" Almost faster than the eye could follow, with all his power behind it, Adam kicked Jeremy in the stomach with both feet.

The wind knocked out of him, Jeremy groaned and stumbled backward, collapsing to the ground even as Adam leaped nimbly to his feet. A swift movement of his one booted foot against Jeremy's head efficiently dispatched him, and even with his hands still bound, Adam easily snatched up the black rifle. An unfriendly smile on his face, he swung instantly around and leveled the weapon in Savanna's direction.

The entire incident had taken only seconds, and Savanna had barely had time to understand her danger before it was too late. The moment she had seen Adam's hand touch the rifle, she had known that there was nothing she could do for Jeremy, and she was already spinning on her heels, seeking escape, when Adam's cold voice stopped her.

"I wouldn't, if I were you," he said softly. "My hands might be tied, but I could still shoot you ... and right now it wouldn't matter to me if it was in the back."

Savanna froze, her thoughts in a wild tumult. Everything had happened so swiftly that she still didn't quite comprehend the enormity of it, but a well-honed instinct for survival kept her locked where she stood, tensely waiting for his next move.

It took Adam an awkward few seconds to free his hands with the knife that Jeremy carried at his side and to keep the rifle on Savanna at the same time, but he did it. Tossing aside the rawhide thongs, he glanced around, knowing that Micajah's return could still upset his plans. To Savanna, he snapped impatiently, "Get over here and tie him up."

Savanna obeyed on leaden feet, and with nervous, fumbling movements, she did as she was told, increasingly aware of her danger. She was relieved to find that Jeremy wasn't dead, as she had feared, only knocked senseless, but all too soon, as she reluctantly followed Adam's terse instructions, Jeremy was tightly bound, his hands and feet fastened behind his back, a gag shoved between his teeth.

When she could delay no longer, she finally turned to look defiantly at her captor. He was not a reassuring sight. He suddenly looked infinitely taller, his shoulders beneath the rumpled, once-white shirt broader, his long legs more powerful, and the expression on his hard face would have caused even a battle-tested warrior to quail. The long black rifle was trained unerringly on Savanna's breast, and with three days of black stubble shadowing his lower features, his thick hair tumbling in dark, rakish waves across his forehead and his sapphire-blue eyes filled with a decidedly hostile glitter, Adam was indeed a terrifying sight.

Quelling the hysterical scream that rose in her throat, Savanna stared unflinchingly back at him, determined not to let him see how fearful she found her situation, and as the uneasy seconds passed, her hands clenched into fists. Precisely what she intended to do she didn't know, but the cold, sardonic smile that flitted across his dark face at her actions frightened Savanna more than anything that had happened so far.

Jutting her chin out aggressively, she demanded, "And now? What do you intend to do now?"

Neither the smile nor the unnerving expression in his dark blue eyes altered in the least. Motioning with the rifle in the direction of the remaining two horses, he murmured, "And now I intend for us to leave before your, er, friend Micajah returns."

Her aquamarine eyes widening with horror, she asked faintly, "Surely you don't mean to . . . ?"

"Take you with me?" Adam finished coolly. "Certainly," His gaze traveled insolently over her lush form. "You and I have a few things to settle between us, don't we?"

Dazedly, Savanna shook her head, the red-gold hair dancing like fire around her shoulders. "But you can't!" she protested stupidly. "You're free! What more can you want?"

Some new emotion leaped in his sapphire eyes, and in an instant Adam closed the space between them. Stunningly, Savanna felt his arm close around her, and his breath was warm against her lips as he muttered, "What more can I want, spitfire? Why, I want *you!*"

His mouth trapped hers, the hard, knowing lips feeding voluptuously on hers, and as he forced his tongue between her lips, ravaging her inner warmth, Savanna was engulfed by the erotic sensations exploding through her body. In dazed compliance, she stood in his embrace, his pillaging lips and tongue making her unbearably aware of the sudden heat of his body against hers, of the instant quickening of her breasts and the powerful jut of his manhood between their locked forms.

The kiss was fiercely explicit and equally brief, and before Savanna could gather her shattered defenses, she found herself thrust brutally away from him. Eyes huge in her white face, her lips swollen from the force of his kiss, she stared up at him.

Adam fought to get himself under control, furious that the desire to taste that sweet, provocative mouth had finally swamped his common sense. His breathing was still ragged, but his face was expressionless as he looked back at her, no sign evident of the white-hot passion with which he had just kissed her. And yet ... he was angrily aware of how very much he wanted to continue kissing her, painfully aware of the size and heat of his engorged manhood. Disliking her intensely at the moment, he drawled, "Now that we understand each other, I think we'd better get the hell out of here!"

Feeling as if she had stumbled into the blackest nightmare of her life, Savanna was dragged ungently toward the tethered horses. It had been mere moments since Adam had first cried out, and Savanna was still shocked by his sudden escape and the naked intent of his kiss. She knew that she had to act immediately, knew that she should scream or fight or make a run for it, but it was as if her brain and body both had become cotton wool and she could only half walk, half stumble in the direction in which he forced her. Frantically she tried to clear her thoughts, to concentrate, to find a way out of this new and horrible dilemma she found herself in. But Adam moved with a terrifying swiftness and efficiency, and before she knew it, her hands were tied to the saddle horn, Adam was astride the other horse, and with the reins of her horse held firmly in his hand, he was plunging them into the forest.

For Savanna, this nightmarish turn of events was all too familiar, almost identical to Micajah's abduction of her, but this time, she raged miserably, it was infinitely worse. Micajah was a devil, a brutal killer, no doubt about it, but this man ... Even knowing that he was a murderer and a scoundrel every bit as bad as Micajah didn't stop this man from arousing emotions within her that she had never felt before and which, perhaps most of all, she found the hardest to stomach. With Micajah, she had lived every second in fear of rape; with this man, she feared that when he decided to take her, it wouldn't *be* rape. . . . Fear mingling with fury, she stared daggers at the back of the tall man on the horse in front of her, certain she hated him more than any man she had ever met!

Adam's thoughts about Savanna weren't any kinder than hers about him either! She was a damned aggravating nuisance that he must have been addle-witted to have brought with him! The trip was going to be treacherous enough without a fractious, red-haired virago-tongued, undeniably beautiful creature like Savanna O'Rourke along. God! He must have been mad! He cursed himself viciously and roundly, but despite being thoroughly disgusted with himself, he didn't cut her loose or turn her free. Nor did his aroused body forget the drugging taste of her lips or what she had felt like crushed against him. . . .

The second time a pine bough slapped him painfully in the face, Adam reflected darkly that it was time to stop thinking about his unwilling companion and to start concentrating on his next move. It had been just luck that he had escaped, and he was quite aware that he was going to need a lot more than just luck if he was to come out of this scrape alive—and keep Jason from falling afoul of Micajah and Jeremy.

Adam's mouth twisted. I should have killed Jeremy when I had the chance, he thought impatiently. Then I'd have only that bastard Micajah to worry about tracking me down!

He frowned, thinking hard. He had discovered a lot about his captors during the past few days, and one thing was very clear—the only real sustained danger appeared to be Micajah. Jeremy might have found the dying Davalos and learned the rest of it, but alone, Jeremy would have accomplished very little. It was when he had joined up with the burly man that Jeremy had become a threat. Adam shook his head. And to think that he had innocently come to Terre du Coeur because he had been bored at Belle Vista! He certainly wasn't bored anymore, but it had to have been the devil's own luck that he had been mistaken for Jason Savage!

Since keeping Micajah from finding out his mistake and going after the *real* Jason Savage was imperative, Adam concluded that until he had managed to either pull Micajah's fangs or kill him, it wouldn't be safe or wise to go anywhere near Terre du Coeur or New Orleans . . . and before he headed for Belle Vista, he would have to make certain that he had completely shaken Micajah off his trail. Adam grimaced, not liking the prospect facing him. His only option, he finally decided, was to lead Micajah deep into Texas, and only when he was certain that he had lost him would he circle back and head for Natchez.

Even while he had been thinking deeply, Adam had also been paying attention to his whereabouts, and when the horses came to a stream, he immediately turned them into the current and proceeded to keep them going at a brisk pace down the middle of the shallow creek. He didn't know how good a tracker Micajah might be, but there was sure as hell no reason to make it easy for him.

Adam couldn't hazard a guess about how much time he had until Micajah was on his trail—he could have minutes or hours; it all depended on how soon Micajah found some game or gave up and returned to camp. An unpleasant smile curved his mouth as he thought of Micajah's reaction when he discovered that the quarry had fled and taken the woman with him. Somehow the notion of stealing Micajah's woman, if Savanna *was* Micajah's woman—and Adam was still undecided about *that*— pleased him almost as much as escaping.

Glancing at the sky, Adam figured he had less than two hours of daylight, and since his whole purpose was to make things difficult for Micajah, he didn't see any harm in following the windings of the stream for the time being. At the moment he was simply content to put as much distance as possible between himself and Micajah—and hide his passing.

In the rush to escape, Adam hadn't wasted time making an inventory of what supplies he had, but over an hour later, having seen no sign of nor heard any sounds of pursuit, and aware of the sudden increase of dark clouds overhead, he decided to take advantage of the rapidly disappearing light to check out what the horses carried in their saddlebags. Bringing the animals to the edge of the creek, Adam dismounted on the muddy shore and made a swift but thorough examination of his stolen goods.

They weren't much: two horses, two saddles, one filthy bedroll, an old pair of slave-shackles with an iron key, a sack of shelled corn, which they'd have to share with the horses, a skillet, a pot, some fire-starter, a small leather bag of shot and powder, the rifle and knife he'd taken from Jeremy and, of course, Savanna. . . .

Staring at her in the gathering shadows, Adam remembered again what her soft body had felt like pressed against his, and a wolfish grin slashed across his face. He could get used to thieving if the booty included a flame-haired, sea-eyed witch like the one glaring warily at him.

Inexplicably satisfied with the situation, Adam swung up into the saddle and once again urged the animals into the center of the stream. The few tracks they had made on the muddy bank would be obliterated by either the rain that was likely to fall at any minute or the rushing water of the creek.

Not ten minutes later, it began to rain softly at first and then with increasing strength. Already tired, hungry and angrily apprehensive, Savanna was now thoroughly miserable as the rain gradually soaked through her clothing. The fading light had almost vanished with the clouds, and she wondered if her captor intended to ride all night. When he urged their horses from the stream a few seconds later, she felt a faint stirring of hope. Perhaps he was planning to find a spot to make camp. But then, as she thought of that blunt kiss he had forced upon her and what might happen when they did finally stop, her spirits plunged even lower.

Despite being every bit as wet, tired and hungry as Savanna, Adam wasn't about to call a halt to their wild dash from Micajah's vicinity. Darkness might be falling, the rain might be damned uncomfortable, but it was a godsend as far as he was concerned: by the time the rain stopped, all signs of their tracks should be effectively erased, and he wanted to take full advantage of that. Micajah might eventually pick up their trail, but it was going to take him days instead of hours, and Adam smiled with a savage satisfaction as he prodded his horse forward.

The darker it became, the harder it rained and the slower their progress was, but beyond dismounting and leading both animals, Adam kept moving steadily through the pines. The ground was fairly level and the thick carpet of needles muffled the sounds of the horses' hooves and left little proof of their passing, but after an hour or so, even Adam had to acknowledge that it would be wise to stop—at least until the rain ceased.

There wasn't much in the way of protection available, and deciding that the driest place they were likely to find tonight was under the sheltering limbs of a tree, Adam finally halted the horses beneath the heavy branches of a huge pine. Despite the downpour, it was relatively dry under the tree, the pine boughs making an effective umbrella.

Dismounting, Adam tied the horses and quickly released Savanna's hands from the saddle horn and, as if she were a featherweight, swung her effortlessly to the ground. Though no longer tied to the saddle, her hands were still bound, but it was so wonderful to be off the back of the horse that she sighed with pleasure.

Hearing that sound, Adam asked softly, "Tired? You should be—it's been a very long day and I'm afraid that it's not over with yet."

In the gloom of the darkness, Savanna could barely make out his lean features, but she could see the gleam of his teeth and the half smile that curved his mouth. The smile both angered and alarmed her— how *could* he smile at a time like this? And how could she find his smile so utterly attractive? Mentally she shook herself. She *was* tired, very nearly exhausted, in fact, and was certainly in no mood to cross wits with the infuriating devil who had kidnapped her, but her temper betrayed her as, shrugging, she muttered ungraciously, "I've felt worse, and I'm sure if I'm forced to spend very much time in *your* company, I'm going to feel a lot worse!"

The smile was wiped from his face. Legs spread apart, thumbs hooked into the waist of his breeches, he made a long, openly brazen survey of her tautly held form, those hard blue eyes stripping her wet gown from her body.

"Perhaps," he drawled insolently, after a humiliating length of time. "But I'm positive that you're going to make *me* feel very good!"

His meaning was obvious, and glaring furiously at

him, Savanna snarled, "I wouldn't count on it—unless, of course, you enjoy forcing yourself upon an unwilling woman!"

His gaze narrowed, and catching each side of her face in his two hands, he tipped her head backward. Brushing his lips against hers, he murmured outrageously, "Ah, but, sweetheart, when I make love to you, you *won't* be unwilling!"

Crushing her soft mouth under his, Adam kissed her hungrily, holding her head firmly imprisoned between his hands when she tried to jerk away. His lips and tongue brooked no escape and he explored and plundered her mouth at will, taking precisely what he wanted, the honied warmth he conquered even sweeter than he remembered.

A bolt of guilty, giddy pleasure shot through Savanna's body at the first touch of his lips on hers, and when his marauding tongue thrust boldly into her mouth, she shivered uncontrollably. The motions of his tongue were pointedly carnal, and to her horror, her nipples suddenly sprang erect beneath her damp gown, deep in her belly an odd sensation of warmth flamed into life and between her thighs she felt a tingling heat. Frightened at how easily he conjured up feelings and emotions that she had only guessed at before his disruptive advent into her world, Savanna began to struggle in his arms. Reminding herself precisely *who* he was gave an added impetus to her movements, and she managed to jerk her mouth from the beguiling warmth of his. Eyes blazing, she spat, "But I *am* unwilling!"

An infuriating grin suddenly tugged at the corners of his lips. "Hmm, you say the words, but your body tells me something far different!"

"It does *not*, you conceited jackass!" Savanna insisted breathlessly.

The grin faded from his face and, his expression intent, he growled, "Call me all the names you like, sweetheart, but don't try to deny *this!*"

His lips crushed against hers once more, and despite all her protestations, as his tongue again began its bluntly demanding exploration of her soft mouth, she was dizzyingly aware of an insidious, insistent fire instantly flicking through her veins. Her mind might reject him, but her young, healthy body clamored eagerly for more of the wanton responses he aroused with such terrifying ease. But she fought fiercely against those powerful emotions, struggling violently in his arms.

Aching to discover all the secrets of her sweet, supple form, Adam easily subdued her thrashing body against his, and he might have gone on kissing her indefinitely, but just then one of the horses threw up its head and snorted loudly.

Instantly alert to danger, Adam jerked his lips from Savanna's and placed one hand over her mouth, while with his other hand he grabbed the rifle. Straining to hear any sound, his gaze piercing the darkness, he searched intently for whatever had caught the horse's attention, but part of his mind was on what had just transpired. Jesus! Another minute and he'd have had her on the ground—and wouldn't *that* have been a ridiculous position for Micajah to find them in! Furious with himself, Adam glanced down at her and, his dark blue eyes deadly, he muttered, "One sound out of you, spitfire, and you'll feel the butt end of this rifle against that lovely head of yours. Understand?"

Staggered by the sudden plunge from the drugging world of erotic discovery to the present, Savanna stared up at him dumbly, grasping frantically at the thoughts and sensations that whipped through her brain and her body. But she hadn't survived by being slow-witted, and despite her stunned condition, she nodded almost immediately.

His eyes softened for just a second, and then he was looking beyond her and she was freed from the mesmerizing power of that hard blue gaze. Astonishing herself, she stood docilely, her head almost cradled against his shoulder as they waited tensely.

The minutes passed and still Adam could detect no sign of what had disturbed the horse. Suddenly there was a rustle to their left, and a smile swept across his face as a small black-and-white creature bustled out of the brush, avoided them by less than six feet and continued on its way.

Together they watched as the skunk waddled away, and Savanna found herself grateful for the animal's timely interruption—the skunk's arrival had completely shattered the amorous intentions of her captor. The creature had hardly disappeared before Adam removed his hand from her mouth and said in clipped tones, "We'd better get some sleep for what is left of the night—I intend for us to be gone from here by first light."

"Gone where?" Savanna asked sweetly. "Nacogdoches?"

Adam shot her a dark look. "None of your business," he growled. "And I think I should warn you—I'm bone-tired and not in a mood to be baited."

A tiny ray of hope sprang into her breast. If he slept soundly enough ...

Almost as if he had read her thoughts, he smiled thinly and drawled, "Forget it, sweetheart. You're not getting free of me until I'm damn good and ready to let you go."

"And while you're asleep, how precisely do you intend to make certain that I don't, um, just slip away?" she asked innocently, her eyes very wide with suspect guilelessness.

Adam didn't reply, but walked over to his horse and yanked out the slave-shackles, oblivious of Savanna's indignant gaze. Before she had fully comprehended his actions, she found her ankle shackled to his! Smiling with what Savanna could only feel was fiendish glee, Adam waved the iron key under her nose and then promptly hung it on a tree branch well beyond her reach.

Ignoring her, he continued to move about, forcing her to follow quickly in his wake if she didn't want her ankle jerked out from under her. Leaving the horses saddled, he fed them some of their precious ration of grain, then passed Savanna a handful of the shelled corn and said, "This will have to do for dinner tonight—we're not advertising our presence by lighting a fire."

Savanna was so famished that she gratefully accepted the corn without a scathing comment. Chewing hungrily on the hard yellow kernels as Adam busied himself with laying out the bedroll, she glanced occasionally but with great longing at the key which dangled temptingly out of her reach.

Adam noticed the direction of her gaze and smiled nastily. "Won't do you any good, spitfire. You won't be making a move tonight that I don't know about, so resign yourself—and hope I don't die in my sleep. Otherwise you're going to be out here all by yourself, leg-shackled to a corpse."

She glared at him and snapped, "I find the idea of your being a corpse very appealing!"

He snorted and walked away, the shackle that bound them together automatically jerking Savanna after him. Stumbling behind him, she cursed viciously under her breath, considering all manner of ugly fates for him. He continued to move about, double-checking the horses and the gear and ignoring Savanna's fulminating presence behind him. Once he was satisfied that everything was in order, he ambled back to the bedroll.

It was infuriating and humiliating for Savanna to be dragged along behind him, to be ignored and treated like some dog on a chain, and her temper finally got the better of her—again. Staring bullets into his broad back as he stood unsuspecting in front of her, she suddenly bent down and grabbed the chain that united them and gave it a savage tug, yanking his ankle out from under him.

With a startled oath, he fell into the bedroll face-first. Savannah's moment of triumph was short-lived, however; swift as a cat, he spun over and, from his supine position, stared consideringly up at her. A smile she didn't like crossed his mouth, and a second later, the side of his foot hit her knee and knocked her down.

To her embarrassment and fury, she fell on top of him, and there were several undignified moments in which she struggled to put as much distance between his hard, muscled length and herself. Eventually, she was lying on the bedroll beside him, and her fury only mounted when she realized that his chest was rumbling with laughter as he lay beside her.

"You're a despicable, murdering gringo bastard, Jason Savage!" she spat wrathfully.

His laughter vanished and, to her bewilderment, he suddenly loomed up over her, his features dark and dangerous as he snarled softly, "Don't call me that!"

"Why? Don't you like the sound of your own name—black though it may be?" she taunted.

Adam was almost angry enough to tell her the truth, but realizing the danger, he exerted control over his temper and threw himself back down beside her. "Adam," he muttered. "Call me Adam—most people do."

Savanna frowned. "Is that your full name—Jason *Adam* Savage?"

"Yeah," he replied coolly. "But all you need to remember is that I answer only to *Adam!*"

Chapter 8

UNEASILY SAVANNA MULLED OVER HIS WORDS, PUZZLED by his angry reaction. Why had he been so *adam*ant about what she'd called him? And it hadn't been the ugly epithets she had hurled at him that had provoked his outburst, but the fact that she had called him Jason Savage.... Was he ashamed of his name?

Lying stiffly beside him on the bedroll, she waited in great trepidation for his next move. To her astonishment, he fell asleep almost immediately. His doing so only added to the puzzle and she continued to think about his odd behavior until exhaustion claimed her. Yawning hugely a second later, she decided sleepily, her eyes closing, that if he wanted to be called Adam, it was fine with her—but it didn't change the fact that he was *still* a murdering scoundrel!

It seemed that she had barely shut her eyes and slept for only a few minutes before "Adam" was shaking her awake again. Sleepily she blinked at him, hardly able to discern his features in the shadowy light.

"Time to get up, sleeping beauty—we're going to be leaving soon," he said briefly before moving away.

It was still dark, dawn still several minutes away, but it seemed that Adam wanted to be riding before first light. Savanna sat up quickly, rubbing her eyes with a grubby fist. She glanced around, surprised to discover that the shackles that had chained her to him all night were already gone, the key no longer hanging so temptingly just out of her reach. Silently she watched her captor in the dawn gloom as, almost ignoring her, he fed the horses with swift, economical movements.

Grimacing wryly, Adam passed her a handful of the corn and commented, "It'll fill our stomachs until I can find something better—which, hopefully, won't be too many hours from now."

Savanna shrugged and ate her corn, too tired and hungry to really put her heart into an argument. For just a minute she let herself dream of hot, fragrant coffee, warm, tender biscuits dripping with butter and crisp bacon . . . oh, and a bath, she added blissfully, since it was only a dream, and a bed—a featherbed with clean white sheets. . . .

Sighing, she glumly swallowed the rest of her corn and stood up and stretched. She ached in every muscle; her gown and her body were filthy, and as for her hair—well, it was so tangled that she'd probably have to cut it all off to ever get it unsnarled. This morning there wasn't even the luxury of cold stream water to splash in her face and wash her arms and neck with, and Savanna decided that if she ever got home again she'd spend at least four hours of every day sitting in a tub of hot, soapy water! Her mouth twisted ruefully; it would no doubt take a month of such a regime to wash away the weeks of dirt that she had accumulated thus far. And as for the plain brown gown she wore . . . burning was too kind a fate for it!

Thoroughly miserable, her stomach growling in

complaint about the meager breakfast it had been offered, she stooped over and rolled up the bedding. She handed it to Adam and he quickly tied it to the back of the saddle.

He flashed a glance around to make certain nothing was forgotten and then turned back to Savanna. She appeared as disreputable as he felt and it occurred to him that if she could arouse him now, looking as she did, Lord help him if he ever saw her clean and gowned properly!

Scowling at his thoughts, he roughly ordered her into the saddle and once again tied her hands to the horn. There were no words between them, Savanna watching him stoically, Adam working silently, ignoring her. Swiftly he mounted his own horse and with the reins of her horse held securely in his hand, he kicked his weary animal into motion.

Adam had no clear idea where he was headed—he only knew that he had to keep moving and that his familiar haunts were closed to him for the time being. He also knew that they needed better horses, food and clothing and more weapons and ammunition than they possessed at the moment—if they were to survive very long in the vast wilderness of Texas.

They plodded steadily westward. Beyond knowing that he had to lure Micajah away from Jason's haunts before heading back to Natchez, Adam was still uncertain of his immediate destination as he grappled with the more pressing needs of food and supplies. The horses they rode had been poor specimens at the beginning of their journey, and by now they were sorry nags indeed! He doubted that he could trade the pair of them for even one fairly decent animal, and without sound horses, any attempt to elude Micajah and Jeremy was doomed to fail. Adam knew that Micajah had horses and more supplies waiting for him at Nacogdoches, but even as the thought of those precious commodities crossed Adam's mind, he dismissed it. Too risky, and he had no way of knowing if Micajah, discouraged by the rain, hadn't decided to head to Nacogdoches first and then, with fresh mounts and supplies, try to pick up their trail.

There hadn't been much conversation between Adam and Savanna, but her curiosity finally got the better of her and she asked waspishly, "Since we're obviously not going to Nacogdoches, where *are* we going?"

"Away from your friends, that's for damn sure," he replied laconically.

Savanna's teeth gritted together and she tried again. "You have to have some destination in mind— where are you taking me?"

He glanced over his shoulder and, blue eyes dancing with mockery, he drawled, "Well, I'd like to take you to bed. . . ."

She glared at him with impotent rage, deliberately ignoring the funny little leap her pulse gave at his words. Since it was obvious he wasn't going to tell her where he was taking her, she decided to lapse into sullen silence.

An hour after dawn the demands of Adam's stomach became too pronounced for him to ignore any longer. Having spied several game trails leading to a narrow stream, he decided to stop long enough to set some snares and see what he could catch—and Micajah could go to hell!

Just the thought of food set Savanna's mouth watering, and in spite of maintaining an outwardly indifferent air, she hoped that Adam was a competent hunter. He was. Skillfully he fashioned several snares and set them along the game trails. It was still early enough in the morning for small game to be moving freely about, and in a rather gratifyingly short time, Adam managed to catch a fat turkey and two plump rabbits.

Animosity momentarily forgotten with the prospect of fresh roasted meat in the offing, Adam and

Savanna quickly produced a credible fire and in a startlingly brief period managed to demolish the two rabbits. Her stomach full for the first time in what seemed like days, Savanna inelegantly wiped her mouth on her sleeve and glanced consideringly at the dressed turkey carcass lying near the stream bank where Adam had left it.

Catching the longing expression on her face, Adam laughed not unkindly and said lightly, "Not yet, sweetheart! I'm hoping that before we have to eat that turkey to keep it from spoiling, we'll pass a dwelling where the inhabitants will be willing to trade the fresh meat for something we can use." His mouth twisted. "And Lord knows we can use just about everything!"

The tension between them had lessened some due to their full stomachs and deciding that his prickly captive was in as amiable a mood as he had seen so far, Adam let his curiosity get the better of him. "How did you hook up with Micajah and Jeremy?" he asked.

Determined to treat his questions as he had hers, Savanna smiled seraphically and murmured, "None of your business."

Adam scowled. "All right," he said reluctantly, "I'll answer any question you ask . . . but you have to answer one of mine. Fair enough?"

Savanna nodded and, staring at him intently, inquired bluntly, "Why did you kill my father?"

It wasn't the question he had expected and it was the one question for which he had no ready reply. He looked across at her for a long time composing his answer, the answer he suspected that Jason might have given. Very carefully he said, "He died because he deserved to die. He killed my friend, would have killed me, but most of all, because he defiled the person dearest to me."

"That's a damned dirty lie!" Savanna burst out furiously. "You're just making that up to excuse your actions!"

Adam shook his head slowly and there was something about the set of his features that chilled Savanna. Was it possible? *Had* her father done those things? Micajah had claimed that Davalos had confessed to killing someone named Nolan . . . didn't that lend credence to what Adam was saying? She didn't want to believe him, everything within her rebelled against it, but there was the unmistakable ring of truth to his words.

Unconvinced, but greatly troubled by his revelations, Savanna looked away from his steady blue gaze and muttered, "What about the gold? Is that a lie, too?"

Adam started to remind her that it was his turn to ask a question, but then he shrugged and admitted candidly, "Two people I trust implicitly have confirmed its existence—they have seen it."

Still grappling with what he had said about Davalos, she drew little comfort from his confirmation of the gold and demanded sharply, "Are you going after it?"

"I think it's my turn to ask some questions, don't you?" he inquired silkily.

Savanna grimaced and shrugged her shoulders.

Taking her actions as an affirmative, Adam queried softly, "What is Micajah to you?"

If Savanna was surprised by his question, she didn't reveal it, and tired of sparring with him, she answered truthfully. "I've known Micajah Yates since I was a child, and for just about all of that time he's been nothing to me but a dangerous aggravation. I'd like to cut out his guts"—she flashed Adam a dark look—"after I've cut out yours, of course, but unfortunately, I haven't had the chance lately."

Ignoring her gibe, Adam frowned. "If there is bad feeling between you, why the hell were you with

him? I would have thought he'd be the *last* person
you'd ask to help you find the gold!"

"No, *you'd* be the last person I'd ask!" Savanna
shot back smartly, rather pleased with her barb.

Adam looked at her, relishing the thought of putting his hands around that slender neck and . . . Rising to his feet, he said coldly, "Since it's apparent
you're not going to keep your end of the bargain, I
see no reason to waste any more time here. Get on
your horse."

Feeling rather chastened and a little guilty, Savanna complied without argument. Her subdued
state didn't last long, however, and they hadn't ridden far before she began to dwell on his crimes.
Hadn't he killed her father and *lied* about him?
Wasn't he one of the most fascinatingly despicable
bastards it had been her misfortune to meet, and
hadn't he made her his prisoner? She knew the answers to those questions, and the question foremost
in her mind right now was how the devil was she
going to get away from him?

Frowning with sudden concentration, she stared at
Adam's broad back as they rode. If only he would
drop his guard for an instant. . . . Her gaze narrowed.
She needed some sort of distraction, something to oc-
cupy him while she attempted to escape or made
him *her* prisoner. A smile tinged with more than a little malice curved her mouth. Oh, yes, she would enjoy having Adam as her prisoner!

He pulled their horses to a sudden halt and her
heart leaped with excitement when she saw what
had caused his actions. Through a break in the trees
in the distance she caught a glimpse of a large clearing with several small buildings clustered around a
square log cabin. A half-dozen hounds, chickens and
a sow with a litter of piglets were scattered out in
front of the cabin, and a couple of black children
played in the red dirt at the side of the building.
The hounds had not yet caught their sound or

scent and Adam was grimly determined for things to stay that way, at least until he had stashed Savanna away somewhere safe. Flashing a dark look in her direction, he growled, "Not one sound out of you, or it will be the last noise you make for quite some time!"

One look at the expression on his face convinced Savanna of the wisdom of obeying him. She would have been willing to risk his wrath if she'd had the least hope of being rescued, but there was such a desolate air about the clearing that she doubted anyone was there who could help her. There'd be other chances, she reminded herself as Adam took them in the opposite direction from the clearing.

When he stopped a few minutes later and, after a short, violent tussle with Savanna, left her gagged, her hands bound and her ankle shackled to a stout oak sapling, Savanna wished heartily that she had screamed the instant she had first spied the clearing. Torn between fury and astonishment, she watched him as he hung the key to the shackles on a small branch high above her head.

"I'm going to see if I can trade our turkey for something we can use but if something should happen to me and I don't return, you should eventually be able to release your hands and reach the key," Adam explained coolly.

Savanna glared at him.

Adam shrugged and walked over to his horse. "At least this way," he continued, "I won't have to worry that I left you to die in the forest." He swung up into the saddle, and glancing down at her from his horse, he said dryly, "Try not to pine for me while I'm gone."

Savanna's magnificent eyes flashed all sorts of retribution, but the insults she hurled at him were muffled by the gag. Adam grinned. "I know, sweetheart. I'll miss you, too."

He disappeared into the forest and Savanna continued to glare at the spot where she had last seen him for several more minutes, before it dawned on her that he had truly left her bound and gagged and alone in the forest. Longingly she looked at the key dangling above her head and began to struggle to free her hands. The rawhide bonds proved unyielding and it seemed impossible that she would ever free herself. Suddenly she found herself praying desperately for Adam's safe return.

Adam was gone nearly all day, and though periodically she fought with her bonds, he had tied her too securely for her to escape easily. Her mouth was dry from the gag and her wrists were raw where she had struggled against the rawhide, and she was just beginning to be really fearful that he had simply abandoned her to die when she heard the sound of a horse's approach. Weak-kneed with relief, she watched as he rode carelessly up to her as if he had left only moments ago and had not deserted her this way.

He was smiling as he swung out of the saddle and immediately untied her gag.

"You bastard!" she raged. "Don't you *ever* go off and leave me like that again!"

"Ah, you *did* miss me," he drawled, a teasing glint in the dark blue eyes. Effortlessly he reached up for the key that had hung so temptingly above her head all day.

Savanna growled something extremely ugly under her breath and Adam laughed.

"I'm sorry," he said as he proceeded to finish freeing her. "I never meant to be gone this long, but you'll be happy to know that I managed to gain us a few much-needed supplies."

"How?" she snapped, rubbing her bruised wrists. "You haven't any money. Or have you added thievery to your list of misdeeds?"

Adam didn't reply, and walking over to his horse, he reached for a medium-sized cloth bundle and tossed it to her. "Treasure these meager offerings—

I labored very hard for them." At Savanna's look of disbelief, he smiled suggestively. "The lady's husband and eldest son have left the plantation and gone to New Orleans for six weeks, taking the huskiest slaves with them, and there were several, ah, *tasks* that only a man with my abilities could accomplish."

Outraged, she glared at him, the image of him lolling around all day in the bed of another woman while she had been left abandoned suddenly leaping into her mind. Beneath the rage, Savanna experienced an odd feeling of something that came perilously close to jealousy at the thought of him with another woman, and turning her back on him to hide her emotions, she tore open the cloth bundle.

Inside she found a heartening array of odds and ends: a tiny packet of sugar, a bit of salt, a small pouch of coffee, a slab of smoked pork and a bag of beans. The food items made Savanna's mouth water, but it was two of the other articles included in the bundle that made her feel like she had discovered a treasure: an old comb and a partial bar of soap. There was also a worn white shirt, a pair of equally worn brown breeches, two scuffed boots, a slightly motheaten wool hat with a floppy brim and a razor.

The razor Adam promptly removed from the pile and said, "As soon as we find a decent stream, I'll have use for this. As for the clothing, I think you'll find it more appropriate for the journey than that garment you're presently wearing."

Savanna had grown to despise her wretched brown gown, but at Adam's words, she decided that she was actually very fond of it and had no intention of getting rid of it—and certainly not to trade it for clothing that he had acquired by spending his time with another woman! Her aquamarine eyes suddenly very green, she glanced at Adam and said haughtily, "If this is all you earned today, you must not have pleased the lady that much!"

Adam's mouth tightened and he shot her a narrow-eyed look that made Savanna's heart pound uncomfortably in her chest. There was a tense moment and then he smiled and ran a finger down her cheek. "Believe me, the lady was pleased," he said softly. "Women usually *are* with my efforts."

There was no mistaking what he meant and Savanna's face blazed rosily as she jerked away from him. Muttering under her breath, she angrily piled the foodstuffs to one side of the clothing, wishing viciously that just for once she could get the better of him.

They spent the night as they had the previous one, and as he had done the morning before, Adam woke Savanna while it was still dark. She had been certain that she wouldn't be able to sleep a wink with him lying at her side, but again that assumption had proved false. Despite his disturbing nearness and the shackles that once more bound them together, Savanna had fallen asleep almost as soon as her head had hit the ground.

No time was wasted breaking camp and, despite the addition to their stores, breakfast had been another handful of corn. When the sun finally rose, they had been on the move for nearly an hour and Savanna was bitterly resigned to another day of hard riding. As the sun climbed higher in the bright blue Texas sky, they continued to ride steadily southwest, and some three hours later, hungry, tired and miserably conscious of the grime on her body, she was concentrating so furiously on what a coldhearted, mean-spirited bastard her captor was that when he reined his horse to a stop, she wasn't aware of it for several minutes. It finally dawned on her that they weren't moving and she glanced resentfully over at him.

"Why are we stopping? Have you caught sight of another lonely plantation mistress who is in need of your *services?*" she asked sarcastically.

Swift as a tiger, Adam reached for her, freeing her hands and jerking her off the horse, he dragged her across the front of his saddle. Though her breasts were pressed tightly against his chest and her arms were held in a viselike grip, she glared unrepentantly at his dark, angry features. His sapphire-blue eyes hard, his mouth thin and his temper barely suppressed, he growled, "Keep taunting me that way and I'm liable to start believing that you'd like to avail yourself of my services!"

Savanna's breath came out in a furious hiss. "Don't delude yourself! I'd *never* want you!"

"Shall we see about that?" Adam inquired silkily the second before his knowing mouth came down on hers. There was nothing seductive about his kiss—he was angry, for a lot of different reasons, and he didn't give a damn whether she wanted his kiss or not. He was driven to have the taste of her on his tongue, to feel her in his arms again, and he was determined to prove to her that she needed his touch just as desperately as he wanted hers.

He might have succeeded in his quest if Savanna hadn't been quite so blazingly furious and hadn't been fiercely promising herself *not* to let his practiced lovemaking blind her to reality again. For just a second, the same wild excitement that his touch always aroused swept through her and her lips parted helplessly under the hungry pressure of his, but then she remembered who he was and who she was and she grabbed handfuls of his dark hair, yanking as hard as she could and viciously biting his marauding tongue.

There was a muffled curse from Adam and then Savanna found herself being tossed to the ground. "Jesus Christ!" he burst out, half enraged, half astonished. "What the hell got into you?"

Ignoring her smarting bottom, Savanna said sweetly, "I *told* you that I didn't want you!"

The blue eyes narrowed and something about the set of that very masculine jaw sent a thrill of fear through Savanna. Cursing her unruly tongue, she was on her feet in an instant, running blindly through the pine woods. So caught up in a primitive need to escape the retaliation she had glimpsed in those hard blue eyes, she simply ran, heedless of the direction, of the vines and branches that slapped and clawed at her, deaf to the sound of the thundering hooves of Adam's horse galloping close behind her.

It was only when Adam's arm suddenly snaked around her waist and she was lifted effortlessly from the ground and thrown across the front of his saddle that sanity returned and she realized how hopeless had been her instinctive urge to escape. It dawned on her with the force of a blow that there *was* no escape, that she was totally at the mercy of this man—and unfortunately, this man had no reason to treat her kindly!

Temporarily swamped by a feeling of helplessness, Savanna only struggled halfheartedly as Adam swiftly guided his horse back to where they had originally stopped. The saddle horn was digging into her belly, and with her head dangling down one side of the horse and her legs down the other, she wasn't in much of a position to put up a fight anyway.

Adam hadn't said a word, and when he pulled his horse to a stop, she waited tensely for the angry tirade she was certain he would unleash upon her— that or something even more terrifying. To her astonishment, he simply dumped her ungracefully on the ground and, dismounting himself, said dryly, "Rape isn't something that I find particularly stimulating, so calm your maidenly fears."

Warily she eyed him as he moved around securing the horses and rummaging about in the saddlebags. Just as if the previous minutes had never been, he threw a packet at her and nodded in a direction behind her. "*That's* why I stopped. Clear water is extremely rare around here, and I don't know about you, but I prefer to bathe in water that I can at least see through."

Savanna turned and a sigh of pure bliss came from her as she stared at the small, tear-shaped pond that lay before her. Unusual for this area of Texas, where the streams and rivers were normally muddy with silt, the pool was nearly crystal clear, except for some patches of duckweed and bladderwort that grew along the far side where a few trees had fallen into the water and the occasional fish and turtle could be seen lazily swimming in its turquoise depths. A series of tiny waterfalls splashed over rocks and cascaded into it at the narrow end, and crowding near, in wildly irregular patches, was all manner of junglelike vegetation—tupelo trees, palmettos, ferns and pitcher plants.

Savanna rose to her feet and, Adam and all the turmoil that he represented forgotten, walked as if she were mesmerized straight into the cooling embrace of the water. She didn't stop until it reached her hips. Oblivious of anything but the prospect of being clean again, she glanced over her shoulder and said imperiously, "The soap. Give it to me."

Adam laughed and reached down for the packet he had thrown at her earlier. Holding the precious bar of soap, he walked to the edge, and when Savanna scrambled toward him, he quickly raised it out of her reach.

"I think," he said slowly, "that we need to call a temporary truce. Enticing though the prospect might be, I don't relish chaining you to a stump while you bathe and wash your gown, nor do I want to keep a constant eye on you while discovering if my skin is the same color it was before I had the misfortune to meet up with you and Micajah." He sent her a hard look. "Have I your word that for the time we are here you won't try to escape?"

"I promise," Savanna vowed instantly, not daring to hope that he was actually going to believe her—

especially since she had no intention of keeping the promise.

Something in her face must have given her away, because Adam snorted and remarked dryly, "Very well, if that's the way you want it."

His hand shot out and she was dragged unceremoniously up next to him. The soap was tossed on the ground as Adam smiled down at her, and there was something in that smile that made Savanna suddenly *very* uneasy. His eyes locked with hers, he drawled, "We could have done this the easy way, but since you seem to want to do it the hard way, I see no reason why I shouldn't get a certain amount of pleasure out of it."

Before she divined his intentions, he had deftly undone the fastenings of her gown and in one swift movement had bared her body to the waist. Savanna gasped with outrage, but there was an odd excitement mingling with her outrage as he boldly looked at the naked temptation before his eyes.

Beneath her gown, her skin was milky-white, only the apricot-tinted areolas of her breasts and her small nipples breaking the smooth, silky expanse of pale flesh. She was the loveliest sight Adam had ever seen, with all that lovely alabaster skin and that bright red hair tumbling about her shoulders, and he stared at her nakedness as if he had never seen a woman before, his gaze roaming in stunned appreciation over her slender shoulders down to the taut, generous curves of her bosom. The upper part of her gown was bunched at her narrow waist, which prevented further exploration on his part, but it didn't matter. His gaze returned instantly to those lovely, lovely breasts. . . .

A note of awe in his voice, he muttered, "Jesus, sweetheart! Who would have suspected it!" He tried to drag his eyes away from those soft, tempting mounds, but he could not and his breathing became ragged as he imagined precisely what those pouting little nipples would taste like. . . .

To Savanna's complete embarrassment, as he stared at her, her nipples suddenly swelled, and the satisfied smirk that instantly curved his lips had her trembling with rage. There was no use fighting the firm grip he kept on one of her arms as he looked his fill, and ignoring the shameful betrayal of her body, in a voice filled with freezing disdain, she said, "If you're through ogling me like some ill-mannered, backwoods *cretin* . . ."

Adam sent her a crooked grin and, shaking his head, murmured, "If you'll remember, sweetheart, you started this. I gave you a chance, but you didn't take it. Besides, for the first time since I made your acquaintance, I'm actually enjoying myself!"

Savanna's eyes flashed dangerously and she lunged at him, but Adam easily avoided her charge and after a brief tussle had events well in hand. Grinning down into her furious face while she thrashed against the strong arms that bound her to him, he said mockingly, "You know, even with that bad temper of yours, I'm beginning to see why Micajah put up with you. Beneath that ridiculous excuse for a garment you've been wearing is a body that men only dream about . . . and I'm rather eager to see if the rest of you is as appealing as what I've seen so far."

Despite Savanna's increased struggles, with ruthless efficiency Adam soon had the offending gown stripped from her body. If he had thought her a seductive baggage before, the sight of her flat stomach and long, shapely legs, coupled with the fire-bright curly triangle at the top of her thighs, made his mouth go dry with a fierce elemental desire he had never experienced in his life. What had been a game until this point suddenly became something else; and, aware of the inferno burning low in his belly and the swollen, rigid weight between his legs, he shook his head as if to clear away the explicit images of her parting those long alabaster thighs and of his body slowly merging with hers. . . .

There was a glazed look on his face that made Savanna struggle even more violently, and fearing the worst, she warned him breathlessly, "Don't you dare touch me, you bastard! I'll kill you if you do!"

Her words brought Adam back to reality and he smiled grimly, effortlessly dodging her flailing fists.

"I'm sure you'd try, sweetheart, but I doubt you'd succeed." Manfully ignoring the nearly irresistible promptings of his body, he gave her a sharp shove and she stumbled wildly backward, trying to regain her balance before falling into the water with a large splash.

The water wasn't deep and Savanna came up sputtering, only to remember at the last moment that she was naked. Instantly she hunkered down, knees to her chest, her hair hanging in wet rat tails down her face and back, and glared at her tormentor.

Her garments, what was left of them, swirled at his booted feet and Adam picked them up and threw the sodden mass at her. "After you've scrubbed them and I've laid them out to dry, I'll give you the soap to use on that delectable little hide of yours."

Muttering, she snatched up the clothing, and retreating a safe distance away from him, she treaded water and stared thoughtfully around her. It was true that she was naked, but she had her clothes in her hands and Adam was still on the shore. If she could swim to the other side and get far enough into the forest before he realized what she was up to . . .

Adam's voice startled her, interrupting her thoughts, and she was even more startled when her gaze swung over to him and she discovered he had gotten the rifle and was aiming it at her.

"Now, then, sweetheart," he said levelly, "I would put any idea you may have of escaping out of your head. Try to swim away and I'll shoot you—not to kill you, let me assure you, but just to slow you down enough." He smiled, not pleasantly, and added, "I promise that it will hurt like the devil, too."

With one last, yearning glance at the far shore, Savanna swam over to the base of the small waterfall, the brown gown floating behind her. Coldly ignoring him, but keeping as much of herself underwater as she could, she used a couple of the rocks nearby to pound her garments, and when everything was as clean as it could be without hot water and soap, she wrung them out and tossed them onto dry ground.

Looking back at him, she asked caustically, "Satisfied?"

A twisted smile curved Adam's mouth. "Not at the present, but I expect that before too much longer I will be . . . gratifyingly so."

Savanna could have bitten her tongue off. Her eyes a dark, stormy blue-green, she was unwilling to leave herself open to further suggestive remarks and snapped, "May I have the soap *now?*"

Adam placed the small bar near the shore and murmured, "It's all yours, spitfire." Turning his back on her, he walked over to where the horses were tied.

She eyed the back of his tall form for several suspicious seconds, but then, deciding that this was the only privacy he was likely to give her, she quickly swam to where the soap was and snatched it up. She had expected a trick, that he would wait until she was half out of the water and then turn and stare at her nakedness, but he hadn't, and she was completely baffled as she retreated to deeper water. She wasted a few moments speculating on his motives and actions, but the sun-warmed pool and the faint lavender scent of the soap soon turned her thoughts to more pleasant avenues.

The water felt wonderful—invigorating, almost bath-hot for a few inches on the surface, but the depths were cool and refreshing, and the soap . . .

She nearly purred with delight as she lathered her dirty hair and rubbed the lavender-scented bar along her skin. For a time, Adam, Micajah, all her troubles retreated and she simply took pleasure in washing away the sweat and grime of the past horrible weeks, never giving a thought to the dangers that might lurk in the pond. Oblivious of everything, she swam and played like a young otter in the middle of the pond, where the water was deepest, and even surprised herself by laughing out loud.

It was Adam's voice shockingly near that brought her painfully back to reality. "Before the soap is all gone, I'd like to borrow it," he said dryly.

She spun around and, to her horror, there he was, not two feet away from her, his hair wet and his naked shoulders rising above the turquoise water. Her gaze dropped and she was stunned at the revealing clarity of the pool waters. It was immediately obvious that he was as naked as she and that there were great differences between her own slender body and his more powerful one. His broad chest and flat stomach were covered with a mat of dark hair that, just below his waist, arrowed seductively downward. She wanted desperately to look away, but she simply could not stop her eyes from following the arrow's path, her gaze widening when she realized that he was fully erect.

Almost accusingly, her eyes swept up to meet his sardonic gaze. "It's not," he said coolly, "something that I have a lot of control over. And if you don't want to find out exactly how *little* control I have at the moment, you'll hand me the soap and keep a safe distance away."

Instantly the soap was proffered and when his fingers closed around it, Savanna immediately put several yards between them. Adam smiled. "It's too bad that you're not always so obedient."

For once, Savanna wasn't going to taunt him. Instinct told her that the situation was far too volatile at the moment and so she contented herself with coldly ignoring him and paddling aimlessly in the water. But though she tried not to think about him, the sounds of his exuberant pleasure as he bathed were hard to ignore, and as the memory of that naked, very masculine form flashed across her mind, she experienced a tingling sensation that had nothing to do with the coolness of the water!

Angry with herself, she wrenched her wayward thoughts away from Adam and began to concentrate determinedly on escaping from him. Speculatively she eyed the distance from Adam to the shore and it dawned on her that for all his seemingly careless enjoyment of the water, he always kept himself between her and the shore, where their garments and supplies were situated. She grimaced. Trust him to leave nothing to chance.

Adam had tried not to leave anything to chance. His clothes, rifle and knife were hidden nearby, just in case someone tried to surprise them; the last thing he wanted was to be caught naked and unarmed by someone like Micajah Yates! Now, if Savanna wanted to attack him . . . He grinned, remembering the expression on her face when she had caught sight of him—and his condition. Lord, but it had been hard not to burst out laughing—that, or do precisely what his body had been prompting him to do practically since he had first laid eyes on her—make exquisitely satisfying love to her!

The sound of something large moving swiftly through the brush sent thoughts of Savanna flying and he plunged to the shore, reaching his rifle just as a large bear ambled out of the forest not six feet in front of him. Whether Adam or the bear was the more surprised would have been hard to say, but the bear took one look at the human and with a startled grunt disappeared back into the brush.

Adam glanced around at Savanna, who was staring in the direction the bear had disappeared with a look of astonishment on her lovely face, and shaking his head in amusement, he put down the rifle and decided that he had dallied long enough. Actually, he hadn't dallied at all—while Savanna had been busy with her own bath, he had draped her wet garments over a bush to dry and had washed his own clothes before he had joined her in the water. Since he had hidden his clothes instead of laying them in the sun, when he reached for his breeches, his mouth twisted wryly. They were far from dry, but ignoring the clammy feel of damp cloth on his wet body, he dragged them on. The shirt he left open, and after pulling up his boots, knife in the waistband, rifle in hand, he picked up the scrap of soap that he had dropped at the shore in his haste to reach the rifle and walked toward the horses.

Adam kept an unobtrusive eye on Savanna as he found the razor and, approaching the pond again, worked up enough lather to shave off the beard that shadowed his cheeks. Afterward, glancing at the sun, he figured it was only about noon, and while the majority of the daylight hours was still ahead of them, Adam wasn't inclined to spend the next several hours in the saddle. Recently they had camped for too many nights without a water source and he wasn't in the mood to do so again. He was looking forward to putting on those beans and pork and enjoying a halfway decent meal. Methodically he began to set up camp.

Since Savanna seemed singularly disinclined to leave the water, Adam quietly continued with his tasks. He gathered wood and started a fire and put the beans and a bit of salt in a pot with some water from the waterfall to start them cooking. Shaking out the bedroll, he eyed it with distaste, and walking to the shore, he threw it to Savanna. "Use the rocks on that—it should dry by tonight, if we're lucky."

Sending him a resentful glance, Savanna nonetheless did as ordered, and shortly the bedroll, looking

considerably more appealing even wet, was laid over
a tree branch to dry in the sun. She had lingered as
long as she could, and she concluded uneasily that it
was time for her to leave the water, too.

Chapter 9

WATCHING HER UNOBTRUSIVELY FROM HIS POSITION under the shade of a large oak tree where he was comfortably sprawled, Adam was well aware of Savanna's dilemma. He'd been anticipating this moment for several minutes now and he waited with growing enjoyment for her next move.

Savanna had swum nearer to shore and was standing in water breast-deep, unaware that the clarity of the water left little to Adam's already far-too-active imagination. She was, he decided reluctantly, absolutely the most glorious creature he had ever seen in his life as she stood there, her flame-colored hair drying in curly tendrils about her face and her delicate white shoulders rising from the turquoise depths of the pool. The clear waters gave him an utterly entrancing view of her lush breasts, narrow waist and shapely hips and he moved uncomfortably beneath the oak tree, his breeches suddenly unbearably tight. Damn her!

Angry at his increasingly familiar reaction to her, he rose to his feet. Telling himself that the sooner she was clothed, the less of a temptation she would be to him, he grabbed up the breeches and shirt he had acquired yesterday and stalked to the edge of the pond. Throwing the garments down a few feet from the water, he snapped, "Put these on when you're ready to get out of there."

Savanna's teeth ground together at his tone. "I'm not coming out and pandering to your perverted tastes by letting you watch me dress. And I'm *not* wearing those clothes! My own things should be dry enough by now."

Adam smiled unpleasantly. "Whether your clothes are dry or not isn't the point, sweetheart! The only things that you're going to wear are these and if you don't want to wear them, then you can damn well go naked!"

The expression on his face and his cold tone of voice told her that there was no budging him, and while she could see the wisdom of the breeches and shirt, sheer stubbornness made her reluctant to follow his orders. And she certainly wasn't going to put on her clothes under the lascivious gaze of those hard blue eyes! But she also didn't have a lot of choice in the matter.

"If you'll allow me the privacy to get dressed, I'll wear the damn breeches and shirt," she offered stiffly, hoping to salvage a little of her pride.

Looking at a point over her shoulder, Adam suddenly said urgently, "Savanna, get out of the water *now!*"

Startled at his tone, she glanced backward and a chill went through her as she caught sight of a pair of ugly, thick-bodied serpents rapidly swimming toward her. Born and raised along the rivers and bayous that they frequently inhabited, she had no trouble recognizing the snakes—they were cottonmouth water moccasins! The cottonmouth moccasin was a deadly and aggressive snake, not taking kindly to being disturbed, and it was obvious that this pair was no different!

The overpowering appeal of the pond had momentarily made Savanna forget about the two dangers that normally lurked wherever there was water in the semitropical warmth of the southern United States—water moccasins and alligators, to be specific— and as she began to swim frantically to shore, she wondered hysterically if a huge alligator wasn't going to suddenly appear, too!

The need to save her pride and the arguments with Adam forgotten, Savanna swam desperately toward him, but she knew in her heart that there was every possibility that any second she would feel the sting of one of the snakes biting her—or both! Anger at herself for not paying attention to her surroundings, as much as fear, helped propel her swiftly through the water, and upon reaching the shallows, she surged to her feet, oblivious of her nakedness, and began to run in the knee-deep water.

To Savanna's astonishment a pair of strong arms suddenly swung her upward out of danger as Adam met her halfway. With her naked body secured in his arms, he plunged to the shore, heedless of the nearing snakes, his only thought to remove Savanna from harm.

The first snake was right behind him as he reached the dry ground, and it was only his quick reaction as he brought his booted heel down on the flat, triangular head of the moccasin that saved him from being bitten. Ignoring the squirming of the dying reptile near his feet, swinging Savanna safely behind him, Adam reached for his knife, and as the second snake gained the shore, with unerring aim he quickly dispatched it.

Shivering with shock, only halfway aware of her nakedness, Savanna stared with horror-filled eyes at the bodies of the two snakes, realizing how close she had come to possibly suffering an ugly death. Her teeth began to chatter and she hugged herself as if she could lessen the chill that was permeating her entire body.

Having made certain that the moccasins no longer represented any danger, Adam turned around to look at Savanna, and seeing her condition, he swore under his breath. Pulling her next to him, he ran his hands soothingly over her body. Her head was pressed into his shoulder and, his mouth bare inches from her ear, he murmured, "It's over, Savanna. It's over. You're safe now."

His body was warm against hers, and as the minutes passed and his hands continued their gentle caressing, his voice rumbling reassuring phrases against her ear, Savanna was gradually aware of a lessening of her fear . . . a lessening of at least *one* kind of fear. Unfortunately, her fear of the snakes was rapidly being replaced by the growing fear of Adam's touch. Not his touch, precisely, but what his touch was doing to her.

Adam's only intention had been to comfort Savanna when he had first put his arms around her trembling form, but as the moments passed and her trembling ceased, he became painfully aware of the demands of his own body. He had been in a constant state of half arousal from the moment he had first looked into those lovely aquamarine eyes, and having her soft and naked in his embrace was far more than he could withstand. Damning himself for being a calculating bastard, but unable to stop himself, he lifted her chin with one hand and brought his mouth down on hers.

He kissed her with all the pent-up hunger inside him, his lips warm and hard as they moved demandingly on hers. For Adam there was no slow slide into passion. The moment his mouth touched hers, he was consumed with the driving urge to touch her everywhere, to explore with his hands and mouth every curve, every sleek inch of her lovely body, to join their bodies together and lose himself in the silken ecstasy he knew he would find.

Adam's body was solid and warm against hers and Savanna instinctively clung to him, her mouth soft and vulnerable beneath the urgent assault of his, her lips parting helplessly to allow the hungry penetration of his tongue. As the kiss deepened, his arms tightened around her, crushing her naked form even closer to him, his hands cupping her buttocks to force her against him, and she was instantly, dizzyingly, aware of his great arousal, of how very badly he wanted her . . . and of how very easy it would be to let him have his way. . . .

His white shirt hung open and her breasts were pressed against his bare skin, the thick dark hair on his chest rubbing excitingly against her nipples. The flame that had sprung to life in her belly at the first touch of his lips on hers blazed hotter and more powerful with every passing second, until Savanna thought it would consume her. Frightened at what she was feeling, stunned at the carnal emotions that seemed to have erupted without warning, she fought against what her body wanted and what her brain told her she should do. She hated him, didn't she? She didn't *want* to feel this way about him, didn't want to respond to him, but her body . . . ah, but that treacherous body of hers desperately wanted his touch, her betraying mouth wantonly sought the plunder of his and she swayed in his arms, a furious battle raging within her.

Frantically struggling against the chains of passion that kept her prisoner in his embrace, she freed her mouth from his and said thickly, "Stop! I don't want this! I don't want *you!*"

His blue eyes nearly black with desire, Adam stared down at her flushed face, his gaze lingering on her rosy mouth, the lips swollen from the force of his kisses.

Nervously she pushed herself slightly away from

him and glared up at him, waiting tensely for his next move. His expression didn't change, nor did his hands leave her buttocks, but his gaze dropped to her breasts and, to her complete humiliation, she could feel her nipples tighten and swell under his gaze.

A crooked smile curved his lips. "Liar," he said softly. "This is something we've both wanted since the first moment we laid eyes on each other."

"No! No, it's not!" Savanna replied desperately, denying the truth of his words, trying feverishly to ignore the appeal of that shockingly pleasurable mouth of his, trying to pretend that the warmth of his hands on her naked flesh didn't fill her with delight, or that his touch didn't arouse a hungry yearning within her. She did *not* want to want him! Nothing had changed between them—he was still the coldhearted bastard who had killed her father, he was still the man who had kidnapped her and nothing could ever change those facts. Except . . . except somewhere in the region of her heart there was a dull ache, an ache that had increased with every passing hour she spent in his company; and then there was her treacherous, *treacherous* body, which ached, too, but with a different ache from the one in her heart . . . a purely physical ache that she knew could be easily satisfied if she gave in to temptation, but that ache was one that she dared not appease. . . .

Adam stared at her for a long moment, those dark blue eyes roaming over her lovely face, lingering on the soft temptation of her mouth before dropping once again to the lush fullness of her breasts, the coral nipples erect and hard, and involuntarily his hands tightened on the firm flesh of her buttocks, pulling her closely against the rigid strength of his manhood. She shivered with reaction and he felt it and tantalizingly brushed his mouth against hers and said again, "Liar. You want me—even if you won't admit it, and I'm afraid that between us the time for talking is past. . . ." He kissed her insistently, his teeth nibbling against her lower lip until her mouth parted to let his tongue explore at will. He kissed her for a long time, his hands sliding caressingly up and down her back, sometimes cupping her buttocks to keep her pressed near him, and it was only when she gave a defeated little moan and put her arms around his neck that he lifted his ravaging mouth from hers. His breathing was labored and, one hand tracing the swollen fullness of her lips, he muttered, "Tell yourself you don't want me, if it pleases you, but never delude yourself that your body doesn't want mine!"

Sweeping her effortlessly into his arms, he carried her to a thick patch of soft green grass dappled with shade. Lying her down gently on the grass, before Savanna's stunned gaze, he swiftly discarded his boots and his breeches.

Savanna had seen naked men before, but none so hypnotically attractive as the tall man who stood unashamedly in front of her now, the sunlight glinting through the leaves of the trees to caress his bronzed skin. From the crown of his dark head to the soles of his feet, he was undoubtedly the embodiment of every sensuous dream that any woman had ever conjured. The broad shoulders and wide, powerful chest gracefully tapered down to a flat belly, narrow waist and slim hips. His legs were long, elegantly shaped and tautly muscled, and as she stared at him, unable to tear her eyes away from the sheer masculine beauty of him, despite everything that was wrong between them, Savanna felt her breath quicken and her heart begin to pound faster.

Nature had not stinted when it had created Adam St. Clair. His tall body was hard and lithe; his chiseled features were handsome and stamped with an arrogant attractiveness that would stay with him until the day he died. Against her will, Savanna felt herself overpoweringly drawn to his potent masculinity, and when her unknowingly caressing gaze stopped at the apex of his powerful thighs, she was shaken by the sight of just how generous nature had been to him . . . and by the bittersweet knowledge that she had brought him to this state.

As Adam came down beside her, Savanna made one last, frantic attempt to escape from him, but it was useless. His arms closed tightly around her and his mouth unerringly found hers. She was shocked at the heat that emanated from his body as he pressed himself against her soft length, shocked at how eagerly her own body responded to that heat and how nearly impossible it was to remember that she hated him.

His lips brooked no barriers and all too soon his tongue was filling her, pleasuring her immensely as it searched and slid rhythmically within her mouth. It was such a simple act, his tongue within her mouth, and yet it seemed that she could feel its thrusting motions throughout her body. His hand touched her breast, the long fingers circling her erect nipples, and she shuddered with the elemental demands that suddenly flooded through her, twisting wildly in his arms, not to escape but to press closer, her lips opening wider to allow him to delve deeper, more insistently. Without thinking, she put her arms around his neck and arched in his embrace, beset by the myriad emotions that his explicit kisses and warm touch had so violently aroused within her.

Her body was afire and yet she was shivering, not from cold but from the urgent sensations that were coursing through her; she pressed even closer to his naked body, the feel of his swollen manhood pushing vigorously between her thighs, filling her with both fear and wild anticipation. When his warm lips left her plundered mouth and slid down to suckle hungrily at her breast, her entire body jumped with shocked, guilty pleasure and deep within her loins there was a sudden clenching, a throbbing ache that had her twisting helplessly in his arms. Oh, God! She *did* want him!

Adam had never had any doubt about wanting Savanna, but even he wasn't prepared for the magnitude of pleasure it gave him to kiss her, to explore the sweetness of her mouth and to taste the honied softness of her flesh. She enthralled him, made him half wild with the longing to plunge himself deep within her and ruthlessly possess her and make love to her so fiercely that the memory of any other man's touch would be banished forever from her mind. These were not emotions he had ever felt for any other woman and they only seemed to increase the intensity of what he was feeling as he held her in his arms and compulsively began to discover all the secrets of her lovely body.

He could not seem to get enough of her, his hands and lips roaming restlessly over her face and breasts, nipping and kissing, fondling and caressing, his hips moving rhythmically against hers in frankly carnal demand. Entrapped as helplessly as Savanna by the frantic urgings of his own flesh, Adam buried his face between her breasts, savoring her clean scent, and let his hands drift sensuously down her body, caressing the indentation of her slim waist, the lush curve of her hip, the flatness of her belly. . . . His head lifted and his lips crushed hers in an uninhibited appeal, his tongue filling her mouth as his hand slowly slid into the tight red-gold curls between her thighs.

Savanna arched up against him in violent reaction to his bold movement, and despite the frantic leap of her pulse and the melting sensation at his touch, for just a moment cold reality washed over her. She shoved hard against his broad shoulders and, tearing her lips from his, pleaded huskily, "Adam! Please! I don't want . . . Please, stop! Please . . ."

The sapphire-blue eyes glittered down into hers, a lock of black hair lay fallen across his dark forehead and Savanna's heart twisted in her breast as she stared up at him. His features were flushed with passion and there was a distinctly sensuous curve to his mouth that made her belly clench with desire. As they stared intently at each other, Savanna's breathing almost stopped as the sapphire-blue eyes darkened with some nameless emotion, and then his head dropped and he pressed a butterfly-soft kiss to the corner of her mouth and murmured, "Oh, I definitely intend to please, sweetheart."

Savanna didn't doubt it—she feared that he would please her far too much, but before she could offer further resistance, his mouth covered hers, his lips hungry and urgent against hers, his tongue brazenly forcing itself between her teeth, deeply penetrating the new territory it had won. His kiss was drugging, and helplessly her hands caressed his dark head, her yearning body wantonly heedless of anything but the mesmerizingly erotic spell he was weaving around her. She ached in places she had never known *could* ache, and when his knowing hand began to gently explore the soft flesh between her thighs, she shuddered with the force of the pleasure he evoked. Savanna writhed wildly under the carnal onslaught that Adam lavished upon her, her mouth was full of him, her swollen breasts were crushed against his hard chest and her untried body was already accepting the seeking thrust of his fingers as he brought her to the very edge of ecstasy.

Moaning with delight, she slid her arms around him, her hands gliding restlessly over his broad back, her fingers digging into the warm skin as the tight, nearly unbearable ache in her loins seemed to spread throughout her entire body. His lips left hers, blazing a trail of fire to her breasts, where his tongue curled possessively around her hard nipples, his teeth gently grazing the tender tips until Savanna thought she would go mad from the sensations he aroused within her. He gave her no succor from his plundering lips and hands and she became frantic for relief from the hungry, mindless need that increased with every second. Powerless against the ever-increasing demands of her body, she thrashed uncontrollably beneath him, desperate to reach some dim, only-guessed-at pinnacle. Totally obsessed by the elemental, unceasing emotions that beset her, Savanna was hardly aware when Adam shifted, nudging her thighs apart to make room for his big body between her legs.

As obsessed as Savanna, Adam was certain that he would indeed die if he didn't soon sink into the slick warmth he knew awaited him. There had never been a woman like Savanna—she was fire and silk in his arms; the taste of her, the feel of her soft flesh against his and her wild undulations so befuddling his brain that nothing existed in this world but the wanton creature twisting in his arms. The savage demands of his own body had him groaning half in pain, half in pleasure when he slipped between her legs, and he was fearful that simply the excitement of entering her would unman him. Deliberately he fought to slow the pace, to gain control of his emotions, but it was a useless battle, Savanna's abandoned movements shattering his resolve. Erotically she pushed up against his swollen manhood, the soft brush of those red-gold curls between her thighs making him curse softly at his helplessness. Contenting himself with one last, hungry tug of her nipple, he unerringly found her mouth and kissed her with all the pent-up hunger within him, his hand slipping beneath her hips to lift her to receive him. Trembling from the power of his need, he slid slowly into her silken sheath, only half aware of the incredible tightness, too lost in his own pleasure at first to realize that something was different. It was only when he broached that final frail barrier and her muscles clenched in instinctive rejection that the truth exploded in his brain, but by then it was far too late, far, *far* too late. . . .

Savanna was adrift with intense, unrelenting sensations; the singularly seductive awareness of him sinking into her flesh and the amazement as her body had stretched to accept the fullness of him filled her with a desperate pleasure. The pain, when it came, was totally unexpected and helplessly she arched up against him, suddenly frantic to escape from him and what he was doing to her. But there was no escape. Adam's hard body was pressing hers into the soft grass, his chest was crushed against her breasts and his flesh was irrevocably joined with hers. They lay there locked together for a dazed moment and then, muttering something savage against her mouth, Adam moved, thrusting deeply, urgently into her again and again. In stunned disbelief, Savanna was swept along with him, every frenzied stroke of his body lessening her pain until there was only the wonder of his unbridled possession. Deep within her the coils of pleasure tightened with every powerful thrust he made, and then, without warning, just as Adam groaned aloud at his own explosive release, an intensely pleasurable sensation rippled through Savanna, leaving her feeling inexplicably languid and faintly astonished. So *this* was what drove men and women to behave so incomprehensibly at times, she thought stupidly, her heartbeat slowing, her body suddenly at peace.

There was silence between them, Adam's warm body still atop hers, his flesh still joined with hers, and it was only gradually that the enormity of what had transpired between them began to dawn on Savanna. She stiffened in horrified denial, her eyes flying open to meet Adam's hard blue gaze.

He shifted slightly, resting the bulk of his weight on his forearms, but he made no move to lessen the contact between their bodies. His breathing and sanity had returned to normal, and with it came the unwelcome knowledge that he had held one *major* misconception about Savanna O'Rourke! Furious at the situation, but unable to tear himself away from her soft, clinging warmth, he stared down at her flushed, lovely face, rage and resentment and, unfortunately, barely slaked desire stirring within him. Clever, manipulative, seductive little bitch! he thought savagely. She had tricked him with a lure as old as time and he, besotted fool that he was, had fallen, nay, *rushed* headlong into her silken trap!

Despite the odd and totally irrational feeling of satisfaction he had that he was her first lover, at the moment Adam's main feelings were those of betrayal and fury. Women who looked like and lived as Savanna did were *not* supposed to be virgins! Hell! He'd been certain that Micajah had been her lover! He'd have sworn unhesitatingly that it was true and yet ... His mouth twisted unpleasantly. He had always made it a point, no matter what their station in life, to give innocent maids a wide berth—sexual congress with that type of woman invariably created problems, one of them being that it usually led to marriage! He was, without a doubt, a rascal with women, but he did have some scruples, and those scruples adamantly forbade what had just happened. If he'd known, if he'd had the slightest inkling, he thought viciously, he would not have touched her with a barge pole! Almost immediately the contrary notion slyly occurred to him—that, virginity or not, *nothing* would have stopped him from taking her! Even now his body tingled with remembered pleasure and he was gallingly aware that it would take little effort on her part to bring him fully erect and eager to lose himself again in her intoxicatingly sweet heat. . . .

Adam wrenched himself away from the dangerous path his thoughts and body seemed intent on taking, his blue eyes darkening with temper. "Why the bloody *hell* didn't you say something? Jesus! A

damned virgin!" he said harshly. Staring suspiciously
at her, he muttered, "Well? Isn't this when you name
your price? Or are you waiting for me to make some
sort of offer to recompense you? Isn't that usually the
way it is?"

Whatever Savanna had expected him to say, it certainly hadn't been *that*, nor in such an infuriating
tone of voice, and she gazed up at him in stupefac-
tion. *He* had been the one who had forced himself
upon her, not the other way around, and if anyone
had a right to be outraged, it was definitely her! Recompense, indeed!

Her mouth tight, she spat, "It was *my* body that
was violated, not yours—I think you have insulted
me enough!"

"Insult!" he snarled, irrationally angry that she
dared to call what they had just shared insulting, and
he lashed out at her. "Sweetheart, believe me, I
haven't even started insulting you! Women like you
have been laying clever little snares for men like me
for centuries, but I'll be damned if you're going to
trap me so easily!" Sending her an unfriendly look,
he growled again, "A virgin! Just tell me one thing—
why did you hide that interesting fact until it was too
late for me to do anything about it?"

Her eyes a furious, glittering blue-green, she
snapped, "Would it have made any difference?
Would you have stopped? I asked you to, if you will
remember!"

Adam winced inwardly and his mouth thinned.
Regrettably, however, her words, instead of making
him feel ashamed, only fed his own rage at the situation, his anger growing with every passing second
as he felt his body already beginning to respond to
their compromising positions. Furious at what was
happening to him, he tore himself away from her all-
too-seductive flesh, and lying on his back beside her,
he stared frustratedly up at the blue sky. Grimly he
replied, "Lady, you wanted me as much as I wanted

you, and don't try to tell me that you didn't enjoy
what we just shared!"

Savanna could hardly believe his words. Lifting
herself up on her elbows, she glared at his recumbent
form, hating him at that moment more than she had
ever hated anyone in her life. "Why, you obnoxious,
conceited, ass-eared son of a bitch! You kidnap me
and terrorize me!" Her voice rose almost to a shriek.
"*Then* you rape me and I'm supposed to have enjoyed it!"

Driven by devils he barely understood, infuriated
that she could dismiss what they had just shared
with such an ugly, inappropriate word, Adam, perhaps for the first time in his life, completely lost his
temper. "Rape?" he demanded with wrathful incre-
dulity, suddenly looming up over her like an avenging god. "I'll show you rape, my dear!"

His mouth came down with hungry brutality on
hers and he took her with few preliminaries, his
body mating fiercely with hers. Savanna fought him,
but it was no use, and while there was no pain, there
was little pleasure, either, in this hostile taking and
she merely endured his possession. It was over
quickly, Adam rolling away from her as soon as he
was finished.

Aghast and utterly disgusted with himself, he
leaped upright and with his back to her, as if he were
ashamed to look at her, he jerked on his breeches. But
despite the sick fury in his soul, he could not bring
himself to either comfort her or attempt to apologize
for what he had done and, his voice deliberately
cold, he said, "*That*, sweetheart, was rape! I'm sure in
the future you'll be able to tell the difference!"

Blind, uncontrollable rage shook Savanna and she
was hardly aware of what she was doing as her fingers curled around a tree branch lying on the ground
near her. Rising up from the grass like a feral tigress
springing after her prey, she swung the branch with
all her might, striking Adam a decisive blow to the

back of his head. With a soft groan, he slumped to
the ground in front of her. Paralyzed with astonishment, she stared dumbly at his fallen body, hardly
able to believe what she had done.

Her paralysis lasted only a moment, and acting on
blind instinct, heedless of her nakedness, in a matter
of seconds she had him securely bound. Satisfied that
he would be helpless upon regaining his wits, sitting
on her haunches beside him, she studied him for a
timeless moment, surprised to find that despite what
had happened, she could still find him unbearably
attractive. Against her will, her gaze traced those arrogantly handsome features, his lashes incredibly
long and dark against his high cheekbones, his nose
bold and well shaped, before lingering compulsively
on the sensuous fullness of his lower lip. . . .

She tore her eyes away from him and rose determinedly to her feet, immediately pulling on the hotly
contested breeches and shirt he had tossed at her
what seemed like hours ago. Finding the boots, she
swiftly dragged them on and then, with a wary
glance in his direction, moved with feverish haste
about their camp, scrupulously dividing all their supplies, packing what she would take with her, not letting herself feel or think at all.

Savanna hadn't really considered what she was
doing, the instinct to escape, to put as many miles
between herself and the man on the ground, the
driving force behind her actions. When she was
ready, seated on her horse, she stared down at
Adam's unmoving form, her expression uneasy.
Shouldn't he be stirring by now? She had deliberately tied his hands in front of him and had left the
knife nearby so that, when he came to, he should be
able to free himself—after all, she didn't want to
leave him to die, although that was what he deserved, she thought savagely. She had left him the
other horse and a fair amount of their food—she
should have no regrets about leaving him. He was a

murderer and—her mouth tightened—he had treated her despicably—she *should* have no compunction about leaving him, should experience no heaviness of spirit, should have no feelings for him except hatred and disgust! Except that even as she swung her horse around and left Adam lying there so still and oddly vulnerable on the ground, she was painfully aware of a strong sensation of despair and regret, almost as if her heart were breaking. . . .

Chapter 10

FOR SEVERAL MILES, SAVANNA RODE ALMOST BLINDLY, her thoughts, much against her will, dwelling on the man she had left lying helpless by the deceptively tranquil waters of that forest pond. What if an alligator attacked him? Or, she thought with a shudder, a water moccasin? Or even some wild beast. Remembering the way Adam had rushed to save her from the snakes earlier, Savanna was smitten by a wave of guilt. He had saved her life and she had left him vulnerable to the very fate that he had helped her escape! Feeling guilty and miserable, she tried to justify her actions.

It was, she knew, highly unlikely for either a gator or a snake to attack him where he lay, but the possibility of attack by other, equally deadly predators couldn't be totally dismissed. She told herself that she didn't care, that he would deserve whatever grisly fate awaited him, and forced herself to coldly dismiss him from her mind. She had other, more important things to think about than the man who had killed her father and raped her!

She pulled her horse to a stop and looked around her in dismay. There was nothing to see but seemingly endless forest, mottled tree trunks, green-hued rampant vines and verdant bushes. She sat there for some time, her mind racing furiously. She was not an *in*adequate woodsman, but the idea of leading herself out of this maze was daunting. Then she shrugged. All she had to do was keep riding in a southeasterly direction and sooner or later she would come to a recognizable landmark—even if she didn't see anything familiar until she reached the Mississippi River!

It was then that she realized that she had fully abandoned any notion of seeking the Aztec gold. Savanna had never hungered after riches in the first place, and although it would have been pleasant to shower Elizabeth with all the elegancies of life if the gold had been found, she and her mother would be just fine without it. Besides, she admitted ruefully, without a map or someone to guide her to it, finding the gold would be a hopeless task, and no amount of gold in the world was worth the danger she would face if she were insane enough to continue on the fool's quest that had ultimately killed her father. Rejoining Micajah was *not* an option, and it was only now that she was free that she realized how incredibly lucky she had been that Micajah hadn't used her far more badly than what she had just suffered at Adam's hands. At least she tried to tell herself that she'd been horribly abused by Adam, but somehow it didn't quite ring true. If she dwelt on that final, angry taking, she could easily convince herself that Adam was no better than Micajah; unfortunately, her mind wouldn't let her forget that first, wondrous joining and the powerful attraction he aroused within her.

Angry that thoughts of Adam had entered her mind again, she kicked her horse into movement. She was going home! She wasn't going to allow herself to think very much about anything that had happened to her since the first moment she had looked up into Micajah's grinning face. She might have allowed herself to be convinced that she had a right to the gold; she might even have allowed herself to think that it was only right and just to kidnap and force the man who had killed her father to lead them to the gold, but no longer. The gold didn't really mean anything to her, and she would content herself with the knowledge that in the end, Davalos had shown his real feelings—that he had truly loved her and her mother. And as for Micajah's threats to spread the truth about Elizabeth's true circumstances . . . Savanna's eyes narrowed. She wasn't certain how she was going to do it, but between now and the next time she saw Micajah, *if* she ever saw Micajah again, she would think of something—she had to, if her mother's respectable life was to continue. With that decision made, she felt her heart lighten a little. She would go home, pick up the threads of her life and forget that she had ever laid eyes on a blue-eyed devil named Adam!

Which was easier said than done, Savanna decided disgustedly as the memory of him lying inert and half naked on the forest floor slipped through her mind again. She should have made certain that he had come to his senses before she left him. She still could have escaped—it would take him some time to fight free of his bonds, and she didn't believe that he would trouble himself to come after her. He would no doubt immediately go back to Terre du Coeur and never give her another thought. The fact that he would be going back to a wife and family suddenly occurred to her, and she was bewildered by the knife-pain in her heart such knowledge gave her.

The fact that he was married was something she had forgotten, but now, in view of what had transpired between them, she was painfully aware of it and she closed her eyes in anguish. How *could* she have forgotten who he was and what he was and allowed herself to have been so shamelessly fascinated by him? How could she have been willing, when all was said and done, to lie in his arms and allow him the freedoms which no man had ever had from her? She cared *nothing* for him! She hated him! Thoroughly ashamed that she had felt such pleasure in his embrace, disgusted that she allowed herself to be beguiled by a man so unworthy of her, Savanna stared dully between the ears of her horse, wishing she had never laid eyes on him.

Well, my girl, she finally told herself firmly, stop dwelling on it; put it behind you and think about how you're going to find your way home. Her rousing little speech worked for a while, and she concentrated fiercely on where she was going and considered various means to supplement her meager supplies, but insidiously, images of Adam's still form kept darting in and out of her thoughts. What if he couldn't escape those bonds and slowly starved to death? If some wild animal didn't discover him first! Suppose Micajah found him? Micajah would torture him to death!

Eventually, Savanna gave up resisting the urge to leave him to his justly deserved fate, whatever it might be, and turned her horse around. She would have to go back, make certain that he *had* regained his wits, and she wouldn't think at all how she would feel if he hadn't; if he were awake, she would have to figure out some sort of plan that would allow her to leave, confident that he could free himself and wouldn't be hot on her trail. She wanted him, she told herself savagely, out of her life, not dead!

It was relatively simple to follow her own trail slowly back to the place where she had left Adam, and she did so with extreme misgivings. Her thoughts were not pleasant or comfortable as she reluctantly made the return journey.

Strangely enough, Savanna didn't regret the loss of

her virginity, nor did she totally blame Adam for his first possession of her. She almost believed that it had been inevitable, but there was no way that she could excuse that second, ungentle taking. He had acted abominably and for that she should leave him to suffer—let alone for what he had done to her father! As for his wife and children . . . she swallowed painfully. He belonged to them and she had not deliberately set out to wrong them. It had happened and she would be sorry for it for a long time.

Her mouth twisted ruefully. Just see what comes from trying to extract revenge, my girl! she scolded herself. How much better off would you have been if you had never allowed Micajah's words to sway you? She grimaced. Of course, she'd never really had much choice in the matter, but she couldn't deny that once she'd realized her position, she hadn't been a willing participant in Micajah's scheme. Well, she was paying for her foolishness now and she only hoped that after ascertaining Adam's safety, she could turn her back on him and begin the journey home—and forget she had ever met Jason *Adam* Savage!

Several hours had passed since she had made her escape, and she was uncertain what sort of scene would be waiting for her when she returned to where Adam had set up camp. Some distance from it, she dismounted and tied her horse to a sapling. Careful to make as little noise as possible, she crept nearer, her emotions and thoughts ambivalent. She didn't want to see her tormentor again, but she was anxious for him, and her heart began to pound thunderously with every cautious step she took.

Creeping to the edge of the camp area, hidden by a clump of tangled foliage, Savanna peered surreptitiously around. Everything looked normal; Adam's horse was still tethered to the same tree, the items she had left were still scattered haphazardly about, but of Adam himself there was no sign. Nothing. The

place was empty of any human habitation. Savanna
closed her eyes, horrible pictures of him being carried off by mountain lions or bears flashing before
her. Forcing down the terror that rose in her throat,
she looked again, this time even more carefully, and
it was then that she noticed that the knife was missing from where she had left it. . . .

Suddenly frightened, telling herself she had done
what she had intended—obviously he had escaped
her bonds—she spun around, intent on swiftly putting as much distance between herself and this place
as she could, and promptly collided heavily with a
warm, hard body she knew all too well. His arms
fastened brutally around her, and despite her fierce
struggles, she was his captive once more.

Adam was still garbed only in his breeches, and
her face was crushed against the heat of his naked
chest, his powerful arms wrapped tightly around her.
There was nothing the *least* loverlike about his embrace, nor in his tone as he drawled coolly, "Come
back to amuse yourself with my death struggles,
sweetheart? Or perhaps you decided to give me a
kinder death than starvation and were going to do
the deed yourself?"

It was so far from the truth that Savanna could
only gape openmouthed at him. How could he think
such a thing? She'd come back to prevent just such
an event! Equally furious that he believed her capable of such utter cruelty and that she had, albeit with
the noblest of intentions, brought this latest calamity
upon herself, she simply glared at him and closed
her mouth with an angry snap. I should never have
wasted a second's remorse on him, she thought viciously; never, *never* risked my own safety to see
about his!

His hands closed around her shoulders and he
shook her ungently. "No answer?" he questioned
grimly. "Too busy trying to think up some sort of
clever lie?"

Her breathing labored as much from temper as from their struggle, Savanna snarled, "You murdering bastard! What else did you expect from me? Kindness? After what you did to me and my father?"

An odd expression—regret? shame?—flashed across his face, but vanished as swiftly as it had appeared. His face cold and remote once more, he drawled icily, "I might have asked you the same question—what the hell did *you* expect from *me*? After all, I am, as you have frequently informed me, an unfeeling monster!"

His words gave her a queer sense of pain and miserably she realized that she didn't, most of the time, think of him in those derogatory terms. But she *should*, she reminded herself fiercely. She should never forget who he was or what he had done! Sending him a contemptuous glance, she stared stonily over his shoulder and muttered, "I don't want to talk about it!"

She felt his shrug. "Not much point," he agreed equitably and, spinning her around, shoved her in the direction of their camp. "Where is your horse and the rest of the supplies?" he asked as he efficiently shackled her to a small willow tree.

Glancing down at the despised chains, Savanna wished vehemently that she had thought to hurl them into the deepest part of the pond while she'd had the chance. Since there was no point in not answering his question, she replied stiffly, "About a quarter mile back, tied to an oak sapling."

Adam nodded and, after shrugging into his white shirt, disappeared into the brush. Savanna stared after him, a mirthless smile curving her mouth. So much for trying to do a Christian act, she thought with bitter regret.

Adam's thoughts were just as bitterly regretful as Savanna's as he swiftly stalked in the direction she had indicated, but for vastly different reasons. He had *never* used a woman as he had Savanna, and the fact that the loss of her virginity had happened only moments before made the act even more reprehensible. Shame scalded through him and he wondered irritably if being in the company of men like Micajah had turned him into the same sort of bestial animal. Though he tried, Adam could find no real excuse for his incomprehensible behavior—at least nothing that satisfied him or lessened his deep feelings of shame and self-disgust. I should never have touched her, he admitted grimly. Never kissed her, never discovered the astonishing fact that she had been a virgin, and he certainly should never, *never* have unleashed his formidable temper in such a despicable manner!

He was an extremely troubled and baffled man as he came upon Savanna's horse and mechanically untied the animal and began to walk back to camp. His head ached abominably and his conscience was tearing viciously at him in a way that it never had before in his life. He didn't regret in the least having made love to Savanna and he would even admit that the knowledge that she had been a virgin filled him with a powerful sense of possession and a bewildering pleasure. Of that second taking he simply would not think, not of the brutal act itself, nor of the reasons behind it.

What he had to concentrate on now, he finally decided, was how to get himself out of his current dangerous predicament—a predicament that could be laid directly at Savanna's damn feet! Despite the earlier events of today, nothing had really changed—he was still a fugitive from Micajah's tender mercies, it was still imperative that no one know that he was not Jason Savage and it was just as imperative that he not lead the chase back to his half brother either at Terre du Coeur or in New Orleans.

Adam sighed. What the hell was he going to do? He couldn't keep riding aimlessly through the Texas wilderness indefinitely, and yet until he felt confident that he had truly eluded Micajah, he didn't want to head for Natchez. And then there were the meager supplies and decidedly *un*spirited mounts! For a journey of any length, he would need better horses and better equipment, but without any money, how the devil was he to accomplish any change?

Coldly he admitted that he should have gotten rid of Savanna at the first opportunity—should have left her trussed up on the ground beside Jeremy! She was an unneeded distraction, a treacherous disruption and a dangerous liability! Having given in to a moment of insanity and taken her with him when he made his escape, he certainly should have regained his senses by the time he had gotten to that plantation, and left her there while he disappeared with both the horses and all the provisions. But even knowing what he should have done and what he should do now, wondering blackly if insanity ran rampant in the family, Adam was furiously aware that for reasons which completely escaped him, he was not going to let that flame-haired, witch-spirited little bitch out of his sight! She was *his!* And she owed him far more than she had paid so far!

When he got back to camp, his mood was bleak and dark. Ignoring Savanna, he retied her horse and unpacked the supplies that she had taken with her. As he glanced at the sun hanging low in the sky, it was, he thought sourly, too late in the day to travel any farther—besides, he had the devil's own headache! They would rise tomorrow before dawn and there would be no more dallying around—he had come to a sudden decision: they would ride for San Antonio, where, as he recalled from the one time he had met the stiffly punctilious old Spanish grandee at Terre du Coeur, Don Felipe Santana lived. Don Felipe was some sort of a cousin of Jason's, and while Adam hated to go begging, he didn't see that he had any other choice. Besides, heading for San Antonio would solve several problems—between here and there they were sure to completely lose

Micajah, and Don Felipe would, even if reluctantly, give them food and shelter and provide Adam with new supplies and horses to finally begin the journey home to Natchez. From now on they would be riding hard and long, and Adam only hoped that he'd be so exhausted at night that the memory of Savanna's softly thrashing body beneath his wouldn't tempt him to seek oblivion in her all-too-seductive flesh.

It was apparent to Savanna that Adam had come to some decision, although what it was she had no idea, but as they set out at a punishing pace the next morning, she could only wonder where he was taking her and if she was ever going to see beloved faces and familiar places again. She had never ridden at such a fierce gait in her life and she had never been as sore, exhausted, dirty or hungry either! From the darkness of predawn until the darkness of dusk they rode, stopping rarely during the daylight hours and then only for Adam to add, when he could, to their frighteningly depleted food supply. There was silence between them as they traveled through the wilderness, but it was not the silence of friendship; it was a simmering, angry, resentful silence, one that would take little effort on either of their parts to cause to explode into something that neither one of them was willing to face.

Without protest, Savanna continued to wear the breeches and other clothing that he had procured for her, and she didn't even murmur an objection when he roughly combed and braided her hair into a pair of thick plaits and tied them on top of her head. She was almost grateful for the coolness it afforded her, until he briskly jammed the old wool hat down on her head, almost to her eyes, and muttered, "At least no one will see that red hair, and from a distance you just might pass for a youth! Let's hope so! We don't need to leave any clues for dear Micajah to find, do we, witch-whelp!"

Adam had considered cutting off that tangled

mane of red-gold hair, but somehow, even with the knife in his hand, he couldn't bring himself to do it, and decided blackly that he was indeed a bewitched fool! The breeches and shirt didn't disguise her femininity as much as he had hoped, the breeches clinging a little too lovingly to her hips and thighs and the shirt, if not hiding her full breasts, at least not calling attention to them. He didn't delude himself about the effectiveness of his efforts to conceal her sex either—only from quite a distance could Savanna ever be mistaken for a young man!

As they rode steadily southwest, deeper into Texas, the terrain began to gradually change. They had left behind the pine forests and had ridden through areas where oak and chestnut trees had been the main wood, swamp willows and a few magnolia trees interspersed among them. Knowing that Micajah, after wasting a certain amount of time trying to pick up their trail, would no doubt head directly to Nacogdoches to resupply himself and Jeremy before continuing the chase, Adam had taken pains to stay well away from that area. Steadily he and Savanna pressed onward, crossing the Angelina and Neches rivers, riding through endless stands of oak and blackjack, a type of small, black-barked, gnarly oak. Just before they crossed the Trinity River some days later, they caught sight of their first prairie of any size. After so many days of wandering through seemingly endless forests, they were happy to have the landscape open up before them.

They approached the Trinity River from a high bluff, and once they had struggled across its rapid, muddy flow, the terrain took on a semitropical appearance. There were dense canebrakes to traverse; an abundant variety of green-hued, immense trees grew everywhere, strung with vines of every kind, huge grapevines dominating, and ghostly Spanish moss clung thickly to many of the trees.

They camped on the edge of the rich bottomland

of the Trinity River that night, and as a result of being in each other's company for so long, they had established an *almost* pleasant routine for setting up camp. Earlier in the day they had surprised a pack of wild pigs, and Adam had expended one of their precious bullets and killed a young gilt. They ate well that evening.

Adam should have been at ease that night: there was no obvious sign of pursuit; his stomach was full for the first time in days; Savanna was not *overtly* troublesome. And yet ... he felt distinctly uneasy. For the past day and a half, the back of his neck had prickled incessantly, and although he constantly glanced over his shoulder, he never glimpsed anything that could explain his increasing sensation that someone or something was following them. Whatever was back there had him greatly puzzled—he took what precautions he could each night against a surprise attack, but if it were Micajah and Jeremy following them, why the hell hadn't they launched some sort of foray against him?

There were other considerations to bother him that night also. They had used up their small supply of food days ago and were reduced to eating only whatever he could trap or shoot; the bullets were diminishing alarmingly, especially in view of their vulnerable situation. With the corn gone, their horses, while able to find a certain amount of forage—and the forage was bound to improve as the grassy prairies became more prevalent—were less and less capable of traveling much farther, at any speed.

Staring glumly into the darkness, Adam knew it was only a matter of time before one of the animals came up lame, or simply lay down and died. And being on the run in the vast Texas wilderness, without horses, soon to be almost weaponless and with no food, made their outlook seem particularly bleak.

He glanced across at Savanna's sleeping form and unknowingly his hard features softened. Her face was gaunt from their ordeal, her hands and arms were scratched and sunburned and her clothing was torn and filthy, but she had endured uncomplainingly, he'd give her that. Of course, he reminded himself cynically, it was *her* fault she was in this position; if she hadn't been a greedy little bitch and joined up with Micajah to go after the gold in the first place, none of this would have happened. She deserved whatever she got.

Adam frowned. The powerful attraction she held for him was unabated, and even though he fell into exhausted sleep each night, his dreams were full of her, the sweetness of her kiss, the softness of her body. Generally he woke up in a foul mood, furious that he could not escape from her even in sleep.

The next morning dawned bright and clear, the sun a hot yellow orb in the brilliant blue of the sky, and the scenery changed again as they rode over small, flat, boggy prairies, raggedly edged by thick timber. The grass was coarse and reedy, and by late afternoon they came upon oaks which changed to blackjack, but Adam had little eye for the terrain. That uneasy feeling that something was on their trail had him increasingly jumpy.

Perhaps it was because he was concentrating so much on what might be behind them that, just prior to dusk, when the ragtag, tiny village suddenly appeared before them, Adam was taken by surprise. From a small stand of timber he stared disbelievingly at the half-dozen or so shabby buildings clustered protectively together in the middle of nowhere. The sight was unbearably welcoming, but, mindful that they were deep in Spanish territory illegally, and not especially inclined to spend his remaining days immured in some godforsaken Spanish prison, Adam hesitated to approach the tattered structures.

In the fading light, he ran his eyes speculatively over the village—a grand name for the pitiful shacks before him. He suspected that it was a military outpost, which didn't exactly bode well. There were several horses tethered about, however, and he spied a rough corral holding a dozen or so more. Situated out here in the middle of nowhere, the outpost would hopefully be well supplied—although he was aware of the deplorable conditions that were normal at most of these remote garrisons. From this distance he could faintly hear the low of a cow and the squawks and squeals of chickens and pigs, so he knew there was *some* food available. The problem was getting it and escaping with his hide intact!

For several seconds he stared consideringly at the outpost. The inhabitants would be soldiers and perhaps a few families of the more senior men. As he watched, it became apparent that one of the larger buildings was a cantina; the sounds of guitar music, the clink of glass and bursts of raucous laughter drifted to him. His eyes narrowed. The men would be bored out here; they would spend the evening drinking and gambling. . . . A wolfish smile curved his mouth.

He glanced back at Savanna. He'd have to leave her as he had when he'd gone to that plantation, and this time there was a very real possibility that he might not make it back if the soldiers discovered him raiding their corrals and storerooms. He frowned. The knots that bound her hands together would have to be tied so that he could be assured that she could escape within a few hours in case something did happen to him. He wouldn't want her starving to death alone in this copse, nor would he want the soldiers to find her. Adam found himself strangely reluctant to be parted from her; uneasy about leaving her alone, but swearing softly at his own folly, he angrily convinced himself it was the only way.

His plans were risky, but he had great confidence in his own abilities and he intended to be in and out of that outpost without the Spaniards ever guessing he'd been in the vicinity. With fresh horses and supplies, he'd return to Savanna before she'd even had time to undo the first knot—unless, of course, he admitted with a grim twist of his lips, he was captured or dead. . . .

Dusk had fallen, and from a couple of the smaller buildings the glow of candlelight spilled out into the encroaching darkness. It would be several hours yet before he dared venture closer, and turning his horse away, he led Savanna back a half mile to a spot they had passed before.

Puzzlement in her lovely eyes, Savanna stared at him as he dismounted and untied her hands from the saddle horn. "Why didn't we approach the village?"

"Because, sweetheart," he said caustically, "we're not exactly welcome in Spanish territory! And there is the fact that those soldiers down there would take one look at you and clarify what constitutes rape even more vividly than I did!"

Savanna drew in an angry breath, but didn't rise to his deliberate baiting. For some reason, he wanted to pick a fight with her, and she wasn't about to give him the satisfaction of provoking her to blind rage. He was up to something, she decided uneasily as she watched him move around the area, only partially unpacking their few belongings. The animosity between them had been kept carefully banked these past weeks—there had been no references to what had transpired by that forest pool until tonight.

Stepping in front of him, she touched his arm, and her eyes locking with his, she asked levelly, "What are you going to do?"

In the dusky light she could barely make out his hard features, the thick black beard that had grown over the weeks hiding the strong line of his jaw and granite chin. The blue eyes were almost black in the murky darkness and the expression in them made Savanna's heart leap painfully in her breast. "You're going back there, aren't you?" she asked incredulously.

He nodded curtly and replied evenly, "It's the only way we're going to get resupplied. I'll wait until after midnight before I risk it—you'll remain here. I shouldn't be gone very long."

Savanna swallowed with difficulty. "And if they capture you? What then?"

Adam smiled derisively. "Well, then you'll be on your own, sweetheart, and you'll have the immense satisfaction of knowing that the Spaniards did the job for you of cutting my throat."

His words stabbed her and she suddenly realized that she didn't want him hurt—despite what she had been telling herself for weeks. Concealing her bewildered anguish, taking refuge in defiance, she muttered savagely, "I only wish I could watch them do it!"

There were no further exchanges between them, and when it was time for him to leave, she stoically endured the bonds he placed around her, telling herself it didn't matter that she might never see him again. It was only when he started to put the gag in her mouth that her composure broke and she lifted pleading eyes to his. "Please," she said, "not that."

He stared for a long moment into her upturned face, the distasteful knowledge that this might be the last time he ever looked into those bewitching aquamarine eyes suddenly coursing through him. It shouldn't have made a difference, but it did, and with a muffled curse he threw down the gag and dragged her into his arms. He kissed her fiercely, his mouth bruising and feverish on hers, and then he thrust her from him abruptly and leaped onto the back of his horse and disappeared into the night.

How long she remained alone in the moon-filtered darkness, Savanna never knew. Time stood still in the beginning, but after a while, she had the uncomfortable feeling that she was not quite alone. It was unnerving to think of something out there in the darkness watching her, waiting. . . . She shrank back against the tree to which she was shackled, telling herself it was probably just some roaming beast and praying fervently for Adam's swift, *safe* return. Then, suddenly, Adam was there before her, leading what seemed to be an inordinate amount of horses. He was grinning when he dismounted, his teeth flashing whitely in the shadowy light, and it was obvious he was very pleased with himself. Kneeling, he immediately undid the shackles. A moment later, her hands were free. "A supply train must have arrived just a few days ago, because their storehouses were well stocked and the animals are in excellent condition," Adam explained as he turned away and began to transfer her saddle to the back of a fresh horse. Flashing her a sardonic look, he added, "As for the soldiers themselves, I'm afraid you'll just have to wait for another opportunity for someone to rid you of me!"

Some of her joy at his safe return ebbed, and glaring at him, she snapped untruthfully, "Well, it can't be soon enough for me!" Adam only laughed at her and began to tighten the cinch on her saddle.

In the excitement of his return, Savanna had momentarily forgotten the uneasy sensations that she'd had earlier, and Adam was too busy concentrating on getting them away from this area as quickly as possible to sense the presence of the man so stealthily approaching the pair of them. Savanna was standing fifteen feet away from Adam as he completed his task, staring daggers into his broad back, when the huge, dark shape exploded out of the underbrush and swung a thick club at the back of Adam's head.

Savanna screamed and Adam was already spinning about when the man struck. The stunning blow caught Adam on the temple and he crumpled in a heap. Like a tigress defending her young, Savanna launched herself at the attacker, only to come to a frozen standstill as the man turned and she recognized him.

Incredulously she stared at features she knew as well as her own. *"Bodene!"*

Chapter 11

"WELL, WHO THE HELL ELSE DID YOU EXPECT?" HER cousin demanded irascibly as he bent over and efficiently tied Adam's hands behind his back.

Savanna laughed tremulously, still not quite capable of taking in the astonishing fact that it was her immeasurably comforting cousin who had struck Adam down. It was only when he stood up and regarded her with that familiar mixture of affection and exasperation that she knew it really was Bodene Sullivan there in front of her and not some mad dream. Smiling and crying at the same time, she hurled herself into his arms and, enveloped in his strong embrace, lost the iron control she had kept over herself and let the too-long-held-back tears stream from her eyes.

When the worst of the storm of weeping had passed, she firmly brushed away the signs of her weakness and smiled, albeit shakily, up at him. "Oh, Bodene! I don't think I've ever been so happy to see anyone in my life than I am to see you right now!" she admitted.

"I should hope so, my dear!" Bodene retorted bluntly. "You've led me the devil's own chase, I can tell you! Now, do you want to explain to me what's going on? I've been tracking you for weeks and the only thing that has kept me going, besides dwelling on the satisfaction it would give me to wring your neck, was that I would find out what the hell happened to cause you to disappear like that! Your mother has been frantic!"

Still smiling mistily up at him, she noted that he made no reference to the fact that *he* had been equally frantic. She sighed raggedly. "It's a very long story—one I'll tell you once we're far away from here."

She sent a worried glance in Adam's direction and, dropping down next to his still body, assured herself that he was only unconscious. An anxious expression on her face, she muttered, "I wish you hadn't hit him quite so hard. It's going to be difficult to get him on a horse in his condition."

Bodene stared at her, thunderstruck. "Excuse me? Do I take that statement to mean we're taking that blackguard with us?"

"We can't leave him here!" she exclaimed. "Anything could happen to him!"

"Well, I should bloody well hope so!" Bodene burst out explosively. "I don't know what has gone on, but it's obvious to me that you didn't leave home with him willingly, nor have you stayed with him because you wanted to be with him. And from the bit of conversation I overheard before I knocked him out, it didn't sound as if your relationship was particularly friendly!"

Savanna grimaced. "I know. It's all so complicated. But he wasn't the one who kidnapped me—at least not in the beginning," she admitted truthfully. "*That* was Micajah!"

Looking thoroughly bewildered, Bodene regarded her silently for a long moment. Then he let his breath out in an exasperated sigh and said, "I think you had better start at the beginning of this tale."

"I will, I promise, but first we had better get away from here—he stole these horses and supplies from a small Spanish outpost about a half mile from here. They'll be looking for us come daylight."

Bodene's chin jutted stubbornly and Savanna feared that he was going to prove to be immovable, but after studying Savanna's strained expression and then glancing consideringly at the man on the ground beside her, he shrugged. "All right. We'll take him with us, but you had better have a good story to convince me that I shouldn't have left him lying here!"

Savanna nodded vigorously, and the next several moments were spent in hurried activity as they swiftly took stock of the animals and goods and tied Adam like a sack of grain over his saddle, which had been placed on the back of a fresh horse. The worn-out mounts which Adam and Savanna had been riding originally, they turned loose. Bodene's horse and pack mule, which he had concealed some distance away, showed signs of the long, hard trek they had just completed, but were in good condition. Not fifteen minutes later, the cavalcade was on its way through the moonlit darkness, Bodene leading his own mule and a packhorse, Savanna leading Adam's horse and the other packhorse Adam had stolen.

There wasn't a lot of conversation between them, for they both were occupied with putting as much distance between themselves and the Spanish outpost as possible, and though the moon greatly aided their journey, it was no pleasure ride. Fortunately, they were crossing territory they had traveled before and they made excellent progress, galloping their mounts as fast as they dared.

They lost some time while Bodene tried to disguise their trail, but eventually he gave that up—the passing of six animals was difficult to obliterate even in daylight, and with only the glow of the moon to help him, it was nearly impossible. Speed, he decided grimly, was the only thing that was going to put them beyond the reach of the Spanish! He kept the horses at a rigorous pace even after the sun had risen, but he knew that they would have to stop by evening—Savanna's pale features clearly defined how very near exhaustion she was, and he cursed under his breath the man who had brought her to this state. Glancing back at the bobbing form of the unconscious man, Bodene promised himself fiercely that the fellow was going to learn to his cost that it wasn't wise to meddle with Savanna! Bodene Sullivan was going to teach him a lesson he'd never forget!

As the day progressed, Savanna kept throwing anxious looks back at Adam's body, fearful that this punishing ride would harm him further. If only he would stir, she thought for perhaps the hundredth time since they had begun their mad dash away from probable pursuit. Why doesn't he wake? Whenever Bodene pulled the horses to a halt for a brief rest or for water, Savanna dismounted and checked on Adam, but by late afternoon, when there still was no sign of his rousing, she was acutely worried.

"Shouldn't he be waking by now?" she asked Bodene with a distressed expression on her tired features.

Speculatively Bodene's gaze went from her face to the limp body of the man on the horse. Savanna was sure damned concerned for that fellow, he thought slowly, and she shouldn't be! He might not know *exactly* what had happened to her, but from his observation before he had made his presence known, it had been apparent they weren't friends! Yet she seemed genuinely anxious about the man. What the hell had happened between the two of them?

Frowning, he asked out loud, "Why do you care? When I found you, he'd left you chained like a slave in the middle of nowhere!" He glanced again at the man. "Something happen between you two that I should know about?"

Wearily, Savanna shook her head. She wasn't about to involve someone else in her argument with Adam—if what lay between them could be identified by such an innocuous term!

Unknowingly, her fingers caressed Adam's dark head and she muttered, "I just don't want him to die, that's all!"

Bodene snorted and, walking over to Adam, made a rapid survey of his body. "Breathing's normal and his color isn't bad," he finally said. "He should wake up this evening sometime—with one hell of a head-ache!"

They remounted and rode steadily eastward, Savanna so exhausted that she simply trusted her horse to follow Bodene's and fell into uneasy naps. It was only when she was in danger of falling off her horse that she would jerk fully awake and for a while would try to stave off the overpowering need for sleep, until the effort became too much and she would doze off again.

Bodene had not been wrong about Adam's head-ache, but he had miscalculated the time of his awakening. Not more than an hour after the conversation between the cousins, Adam gradually became aware of his situation. His head did indeed ache—atrociously so—and to find himself roped to a saddle like a sack of grain, his head hanging down on one side of the horse, his feet on the other, did not add to his comfort! Sourly Adam decided that he was getting damn tired of being hit in the head!

Beyond realizing that once again someone had knocked him out, at first he was slightly disoriented, but with every jarring step the horse took, memory came flooding back. The events of the previous night were suddenly vibrantly clear to him, and it didn't take a genius to figure out that someone—Micajah?—

had struck him from behind and trussed him up this way.

As much not to give away his recovery as not to increase the pounding in his temples, Adam moved his head cautiously, looking around as best his bonds permitted. He couldn't tell a great deal from his position, but it appeared that Savanna was leading his horse as well as one of the packhorses and that she was following someone else. Who? Micajah? The thought was a chilling one, and almost gratefully, Adam slid once more into unconsciousness. He woke several times more during the rest of the day, each time staying awake longer and becoming more and more alert. It soon became apparent, from the little conversation he overheard between Savanna and the other man, that it hadn't been Micajah who had given him the blow to the head. That information didn't comfort him very much, because it was also obvious that whoever had knocked him out was someone Savanna knew—which didn't bode well for him!

It was nearly dark when Bodene finally decided that they should stop for the night. He chose a small tree-dotted bluff which gave a clear view of the wide prairie they had just crossed and which he hoped fervently would allow him to spot any pursuers in time to take defensive action. A good-sized stream ran near the base of the bluff, and the grass was long and sweet for the animals.

Savanna slid exhaustedly from her horse, and watching her stiff movements as she tied her mount and began to unsaddle it, Bodene said in a gruff voice, "Leave it, brat! I'll take care of it. You see how our companion is doing and then just rest a while."

For once in her life, she was too worn out to argue. She sent him a grateful smile and approached Adam's horse. Almost tenderly, her hands cupped his face as she lifted his head to examine his features. Finding herself being coolly studied by those hard blue eyes was a shock and she gave a small, startled gasp.

Dryly Adam asked, "Going to kiss me awake, sweetheart? Or perhaps you intend for your friend to knock me in the head again?"

Savanna's mouth tightened. "It's only what you deserve!"

Adam's brow rose. "A kiss?"

Savanna let his head drop, and turning away, she said viciously, "No! A knock in the head!"

Bodene looked up from his task and walked over as Adam lifted his head and stared back at him. Catching his first real sight of his captor, Adam almost groaned out loud. He had seldom met a man whose size gave him pause, but taking in Bodene's massive presence, he whistled soundlessly. Jesus! Wouldn't you just know that Savanna's rescuer would be a bloody giant!

Sending the other man a grim smile, Adam inquired, "Do I have you to thank for this abominable headache?"

Bodene nodded his dark head and returned laconically, "Yep! Figured it was the simplest way to get her free. I'd have shot you, but then Savanna might have gotten hurt—didn't want that."

"Of course not," Adam replied politely, just as if he were in a grand ballroom and not in his present ignominious position. He sent the object of their conversation a black look and added with a cutting edge to his voice, "Under no circumstances would we want *her* hurt!"

Bodene quirked an eyebrow. It was obvious the man meant exactly the opposite, and Bodene wondered again just what the hell Savanna was involved in. Glancing over at her, he commented, "Your friend here seems to have recovered without any permanent damage, honey. Doesn't seem to care much for you either, does he? Who is he?"

Savanna flashed an unfriendly look at Adam. "Jason Savage—Micajah and Jeremy Childers kidnapped him from his home at Terre du Coeur."

"That so?" Bodene replied in a cool voice.

Something in the other man's voice made Adam look at him sharply. A shiver of unease slid down his spine. Was it possible that Savanna's giant actually knew Jason?

When the other man turned away and began to start a fire, Adam sighed with relief. Perhaps he'd been mistaken.

It was only after camp had been completely set up, and a pot of coffee and one of beans were bubbling merrily on the fire, that Bodene's attention turned to the man still slung over the saddle of his horse. All the other horses were hobbled and grazing nearby. Savanna was slumped on the ground, leaning back against a log, her eyes fixed sleepily on the dancing flames of the fire.

Approaching Adam's horse, Bodene swiftly undid the bonds that tied Adam to the saddle, leaving his hands and feet still roped tightly together, and with a grunt, hefted Adam's not inconsiderable weight onto his massive shoulders. Then he moved toward one of the trees near the leaping fire and dumped Adam unceremoniously on the ground. Turning away, he unsaddled that last horse and, after hobbling it, watched for a long moment as the animal ambled away to join the others. Then he walked back to Adam and stood there looking down at him.

There was nothing friendly in the glance he sent Adam, and Adam cursed his helpless position. Braced for whatever punishment he might receive, he stared coolly back at the bigger man.

Bodene looked him up and down again. "Jason Savage, eh?" He glanced over his shoulder at Savanna. "Seems that not only is your friend here a kidnapper, but he's a liar, too!"

A faint frown etched Savanna's forehead. "What do you mean?"

Bodene hunkered down next to the fire and, picking up the cool end of one of the pieces of burning wood, held the flame closer to Adam's face. Adam stared back unflinchingly.

Savanna had gotten up and crossed to stand next to Bodene. Her hand on his shoulder, she shook him slightly and asked, "What do you mean by that? A liar?"

"Only that I know Jason Savage by sight—and whoever this fellow is, he sure as hell ain't Jason Savage!"

"*What?*" Savanna demanded incredulously. "But he has to be!" she protested wildly. "He was at Terre du Coeur and he admitted that he was Jason Savage! Micajah kidnapped him and was going to torture him—if he isn't Jason Savage, why wouldn't he say so?"

"I don't know," Bodene replied equitably. "Why don't you ask him?"

Savanna turned accusing eyes upon Adam. "Well?" she demanded.

Adam shrugged his broad shoulders, having decided that silence might be his best defense for the time being.

Indecision clouded Savanna's features, and shaking Bodene's shoulder, she asked uneasily, "Bodene, are you certain he's not Jason Savage?"

Bodene tossed the flaming branch back into the fire. "Yep. I'm sure. Jason Savage is a well-known figure around New Orleans. I've had him pointed out to me several times—he's even come to my place and done a little gambling. Had the devil's own luck that night, too, I might add."

Her confusion evident, Savanna said breathlessly in a dazed tone, "But if he isn't Jason Savage, then *who* is he? And why would he put his life in such danger by pretending to be Jason Savage?"

Bodene looked thoughtful, his gaze never leaving Adam's carefully blank face. Rubbing his chin,

Bodene finally said slowly, "I expect that he knew Micajah would slit his throat once the truth came out, and as for the other . . . maybe he was trying to throw Micajah off the scent of the *real* Jason Savage."

"Is that true?" Savanna asked Adam, her eyes locked painfully on his.

Adam remained silent, his thoughts racing. If this fellow Bodene knew Jason, Adam was grimly aware that he didn't have a snowball's chance in hell of maintaining even a semblance of doubt about his identity. Consideringly, his gaze went over Bodene. He could see no overt resemblance between Bodene and Savanna, and yet there was something about the man that made Adam uneasily suspicious that he was the prisoner of Savanna's relative . . . a relative, it was obvious, who didn't take kindly to Savanna's kidnapping . . . a relative who might take a very dim view of Adam's actions with Savanna—particularly those that had taken place by that forest pond! Studying the hard jaw and unwavering gaze of the powerful young man in front of him, Adam suddenly concluded that he had stood a better chance of survival with Micajah than he did with this giant of a man.

Bodene's eyes had never left Adam's face as the moments spun by, and Bodene finally asked silkily, "Going to answer the lady's question?"

"He'd better!" Savanna said fiercely. "Is what Bodene said the truth? Tell me, damn you!"

Adam sighed. Well, he'd run this rig for as long as he could, and there was nothing more to be gained by keeping his mouth shut. Curtly he admitted, "It's true. I'm not Jason Savage."

Savanna stared at him, stunned. The knowledge that Micajah had not kidnapped Jason Savage, that it had not been Jason Savage who had made love to her and had so tormented her thoughts and dreams, utterly devastated her. She was appalled, relieved, frightened and angry all at the same time. Who *was* this man, this stranger who had turned her life upside down? She almost feared the answer. At least believing him to be Jason Savage had meant that she'd known what she was up against, but to have that knowledge torn from her left her feeling vulnerable and angry.

Her jaw set, her aquamarine eyes hard, she demanded, "Is your name even Adam?"

"Oh, yes," Adam answered calmly. "My name really is Adam. Adam St. Clair, to be exact. Jason is married to my half sister, Catherine, and I was staying at their house while they were in New Orleans when Micajah so, ah, eloquently convinced me to join your little band."

Bodene smiled with satisfaction. "Thought that was who you were! Saw you once, but I wasn't sure that it was really you under that beard! Now then, want to tell me, since you obviously got free of Micajah, why you were heading west with Savanna?"

Adam tiredly rested his head back against the tree, his eyes closed. Resignedly, he muttered, "I didn't want to lead Micajah back to New Orleans and Jason. It was the only way I could think of to keep Jason safe."

Bodene nodded his dark head, understanding perfectly Adam's motive. "But why take my cousin with you? Why not leave her with Micajah?"

Adam moved restlessly. Even if he were willing to explain his reasons, he wouldn't have been able to— hell, *he* didn't even know why he had taken her with him! His eyes opened and he asked suddenly, "Would *you* have left her with Micajah?"

"She's my cousin," Bodene answered calmly, "I'd be honor-bound to take her with me." He cast Savanna a half-teasing, half-exasperated look. "Aggravating little wretch that she is!" He glanced back at Adam. "But that doesn't explain your reasons."

Adam smiled without mirth. "Let's just say that I,

too, found her equally aggravating and decided that she deserved to be taught a much-needed lesson!"

Bodene nodded, apparently understanding and agreeing thoroughly with Adam's explanation.

Feeling much like a fractious child whom they were discussing, Savanna roughly punched Bodene's shoulder and muttered, "It doesn't matter *why* he did it—the point is that he's a lying bastard who doesn't deserve the least bit of kindness from us."

"Oh, that so?" Bodene replied levelly. "Knowing you feel this way makes me wonder why you wanted to bring him with us. If I remember correctly, I was all for leaving him back there near the Spanish outpost, but you wouldn't have it! Said you were afraid something might happen to him."

Adam flashed her a quizzical look and Savanna's cheeks flamed. "It doesn't matter!" she said through clenched teeth. "Just don't get any ideas that he's some poor, abused, innocent bystander! He's not!"

"Maybe so," Bodene said as he rose to his great height. "But it seems to me that you have quite a few questions to answer yourself, brat. Now sit down and eat your beans, and when we're through eating, you can tell me exactly what's been going on since you disappeared."

Resentfully, Savanna did as Bodene had commanded, but she wasn't happy about the change in circumstance. She wasn't certain how it had come about, but somehow it seemed that *she* was being held responsible for what had happened! Some of her resentment had faded by the time her stomach was full and she was sipping her second tin mug of coffee. Despite knowing his true identity and, Savanna suspected, having a sneaking bit of sympathy for him, Bodene had not released Adam from his bonds. He'd only loosened them enough for Adam to eat and drink and then had carefully retied them. The fire was lower now, and watching as Bodene cleaned up—he'd waved away her offers to help—

Savanna knew that any minute her big cousin was going to demand a thorough and detailed explanation of how she'd come to be in the situation in which he had found her.

Moodily she stared at the rich darkness of her coffee. The bare facts of her abduction, first by Micajah and then by Adam, were simple enough to relate; less easy to explain was how or why she had allowed herself to be caught up in Micajah's scheme to go after the Aztec gold. As for Adam St. Clair . . . She shot him a dark look from beneath her lashes. There were some things that were none of Bodene's business! And how she felt about Adam and what had transpired between them fell squarely in that category.

Consequently, when Bodene pressed her a few minutes later for an explanation, she gave him a considerably pared-down version, telling him just the bare bones of what had happened to her. All the while she spoke to her cousin, she was uncomfortably aware that Adam was listening intently to every word, and she wondered uneasily what he would make of all the things that she deliberately left out of her narrative, such as the animosity that existed between them and the torrid mating that had taken place near that tear-shaped pond deep in the forest.

When she had finished, there was a long silence, and after poking at the dying fire, Bodene glanced from her to Adam. "Seems to me," he said slowly, "that Mr. St. Clair here is more sinned against than sinner!"

Savanna's face tightened. "How can you say that! He kidnapped me and treated me wickedly!"

"But only after you and Micajah had kidnapped him first and no doubt treated him equally wickedly!" Bodene replied sharply. "Seems to me you are as much to blame for what happened as he is!"

Adam's appreciative grin did nothing to cool her temper, and, eyes flashing, she snapped, "I might have guessed you'd take his side! Next, I suppose you're going to congratulate him and turn him loose!"

"No, I'm not going to turn him loose . . . yet," Bodene answered calmly. He glanced over to Adam. "I don't know where you were heading with Savanna, and until I'm certain that you won't try to get the drop on me and take off with her again, I'm afraid you'll have to suffer being tied. But you have my word that I'll not treat you unkindly, and as soon as you prove to me that you are no danger to us, I'll set you free. In the meantime, we're all heading back to New Orleans!"

Adam nodded. "Seems fair enough. . . . I hate to inject an unpleasant note into these proceedings, but what about Micajah?"

Bodene shrugged. "From the tracks I found at the campsite where you made your escape, I'd say that Micajah and Jeremy headed to Nacogdoches, and where they are now is anybody's guess!"

"How did you find us?" Adam asked curiously. "I thought I'd covered our tracks fairly well."

"You did a damn good job, almost too damn good!" Bodene said acidly. "There were far too many days when I was certain I'd lost your trail entirely. And from the time your tracks split from Micajah's, I'd never been positive that I made the right choice. Faced with the split in the trail and not knowing who was who, I just flipped a coin—couldn't see anything else to do. The toss came out that I ignore the tracks leading in the direction of Nacogdoches and follow the one that disappeared into the forest. Damn lucky toss!" Bodene smiled widely. "Lost you several times, and most of the time I feared I was chasing the wrong people—gave me several nasty days while I wondered if I should have followed that other trail. Even when I caught sight of you a couple of days ago, I still wasn't certain I'd tracked the right quarry. Wasn't until late yesterday, when one of Savanna's braids fell out from under her hat and I glimpsed that red hair, that I knew I'd had the devil's own luck!"

There wasn't much conversation after that, and it was only when they were preparing to retire for the night that Bodene brought up something that had been troubling him. Looking at Adam, he asked, "How likely is it that those Spaniards will come after us?"

Adam shrugged. "No telling. Before I left I turned loose all their animals in the hopes that by the time they gathered them up in the morning and discovered that four of them were missing, our trail would be too cold and too obliterated by the wanderings of their own horses for them to give chase. I *think* we're fairly safe."

Bodene grunted and, after throwing a blanket over Adam, settled down with his own blanket, resting his head on his saddle. He had chosen to sleep at the edge of the camp, near Adam, while Savanna had bedded down close to the coals of the dimming fire. In a matter of seconds, all was quiet as sleep claimed them.

Precisely what woke Savanna, she never knew. She was only aware that she had awakened from a deep sleep, with her heart pounding wildly and all her senses screaming that something dangerous had found them. She lay frozen on the ground, her ears straining to hear the first hint of what had woken her so violently, but all seemed to be quiet. The sky was just beginning to bloom with brilliant streaks of gold and rose, and she knew that dawn was seconds away. She tried to tell herself that she had awakened naturally, but that didn't explain the frantic beat of her heart or the strong sensation that something was wrong. Hardly daring to breathe, she inched her fingers nearer the long black rifle that lay on the ground beside her, and she felt a thrill of exhilaration when her hand closed comfortingly around it.

A sound, a soft groan, wafted across the campsite

from Bodene's direction, and not giving herself time to think, in one easy movement she swung up and around, the rifle primed and ready in her hands. To say which of the five people caught in the tense little tableau that dawn was the most surprised was impossible to determine. Certainly Savanna was surprised to see a huge Indian with thick black braids deftly cutting through Adam's bonds, while an emerald-eyed, powerfully built man twisted Bodene's arm behind his back; that they were equally surprised to be confronted by a flame-haired, rifle-toting Amazon was obviously apparent, and everyone froze, no one moving a muscle.

The emerald-eyed man seemed to recover first, and holding a knife blade to Bodene's throat, he said in a menacing tone, "Drop it, lady! Drop it or he dies!"

Savanna hesitated less than a second and then pointed the rifle at Adam's breast as he stood there by the tall Indian. "I think not!" she said coldly. "If you kill him, then Adam dies."

An unwilling smile of admiration curved Adam's mouth. "She's serious. I think we have a stalemate—you'd better let her cousin, Bodene, go, because there is nothing that Savanna would like better than to put a bullet through me!"

The green-eyed man frowned slightly, but his hold on Bodene lessened. Dryly he asked, "Ah, has your fabled charm deserted you? I warned you that one day it would." Glancing over at Savanna, Bodene's captor ran an assessing look up and down her, those jewel-toned eyes missing nothing. "Well, madame," he said at last, "it seems that we must trust each other, you and I. If I turn your cousin loose, do I have your word that you will not fire on us?"

Savanna shook her head. "Release Bodene first."

Adam and the green-eyed man exchanged glances, Adam's dark head nodding affirmatively. The other man shrugged and, after releasing Bodene, stepped back. The Indian had remained silent, his arms folded across his naked chest, his black, knowing eyes missing nothing, but Savanna watched him uneasily as Bodene walked over to her, rubbing his arm.

Moving past her, Bodene kicked the smoldering coals into the fire and then put his hand on the barrel of Savanna's rifle and said, "It's all right, Savanna. Put the rifle away. I know this man and I suspect that he has been doing exactly the same thing that I have and for the same reason—to find and free a kidnapped relative!"

Savanna's eyes widened, comprehension dawning, comprehension deepening when Adam smiled, albeit cynically, and, approaching with the green-eyed man and the Indian on either side of him, said mockingly, "Yes, indeed, you have been quite determined to meet him—allow me to introduce you to Jason Savage and his blood brother, Blood Drinker!"

Chapter 12

WOULDN'T YOU JUST KNOW, SAVANNA THOUGHT BITterly as she stared into the emerald depths of Jason Savage's eyes, that Micajah would snatch the wrong man!

Her jaw firmed. She could not undo the past, she could only go forward from this moment. Her head held at a haughty angle, she said coolly to Jason, "I won't say that I'm pleased to meet you ... or that I have *enjoyed* my encounter with your brother-in-law!" Glancing at Adam, she added icily, "I suppose that I must apologize for mistaking you for Jason Savage. However, I'm sure you will admit that you did everything you could to make us believe that you *were* Jason Savage! You have no one to blame but yourself for the continuation of our error!" Her bitterness seeping through, with angry, accusing eyes she stared at Adam's dark features as she said, "I think you and I are even!"

Adam's face was expressionless as he stared back at her, but he acknowledged her statement with an almost imperceptible nod of his head.

The exchange was watched with interest by the other three, and it was only when it became apparent that no more fascinating revelations were forthcoming that Jason stepped forward and, with a quizzical gleam in his green eyes, asked gently, "Since you have the advantage over me, perhaps you would like to introduce yourself?"

Savanna smiled tightly. "It will be my pleasure, but I doubt the name Savanna O'Rourke means anything to you. I *do* think the name Blas Davalos is well known to you—he was my father!"

Jason's face froze, the expression in his eyes hard to define. "I see," he said slowly, his gaze roaming over her set features as he searched in vain for any resemblance to his most hated and deadly enemy. "I'm afraid you don't have the look of your father."

Savanna's lip lifted in a sneer. "Your brother-in-law said the same thing, but it still doesn't change the fact. Blas Davalos *was* my father!"

Jason and Blood Drinker exchanged a look. "Blas never made mention of a wife or a child," Jason finally said.

A bitter smile crossed Savanna's expressive face. "That's because he didn't have a wife—he never married my mother!"

Bodene broke into the tense atmosphere by saying calmly, "I believe that this story is going to take a while, and I don't know about anyone else, but I'd sure like to put something into my belly and have some coffee—it's been one hell of a morning!"

Adam smiled faintly and Jason nodded absently, his eyes never leaving Savanna's face. Blood Drinker appeared indifferent to anything but the tall young woman with the flame-colored hair, and as Bodene and Adam began to busy themselves about a fire, Blood Drinker said abruptly, "Your father was a bad man—I killed him and would do so again. He was evil and did evil things to my blood brother, Jason, but I see no sign of his wicked nature or his many weaknesses in your face. There is little of him to be seen in you, and despite the evidence, I see none of the consuming greed which led to his death by my hand."

Savanna's features had whitened with every word Blood Drinker spoke. Blind, *stubborn* loyalty to Davalos had hot words of denial surging to her lips, but caution made her hold her tongue. Her fists clenched at her side, she muttered, "No matter what you say—there is no excuse for such a cruel act!"

Blood Drinker stared at her for a long, unnerving moment. "My act was no crueler than what he inflicted upon my blood brother and his wife," he said calmly. His black eyes boring into hers, he added, "Davalos *deserved* to die! And in the manner that I killed him!"

No matter what sort of confused emotions Savanna might have held for her father, coupled with everything else that had happened to her over the past weeks, she needed someone to strike out at, and Blood Drinker's words were simply too much. With blazing aquamarine eyes, she charged toward him like an angry tornado, her intention to claw his eyes out obvious.

Adam, who had been watching the scene intently from the sidelines, deftly intercepted Savanna's heedless charge, and catching her in his arms, he shook her slightly, saying bluntly, "Calm down! Before you go flying off in Davalos's defense, perhaps you ought to hear our side of the story."

Taking a mug of steaming black coffee from Bodene, Jason blew on it and said with commendable restraint, "He's right, you know—there are usually two sides to every story, and while Davalos may have painted himself innocent in this affair, the truth is far different."

Savanna thought she would choke on the rage that consumed her at Adam's interference, and ignoring the way her heart had leaped when his hands had closed around her upper arms, she glanced coldly at the hands that still held her prisoner and snarled, "If you wouldn't mind? The time when you could treat me as you liked is long past!"

Adam's mouth tightened, but his hands dropped away. "Listen to what they have to say, Savanna," he urged harshly. "Even you might find it illuminating!"

Before Savanna could reply, Bodene came up and shoved a mug into her hand. "Drink this, brat! And then sit down on that log over there and let them talk." He cocked an eyebrow at her. "You're not in the best position you know—after all, you *did* take part in Adam's kidnapping, and if they want to bring charges against you, I wonder how a judge would view the case."

Bodene's words took the wind right out of Savanna's sails. The fact that she could possibly face criminal charges had never occurred to her, and she was suddenly very aware of her invidious situation. Staring at the black liquid in her tin mug, she wondered bleakly how everything had gone wrong and she sighed. She was so bloody *tired!* So weary of the seemingly endless days of little food and the never-ending nights of sleeping rough on the ground; so exhausted from the fierce, unrelenting battle that Adam had aroused within her breast that all she wanted to do was crawl away and sleep until everything faded from memory.

Becoming aware that she was the object of four different pairs of masculine eyes made her sit up straighter, her expression carefully blank. Taking a sip of the coffee, she muttered, "Go ahead. Tell your damn story."

Jason shook his dark head. "No," he said evenly, "I think we should hear your story first."

Savanna shrugged. It didn't matter to her. Nothing seemed to matter to her. Since she'd already told Bodene what had happened and why and how she had come to be here with Adam, the second telling was easier. Like the story that she had told her cousin, this rendering of it also deliberately left out any references to the emotional storm and incomprehensible attraction that existed between her and Adam. Painfully aware of Adam's presence, she again deleted the fateful stop at the forest pond. Her eyes fixed on some spot in the distance, she spoke in a flat tone of voice, giving no hint of what she might or might not have felt during that wild odyssey. She ended her tale with Bodene's appearance and the flight of the three of them from the Spanish.

Jason looked thoughtful when she finished speaking, and a curious gleam appeared in his eyes, as he glanced at Adam. "Why did you take her with you when you escaped? Wouldn't it have been simpler to leave her behind?"

Adam's mouth thinned. The look he sent Savanna was baffled and hostile. "Let's just say that she irritated the hell out of me and I felt that it was time that someone taught her a lesson!"

That seemed to satisfy Jason, although there was an odd quirk at the corners of his mouth as he turned back to Savanna. The quirk faded as he gazed at her and a frown marred his broad forehead. *Davalos's daughter!* Good God, but it was hard to comprehend!

Jason had not thought of Davalos in years, but the enmity and hatred he felt for the man who had once been his friend was unabated, and all too clearly he could remember that terrible dawn when he had held his wife in his arms and watched as she had lost the baby she had carried; had watched the ground darken with her blood; had watched so helplessly and feared that she would die—and for it all, he had Davalos to thank! It was only later, when it was apparent that Catherine would live, that he had been further shattered to learn that during her terrible ordeal after Davalos had kidnapped her from Terre du Coeur, Davalos had also brutally raped her. There were some things that a man never forgot or forgave, and the murder of his unborn child and the rape of his wife certainly ranked high among them! Time might have dulled the pain and horror, but the scars were still there, deep and ugly in his heart, and Jason could not help the wave of antagonism that swept over him as he stared at the daughter of the man who had inflicted so much suffering on him and his family. His feelings were totally unfair, even he would admit that, but although he could admit that Savanna was an unusual and intriguing young woman, the fact that her father had been Blas Davalos made her as appealing to him as a twelve-foot timber rattlesnake! And there was the further damning fact that she had taken part in the abduction of Adam and had been, it would appear, as equally driven to find that lost Aztec gold as her father!

A touch on his arm startled him and he glanced over at Blood Drinker. Blood Drinker's expression was filled with understanding as he stared into Jason's eyes. For Jason's ears alone, Blood Drinker said softly, "It is hard, my brother, but do not condemn her for the sins of her father. *She* had nothing to do with those events that caused us such pain so many years ago! She was a mere infant when Davalos killed Nolan and stole the golden armband and began the terrible chain of events that linked us all together. We took our vengeance on Davalos—there is no need to punish her for what she cannot help."

Jason took a deep breath. A faint smile curved his mouth. "As always, my friend, you are right, but it will not be easy for me to look at her and not remember what her father did to us."

Blood Drinker nodded, the long black braids swaying slightly on his powerful chest. "But you will have to overcome it . . . there is Adam to consider now."

Jason grimaced, well aware of what Blood Drinker alluded to. That his harum-scarum half brother was deeply attracted to Savanna had not escaped him, and it created problems that he would rather not have faced. Why in hell, Jason wondered angrily as his gaze wandered between Adam and Savanna, couldn't Adam have chosen to lose his heart to someone other than the daughter of Blas Davalos? Good God! Catherine was going to be devastated when she learned of Adam's unfortunate infatuation, and for that alone, Jason was already wishing that he had never laid eyes on Savanna O'Rourke!

While Jason and Blood Drinker had been speaking quietly to each other, Bodene had been busy concocting breakfast for all of them. Having found a slab of smoked bacon amongst the supplies that Adam had pilfered from the Spanish, Bodene had sliced the entire hunk since it would not keep long and tossed it into a pan, and very soon the mouth-watering scent of frying bacon was wafting through the camp. It was eventually served with the ubiquitous cornmeal mush, but no one seemed to mind—the food disappearing shortly after it was dished out.

Conversation was coolly polite at the beginning of the meal, everyone apparently deciding privately that breakfast should be eaten in relative tranquility. Gradually the atmosphere lightened and soon Jason was skillfully asking questions about the cousins— how they came to be together and where they had lived as children. Expertly he gathered general information about them and their lives. Savanna and Bodene were careful of what they said, but Jason and the others deducted more than enough to get a clear picture of the wretchedness of their early lives— unknowingly, the cousins revealed more by what they *didn't* say than by what they did say. It was only after their stomachs were full and the clutter from breakfast had been cleaned and repacked that Jason settled back against a scrubby oak tree and began to talk about his own relationship with Davalos.

"My grandfather's plantation, Beauvais, adjoins

Campo de Verde, did you know that?" Jason asked quietly as he looked at Savanna.

They were all scattered about the camp in various positions of relaxation, except for Blood Drinker, who stood half hidden in the thicket of trees behind Jason, his black eyes missing nothing as he scanned the horizon near and far. Savanna and Bodene were sitting side by side on the ground to the left of Jason, their backs resting against a fallen log; Adam was lounging comfortably directly across from his half brother, his broad shoulders, like Jason's, propped comfortably against the trunk of a tree. All of them, except Blood Drinker, were enjoying one last cup of coffee, and while most of the initial hostility had been banished, there was still an air of constraint about the group.

Glancing up from her deep contemplation of the dark liquid in her cup, Savanna met Jason's gaze and shook her red-gold head. "No, I didn't. I knew some old man lived next door, but that's all."

At her reference to "some old man," a faint smile crossed Jason's face. "Armand, my grandfather," he said lightly, "will not be pleased to be called an *old* man! He celebrated his eighty-third birthday this past February and still exerts a vast charm for the ladies!"

Savanna shrugged. "Perhaps—but I have never met him, although it's possible that my mother has been introduced to him."

"I doubt it," Bodene interjected dryly. "I'm afraid you'll find that this branch of O'Rourkes doesn't move in such exalted circles."

Jason didn't argue the point. Taking a swallow of his coffee, he said slowly, "Because of the location of my grandfather's plantation and the fact that I spent most of my youth with him, it was natural that I became extremely intimate with his neighbor's son— Blas Davalos. We were close in age and in those days were consumed with many of the same pursuits." Jason smiled wryly. "Mostly horses, women and gaming. Our friendship might have continued unabated except for the fact that in the late 1790s, the indigo crop failed and the Davalos fortune was wiped out." Jason looked grim. "Blas took it hard and he was bitterly resentful that in a matter of months he had gone from being the heir to a large fortune to having to work for a basic living. The last of the ready cash of the family had been spent in procuring him his rank in the Spanish army." Jason sighed. "While another man would have gone on and put the past behind him, Blas couldn't seem to—he blamed everyone for his sudden reversal of fortune and was particularly bitter against me and my family. We escaped the indigo crisis because we had switched to the growing of sugarcane a few years previously." Jason sighed again, staring blindly off into space. "It was a difficult time for him, and I'm afraid that while I sympathized with him in the beginning, after a while I grew angry and irritated at his constant complaints about his financial predicament. Gradually we grew apart—a little because Blas could no longer afford the pursuits that were still available to me, but mostly because of his deep bitterness and resentment at the blow fate had dealt him. He became sullen and unpleasant and began to chase after quick, often unlawful schemes to regain the family's lost fortune."

Jason was silent for a long time, his thoughts dwelling painfully on those events of long ago. Eventually he shook himself and said softly, "I had another friend, Philip Nolan. Nolan was my hero and my mentor, and Blood Drinker and I had many adventures with him. He was older and perhaps not any wiser than we, but he certainly seemed a font of wisdom to me—I loved Nolan."

Again Jason stared off into the distance, and it was obvious to Savanna that this conversation was exceedingly painful to him in spite of the fact that he was speaking of events that were decades old. Jason took another long swallow of his coffee and then in his compelling voice he effortlessly wove a spell around the others, telling of that fateful trip to trade with the Comanches and of the hidden Aztec treasure they had accidentally found. In detail he described the twin gold-and-emerald armbands that they had discovered on the grisly remains of the last victim of the Aztecs' priests, the same armbands that he and Nolan had carried away with them when they had left the hidden valley and the treasure. Rolling up his sleeve, he showed them the gold-and-emerald band that still adorned his own arm, and Savanna stared at it mesmerized until Jason abruptly pulled down his sleeve and began to speak once more.

Still half dazed by all that she had heard, Savanna couldn't help interrupting. Her eyes fixed on Jason, she asked huskily, "Why did you leave the treasure? Haven't you ever tried to go back for it?"

Jason smiled faintly. "We had only the horses we rode, and with a pack of Comanches intent upon lifting our scalps searching for us, I'm afraid that taking any treasure with us, beyond the armbands, was out of the question. As for returning for it . . ." He glanced across to Blood Drinker.

A brooding expression on his darkly chiseled features, Blood Drinker said slowly, "It was an evil place, not a place that I or my blood brother wanted to find again. And we had no need of the gold. Jason has always had a great fortune—what would he have done with more? My family is wealthy even by the white man's standards and my wants are simple. The gold of the Aztecs had no usefulness to me."

Intently Savanna stared at Blood Drinker. "But *could* you find it again?"

Very slowly, Blood Drinker nodded. "If I wished," he replied distantly.

His own curiosity evident, Bodene asked, "Do you think that Nolan returned to it?"

Jason shrugged. "I think he may have planned to." He glanced at Savanna. "Unfortunately, he met up with your father."

There was an uncomfortable silence for a moment and then Jason continued his tale, his anguish clearly revealed when he spoke of Nolan being led away in chains and shackles by Davalos, never to be seen again.

The very fact that Nolan had disappeared while in Davalos's custody was damning, but Savanna knew that her father had indeed killed Jason's friend; she had Jeremy's story of Davalos's dying words to shatter whatever doubts she might have wished to harbor about her father. Her mouth twisted bitterly. What a wonderful legacy Davalos had left her!

But the story became even more horrifying and ugly as slowly, haltingly, Jason spoke of his wife, Catherine, and what had happened when Davalos, still intent upon finding the Aztec gold, had stumbled across her and taken her captive. Blood Drinker and Adam knew the terrible tale, and their faces were stony when Jason finally reached the point of Catherine's escape after suffering Davalos's brutal rape and the subsequent loss of the child she had been carrying.

There was utter silence in the camp when Jason stopped speaking and the atmosphere was dark and full of remembered pain. Savanna's tender heart bled for Jason and Catherine, and knowing what her father had done to them, she could *almost* forgive Adam's treatment of her. Certainly she never doubted that she had finally heard the truth—not some fanciful tale concocted by Micajah to sway her to his side. Ashamed and horrified that she had ever allowed herself to be part of the repugnant scheme that Micajah had proposed, she stared miserably at the bottom of her mug, wishing that there was something she could do or say that would make even the smallest amend for her actions. As for what her father had done . . .

Tiredly Savanna realized that there was nothing that she could say to excuse or explain either her own rash actions or her father's far more brutal ones, and, her face revealing none of her inner torment, she bravely met Jason's cool gaze. Her chin lifted slightly at the condemning expression in his eyes. "It would seem that the Davalos family has sinned against you one more time," she said gravely.

Jason nodded slowly. "It would appear that way."

His tone made Savanna writhe with guilt and she felt compelled to add something in her defense. "I have no *real* excuse . . . except that I believed totally in what I was doing—I believed that I had *right* and justice on my side—I *believed* that I was avenging my father's death and that I had a moral right to the gold."

Remembering Catherine's distraught face at Terre du Coeur when he and Blood Drinker had left to search for the missing Adam, and his own fear that he would never see his half brother alive again, Jason appeared unmoved by her words. He merely snorted and said, "For your sake, I hope that a judge will look kindly on that feeble excuse. As for myself, the sooner I can turn you over to the authorities and wash my hands of you, the better I will feel!"

Adam had listened to this exchange silently, but at the mention of authorities, he stood up and stated forcibly, "She is not going to go before a judge!" Looking grimly at Jason, he said harshly, "This episode ends right here! I do not intend to press any charges against her and I'll deny everything if you try to ride over the top of me!"

For a long minute the two men stared at each other, and seeing the fierce determination in Adam's blue eyes, Jason shrugged. "It's your decision and I won't argue with you—I only hope to hell you know what you're doing!"

Adam smiled crookedly. "I doubt that I do, but I think it would be simplest for all concerned if we let well enough alone." His smile faded and he added bluntly, "While Savanna may have taken part in Micajah's plan, she was as much his prisoner as I was. Certainly she's not had a pleasant time of it, and I see no reason to persecute her further."

While Savanna was horrified at what her father had done to Jason and his wife and thoroughly ashamed of her activities in furthering her father's terrible wrongs, after the way Adam had treated her, she was outraged at his daring to act as her champion. She wanted nothing from him! And despite her best intentions, that unruly tongue of hers got the better of her. Aquamarine eyes a stormy blue-green, she surged to her feet and snapped, "If there is one thing I don't need, it's *your* help! I want nothing from you, and that includes your mawkish support!"

Flashing a furious glance at Jason, she said hotly, "Take me before a judge—I'll be damned if *I* care!"

"But I'll care, and so will your mother," said Bodene quietly, entering the conversation once again. "And if you'll cool down and think about it, I'm sure you would rather *not* have this unpleasant little affair go any further! Nor do I think that you would enjoy the notoriety that would accompany your appearance in court!"

"Yes!" Adam added with a mocking twist to his lips. "For once, why don't you shut that lovely mouth of yours and let us settle this thing peaceably!"

Savanna shot Adam a scalding look, but Bodene's mention of her mother knocked the fight right out of her. Hadn't it been to keep her mother safe from scandal that she had gone along so meekly with Micajah in the first place? And while Micajah's threat was still very real and she hadn't yet decided precisely how she was going to deal with him, if he showed up again, was she willing to subject Elizabeth to ugly speculation simply to defy Adam St. Clair? Savanna was hot-tempered in the extreme, but she wasn't stupid, and with a defeated shrug of her slender shoulders, she turned away. "Do what you want," she muttered dully. "It makes little difference to me."

Looking at Adam, Jason inquired dryly, "Having settled that little problem, what are we going to do about our friend Micajah?"

Adam grinned. "First Micajah has to find us!"

Not amused, Jason sent him an exasperated look. "And when he does? What do you intend to do?"

Adam's grin faded and he said seriously, "For the time being, we can do nothing—we go baying to the authorities for justice, and when and *if* they ever lay hands on Micajah and he is brought to trial, the whole nasty story will come out—you can wager on that! Micajah will see to it and relish pulling Savanna down with him." Adam's eyes met Jason's. "We have no idea where Micajah even *is*—he could have gone back to Natchez, or stayed in Nacogdoches, or he could have gone after the gold himself, hoping that Jeremy can lead him to where Davalos died. He could even be dead or lost in the wilderness, trying to follow my trail. I certainly don't intend to waste *my* time trying to find him, and until he makes his presence known, there is little that we can do— beyond taking safeguards against being surprised. But once we do know where is he is . . ." Adam smiled, not a nice smile. "Why, then I guess I'll just have to let him force me to kill him."

Jason nodded slowly. "Of course, you'll allow me that same pleasure if he just happens to come looking for the *real* Jason Savage?"

"Of course," Adam replied cordially, a glitter in his blue eyes making Jason fairly certain that his half brother was lying through his teeth.

"Well, then," Bodene said amiably, "since we have settled Micajah's fate and since breakfast is past and the sun is rising high, I would suggest that we saddle up and get riding—we have a long way to go."

It had been decided that the five of them would continue to ride together; they would be able to share their supplies, and in case of danger, five together would stand a better chance than two smaller groups. They traveled swiftly during the next several days and as each mile brought them closer to the Sabine River, there was a gradual relaxation to be discerned amongst the group. Soon they would be out of Spanish territory and out of at least one sort of danger.

An easy comradeship sprang up between the four men, but it was only in Bodene's company that Savanna felt totally at ease. Shame kept her from accepting the few overtures of friendship made by Jason and Blood Drinker, and as for Adam ...

To her utter fury, whenever she looked around and caught those hard blue eyes watching her, her traitorous heart would leap in her breast, and not necessarily with fear. Just the very sight of him walking with that animal grace of his across the campsite at night, his tall, broad-shouldered form outlined by the flickering firelight, would make her remember vividly the feel of that long, muscled body moving on hers, possessing her completely, and she hated him for so effortlessly arousing the memory of something she wanted desperately to forget ... to pretend never happened.

Savanna longed most fervently to go back to being the young woman she had been before Adam St. Clair had entered her life and made her achingly aware of the pleasure that one man's touch, one man's kiss, could give a woman. She had prided herself on being unmoved by the men who had previously crossed her path, but Adam had shattered all her most dearly held beliefs about herself and she was not the least grateful for it. She hated him, she told herself repeatedly; hated that arrogance of his;

hated that mocking smile on that long, sensuous mouth; hated the emotions that a glance from those brilliant blue eyes could arouse within her. And she was afraid of him ... afraid that this dark spell he had cast over her would set her feet on the same path that her mother had followed. And if there was anything that Savanna truly feared, it was loving a man as her mother had loved Davalos—and suffering the degradation that had come with that love. But she also had another fear, and it was one that gnawed with increasing ferocity at her very vitals: not once since she had first been abducted by Micajah had she experienced her monthly flow. . . .

In the beginning she had not been overly worried, convinced that the physical ordeal and strain that she had suffered was reason enough for its cessation, but ever since Adam had made love to her, the terror had grown that there was now an extremely tangible reason for her lack—she could be pregnant with his child! It was an appalling thought, and though she tried frantically to push it away, it remained foremost in her mind and gave her an added reason to fear and resent Adam St. Clair.

They crossed the Sabine River early in the morning on the twenty-second of June, and after they had made camp that night, the knowledge was in everyone's mind that at daybreak tomorrow the group would separate. Savanna and Bodene would make their way to Campo de Verde, situated in the south of Louisiana, and the others would ride to Terre du Coeur in the north.

There had been no private conversation between Adam and Savanna since the others had joined them, but Savanna was uneasily aware that Adam seemed to watch her continually, the expression in those sapphire-blue eyes hard to define. There had been several occasions during the past few days when he had attempted to speak with her alone, but she had deftly avoided him. There was nothing, she told herself fiercely, that she had to say to Adam St. Clair, and she could not imagine that he had anything to say that she wanted to hear—not even an apology! There was nothing that he could say to undo what he had done to her, just as she could never undo what her father had done to Jason and Catherine. They were quits and she wanted it to stay that way—no matter what might or might not be going on within her body!

Savanna did not sleep well that night, tossing and turning on the hard ground, and she was relieved when the sun finally rose the next morning. After the breakfast chores were done, she slipped away for a moment of privacy as the others enjoyed a final cup of coffee before they all separated. Grimly she told herself that today would be the last day she would have to put up with Adam's disruptive presence and that she was overjoyed by that fact!

She was reluctantly making her way back to join the others when she caught sight of Adam's tall form leaning against a tree, his arms folded across his chest, and the blood suddenly thundered in her veins. He was directly in her path and she acknowledged him with a cool nod of her red-gold head. She had hoped he would let her pass unmolested, but that hope died when his hand closed around her upper arm and he said tautly, "I think it's time that you and I had a word together."

Stonily Savanna stared at his dark features. "I have nothing to say to you. *Nothing!*"

His eyes narrowed. "Now, I tend to disagree with that statement, sweetheart," he drawled insolently, his gaze roaming over her, his lips tightening as he saw the all-too-apparent signs of the deprivations she had suffered these past weeks. Her clear aquamarine eyes looked too large for her lovely face, whose thinness intensified the slant of her high cheekbones and the fine-boned elegance of her jaw and chin. A muscle twitched in his cheek as he tore his gaze away from the still far-too-tempting curve of her mouth and forced himself to look at the changes that he was at least partially responsible for: the almost frail slenderness of her body, the delicacy of her collarbone where it showed at the opening of her shirt and the heartbreaking fragility of the bones in her wrists.

There was an odd ache in his chest as he stared at her, but his expression and voice were bland as he stated grimly, "I think there is one topic that needs discussing before we part today, and for once you're not going to shy away from me like a scalded cat!"

Painfully aware of the pull of attraction he still exerted on her, Savanna eyed him resentfully. "I can't imagine what it is," she finally said as indifferently as she could, stubbornly ignoring the beguiling warmth of his hand on her arm.

Adam smiled mockingly, the smile not reaching his eyes. "Oh, I imagine you know exactly what I'm talking about—women usually do." When Savanna remained obstinately silent, Adam asked bluntly, "Are you pregnant?"

Savanna gasped and her eyes clung fearfully to his for a shocking moment. Then her chin lifted and she said sharply, "It makes no difference if I am!" She smiled nastily and asked, "Why do you want to know? Did you perhaps intend to do the honorable thing and offer marriage?"

Adam smothered a curse, and dragging her closer to him, he kissed her devastatingly and then muttered against her mouth, "Damn you! That's *exactly* what I had in mind!"

Part 3

Dangerous Desire

*What's affection, but the power we
give another to torment us?*

Darnley
Edward Bulwer-Lytton

Chapter 13

STUNNED, SAVANNA STARED UP AT ADAM'S DARK, UNRE-
lenting features, hardly able to credit his words. Her
lips tingled from the force of his kiss and she was unbearably aware of the long, warm length of him
pressed closely against her, but there was no joy
within her. It would seem that Adam St. Clair was,
unlike her father, she admitted sadly, an honorable
man. He suspected that she might be pregnant and
so felt compelled to offer marriage to a woman he
might desire, and Savanna didn't doubt that he did
desire her—at least, at the moment—but she was
miserably certain that she aroused no deeper, finer
emotions within him. The question of her father
aside, what sort of a marriage would it be with him
shackled to a woman far below him in wealth and
social standing, a woman who under normal circumstances would never even have crossed his path? If
there were love between them, they might overcome
the chasms that separated them, but with only his
desire for her body to bind them together, she could
see nothing but unhappiness ahead for either of them

if she were foolish enough to marry him. And then there was her father . . . would Adam or *any* of his family ever be able to look upon her and not think of Davalos and the horrible ordeal he had forced them to endure—and not hate her for it? For the sake of a child, could she bear to marry Adam, knowing the ugly circumstances that had brought them to this point; knowing that nothing but lust bound them together; knowing that her father had done grievous wrongs to his family? Surely, once his fascination for her body had waned, and Savanna never doubted that it would, he would hate her . . . and the child she might bear. . . .

Savanna's heart clenched painfully. Adam's scorn and hatred for her she could withstand, but what about his scorn for their child? Hadn't she herself suffered because of Davalos's indifference? How much worse would it be when the father actually hated the mother, and that hatred included a child?

When she remained silent for so long, her eyes locked in his, Adam grew impatient. Shaking her slightly, he demanded, "Well? Are you going to marry me?"

Savanna took a deep breath and carefully extricated herself from his arms. Not looking at him, she brushed a leaf from her worn breeches and said softly, "No."

Adam stared at her incredulously, the unexpected ache in his heart at her answer almost driving him to his knees. "Excuse me?" he said in a dangerous tone of voice once he had gained command of himself. "Are you telling me that you refuse? That you're not going to marry me?"

Savanna nodded stiffly, unable to look at him for fear her resolve might weaken.

A wave of impotent rage swept through Adam and, his hard blue eyes boring into her, he wanted to curse, shake her senseless and kiss her into acquiescence all at the same time. Jaw clenched, hands on hips, he surveyed her with open dislike. "And would you mind," he finally snarled, "telling me why in the hell not? You sure as the devil aren't likely to get a better offer!"

Savanna's head snapped up at that and, suddenly just as angry as he, she spat, "I don't have to give you a reason—but I could point out that you haven't shown me any cause to want to spend the rest of my life with you! You're an overbearing, arrogant swine! Why the hell *should* I want to marry you?"

The truth of her words hit him like a blow, and his hurt and rage at her refusal ebbed slightly. God knew their courtship, if what they'd shared could be called that, certainly had not been gentle! He'd never asked a woman to marry him before in his life, had never *wanted* to marry anyone before now, and while he would admit that the circumstances were not the best, he had been convinced that Savanna would see that marriage was the only answer to their dilemma. That he might have other reasons for wanting her as his wife than just to give his child a name, he single-mindedly pushed aside. She had to be made to see sense! The facts surrounding his own birth made him particularly sensitive to the notion of a child being born out of wedlock, and he was grimly determined that no child of his was going to suffer that fate—not even if he had to drag the mother hog-tied and gagged to the altar! Savanna *was* going to marry him! She just didn't know it yet! And he was willing to pull every underhanded trick he knew to make her realize it. . . .

Catching her off guard, he jerked her into his embrace and his lips unerringly found hers. He kissed her an endless time, all the passion and pent-up longing within him behind the seductive crush of his mouth on hers. Ah, Jesus, he'd missed having her in his arms, he admitted with angry bewilderment; missed the warmth of her soft body against his; missed the intoxicating sweet taste of her on his tongue, the soft, exciting sounds she made when he kissed her.

Savanna fought against the hungry desire that surged through her as Adam's mouth worked its dark magic on her, but her attempt was futile, and with a faint moan of defeat and despair she finally melted against him, hating herself just as much as she was convinced she hated him. . . . His tongue moved with sensuous abandon within her mouth, making her weak with longing, arousing sensations and emotions she didn't want to feel but was powerless to control. To her shame, she pressed nearer, her own tongue curling warmly about his, her breasts pushing wantonly into his hard chest.

Helplessly entangled in the web of desire that bound them together, they clung desperately to each other, for the moment all the difficulties and hurts and misunderstandings that lay between them forgotten. There was only this: the demanding hunger of each other's kiss, the giddy sensation of their bodies crushed together as they stood there locked in a passionate embrace.

They remained lost in each other's arms until the sound of Bodene's voice in the distance brought Adam slowly back to the present. Dazedly he lifted his plundering mouth from Savanna's but recovered himself almost instantly to allow a crooked grin to slash across his face, and he glanced down into her bemused features and drawled mockingly, "I think we've just thoroughly demonstrated one of the reasons why you should want to marry me."

Savanna had been drowning in the sweetness of his kiss, but his words were like an icy douche, all the problems and obstacles between them exploding through her, and before she had time to think, her hand shot out and she gave him a ringing slap on one lean cheek. Bosom heaving, she glared up at him. *"That,"* she said frostily, "is not reason enough for me!"

Adam's face darkened and he took an angry step forward. Grasping her arm, he shook her roughly and growled, "You know, I've suffered about all the physical abuse from you that I'm going to—you've hit me for the last time, sweetheart. Next time you lay a hand on me that way ... I'm going to beat the living hell out of you!"

"Try it!" she snarled back. "And I'll skewer your liver and feed it to the gators!"

Hearing this last bit as he walked up to them, Bodene smiled and murmured, "Ah, how sweet the lovebirds sing!"

Two pairs of furious eyes nailed him where he stood, and almost in unison, with equal amounts of loathing obvious in their tones, Savanna and Adam repeated scathingly, "*Lovebirds!*"

Bodene pulled on his ear and, bending his head, looked suitably chastened, but a smile lurked at the corners of his mouth as he said with suspect meekness, "My mistake! I apologize." Glancing quizzically at them, he added, "We're ready to break camp— you'd better come back now, or you'll have Jason and Blood Drinker coming after you."

Throwing Adam a fulminating look, Savanna said tightly, "Believe me, we can't break camp soon enough! There are *some* people I'll be glad never to see again!"

Adam took a deep breath and grabbed hold of her arm. "We haven't finished our conversation yet," he said stubbornly. Never taking his eyes off her stormy face, he added to Bodene, "Tell the others we'll be there in just a moment. We have something to settle between ourselves."

Seeing the grim line of Adam's jaw, Bodene decided that now was not the time to argue with him. He shrugged his shoulders and disappeared into the brush.

Equally furious with her cousin for deserting her so easily and with Adam for his high-handedness,

Savanna glared at Adam and muttered, "I don't have anything to say to you. Let me go!"

Gently he turned her to face him and said urgently, "Savanna, whatever you may feel for me, there is still the matter of the child—you can't want it to be born out of wedlock!"

Savanna bit her lip and averted her eyes from him. Mutinously she said, "I don't know if I'm pregnant. I might not be, so until I know for certain, there is no question of marriage!"

"Look at me!" Adam said tightly, his grip on her arm increasing. When her eyes were fastened angrily on his face, he asked heavily, "If you do discover you are carrying my child, can I trust you to tell me?"

Exhausted by the events that she had endured so recently, and worn out from the turmoil within herself, she felt some of the fight go out of her. But pride would not let her abandon the stance she had taken, and she said tightly, "Adam, even if I am pregnant, it will *not* change my answer. I will *not* marry you!" Her chin lifted defiantly. "And you can't make me!"

A dangerous glint entered his sapphire-blue eyes and he added silkily, "Well, sweetheart, we'll just see about that, won't we?"

Releasing her abruptly, he pushed her in the direction of the camp. Uneasily aware of him walking behind her, Savanna quickly made her way to where the others stood waiting. The speculative look that Jason gave the two of them as they approached brought a wave of color burning into her cheeks. She mumbled some sort of greeting and with relief set about double-checking the gear on her horse.

A few minutes later they were all mounted, and there was a brief, awkward moment before Bodene touched the rim of his hat and said cordially, "Gentlemen, we'll bid you good-bye and Godspeed!"

Jason nodded and he and Blood Drinker turned their horses to the north and, taking one of the pack-horses with them, began the journey to Terre du

Coeur. Only Adam remained with the cousins. He smiled at Bodene and murmured, "When next I am in New Orleans, I plan to visit that establishment of yours!"

Bodene grinned. "And lose a tidy sum at the tables, I trust?"

Adam shook his head, mockery brimming in his eyes. "I doubt it—I'm reputed to be very lucky!"

Both men laughed and, the laughter dying out of his face, Adam looked directly at Savanna. Huskily he said, "Any message you wish to send to me will reach me at Belle Vista, near Natchez."

Savanna averted her face and said stiffly, "I cannot imagine *any* reason why I would have to send you a message." Not waiting for a reply, she kicked her horse into motion and disappeared into the brush.

Bodene exchanged a look with Adam. "She's very proud—and stubborn as the devil!" he said ruefully.

"I had noticed," Adam replied dryly. Fixing an intent gaze on Bodene, he added, "If there should be any difficulties . . . will *you* let me know?"

Bodene nodded and then, tipping his hat and pulling their packhorse after him, he quickly followed in Savanna's direction. For a long time after Bodene had ridden away, Adam stared at the spot where he had last seen Savanna, every instinct within him shouting for him to follow after her and make her agree to marry him, but he knew that he would be chasing a fool's errand. At the moment, her mind was obstinately set against him, and he could only hope that time would bring about a change in her attitude. Muttering about the contrariness of women, one certain redheaded witch in particular, Adam swung his horse around and urged it in the direction that Jason and Blood Drinker had ridden.

It didn't take Bodene long to catch up with Savanna, and after taking a look at the closed expression on her face, he concluded that she was in no mood to talk—about anything! They rode in silence for several hours, the only exchange of words having to do with the direction they were going in or the terrain and the best way to get around or through the various natural obstacles they came across.

It was well after noon when Bodene finally suggested that they stop and give their horses a rest, as well as eat something themselves. Savanna nodded and, quietly dismounting, wondered bleakly why, now that she was finally away from Adam and on her way home, she should be so miserable and unhappy.

Bodene quickly lit a small fire and boiled some coffee. Having saved some of the cooked cornmeal mush from breakfast, he fashioned it into a pair of patties and set them in a pan to bake near the fire. Handing the finished product to Savanna a short while later, he grinned at her and murmured, "You know, once we get back to Campo de Verde, I don't think I'm ever going to eat anything with corn in it as long as I live!"

Savanna smiled faintly and, nibbling at her patty, admitted wryly, "I don't think I even want to *see* corn! Not that there haven't been times recently that I haven't been grateful to have it."

That Savanna had suffered during this wild odyssey was obvious—there was a fine-drawn loveliness about her that hadn't been apparent previously, but even in the worn and grubby youth's clothing, she was undeniably a striking woman. She had set her hat aside for the moment, and the sunlight struck fire in the red-gold braids worn on top of her head and caressed her smooth, tawny skin, intensifying the vividness of her coloring. Bodene studied her for several moments and noticed that the tenseness about her mouth had finally disappeared. He asked quietly, "Do you want to tell me what *really* happened between you and Adam St. Clair?"

Savanna's head shot up, a wary expression coming into her clear blue-green eyes. "I don't know what you're talking about," she said after a brief pause. "I've told you everything."

Bodene shook his dark head. "No, you haven't— and don't try to lie to me. You might be able to fool some people with your denials, but I've known you all of your life and it's obvious that there was something between you two. It would have taken an idiot not to recognize the explosive atmosphere whenever you and Adam got within ten feet of each other, and while I've been called a lot of names, 'idiot' hasn't been among them so far."

"Was it that obvious?" she asked painfully, writhing inside that her reaction to Adam had been so apparent.

Bodene nodded. "Let's just say that the way you two acted brought a speculative glint into other pairs of eyes besides my own."

Savanna bent her head. In a voice that he could barely hear, she asked, "Adam?"

He snorted. "I think that Adam was too busy watching you to be aware of anything else going on around him!"

"He hates me," she said dully, still not looking at her cousin.

"Somehow I rather doubt that! Now, are you going to tell me what happened or not?"

"Oh, Bodene!" she burst out unhappily. "I can't explain it! One minute I hate him and I'm certain he's the most arrogant, infuriating, overbearing bastard I've ever met, and the next . . ." She swallowed painfully. "The next, I think I'll die if I can't be with him!" A defiant expression on her face, she muttered, "There! Is that what you wanted me to say?"

"Not exactly—your admission doesn't come as any surprise! But what I'm more interested in is if there are going to be any further repercussions from this little fiasco . . . and I think you know *exactly* what I'm talking about!" There was a determined cast to his chiseled mouth as Bodene finished speaking. He might have been favorably impressed with Adam St. Clair so far, but he wasn't about to meekly stand by and watch Savanna suffer the same fate as her mother. He'd have no compunction about putting a pistol to Adam's head if that was what it would take to save Savanna from further disgrace.

"I don't know!" she said sharply. "Ever since Micajah kidnapped me, the normal signs haven't been there, so I have no way of telling!"

For a moment Bodene's face was white. "Are you telling me," he went on in a menacing tone, "that Micajah . . . ?"

Her eyes huge in her sun-dusted face, Savanna spat out fiercely, "Good God, no! I'd have killed him!"

His color returning, he asked dryly, "But you didn't kill Adam?"

Savanna sighed, a confused look on her face. "No," she said in a soft, shaken voice. "I didn't kill Adam. . . ."

"Do you want me to?" he inquired, the deadly gleam in his gaze making it clear that he was perfectly ready and capable of doing so if that was what she wanted.

Shaking her head vehemently, she replied hotly, "*No!*" A flush stained her cheeks, and averting her eyes, she muttered, "He didn't do anything that I didn't want him to do."

Far from satisfied with her answers, Bodene stared at her for a long moment. "So what do we do now?" he finally asked.

"We go home and take up the threads of our lives."

"And if you are pregnant? What then?"

It was obvious that Bodene wasn't going to let the topic rest, and wearily Savanna admitted, "I don't know what, but before you go hurrying off after Adam, I think you should know that he asked me to marry him and I refused!"

In angry, stupefied dismay, Bodene stared at her. "Why in the hell did you do a damn fool thing like that?" he snarled when he could finally speak, having decided that she had truly lost her wits.

"I don't have to explain myself to you!" Savanna snapped, and standing up, she glared at Bodene. "But answer me this: what sort of a life do you think I would have, married to a man who'd only married me to give his child a name? A man who has good, *just* cause to hate me? Do you think that he could ever forget who I was and what my father had done to his sister? Do you think that my background—or rather, my lack of it—would ever be forgotten? Do you think that his fine, wealthy friends and family would welcome me and my child into their society?" Tears glittering in her eyes, she vowed passionately, "Before I would subject myself and Adam to such a hellish life, I'd raise the child alone—and the rest of you and the world be damned!"

Bodene grimaced. Every question she'd asked had an ugly answer, and crossing over to her, he touched her shoulder in awkward commiseration. "I'm sorry, brat. I didn't stop to think. You're right. And don't worry—if there is to be a child, you won't be alone. I'll stand by you and see that you have everything you need."

Furiously blinking back tears, she buried her face in his shoulder and muttered, "Oh, Bodene! What would I do without you?"

"Damned if I know!" he answered teasingly, trying to inject a light note. "But there is one thing I do know—if we want to make any distance today, we had better get riding!"

The remainder of their journey to Campo de Verde was accomplished without incident, and the afternoon that they finally arrived at the plantation, Savanna experienced a strong feeling of refuge. For the first time in her life, Campo de Verde was precisely where she wanted to be. Whatever sense of adven-

ture had driven her from it at eighteen had been, by
the events of these past months, thoroughly and irrevocably banished. As they rode down the shady
driveway that led to the main house, she realized
suddenly that, whereas before she had scorned her
mother's life and the social restraints put upon her
by Elizabeth, now she yearned only for a return of
those days. A return to a time that didn't contain
memories of Adam St. Clair and his devastating possession of her. . . .

There was one good thing, Savanna admitted painfully, that had come out of her meeting with Adam
St. Clair—she no longer held her mother in loving
contempt for her steadfast love of Davalos. Before
Adam, she had never understood what a cruel trick
one's emotions could play on a person, and she had
always viewed her mother and others like her with a
cheerful disdain, certain that *she* would never fall victim to those same elemental feelings. Her mouth
twisted sadly. She wasn't ready to admit that what
she felt for Adam St. Clair was love; she only knew
that there had never been anyone like him in her life
before and that these past few days she had missed
him intolerably—and that infuriatingly mocking grin
of his! She was shamefully aware that, despite her
best intentions and grim exhortations to the contrary,
given the chance, she would think twice before flinging a proposal of marriage back into his face.

It was a bitter, frightening admission for Savanna—made more so by the vivid memories of what
her mother had suffered for loving the wrong man.
And despite whatever she did feel for Adam, she
was also dead positive that only Murdering Micajah
would be a worse choice for a woman to waste any
emotion on!

The sight of her mother's face as Elizabeth raced
down the broad steps to reach them when they
stopped their horses in front of the house brought a
lump to Savanna's throat and she was suddenly,

deeply aware of a feeling of love and, for the first time, compassion and understanding for what Elizabeth had endured. Flying out of the saddle, oblivious of the tears in her eyes, she flung herself into her mother's outstretched arms and fiercely hugged Elizabeth's small form to her, appreciating and loving her as never before.

Elizabeth's aquamarine eyes glittered with tears. "Oh, darling! I have been so worried! Just frantic! I feared that I would never see you again! What happened? Why did you disappear that way?"

Savanna dropped a soft kiss on her mother's head and said huskily, "Shush, sweetheart! I'm fine and I didn't disappear on purpose—Micajah found me and kidnapped me!"

In horror Elizabeth stared at her. "Oh, my God! That awful beast!" Shaking Savanna's shoulders gently, she asked urgently, "Are you certain that you are all right?"

Savanna smiled. "Certain, Mother! I know it's hard to believe, but Micajah didn't harm me . . . in *any* way. He frightened me, but he didn't force himself on me."

"No," Bodene said dryly as he came up and dropped a kiss on Elizabeth's cheek. "We have a gentleman by the name of Adam St. Clair to thank for that!"

Elizabeth's eyes went round, darting uneasily from one young face to the other. "What do you mean by that?" she demanded. "Who is this Adam St. Clair, and what does he have to do with Micajah and Savanna?"

Savanna glared at Bodene, who stared levelly back at her. She would have liked to keep the full truth from Elizabeth—at least until she knew whether she was indeed pregnant—but Bodene had forced her hand—damn him! Giving Elizabeth another hug, she said wearily, "It is a very long story, Mother. One I'd prefer to tell after I've had a long, long, *long* bath and something other than pork and cornmeal to eat!"

Elizabeth glanced from one to the other again, and smiling, albeit a little uneasily, she said warmly, "Of course, darlings! I'm sure you both must be longing for baths and a change of clothing." Ushering them up the steps, she went on eagerly. "I'll have Cook put on a nice plump chicken, and you shall dine tonight on chicken and tender dumplings with fresh green peas and carrots from the garden. And for dessert— why, I believe that a pie of blackberries with clotted cream will finish off the meal delightfully."

Savanna and Bodene looked at each other and moaned with pleasurable anticipation, their mouths watering. The meal was every bit as delicious as it had sounded, and some hours later, her stomach full, her face shiny with cleanliness, her red-gold hair flowing brightly about her shoulders, wearing a gown of soft, pale green muslin, Savanna sank blissfully into the down-filled cushions of the slightly worn sofa in the back parlor. Bodene joined her on the sofa, his long legs stretched out in front of him. Elizabeth sat across from them in a high-backed chair covered in chintz, a low oak table in front of her. She was busy pouring fragrant black coffee into the cups that were set out before her.

It was only after everyone had been served and had begun to sip the beverage that Elizabeth demanded an explanation. Her eyes shadowy with worry, she stared at the two young people across the pleasant room from her and said firmly, "Well, now, I think that I have been exceedingly patient. It is time that you tell me everything."

And so it was that Savanna began to speak of the ordeal that she had endured and of the advent of Adam St. Clair into her life. Since Bodene had forced her hand, she kept nothing back concerning her relationship with Adam, although she told only the barest details. When she finally finished speaking, there was utter silence in the room.

In a voice full of outrage and pain, Elizabeth exclaimed, "Oh, my dear! How could you have put yourself in danger in order to spare me a bit of scandal? *You* are worth far more to me than my good name! *Never* allow Micajah to force you to do anything to spare me!"

"But the talk . . . people would stare and gossip, and your friends . . ." Savanna protested.

Elizabeth drew herself up in a regal manner. "My *real* friends would continue to be my friends no matter what that vulgar Micajah would say! And as for any others . . ." She sniffed disdainfully. "I have endured worse than stares and gossip in my day, and as for those mean-spirited souls who would listen and *believe* Micajah, why, I don't care a fig for them!" She smiled tenderly at her daughter. "Never forget that *you* are the most important thing to me and that together"—her warm glance included Bodene—"we can survive anything. Haven't we done so in the past?"

A little misty-eyed, Savanna nodded and said softly, "I wish that we had known more about the gold and what Davalos had intended to do once he found it."

A worried expression crossed Elizabeth's face. "Darling, promise me that you will give up any notion of finding the gold—it caused your father's death and I couldn't bear it if you allowed it to obsess you the way it did him. Promise me!"

Savanna made a face. "I already have. It has caused far too much destruction already, and after hearing Jason's story, I have no desire whatsoever to search for it."

Elizabeth's lips tightened at the mention of Jason Savage, and seeing her reaction, Bodene said lightly, "Liza, I don't mean to speak ill of the dead, but you know yourself that Davalos frequently lied to you—

certainly he didn't tell you the truth about Jason Savage. Jason treated us very well and he had good reason not to. I know from having met him previously that he is a fine and honorable man, and this latest meeting with him only confirmed my earlier opinion. He may have been Davalos's enemy, but only because Davalos drove him to it."

It was plain that Elizabeth didn't like Bodene's words, but it was also obvious that she was trying to be fair. Smiling at her, Bodene said coaxingly, "If you remember that Davalos had his own reasons for twisting the truth, I think that when you do finally meet Jason Savage, you will find that he in no way resembles the monster of Davalos's ramblings. I like him and I think you will, too."

"Certainly better than that bastard Adam St. Clair!" Savanna said darkly.

Savanna never realized how much she revealed by those harsh words, but Elizabeth's face was full of understanding as she stared at her daughter's set features. Hurrying across the room, she sank down on the sofa beside her. "Oh, darling!" Elizabeth said unhappily as she grasped Savanna's hands in her own. "It is almost worse than I feared." Peering into Savanna's face, she asked hopefully, "Are you very certain that you don't want to marry this Adam St. Clair? Have you really given the matter enough thought?"

Glancing away from the love and fear she glimpsed in her mother's eyes, Savanna said huskily, "I might not be pregnant, and until we know for certain that I am, I think we should put the matter from us." She looked back at Elizabeth, smiling mistily. "And if I am, how much better off I'll be than you were . . . unless you plan to imitate your brother and throw me penniless out of the house."

Elizabeth hugged her fiercely. "As if I would, darling! As if I would!"

Nothing more was said on the matter, although in

the days that passed, Savanna was aware that her mother watched her anxiously. Bodene had made a lightning trip to New Orleans to see that all was in order at his gambling hall, The Golden Lady, returning to Campo de Verde almost immediately. He, too, watched Savanna, the same flicker of concern in his eyes that Savanna caught all too often in Elizabeth's gaze. And yet, the question of her pregnancy or lack of it aside, the days were pleasant and tranquil and Savanna was surprised at how easily and comfortably she slipped into the routine of the household. She was exhausted from the long journey and during the first week spent hours and hours either in bed asleep or lounging about the house, talking idly with her mother and Bodene. For the moment, she was content to drift. She ate prodigiously and gradually the gauntness left her features, and as the signs of strain began to fade she threw herself into helping Elizabeth with the running of the plantation and one hot, sunny day blended into another.

Every day she prayed for a sign that she was not pregnant, but there was nothing. She was aware that her breasts seemed more tender, perhaps even fuller, but she told herself that it was only a precursor to the one sign that she most desperately wanted to appear. Finally, on a morning some three weeks after she had returned to Campo de Verde, her body gave proof of her condition. She woke early and, rising from her bed as usual, felt the room tilt wildly and became thoroughly, violently, ill. The nausea passed, but as she stood there staring blindly into space, she recognized the truth, the terrible truth that she had tried so frantically to deny: she was going to bear Adam St. Clair a child. . . .

Chapter 14

It took Savanna several more days before she could bring herself to tell her mother and Bodene. She had frantically hoped that she had been mistaken, that her morning attack of illness had been merely an aberration, but such was not the case; and on the twelfth morning in a row when she woke to the now familiar dizzy sensation that preceded the horrible gagging which inevitably followed it, she knew that there was nothing to be gained by keeping her mouth shut.

Neither Elizabeth nor Bodene seemed surprised when she finally admitted her condition that evening as they all sat in the back parlor, the ladies sipping a final glass of lemonade, Bodene nursing a tumbler of whiskey. Elizabeth paled at the news, but patting Savanna's hand gently as she sat on the sofa beside her, she said bracingly, "Well! My very first grandchild! I shall look forward to its arrival."

Bodene, lounging in the chintz-covered chair across from them, sent a sour look in their direction. His gaze locked on Savanna's rigid features, he asked harshly, "Have you written to Adam?"

"No!" she stated tightly. "And I don't intend to!" She looked down at her hands, which were clenched in her lap, and in a tone of bitter unhappiness, she added, "What happened between us meant nothing!" Honesty forcing her to say, "At least to him, and I see absolutely no reason to write to him! If there wasn't going to be a child, you could wager The Golden Lady on the fact that Adam St. Clair wouldn't *ever* come within a crooked mile of me! Just *because* I'm going to have his child—a child he never planned on or wanted in the first place—doesn't change my mind about him—or his about me! What happens now is no concern of his!"

"He's the child's father, for God's sake!" Bodene exploded angrily. "Don't you think that gives him at least the right to know of it?"

Savanna's chin jutted stubbornly. "We've been here at Campo de Verde for a month—if he were the tiniest bit interested," she said painfully, "don't you think that he would have made some attempt to write or find out for himself?"

"If I remember correctly," Bodene replied with an effort, "he asked that you write *him!*"

"Yes, darling," Elizabeth broke in gently, "I remember distinctly, the evening you explained everything to me, that you and Bodene both mentioned that Adam had asked that you send a message to him." Peering into Savanna's unhappy face, she added softly, "Don't you think that would be a good idea? Now that you know for certain you are carrying his child? At least to let him know of it?"

Savanna's eyes closed in anguish. She had no ready argument to fling back at them and miserably she admitted that their questions were both logical and valid—hadn't she been struggling to answer those same damnable questions since the moment she had discovered that she was pregnant? One part of her acknowledged fairly that Adam *should* be informed of his impending fatherhood, but there was another part of her that shrank instinctively from such a step. Every fiber of her being cried out against telling Adam, because she knew that once he learned of the coming child, he would move heaven and earth in his attempts to force her to marry him ... and she was very aware that in a moment of weakness she might give in, making an unhappy situation utterly unbearable for all of them!

Realizing that the others were still waiting for a reply, she stared at her hands and muttered, "I'm sorry! I know you both want what you think is best for me and the child, but I don't believe that informing him is the best solution. I—I don't want to be forced into marriage by anyone, not you, not Adam St. Clair." She raised her eyes and stared at Bodene. "And I want your promise that you will not tell him."

Bodene fixed a long, speculative look on her, noting again the fine-drawn loveliness of her face, the fierce, stubborn pride that was evident in every stiffly held line of her body. It was obvious that further argument was useless, and equally obvious from the glint in her eyes that she wasn't going to leave him alone until he gave his word. His mouth hardened. "Very well," he muttered at last, his eyes not meeting hers.

Savanna didn't trust him, and leaning forward tensely, she demanded urgently, "Say it!"

Bodene took a long swallow of his whiskey and, slamming the tumbler down on the oak table, growled, "I will not say a word to Adam St. Clair— there, are you satisfied?"

She still wasn't quite satisfied, but she could tell from the set expression on his face that he had offered her all the reassurance he was going to, and she would have to be content. Some of the tenseness drained slowly out of her body and she sank back against the sofa. "Thank you, Bodene," she said softly. "I know you think I'm wrong"—she glanced fondly at her mother—"and you, too, but nothing has changed. Adam never cared for me—nor I for him," she added hastily. "Even though I am definitely pregnant, all of the reasons I stated in the beginning about why I didn't agree to marry him when he asked me are still valid."

Bodene snorted disgustedly and, rising to his feet, said grimly, "Well, if you ladies will excuse me, I'm going to spend a few hours in the office and see just what I can do to make the next generation's future a bit better than ours has been so far!"

Twenty minutes later, he glanced up from the letter he was writing to see Elizabeth peeking around the doorframe. A distracted expression on her face, she came in quickly and shut the door behind her.

The office had originally been a small storeroom at the side of the house, but under Elizabeth's guidance, it had been transformed into an extremely pleasant and functional place to handle the affairs of the plantation. A couple of oak bookcases were situated along one wall; a wide, long table with various small farming implements scattered across it, as well as a tray with glasses and liquors, graced the other; and at one end of the room were the big desk and leather chair where Bodene sat. There were two comfortable chairs in worn velvet in front of the desk, and slipping into one of them, Elizabeth fixed worried aquamarine eyes on Bodene's face.

She looked, he thought tenderly as he stared at her, very lovely in her gown of blue sprigged muslin, the strawberry-blond hair caught up neatly in a bun which lay on the nape of her neck. But instead of the normal tranquility he usually saw in her eyes, they were full of anxiety; and ever ready to shelter her from any blow that he could, Bodene said softly, "Don't look so worried, Liza—everything will be just fine! You'll see!"

Elizabeth stared at him uncertainly, biting her full lower lip. "Oh, Bodene! How can you be so certain?

I've prayed and prayed that she would find a nice, ordinary man and marry and live a *happy,* respectable life. And now this! I don't think that I can bear to watch her suffer the contempt and scorn of all of our friends and neighbors once the truth comes out."

Elizabeth glanced away, tears glistening in her eyes. "It is horrible to have people look at you as if you were some sort of filthy rubble beneath their feet. And the men! They think that you are a shameless slut—always ready for a tumble and eagerly craving their crude advances! I simply cannot endure the thought of Savanna having to go through that! There must be a way that we can spare her the shame and degradation that will come. We *must!*"

Moved by her words, Bodene came to kneel on one knee at the side of her chair. Taking one of her slim hands in his, he murmured, "Liza! Don't fret so! I promise you that no one is going to dare put Savanna through what you suffered! I wasn't old enough to protect you in the beginning—but let one man *dare* treat Savanna that way, and he'll have me to answer to!"

There was such savage determination in his deep voice that Elizabeth regarded him with love and dread. "Bodene, I know you would lay down your life for both of us, but you cannot always act as a buffer for us against the world." She sent him a searching look. "How do you think Savanna would feel if you were to die in a duel because of her?"

Bodene smiled wickedly. "I'm very good with both the pistol and the sword, my dear—in my business one has to be—and so I think it highly unlikely that I would be the loser in any contest on the dueling field. But to set your mind at rest . . . I don't believe that I am going to have to risk my life for Savanna's honor. Savanna will *not* face what you did—rest assured of that!"

Puzzled, she stared at him, his words ringing with clear conviction. "How can you be so sure?" she asked huskily. "If Savanna will have nothing to do with this Adam St. Clair, I cannot see anything but unhappiness ahead." Suspicion suddenly narrowing her gaze, she demanded sharply, "What do you know that I don't?"

Rising to his feet, Bodene grinned, and crossing his arms over his broad chest, he said, "Savanna has given you a distorted idea of the relationship that exists between her and Adam. You didn't see the pair of them together—they're both half in love with each other, and I'd be willing to wager a considerable sum on the fact that once Adam learns that he is to be a father, he'll *make* Savanna marry him! Propinquity will do the rest! If all goes as I suspect, your daughter will soon be married to a wealthy, well-bred, well-connected gentleman! He won't be the *ordinary* fellow you may have wished for her, but I think that you will find your future son-in-law to be just the sort of man every woman longs for her daughter to marry. When you meet him, you will like him very much, Liza."

Elizabeth sent him an exasperated glance. "That's all very well, Bodene! But tell me—how am I ever to meet him if Savanna is unwilling to let him know of the child, and if she has made you swear not to tell him?"

Bodene's grin widened and, a dancing light in his eyes, he drawled, "I'm taking care of that little detail right now. Savanna made me swear not to *say* a word to him—she didn't say a damn thing about *writing* to him!"

Elizabeth's eyes grew round. "Oh, Bodene!" she finally said with a soft chuckle. "You *are* a sly boots! Is that what you are doing? Writing to Adam?"

He nodded. "Yes, and the letter will go by Isaac on one of my fastest horses, at first light tomorrow. And if I have judged Adam right, before another month passes, your daughter will be Mrs. St. Clair!"

Bodene wasn't quite as optimistic as he sounded. It

was possible that, once Adam had returned to his usual friends and surroundings, he would prefer to forget about the whole incident with Savanna and would merely read the letter and carelessly toss it aside. Many men in his position would; after all, what did the pregnancy of some little backwoods baggage mean to them? They would shrug their shoulders and go about their business, conveniently putting the matter from their minds. Bodene didn't think Adam would treat the news of impending fatherhood that way, but then again, what did he really know about the man? And then there was Savanna. . . . She was going to be furious with both of them and she had made it blazingly clear that she had no intention of marrying Adam St. Clair! Changing Savanna's mind when she was set on something was such a formidable task that most men would simply quail and walk away. Bodene grinned faintly. He didn't in the least envy Adam the wooing of a stubborn, prideful, hot-tempered virago like Savanna!

Adam received Bodene's letter at dusk on August the ninth, and for a long time after he had read the blunt message, he stared out the window of Belle Vista's elegant library at the purple-shadowed lands across the Mississippi River, torn between jubilation and angry despair. Bodene had made it explicitly apparent in his letter that, in spite of her condition, Savanna was just as adamantly opposed to marriage with him as she had been when he had first broached the question. Adam's mouth twisted wryly. Savanna's continual aversion to marriage with him shouldn't have surprised him, but to a certain extent it did. Without conceit, he knew his own worth; for years scintillating, sophisticated women from some of the finest families in the area and beyond had been vying for his hand, and he found it bitterly ironic that when he had finally asked a woman to marry him, she wanted none of him—even when she was carrying his child!

The idea that he was going to become a father was unsettling and his feelings about the child were ambivalent. He was joyful at the news, but he admitted with brutal insight that most of his joy had to do with the knowledge that the pregnancy gave him a weapon—enormous social pressure would be put on Savanna to accept him in marriage. The letter made it obvious that both Bodene and Elizabeth were firmly in his camp as far as the necessity to have Savanna respectably married was concerned, which gave him another, more powerful weapon—society aside, even Savanna's loved ones were going to push his suit. He shook his head disgustedly, wondering how he had gotten to this point—eager to use any weapon or method he could to have Savanna in his arms.

Wandering away from the window, he poured himself a snifter of brandy from a crystal decanter, and savoring the bouquet as he swirled the amber liquid around, he sat down in a tufted red leather chair and stared off into space, brooding over the irony of fate. A sardonic grin suddenly broke across his lean cheeks. Adam St. Clair married and the father of a child! Five months ago he would have sworn vehemently that that was impossible ... but, of course, that had been before a certain utterly beguiling, red-haired, witch-eyed temptress named Savanna O'Rourke had thrust herself violently into his life!

Tossing down a healthy swallow of the brandy, Adam contemplated the past several weeks and the aching emptiness that had been his constant companion since he had watched Savanna ride away from him. The journey to Terre du Coeur had been uneventful. The reunion with Catherine had been a tearful—on her part—ecstatic moment, but, beyond being glad to be alive and safe and back amidst his own world, Adam was bitingly aware that, for him, something vital was missing. He discovered to his dismay and utter fury that the future suddenly seemed very bleak and unexciting and he did not have far to look to uncover the cause of his singularly apathetic state—Savanna! It was a galling admission, and seeking escape from anything connected with her, hoping desperately that a return to his home and his usual pursuits would bring back his normal sanguine outlook, he had stayed only long enough with Jason and Catherine to convince his sister that he had suffered no lasting harm, before he had mounted a fresh horse and left for Belle Vista.

Getting up from his seat, Adam poured himself a second snifter of brandy and walked once more over to the long windows which graced the library. Staring moodily out into the deepening shadows of night, he conceded that several weeks of frenetic activity, of days jammed to the brim with the many details of running an estate the size of Belle Vista, of evenings filled with visiting and entertaining friends and attending glittering social events, of even later nights which he had spent in reckless abandon, drinking and gaming, had done nothing to alleviate the painful hollowness that Savanna had left within him.

She bewitched me, he admitted reluctantly, from the first moment I regained my senses and stared up into that unforgettable face of hers. Bewitched me and has made my life untenable without her presence. He walked over to where he had tossed the letter and read it again, a grim smile curving his full mouth. From the terse quality of Bodene's letter, it was abundantly clear that getting Savanna to marry him was going to be a monumental undertaking, but Adam suddenly found his spirits rising at the prospect.

Actually, the arrival of Bodene's letter made little difference to Adam's immediate plans. Having al-

ready decided some days ago, about the time he realized that drowning himself in liquor was folly, that
he was not going to let the situation with Savanna remain in its current unsatisfactory, unresolved state,
Adam had been busy making plans to leave Belle
Vista for New Orleans and a confrontation with the
red-haired spitfire who haunted his dreams. Bodene's
letter only brought that date closer, and doing a swift
calculation of what needed to be accomplished before
he could once again leave his plantation and affairs
in the hands of his very competent overseer and agent for an indefinite period of time, Adam concluded
that he could depart for New Orleans no later than
Monday. In the meantime, after a day of rest, he
would send a letter with Isaac on a riverboat back to
Bodene, who would be awaiting a reply at The
Golden Lady. Adam's mouth twisted. How wise of
Bodene to suggest that all communication between
them take place at the gaming establishment in New
Orleans. At least that way there would be no chance
of Savanna getting a whiff of what was in the wind!

Several days later, as Bodene sat in his office at the
rear of The Golden Lady, he glanced up at the sound
of an altercation just outside his door. He was on the
point of rising from his chair when the door was per-
emptorily pushed open and Adam strolled in, looking every inch the wealthy, assured gentleman that
he was. His elegant appearance was quite a contrast
to the grubby, hard-eyed rogue whom Bodene had
first met, and he gawked at the difference. From the
crown of his top hat to the soles of his gleaming
black boots, Adam looked to be the very picture of
sartorial excellence, his dark blue coat fitting his
broad shoulders superbly, the pale-blue-striped Mar-
seilles waistcoat blending attractively with his gray
pantaloons. As was fashionable in New Orleans, he
carried a short cane, which concealed a small sword;
strolling over to stand in front of Bodene's ornately

fashioned walnut desk, he smiled and murmured, "I'm afraid some underling of yours wanted to announce me, but I, er, convinced him that I needed no introduction."

Bodene laughed and, glancing at the man who bobbed in the doorway, nursing an obviously sore jaw, said dismissingly, "There is nothing to worry about, Jake. This gentleman is a friend of mine, and until I tell you differently, he has free access."

Jake nodded his sandy head and, grumbling something about "the gent being right handy with his fives," shut the door.

Making himself comfortable in one of the brass-studded leather chairs which were scattered about the spacious room, Adam leaned back and raised a quizzical eyebrow. "Well? Has the situation changed since I received your letter?"

Bodene shook his head disgustedly. "No! She is just as adamantly opposed to your knowing about the baby as she ever was, and I've had the devil's own time keeping my hands off her and beating some sense into her."

Adam grimaced and said, "It doesn't change the outcome—she *is* going to marry me before the month has ended, but it would be pleasant to start out life together in something less than all-out war!"

"Would you mind telling me how in hell you're going to accomplish that fact?"

"The marriage or less than all-out war?" Adam asked with a mocking light in his eyes.

"The marriage!"

There was suddenly an implacable cast to Adam's face. He didn't honestly know how he was going to make Savanna marry him; he only knew that his life would be desolate indeed without her and that he'd either wring an agreement to marry him out of her or wring her neck! Smiling wryly at his own thoughts, he muttered, "Blast her stubborn hide! Why must she make this as difficult as possible?"

Bodene looked uneasy, suddenly wondering if writing to Adam had been such a wise course after all. Bluntly he asked, "If she wasn't pregnant, what would you do? Would you still marry her?"

"That's a damn-fool question!" Adam replied testily. "Of course I would! I had already made arrangements to come to New Orleans with the intention of wooing Savanna before I received your letter. The baby only means that I'll have to move faster than I had planned." He looked steadily at Bodene. "I'll be honest with you—she drives me half mad—I'm either thinking of kissing her or wringing her neck, and while I'm certain that I shall spend the rest of my life torn between those two emotions, there is no other woman whom I want for my wife . . . whom I've *ever* wanted for my wife."

Adam had not admitted that he loved Savanna, but his words reassured Bodene that he was not consigning Savanna to a loveless union. Of Savanna's feelings Bodene had little doubt, and after listening to Adam, he decided that his original reading of the situation was correct: the only people who didn't realize that they were in love with each other were Adam and Savanna!

Satisfied, Bodene settled back in his chair. "How do you intend to get her to agree to marry you?"

A wicked smile curved Adam's lips. "Why, charm her, of course! Despite her avowals to the contrary, I know that she is not indifferent to me. She came into my arms willingly once, so surely she will again. And I *do* have much to offer her—while not meaning to sound like a braggart, I am *not* some beggarly ruffian!" A mocking twinkle in his blue eyes, he added teasingly, "How can she resist me?"

Silently Bodene agreed with him. If anybody could change Savanna's mind, it was Adam St. Clair. Thinking of the tempestuous wooing that was going to take place caused a small smile to lurk around his mouth. "You can count on my help! Elizabeth's too.

I shall return to Campo de Verde in the morning and alert her to what you plan."

Adam frowned slightly. "Is Elizabeth fully committed to my marriage to Savanna? She knows nothing of me." His mouth twisted. "Except what her daughter may have told her, and I doubt that Savanna has anything complimentary to say about me! And certainly, considering the circumstances . . ."

Bodene was quick to reassure him of Elizabeth's support and the two men continued to talk until the late hours. They had much to discuss—not the least of which was what they would do if Savanna did not succumb to Adam's charms! The comradeship that had sprung up during the journey back from Texas remained unabated, and in these more pleasant surroundings it flourished dramatically. As the hours passed and they conversed on a variety of subjects, each man was more and more warmly impressed by the other, and any awkwardness that could have attended their growing relationship was banished.

It was only as dawn was breaking that they discovered to their astonishment that they had talked the night away. Rising from his seat and stubbing out the remains of a long black cheroot that he had been smoking, Adam remarked amicably, "Seldom have I spent a more enjoyable evening. Once I am respectably married to your cousin, we must do this again."

Bodene concurred, and escorting Adam through the darkened, now deserted rooms of The Golden Lady, he said, "I agree—and hopefully it will be soon!"

Adam laughed and was on the point of walking through the elegant mahogany doors of the establishment when he asked casually, "Have you heard or seen any sign of Micajah or Jeremy since you have returned?"

Bodene shook his dark head. "No. I've ordered several people that I trust to keep their eyes and ears open, but so far there has been nothing. It is as if that pair of scoundrels simply vanished. What about you and Jason?"

Adam shrugged. "It's not me that Micajah wanted in the first place—I doubt he even knows of my existence—so there is no reason for him to be looking for Adam St. Clair of Natchez. Now, Jason Savage is another matter, but since we know what they are up to, Jason is forewarned and armed and ready for any plan they may spring—if they are foolish enough to return to Terre du Coeur or any other place that Jason inhabits!" Adam smiled grimly. "Jason can take care of himself, and Micajah and Jeremy no longer have the element of surprise to their advantage."

The two men began to stroll in the general direction of Adam's hotel. Having been mistaken once for his half brother and not wishing to experience that dubious pleasure again since Jeremy and Micajah were still unaccounted for, Adam was not staying, as was his usual wont when in New Orleans, at the Savage town house! He had taken a set of rooms in one of the very elegant hotels in the fashionable part of the city, and as they ambled in that direction, they continued to speak of Micajah and Jeremy. Both men were convinced that, having failed in their attempt to extract the information they wanted from the man they believed to be Jason Savage, and being unable to follow the twisted trail that Adam had left, they had no doubt continued on their quest for the gold and were probably either dead or hopelessly lost on the endless plains of Texas.

Neither man would have been quite so casual about this subject if he had known that, far from being in Texas, Jeremy and Micajah were in fact nursing their frustration and disappointment in one of the notorious saloons along Silver Street in Natchez, and that Adam St. Clair was the very topic of conversation!

Micajah had been nearly convulsed with fury when he had returned to camp and discovered what had happened, and for one very long moment, in his rage and disgust at finding that Savanna was gone along with the only person who could lead them to the gold, he had coldly considered cutting Jeremy's throat. Only one thing had stopped him—Jeremy at least knew the area where Davalos had died. Little time had been wasted trying to pick up Adam's trail—they'd needed to be refitted before attempting any sort of elaborate search. Riding hard for Nacogdoches, they had traded in their worn and wind-broken mounts for new horses and, resupplied, had returned to search for Adam and Savanna, casting desperately about in ever-widening circles for some trace. In the end they had faced defeat and the unpleasant fact that they were lost. It had taken them several miserable weeks before they stumbled into an area that looked vaguely familiar, and it was with heartfelt relief that they'd eventually managed to find their way back to Nacogdoches. Their supplies, money and horses had been exhausted by now and they had had to remain skulking in that area for some time, robbing and killing anyone unfortunate enough to cross their path. They had finally slain a rich Spanish merchant who carried a tidy sum of gold, and, mounted on the dead Spaniard's fine horses, his gold jingling in their saddlebags, they had lit out for Natchez, arriving in the nether regions of that lovely city two days after Adam had left for New Orleans.

Having spent the past several months living in the utmost squalor—even for them—they had both gotten roaring drunk and, with the help of a pair of harlots, stayed in that condition for nearly a week. They had only sobered up and faced reality when their money was nearly gone.

Micajah had not given up on going after the Aztec gold—he might have been a reluctant partner in the beginning, but some of Jeremy's blind lust for that hidden cache of gold had infected him. He had become convinced that he deserved the gold; that in view of the misfortunes that had plagued him since Savanna and that damned blue-eyed bastard had disappeared, he was *owed* that gold!

The loss of Savanna had been an infuriatingly bitter blow for Micajah; he had lusted after her for so long, and to have had her in his power and not to have tasted her soft, silky flesh ate at him like a cancer. So obsessed was he by her that there were even times when Micajah actually spared a thought about her fate—he suspected that she was dead, that her captor had used her until satisfied and then had slit her throat and dumped her somewhere in the vast untracked wilderness, as he'd half planned to do. It bothered him, though, the idea of Savanna being dead, and he had cursed himself roundly for not having slaked himself on her body when he'd had the chance. His cold blue eyes hard, he vowed that if Savanna was alive and if luck ever shone on him again and brought her into his clutches, he'd not hesitate to finally have her writhing beneath him.

But dreams of what he'd do to Savanna O'Rourke didn't help him right now, and as he and Jeremy were hunched over a battered table at The White Cock, nursing a glass of cheap whiskey, he muttered, "We need money. And there's only one way that I can think of laying our hands on it in a hurry."

Bleary-eyed, Jeremy glanced at him. Micajah smiled cruelly. "I think," Micajah said slowly, "that it's time I seriously set about finding Adam St. Clair and earning the other half of the money that is owed me. . . ."

Chapter 15

Jeremy continued to stare at Micajah, the whiskey fumes making his already slow thought process even slower. But eventually the meaning of Micajah's words came through, and there was a spark of interest in his drink-dulled eyes until something unpleasant occurred to him. Uncertainly he said, "But you were supposed to do that months ago—will the fellow still be willing to pay?"

Micajah shrugged and took a big swallow of his whiskey. "If he wanted St. Clair killed bad enough to hire me to do it in the first place, I can't see that the passage of a few months will have changed his mind."

But Micajah had made one little miscalculation—he had no idea how to find the man who had originally contracted with him to kill St. Clair! Rubbing his rusty-stubbled jaw, he considered his problem. When he had been given the first installment of gold at Spanish Lick, it had been agreed that, once the deed was done, the remainder of the money would be hidden at Spanish Lick. How could he have been so stupid? What if he had killed St. Clair and the rest of the money hadn't been forthcoming? He'd have no recourse, nor any way to take revenge on the man who had cheated him, and he wondered sourly where he had left his wits.

Furious with himself for his lack of foresight, Micajah scowled. He'd look up Jem Elliot and see if Jem knew more about the fair-haired gentleman than he did. And he could find out if St. Clair was back in residence at that fancy estate of his, Belle Vista. If worse came to worst, he could go ahead and kill St. Clair and hope that the gentleman would keep his end of the bargain. And if the gent didn't . . . Micajah shrugged. At least he'd gotten two thousand dollars for the job, and he'd killed for a damn sight less than that on more than one occasion.

Finding Jem Elliot proved easy enough, and Jem did have some interesting news to relate. Micajah and Jeremy found their cohort in a favorite haunt of his, another shoddy tavern farther down Silver Street. Jem was seated in a corner, hunched morosely over a glass of whiskey, and when he looked up and caught sight of Micajah and Jeremy, a grin crossed his face. "Well, well, if it ain't my good friend Micajah Yates! Where in hell you been?"

"Don't matter," Micajah growled, sliding into a chair beside him. "I want to know more about that gent you introduced me to—the one who wanted that Adam St. Clair killed."

"Why?" Jem asked with a hard gleam in his hazel eyes. "You disappeared with the money and left me to face a very unhappy client."

"You saw him again?" Micajah asked excitedly. "Did you get a name?"

"No, I didn't get a name!" Jem replied sharply. "What I did get was an angry tirade about what base-born, lying, cheating rogues we are! The gent was so furious that you had taken his money and not killed St. Clair that I think he seriously considered laying the whole matter before a magistrate—*that's* how mad he was!" Jem sent Micajah a dark look. "You didn't do my reputation any good and you can be sure that we'll not have any other jobs to do for that particular gent or any of his friends either!"

Micajah grunted. "Think it would turn him up sweet if I finally completed the task? More importantly, do you think he'd pay the rest of the money?"

Jem sat up straighter, a bright gleam of avarice in his eyes. "Are you going to do it?"

"Might . . . if I thought the money would still be forthcoming."

Jem licked his lips in anticipation. "I'll see what I can find out. You still staying at the widow's place?"

Micajah nodded. The three men talked briefly abut the latest happenings in Natchez—Micajah and Jeremy adding little to the conversation. They did not remain there for long, and soon they parted from Jem and made their way to the widow Blackstone's boardinghouse.

The lack of money was a pressing issue, and early the next morning they left the immediate area and disappeared into the vast wilderness along the Natchez Trace. The Trace was a dangerous area, notorious for the thieves and murderers who lurked in the heavy underbrush and canebrakes waiting for the unwary traveler. Micajah and Jeremy had ridden up the Trace specifically with robbery and murder on their minds and they didn't have long to wait. Two days later, a father and son, well-to-do merchants from Nashville, traveling homeward from New Orleans, had the misfortune to cross their path. Since dead men told no tales, Murdering Micajah lived up to his name and viciously dispatched both men, hiding their bodies deep in the underbrush. The saddlebags revealed nearly four thousand dollars in gold, and with money in their pockets once more, Micajah and Jeremy returned to Natchez to consider their next step.

Jeremy was all for resupplying themselves and even without a map heading immediately into Texas, but while Micajah was eager for the gold, too, he was also not so keen to subject himself again so soon to the rigors of the trail—and without the information in that blue-eyed devil's head! Micajah had brooded a lot about the escape of Jason Savage and, bitterly aware that they had lost the element of surprise, he doubted that they'd ever have another chance of getting their hands on the man. And without Jason Savage, Micajah was going to have to rely on Jeremy to lead them to where the Spaniard had died, and from there he could only hope that they would find some clue that would lead them to the treasure. Micajah wanted the gold, now almost as badly as Jeremy, and though he hadn't given up on it, he wasn't looking forward to the prospect of months on end of being led through the wilds of Texas by Jeremy! With ample gold jingling in their pockets, Micajah saw no reason why they couldn't travel to New Orleans and enjoy themselves for a while before setting out for Texas. And though he would have torn out his tongue before admitting it, Micajah wanted to talk to Bodene Sullivan about Savanna. It would be a damn tricky conversation, but he was confident that he could find out what he wanted to know without revealing his part in Savanna's disappearance. And if anyone would know about Savanna, if she was alive or dead, it would be Bodene Sullivan!

Jeremy was not best pleased with Micajah's ideas, but he also wasn't immune to the lure of the flesh and drink that Micajah spoke of so winningly, and he finally caved in and grumpily agreed to the delay. Ensconcing themselves in carnal luxury at Micajah's favorite whorehouse, they drank and whored and made drink-sodden plans to take care of Mr. St. Clair—if Jem gave them the good news that their gentleman was still willing to pay. Once the St. Clair matter was settled, they would then travel to New Orleans to visit with Savanna's cousin. . . .

Arriving at midmorning on Tuesday at Campo de Verde, Bodene would have gladly welcomed a visit from Micajah and Jeremy rather than have to face Savanna's wrath when she found out how he had betrayed her. Elizabeth's unabashed delight, however, when he told her of the meeting with Adam and what Adam planned to do, lightened his spirits considerably and he was soon *almost* looking forward to Adam's arrival. It had been decided that Adam would simply arrive at Campo de Verde, Savanna was to have no warning and Bodene and Elizabeth were to make themselves scarce before Adam showed up. It was planned for Adam to arrive that afternoon, and Bodene and Elizabeth went to great lengths either to avoid Savanna or, when forced to be in her company, to act as naturally as possible.

If Savanna noticed that there was a soft gleam of excited anticipation in her mother's eyes or that Bodene's lips twitched now and then with a secretive smile, she gave no sign of it. Actually, Savanna was so lost in her own misery that she was barely aware of what was going on around her. The enormity of the burden that she had taken upon herself had painfully dawned on her the morning after she had so proudly stated that she wanted nothing to do with Adam St. Clair, and she was grappling with the grim reality of her position. It was not pleasant, and it occurred uncomfortably to her that the child deserved a better future than the one that she was busy creating for it. Not only would Adam be able to provide more materially for the child, but she remembered with painful clarity her own childhood and the scorn and the contempt with which others had looked at her because her parents hadn't been married. Was she right in condemning her own child to that fate? And what about her mother? Was it fair to make

Elizabeth suffer the embarrassment of having her friends and neighbors know that her daughter had borne a bastard child? Wouldn't that shameful revelation lead to the crumbling of the respectable facade that Elizabeth had created over the years for herself? Did Savanna dare risk even one tiny crack in that facade?

And then there was Bodene. She might pride herself on her independence, but it would be more than just cowardice if she tried to ignore the fact that it was Bodene's money that would be supporting her and the child for the next several months. Bodene was very discreet about it, but Savanna was very aware that for years he had been generously spending his own money to shore up their meager finances, and that if Elizabeth and the others had to live *solely* on the proceeds earned from Campo de Verde, life would not be quite as comfortable as it was now. One of the reasons she had left Campo de Verde in the first place had been so that she would not be a burden to *either* Elizabeth or Bodene. And now to return nearly penniless and pregnant? To what depths was she willing to sink to keep her pride? And how could she even lay any claim to pride if she merely exchanged one keeper for another? Bodene for Adam?

Miserably aware that she might have painted herself into a very lonely and empty corner, Savanna only picked at lunch that afternoon, her thoughts on the wretched future that seemed to stretch out interminably before her. Would it, a sly voice in her brain asked, be so *very* terrible to be married to Adam St. Clair? Your child would have a name and be the *legitimate* heir to a respectable, possibly vast, fortune. It was true that there might be those who would turn up their noses at *her* antecedents, but Adam's acknowledged child was unlikely to face such prejudice. Was she fair in denying the child its rightful place?

After lunch, when Bodene proposed accompanying Elizabeth on a visit to some friends, Savanna's thoughts were in such a turmoil she barely paid them any heed. It didn't even occur to her that they hadn't extended an invitation to join them and that they departed somewhat hastily. After they had driven away in Bodene's snappy new red road cart, she wandered desolately about the oak-studded grassy area that lay in front of the house. Even though she was preoccupied, she was careful to remain in full sight of the house—she wasn't going to risk having Micajah rise up out of nowhere to whisk her off again! Selecting a spot of dappled shade beneath one of the huge trees, she sat down on the grass, her back resting against the gray-brown bark of the trunk. Her legs were tucked demurely under the flowing skirt of her apple-green cambric gown, the high neck with its standing ruffle framing her lovely features. With her glorious red-gold hair half tamed by a loose knot and a ribbon in the same shade as her gown on top of her head, she hardly resembled the grubby, boy-clad, young Amazon of Adam's memory!

After Adam and Bodene had parted in the early hours of the previous morning, Adam had found himself strangely restless despite his lack of sleep, and instead of seeking out his bed, after refreshing himself he had strolled aimlessly about the city. But mostly his thoughts had been on Savanna and the need to make her see the sense of their immediate marriage. His mind full of images of her and the way she had looked that last time he had seen her, he'd happened to pass the discreet shop of a well-known New Orleans modiste and his steps slowed. . . . A grin suddenly crossed his handsome face. Savanna was going to be furious with him no matter what he did, and so he might as well please himself! A gleam of anticipation in his blue eyes, he had blithely entered the shop.

The next morning, Adam, having elected to ride along the River Road instead of traveling by boat down the Mississippi River as Bodene had planned, left the city several hours ahead of his co-conspirator. They had decided that Bodene needed to arrive first so he could alert Elizabeth of their scheme, and since Adam had no inclination to lurk in the underbrush for a few hours, the separate means of travel seemed ideal. Besides, Adam needed the time to get his thoughts in order before he faced Savanna. But even as he turned his horse onto the rutted road that Bodene had explained led to the main house, Adam still wasn't precisely certain what his first words to Savanna would be. Certainly he had not expected to come across her sitting on the soft green grass like a beguiling wood nymph beneath the outspreading arms of one of the many oaks that dotted the area.

It was obvious from her distracted expression that she was totally unaware of the horse and rider on the roadway, and taking advantage of her abstracted state, Adam quietly halted his horse and dismounted. Leaving his horse to crop grass at the edge of the road, he walked slowly toward her. With stunned appreciation, his blue eyes roamed across her sun-kissed features, noting the finely arched brows, the patrician cast of her nose and jaw, the full, inviting curve of her mouth, before his gaze dropped to the generous lines of her body that the gown modestly revealed. Staring at her, he found himself oddly breathless, as if he had run a great distance, and his usual sangfroid utterly deserted him.

He must have made some sound because Savanna suddenly looked up, her incredible aquamarine eyes widening in shock as she recognized him standing there before her. If Adam had been startled at her appearance, the same could be said for Savanna at her first sight of him. Gone was the shaggy-bearded, ragged-haired, unkempt rogue who had kept her captive, and in his place stood a well-dressed, ex-

tremely handsome man. The thick black hair waved
attractively back from his broad brow; the bronzed
skin was clean-shaven, revealing once again the chiseled perfection of his hard jaw and prominent cheekbones, the carnal slant of his lower lip and the proud
set of his head. He was dressed impeccably, the
bottle-green jacket molding the powerful shoulders
and arms, the pale brown, figured waistcoat con-
trasting nicely with the yellow nankeen breeches
which clung tightly to the long, strongly muscled
legs. The only thing that hadn't changed, she realized
half dreamily, half angrily, was the mocking expression in those unforgettable sapphire-blue eyes and
she stiffened, all the reasons that she shouldn't be
happy to see him flooding through her—that and the
fact that her cousin was an underhanded, lying, conniving son of a bitch!

Her jaw clenched and, the light of battle blazing in
her eyes, she glared up at him and in a voice filled
with loathing said one word: *"Bodene!"*

Adam smiled grimly. "Of course." Ignoring her in-
drawn hiss of wrath, he settled himself on the grass
beside her and continued dryly, "I'm grateful that at
least *one* of you has shown some sense and had the
wisdom to inform me of my impending fatherhood."

His words and brazen air, as well as Bodene's flagrant betrayal, rankled, and Savanna struggled manfully to keep her volatile temper under control. She
would have liked to pretend that his unexpected
presence meant nothing to her, that she hadn't
wished for just such an incident, but she would have
been lying—and Savanna was usually very honest in
her dealings, even with herself. Angry as she was at
Bodene, the fact that Adam was here beside her sent
a dizzying thrill careening through her veins and to
her horror, she had to fight an almost overpowering
urge to fling herself into his arms. But Adam's words
were not precisely conciliatory, and forgetting for the
moment all the doubts that had beset her lately about

her decision not to tell him of the child, she replied stiffly, "There was no reason to inform you. I am perfectly capable of raising my child myself—without your help!"

Adam sent her a long look. "You know," he said casually, "when you make stupid statements like that, I'm never certain whether I want to beat you or kiss you senseless."

Savanna glared at him. "Try either and you'll wish you hadn't," she warned, her eyes promising all kinds of trouble.

Propped up on one elbow, he stared at her, exasperation and admiration in his gaze. God, but she was lovely, the loveliest creature he had ever seen! he thought moodily as his eyes slid slowly down her face and body.

Infuriated by his slow appraisal, Savanna clenched her fists and muttered, "Would you mind not stripping me with your eyes? You may have had me in your power once, but I'll be damned if I'll let *that* happen again!"

"Why?" Adam inquired silkily. "Afraid that you might learn to like it?"

From the furious expression on her face, it was obvious that she was not going to rise to his teasing, and Adam discovered uneasily that her unbending attitude toward him had the ability to hurt. Rejection was not something that had come his way very often and he found it galling that in spite of her hostile manner toward him, he could not negligently shrug his shoulders and simply walk away from her. Almost absently, he said aloud, "I just can't understand why in hell I find you such a fascinating baggage!" His mouth curved wryly. "Oh, you're beautiful, I'll grant you that, and I'll even admit that I find you vastly appealing, but you are also aggravating beyond belief! You have the witch's own tongue and temper, and with one lift of your eyebrow you can infuriate me faster than anyone I have ever known."

He shot her a dark look. "I wasn't completely jesting when I said I never know whether to beat you or kiss you, but one thing I do know—when I'm away from you I feel only half alive, almost as if part of me were missing. . . ."

To say which of them was the more startled by his unexpected admission would have been hard to do. Certainly Savanna's stunned features revealed her reaction, but it was Adam who was shaken to his very core by the enormity of what he had said and what it implied. With the suddenness of a thunderbolt, it dawned on him precisely *why* Savanna seemed to have such power over him—*he loved her!*

His heart slammed painfully into his ribs at what he was admitting and, torn between abject terror and a strong sense of injustice, he glanced away, grappling with this new, unexpected and unwanted knowledge. Jesus! It would have to be her, he thought sourly—the daughter of the one man he hated above all others; the one woman whom he truly wanted and who had made it clear she wanted nothing to do with him! An ironic smile curved his mouth. Probably my just deserts, he admitted with black humor, recalling vividly some of the unflattering things that certain young women had hurled at him in the past when he had deftly eluded their traps. Oh, God, wouldn't Betsey Asher enjoy his predicament!

Adam was silent for several seconds as he struggled to make sense of what had befallen him. Unfortunately, his own introspection gave Savanna enough time to gather her scattered wits about her. His words had wrapped her in a decidedly rosy glow until, insidiously, the thought occurred to her that Adam had a very good reason for making such an astounding statement—he had come here because of the baby, and because of the baby, he was intent upon making their liaison respectable. What better way to get her to go along with him than to offer the dazzling lure that he might actually *care* for her?

Unable to contain the wrath that coursed through her at the idea of his mendacity, she said furiously, "Of all the underhanded, conniving, rascally non-sense! Do you really think that I'm so green that I don't know what you're up to?"

Startled, Adam stared at her. "What the hell are you talking about?"

"You know exactly what I'm talking abut—the baby! The only reason you're here! Don't deny that you came here to convince me to marry you!" she stated passionately. "You're so damned determined to get your own way that you're willing to spout the most outrageous lies! No matter what you say, I have no intention of letting you browbeat me or trick me into some boring marriage of convenience!"

Adam's eyes narrowed dangerously and for one moment Savanna thought she had pushed him too hard. But then, with an effort, he got his temper under control and there was suddenly a gleam in those eyes that made her distinctly uneasy. "Well, at least you got some of it right!" he admitted dryly. "I have come here to convince you to marry me and I'll even confess that I always *used* to view marriage as a trap." He shook his head ruefully. "I was certain that marriage would herald the end of my youth, for a wife would shackle me and curtail my wanderings. But marriage to you would be something entirely different—in fact, I've come to believe that if I have to get married, you're *precisely* the sort of woman I'd want for my wife!"

He couldn't have made his meaning clearer as far as Savanna was concerned. He didn't want a woman of his own class who might have the temerity to question his comings and goings, who might meet him on an equal footing. No! He wanted someone like her—a backwoods baggage he could safely stash in the background and whom he could manipulate at will. Oh, she knew very well what he meant by saying she was precisely the sort of woman he wanted for a wife! Hurt and thoroughly insulted, Savanna drew herself up haughtily and snapped, "Well, I'm afraid you've chosen the wrong woman! I have no intention of marrying—you or anybody else! Forget about me! Forget about the baby! We don't *need* you! We'll do just fine—and without any help from you!"

"If I remember correctly, you didn't get into your situation all by yourself!" Adam drawled calmly, although there was a warning glitter in his blue eyes. "I can even vaguely remember doing my part enthusiastically!"

Savanna's lips thinned. "I don't deny it! However, that one unfortunate event is not reason enough for me to spend the rest of my life locked into a dull marriage with *you!*"

Adam sighed, thinking again that he'd like to either beat her or kiss her. . . . Speculatively he eyed her. He'd never had trouble charming a woman before, and now, when it was so important, when he had practically laid his heart at her feet, he seemed unable to convince *her* of that fact! Growing just a little angry, but persevering gamely, Adam said bluntly, "Before meeting you, I'd always thought of marriage much the same way. I thought it would be a sentence of years of boring domesticity, but with you . . ." He grinned suddenly, thinking of the years and years of hot-tempered wrangling and passionate lovemaking they would share—once he'd convinced her to marry him, of course! "With you," he continued mischievously, his good humor restored, "it would *never* be boring!" Blue eyes dancing with mockery, he added provokingly, "In fact, it would be a damned bloody *challenge!*"

Savanna was certain she was going to burst with fury and, heedless of anything but the desire to vent just a little of the rage within her, she slapped him. Hard. To her astonishment, he laughed aloud, and before she had a chance to realize what he was up to, he lunged for her, catching her shoulders in his hands and jerking her away from the tree, pressing her down into the grass. For a long second he stared into her furious eyes. "Sweetheart, I'd hoped to make you see reason, but I guess the time for words is over. There seems to be only one way I can make you see sense!"

Adam brought his lips down firmly on hers, his mouth and body starving for her after their weeks apart. He was half lying on her, and her angry struggles to escape only aroused him further, making him forget everything but the sheer ecstasy of having the woman he loved once more in his arms. Desire, elemental and inexorable, coursed through him and he crushed her into his powerful embrace as if he would never let her go, as if he would absorb her into his very being and make her part of him.

At Adam's touch, Savanna was pitched into a turmoil. Wondering bleakly how she could hate a man who made her feel like this, hate the father of the child she carried beneath her breast, she fought against the treacherous emotions that threatened to overpower her. Even as she struggled to keep her thoughts focused and not give in to the sweet pleasure that was insidiously sweeping through her body, she was dimly aware that she could never hate him, *had* never hated him. . . . The reason for Adam's inexplicable power over her, the reason why he could so easily shatter her emotions, suddenly burst across her brain. Why, *I love him*, she thought in utter astonishment.

The knowledge that she was in love with Adam didn't find any more favor with Savanna than his awareness that he was in love with her had originally found with him, but if Adam had finally and joyfully embraced the idea, Savanna shrank from it—her mother's example of what misplaced love could bring a woman was too painfully ingrained within her to be ignored. If anything, the knowledge that she loved him made the situation all the more painful and unendurable. Terrified of what loving him could do to her, she tried frantically to gain control of her unruly body, to ignore the fierce delight of his kiss and touch.

But his mouth was too delectably hungry and too wantonly urgent as it moved on hers, and with a small, hopeless moan, she gave him what they both desperately wanted and opened her lips. His warm tongue surged explicitly into her mouth, evoking memories of his big body plunging into hers that exact same way. Dizzyingly aware of the hard length of his swollen manhood pressed between their bodies, Savanna tightened her arms convulsively around his broad shoulders and was instantly as hungry for him as he was for her.

At her surrender, Adam groaned, his hand closing gently around her breast, thoughts of the years together that they would have to share this rare pleasure making him tremble violently. It also brought him forcefully back to reality and made him aware of where they were. With a tremendous effort, he brought himself under control, but he could not bear to stop touching her just yet and, his mouth against hers, he murmured, "Marry me, Savanna! Let me take care of you and the child."

Jerked back to earth by his words, Savanna was humiliated at how easily he had caused her to forget the basic issue between them. How stupid of her to forget that if it weren't for the child and Bodene's meddling, she would never have heard from him again. Dying a little inside, she turned her face away, afraid he might see the love she felt for him and use it as another weapon against her. Struggling out of Adam's slackened grasp, she sat up and, still not looking at him, asked painfully, "Is that what this is all about? A further ploy to get your way?"

Adam's gaze narrowed and his mouth thinned.

"Do you know," he said conversationally, "that there are times I really would like to beat you soundly?"

Her chin lifted and she glared at him. "Lay a hand on me and—"

"I know," Adam interrupted coldly. "You'll skewer me and feed my liver to the gators!"

Savanna smiled sweetly. "Precisely!"

Getting to his feet, Adam dusted a blade or two of grass from his breeches and said dryly, "I had harbored the notion, foolish though I knew it to be, that you might be willing to listen to reason." He shot her an unfriendly look. "Stupid of me, I know. You're determined to be as obdurate and idiotic as you know how to be, aren't you?"

All of the doubts that had beleaguered her lately suddenly leapt to the forefront of her mind and she tamped down the spurt of temper at his words, determined to prove him wrong, determined for the sake of her child to attempt to make some sort of future for them all. "Not exactly," she began honestly. "It's just that . . ."

Perhaps if Adam had been paying more attention, if he hadn't still been wrestling with the stunning knowledge of his love for her, if he had looked, really *looked* at Savanna at that moment, he might have glimpsed all the doubts and uncertainties that were revealed in both her eyes and her voice, and his next words might have been totally different. But for the first time in his life, his deepest emotions were involved, and he *was* certain that she probably hated him and the fact that he had fallen in love with her *did* continue to make him half stupefied, so he missed the subtle change in Savanna and blundered on. His face set, he snapped, "Unfortunately, that's *exactly* the situation! You're so bloody determined to put all of us in an invidious position simply because it's *me* asking you to do something sensible!" The blue eyes hostile, he growled, "Goddammit, Savanna, you're such a *stubborn* minx! You're not listening to what anyone has to say—you won't listen to your mother or Bodene, and anything I say you view with the utmost suspicion." His face softened for a moment. "I know you're being rushed into this and believe me, if the baby weren't already on the way, I swear to you that I would court you in the manner you deserve."

"Would you?" Savanna asked intently. "If you hadn't known about the baby, would you have come back?"

"Yes," he said quietly. "I had already made arrangements to come to see you *before* I got Bodene's letter."

Unhappily Savanna stared at him, wanting desperately to believe him, but the notion that Adam St. Clair, handsome, sophisticated and wealthy, a man who could have nearly any woman he wanted, truly wanted to marry *her* was simply inconceivable. Look at how they had met, for heaven's sake! And that didn't even take into account what her father had done to his sister! He was probably telling the truth about coming back to see her . . . but only, she thought miserably, to see if she was indeed pregnant! She was convinced that there could be no other reason. She knew, too, that he was an honorable man, and like an honorable man, he was determined to do the right thing—even if it meant marrying the rustic, bastard daughter of a man he detested! Savanna shivered. Never!

Her shoulders squared, she said tightly, "It doesn't matter. The fact still remains that I am *not* going to marry you and you can't make me!"

Torn between despair and anger, Adam stared at her. He had tried everything. Reason. Seduction. He had even confessed some of his deepest feelings for her—feelings he hadn't even known himself until he had said the words aloud—and *still* she refused him! She had battered his pride and hurt him as he had never thought he could be hurt, and a savage determination to meet the challenge she had thrown down boiled up through him. With mingled rage and exasperation he glared at her, and for one of the few times in his life, Adam thoroughly lost his formidable temper. Where the words came from, even he didn't know, but he suddenly found himself snarling, "The simple fact is, my dear, that you *will* marry me! Either you will marry me within the week or I shall destroy your mother's nice little world! I wonder how you will feel when I tell all her neighbors and friends that she is not the widow of Blas Davalos, but merely a little ladybird whom he never bothered to marry! And that her illegitimate daughter is following in her mother's footsteps!" His words were deliberately cruel, but he was fighting for his future—and hers, if she would only realize it—and not letting himself be moved by Savanna's white face and shocked expression, his blue eyes cold and hard, he demanded, "How do you think she'll like that? Hmm, sweetheart?"

Savanna nearly choked on the rage that erupted within her, and springing to her feet, she went for Adam, murder blazing in her eyes. "You blackhearted devil! I'll kill you before I'll ever let you do that to her!"

Adam caught her wrists and they fought wildly for a moment before he was able to jerk her to him and kiss her angrily. "No," he said finally, when he had lifted his mouth from her stinging lips, "you won't kill me!" A derisive smile crossed his dark face. "Kill the father of your unborn child? I hardly think so! What you're going to do and do damn shortly is *marry* me!"

Chapter 16

ADAM'S PROPHECY PROVED CORRECT: FOUR DAYS LATER, on a bright, sunny afternoon, with a tearfully beaming Elizabeth, a grimly satisfied Bodene and a grinning Sam Bracken looking on, Adam St. Clair married Savanna O'Rourke. The need for secrecy had forced the quintet to travel some distance from Campo de Verde—Sam driving the ladies in an old-fashioned phaeton, Adam and Bodene riding astride. The ceremony went smoothly; on his way to New Orleans, planning for this eventuality, Adam had stopped at a small hamlet north of the city and spoken with the pastor of the tiny church therein and made the arrangements for the wedding. If the pastor noticed that the bride seemed to view her intended husband with something akin to loathing, he allowed the pleased gratification on the other four faces of the wedding party to overcome his misgivings—that and a generous donation by the groom to the Orphans and Widows Fund!

More for the women's sake than for his own, and to avoid as many raised eyebrows as possible when

Savanna's child was born, Adam had declared that there would be no formal honeymoon, nor an announcement of the wedding. As news of their marriage spread by means of various friends and acquaintances, there would be no mention of the *actual* wedding date. As far as anyone was concerned, the marriage was indeed recent, but *how* recent was nobody's business!

But while the honeymoon was going to be forsaken, Adam did insist that he and Savanna have some time alone before they returned to Campo de Verde to visit for a few weeks before undertaking the journey to Belle Vista. Savanna appeared as coldly indifferent to the idea of a honeymoon as she had to everything he had proposed since the afternoon he had stated so vehemently that they *would* marry, and Adam felt a strong urge to throttle his dearly beloved.

On their wedding night, when the travel-weary little party stopped for the evening at a respectable but rather rough tavern several miles north of North Orleans, Adam suggested that the two ladies share the lone bedroom they were offered and that the gentlemen sleep on blankets outside the door to their room. He had the immense satisfaction of seeing Savanna's eyes widen with astonishment and he was happily aware that for the remainder of the evening, she watched him with a puzzled expression on her lovely face. As much as Adam would have enjoyed making love to his bride, he wanted a far more seductive setting than a tiny room with paper-thin walls and a lumpy bed!

It didn't do Savanna's temper any good to listen that evening, as they prepared for bed, to her mother prattle on about what a considerate, *charming* young man she had married. Outraged and bitter at Adam's underhanded methods to gain her consent to the marriage, Savanna was in no mood to hear anything good about him! Her eyes glittering with suppressed temper, she opened her mouth to state precisely what sort of an arrogant, crafty bastard Adam St. Clair really was, when she caught sight of her mother's happy face and shut her mouth with a decided snap. Elizabeth was thrilled with the marriage! Absolutely delighted that her daughter was safely, *respectably* married to a handsome, generous, well-bred, wealthy young man, and Savanna didn't have the heart to disillusion her. Besides, her argument was with Adam and there was no reason to involve Elizabeth. Giving her mother a fond kiss on the forehead, Savanna rolled over in the small bed and, stifling a yawn, decided that this was probably the oddest wedding night of any bride—imagine sharing a bed with your mother while your groom slept on the floor outside the door! Savanna smiled. Served the insolent devil right!

When Adam had first mentioned the stay in New Orleans, Savanna had viewed it as another sign of his high-handedness, but realizing that as long as her mother was hovering nearby she would have to keep a civil tongue in her mouth, she was now actively looking forward to the instant the two parties separated. Consequently, the next afternoon, when the little group split up, the new couple taking the two horses and detouring to New Orleans while the rest, riding in the phaeton, returned to Campo de Verde, Savanna was almost smiling, the light of battle shining in the depths of her aquamarine eyes.

Adam had kept his suite of rooms at the hotel and it was there that he took his not-so-loving bride. If Savanna was impressed with the gracious rooms and elegant furnishings, she said nothing. She was *not* going to let herself be distracted by such frivolous things as thick, jewel-toned carpets, gilt-edged mirrors, damask-covered sofas, gleaming crystal chandeliers and silk-hung beds!

Privately she admitted that the rooms were gorgeous, and under different circumstances she would

have been wide-eyed with delight and absolutely en-
chanted with her surroundings. Standing stiffly in
the center of the elegant sitting room, she glared resentfully at Adam as he shut the double doors behind him, wishing he didn't look quite so devilishly
attractive in his dark blue coat and buff breeches.
Her wardrobe had always been extremely limited,
and though she had never longed for frilly gowns of
silk and lace, at least never *really* longed for them,
she felt slightly out of place in such grand surroundings wearing her old-fashioned riding habit of plain
gray cloth. That Adam, despite their days on the road
was garbed in the height of fashion, from the pristine
whiteness of his neatly tied cravat to the bright shine
on his black boots, didn't make Savanna feel any
more comfortable. In her present mood, his very elegance was just one more fault in his already vastly
flawed character.

Reaching up and destroying the cravat that
aroused such black feelings within his bride by tearing it from his neck, he tossed it carelessly on one of
the marble-topped tables scattered around the room
and eyed her consideringly. She had been singularly
docile during their ride into the city, but he wasn't
fooled—she was pining for a fight. Adam wasn't exactly averse to letting her vent her spleen—after all,
in front of her mother she'd had to keep a smile
pasted on her face and, though it had choked her,
speak to him in polite tones. He grinned. Knowing
his bride, he thought she was probably about ready
to explode from having had to be nice to him.

Settling himself down comfortably in a deep chair
of straw silk, Adam rested his hands behind his head
and stretched out his booted feet in front of him.
"Ah, my dear, alone at last," he drawled madden-
ingly. "Shall we begin to bill and coo like the lovebirds we are supposed to be?"

"I don't," Savanna ground out with eyes blazing,

"love you! *I hate you*—you underhanded, calculating bastard!"

Adam smiled, but it didn't quite reach his eyes. "Oh, I'm sure you do! After all," he went on silkily, "all I've done is save you from disgrace and provide my child with a name. Such a despicable crime I've committed!"

Savanna looked away, embarrassment and guilt crawling through her. There was too much truth in his words for her to ignore—even in a temper and spoiling for a fight, she found herself with no weapons against him. His words bit deep and the anger she had erected as a shield against him suddenly crumpled. He didn't fight very fair, she thought crankily. How could she possibly rail and shout at him when in the deepest recesses of her heart she knew that she *should* be grateful for what he had done? Sighing, she walked over to one of the wide velvet-draped windows and looked blindly down at the street below. The words stuck in her throat, but she managed to get them out. "You did an honorable thing, I can't deny it, and m-m-most men in your position wouldn't have gone to such lengths." Her eyes suddenly glittered with unshed tears and she declared passionately, "Unfortunately, you have also chained us together for the rest of our lives! Beyond the child, we share nothing, no real feelings for each other!"

She heard Adam get up from his chair and she stiffened as he walked up behind her. He was standing so close to her that she could feel the heat of his big body against her back, and her pulse leapt when his hand rested gently on her shoulder. His warm breath caressed her ear as he bent nearer and said quietly, "Savanna, I do have feelings for you. I know that we started off badly, but since we have managed to create a child between us and we *are* married, don't you think we might try to deal better together than we have so far?"

Savanna bit down hard on her lip, battling back her tears. Adam in a kind mood played bloody havoc with her reasoning and made it difficult for her to remember that he was an unprincipled monster who had blackmailed her into a marriage she most decidedly had not wanted. She wanted to fight with him, to hurl angry words at him, but the urge to spin around and throw herself into his arms and seek comfort from his embrace was nearly overpowering and she fought hard against it. She was *not* going to give him a weapon to use against her! It was impossible, however, considering the state of her treacherous emotions, not to take the olive branch that he so generously offered. The thought of living in a state of constant warfare was definitely not very appealing, and logic told her that in order to survive they must find some way of living peaceably together. Still keeping her back to him, she admitted huskily, "It will not be easy—our backgrounds are very different ... and I don't believe that your family will quickly forget what my father did to them."

Adam's hand tightened on her shoulder. "I'm not going to pretend to you that Jason and Catherine will be overjoyed with our marriage, but they are reasonable people. Once they are convinced that you mean neither them nor me any harm, they will accept you gladly for who you are, *not* for who your father was! As for our different backgrounds ..." Adam smiled and, slowly turning her around, linked his hands behind her waist. "Did I ever tell you of my life with the gypsies?"

Instantly distracted, as he had known she would be, Savanna stared at him, lively curiosity in her eyes. "Gypsies? What are you talking about?"

Laughter flashed in the dark blue eyes. "Why, my dear, only that I am not quite the pillar of respectability that your mother believes—my early years were equally as harum-scarum and unorthodox as yours! Come, sit on the sofa beside me and let me tell you of Clive Pendleton, Reina, Manuél and Tamara—Catherine's name when we lived with the gypsies."

Fascinated, Savanna sat beside him on the damask sofa and listened with wide eyes as Adam told her of those long-ago years he and Catherine had spent living with the gypsies. Adam could tell a good story, and since he had considered the entire experience a huge adventure, Savanna found herself listening to an exciting tale. When he finished speaking, Savanna sat there staring at him and he was astonished to see a tiny flicker of respect in the depths of her gaze.

She lifted a hand and startled him by gently caressing his cheek. "Was it very hard for you when Reina returned you to the earl?"

Delighted with her reaction, Adam caught her hand and kissed her fingertips. A quizzical gleam in his eyes, he said carefully, "Not as hard as convincing you to marry me."

Her face closed up immediately and she glanced away from him. Cursing his impetuousness, Adam rose from the sofa. Loving her as he did, it was all he could do to prevent himself from dragging her into his arms and forcing the response he wanted from her, but, determined to win her heart, he tamped down his baser instincts.

Adopting a casual air, he said easily, "I suspect that you are longing for a bath and then perhaps a nice dinner, served here in our rooms?"

Savanna looked at him gratefully, glad that he had introduced such a mundane topic. She was emotionally exhausted and the thought of a long, luxurious bath, followed by dinner in this elegant setting, was extremely alluring. Smiling shyly at him, she murmured, "That sounds lovely!"

Adam grinned at her and walked over to a corded bellpull. "Madame's wish shall be my command! Especially since the staff of this hotel are noted for their excellence and I have to do nothing but make your desires known to them!"

Adam remained available until everything was in readiness for Savanna's bath; then, casually telling her that he felt like stretching his legs and wandering around the lobby for a while, he departed, leaving Savanna in sole occupancy of the suite. Marveling at how splendidly events were swiftly moving, Savanna wafted dreamily into the large dressing room which adjoined the bedroom and where her bath had been prepared. It wasn't until she was decadently ensconced in the deepest, fullest brass tub of lavender-scented water and frothy bubbles she had ever enjoyed in her life that it dawned on her that Adam was sure to demand intimacy during the coming evening. Thinking of dining alone with her husband in their private set of rooms, and especially of what would happen later, suddenly had her heart beating faster and, to her utter dismay, her nipples and loins fluttering with anticipation.

Seeking escape from the erotic images in her mind, she hastily dunked her head under the water, cursing her vulnerability to him. She forgot to close her eyes or mouth and came up spitting out bubbles and with stinging eyes. That, my girl, she thought crossly as she wiped the soap out of her eyes, is what you get for being such a lascivious little slut!

A few minutes later, her wet hair and body each wrapped in its own towel, she left the dressing room and walked back into the bedroom, intending to find her cleanest and least-crumpled gown to wear for the evening. She stopped in astonishment as her gaze caught the incredibly lovely garments laid out temptingly on the huge bed.

The negligee was the most delicate, feminine concoction she had ever seen in her life. Of the finest-spun gossamer silk, in a shade that rivaled the color of her eyes, with a deep inset of blond Mechlin lace across the bosom, it was undoubtedly a very wicked garment—designed with blatant seduction in mind. Savanna stared at it with longing and trepidation.

Did she dare to put it on? Almost mesmerized by the negligee and the peignoir, she approached the bed in a daze. Wonderingly, her fingers ran over the soft, supple fabric of the peignoir, an equally seductive creation in a darker shade of aquamarine with a narrow gold stripe interwoven in the heavy silken material. A wide ruffle of more blond Mechlin lace flowed around the opening and across the hem of the peignoir, and there was something so delightfully appealing and feminine about the garments that Savanna, accustomed all her life to the plainest, most practical clothing available, suddenly gave in to temptation.

Throwing her towels aside, she slipped the negligee over her head, sighing as the incredibly delicate fabric whispered over her skin. Heedless of her damp hair falling in wild disorder around her face, she raced over to the cheval glass in one corner of the room, her mouth forming a startled O at the sight reflected in the glass. The negligee clung lovingly to every line of her body, every curve, every swell of her lush form clearly outlined, the milky whiteness of her smooth flesh intensified by the rich color of the garment. But it was the placement of the inset that caused her the greatest alarm—her bosom was covered only by a flimsy band of lace, and through the hazy material the tips of her rosy nipples could be glimpsed.

As she stood there confused and undecided, she heard the outer door to the suite open and shut, and with something akin to panic she grabbed the peignoir and slipped it on. If the negligee clung and revealed, the peignoir was voluminous, almost modest, the fabric a heavier, totally opaque silk which completely hid the seductive garment beneath it. Mindful of the disheveled state of her wet hair, wishing bitterly she had not given in to temptation to try on the garments, Savanna nervously pushed the fiery mane back from her face.

At least the peignoir effectively hid the disgraceful negligee and gave her some degree of composure. But only *some* degree. She had always taken her own body for granted, but she was suddenly aware of herself in a way that she had never thought possible. The friction of the negligee against her flesh made her remember the feel of Adam's hands on her body and she shivered, liking the sensation of the silk rubbing next to her sensitive skin far too much.

Hearing the measured footsteps coming toward the bedroom, she froze, her heart beating thunderously in her breast. Embarrassed and uneasy, Savanna faced the doorway, her chin lifted pugnaciously, one hand gripping the neckline of the peignoir tightly together almost as if her life depended upon it.

Adam paused in the doorway, the sight of Savanna standing there as he had imagined her so often in his dreams stunning him. He had partially expected to find his gifts torn to shreds and lying on the floor; that she had been unable to resist the allure of the garments pleased him inordinately. She was utterly adorable as she stood there, half poised for flight, half eager to fight, and Adam was suddenly fiercely glad that she was his wife—no matter what underhanded schemes he'd had to concoct to marry her!

Desire pulsed through him as he stared at her, knowing that under the concealment of the voluminous peignoir she was wearing the oh-so-seductive negligee he had ordered from the modiste. The lace of the peignoir framed her lovely features, caressing the clean lines of her cheek and jaw, the heavy silk falling in graceful lines to the floor, where her bare feet peeped out from underneath the lacy hem. The glow of her red-gold hair was tempered just now by dampness, but here and there the flickering candlelight picked out the gleam of fire in a drying tendril. Even with her hair falling in damp disorder about her slender shoulders, Adam was certain that she had never looked more beautiful or desirable than she did at this moment, and his heart swelled.

They stared at each other wordlessly for a long moment, and then, fighting to act normally when his every instinct cried out to take her in his arms and kiss her passionately, Adam said prosaically, his voice oddly husky, "Ah, I see you found the clothes. I trust that you like them? If you don't, we can always order something else."

Savanna swallowed, grateful that he was making this so easy for her. Her hand caressed the heavy silk and, almost shyly, she admitted, "They are lovely. I—I've never seen anything so l-l-lovely. Thank y-y-you."

Another silence fell. Adam couldn't take his eyes off her, and the desire to make love to her was nearly overpowering, but he was exceedingly aware of the way he had taken her that last time by the pond and he didn't want to repeat it. He wanted desperately to erase that shameful memory from her mind, for her to remember his lovemaking with pleasure. Pouncing on her and ripping the clothes from her body and burying his flesh deep within hers at the first opportunity was not, even he knew, the way to accomplish his aims—despite the urgings and readiness of his body to do just that!

Manfully ignoring the ache in his groin, clearing his throat nervously, Adam finally said, "Well. I'm pleased that you liked them. I shall leave you to complete your toilet. When you are finished, let me know and I shall order up my own bath." Mentally cursing his own inept tongue and knowing that he was babbling like a fool, but unable to stop himself, he went on. "Our meal will not be served for some time yet, so I shall be able to bathe and refresh myself also before it arrives."

Adam had never felt this way before, had never found himself groping for conversation with a woman, and he was as gauche as any youth falling in love for the first time. Gone was his famous address and sophisticated patter, and feeling very much like a backwoods oaf suddenly faced with a queen, he muttered some other inane comment and beat a hasty retreat to the outer room.

Savanna had been too confused by her own conflicting reactions to him to realize that he was not acting in his usual confident manner, but she was unbearably aware that something vital and exciting had left the room with him. He had looked so handsome and dear standing there in the doorway, the unruly black hair curling rakishly near his temples, the blue eyes bright with some undefined emotion as he had stared at her. She had been both thrilled and ashamed that he had found her wearing the negligee and peignoir—one part of her wanting to flaunt her body in front of him, wanting to let the peignoir fall open, giving him a glimpse of her nipples straining against the lace inset, eager as she was to see the flame of desire leap into his gaze; the other part wanting furiously to fling the garments at him and hurl all her pent-up anger and resentment at his high-handed blackmail back into his arrogant face.

But it was too late to throw the clothing at him. Disgusted with her wayward emotions, she walked over to a satinwood dressing table with a matching mirror and, seating herself on the velvet-covered stool in front of it, proceeded to stare glumly at her reflection. What the devil was the matter with her?

Savanna looked away, not seeing the lovely room in which she sat. She knew the answers to her questions. It was all tangled up with the way her mother had loved Davalos and what she had endured for loving the wrong man. There wasn't much that frightened Savanna, but right now she was terrified of being weakened by love, of allowing her love to let her be utterly controlled by a man who had married her only because she was carrying his child.

She sighed and absentmindedly picked up the silver-backed comb and began to bring her rapidly drying hair into some sort of order. Adam was being exceedingly kind to her, she couldn't deny that. Having ruthlessly engineered their wedding for the sake of the child, he could still have been cold and cruel to her, but he hadn't—the very clothes she was wearing and the room she sat in were proof of his kindness and thoughtfulness. She tried desperately to remind herself how *lucky* she was. A bitter smile curved her full mouth. Oh, she was lucky, all right—at least she wouldn't have to endure the hell Davalos had inflicted upon Elizabeth, but wasn't she letting herself in for the same thing by falling love with Adam? Hadn't it been *because* Elizabeth had loved Davalos that he had been able to hurt her so deeply?

Savanna stood up abruptly. Dwelling on the past, brooding over events that she could not change, accomplished nothing—except to make her feel even more dejected and trapped than she already did. Women had faced worse fates than the one that lay before her, and she was just going to have to make the best of things!

A resolute gleam in her eyes, she stared at herself in the mirror. She *would* make the best of things! Shoulders squared, chin lifted proudly, with queenly grace she walked from the bedchamber into the sitting room, the peignoir flowing grandly about her bare feet.

Those bare feet were the first things that Adam noticed and a smile touched his lips. Laughter glittering in his gaze, he looked at her, his expression inviting her to share his amusement as he murmured, "I believe that in the morning we shall have to go shopping for some slippers and perhaps some more items to add to your wardrobe . . . although I must admit that I find the sight of those pink toes of yours vastly appealing."

Savanna glanced down at her toes peeking out from underneath the lacy hem, a smile touching her own mouth. "Good! Because I doubt that my normal footwear would compliment such lovely clothing." The words left her mouth before she'd had time to think about them, and she could have bitten her tongue off. It was bad enough that she had allowed herself to be seduced by the lovely garments, but here she was boldly agreeing to let him buy her other things. Having forced her into marriage because of the child, was Adam now attempting to *buy* her compliance?

Angry with herself and reminding herself grimly that it had only been moments before that she had sworn to make the best of things, Savanna managed, barely, to keep a smile on her face.

Seeking to change the subject, she came further into the room and asked lightly, "Have you ordered your bath?"

"Yes, some minutes ago," Adam answered. "After last night's accommodations, I am looking forward to it."

Even as he finished speaking there was a tap on the door. Adam's bath had arrived. Left alone in the large salon while he disappeared to bathe, Savanna moved restlessly about, wishing that the conflict within herself would abate. She was suddenly dreading the evening ahead of her and she wondered how she was going to endure years of Adam's lovemaking, knowing that it was merely lust that brought him to her bed, that there was no love in his possession of her body. Worse, she admitted bitterly, was that while her heart yearned for love, it didn't matter to her treacherous flesh that he did not love her—all he had to do was reach out and touch her and she was lost, her body turning into liquid fire, rapturous to experience again the sorcery of Adam's possession.

But it *did* matter, Savanna thought desperately. It mattered almost more than anything else in the world to her. . . .

Adam returned refreshed from his bath to find Savanna curled up in one corner of a sofa, her feet tucked under her, her expression grave. A quizzical smile lurked at the corners of his mobile mouth, and seating himself at the other end of the sofa, he asked easily, "Why do you look so? Have you found disfavor with the robe? If you have, throw it away and I shall buy you another that pleases you."

Adam meant to tease her, to bring a smile to her face; he was also a generous man—*his* wife would never want for anything, and knowing the poverty of her childhood, he was looking forward to indulging Savanna and himself in the process. He certainly hadn't expected the reaction he got!

Her face paled at his words, the invidiousness of her position twisting painfully through her. Rather than let him realize how easily he could hurt her, she took refuge in anger, and leaning forward, her eyes blazing, she said, "I am not a child to be pacified with presents! You may have forced me to marry you, but since ours is not a normal marriage, I see no reason for you to be so bloody *generous* with your fortune!"

Adam's jaw tightened, but he said evenly enough, "But you are wrong, my dear. Make no mistake, our marriage will be normal in *all* facets!"

Savanna glared at him, glad of the rage that was coursing through her veins, glad that she could hide her love behind a facade of angry disdain. Rising to her feet, she glanced coolly at him. "Forgive me, but I think it is *you* who has made the mistake!"

Adam surged to his feet, and jerking Savanna into his arms, he kissed her with an angry, urgent passion. Lifting his head, he stared grimly down into her face, his hands tightening on her shoulders. "No, sweetheart, I don't make mistakes, and you have erred badly if you think that I don't intend to avail myself of one of the *few* pleasures of marriage— making love to one's wife!"

Chapter 17

Savanna's gasp of outrage was lost under the hungry onslaught of his demanding mouth, his strong hands pulling her up against his lean body, making her vividly aware of the fact that he was already aroused and ready. She fought him and herself, trying desperately not only to escape from the seductive spell he could weave so effortlessly around her, but to quell the powerful urge to surrender that clamored through her veins at the first touch of his mouth on hers. It was an elemental demand that swept through her, her entire body suddenly electrified by the explicit probing of his tongue and the feel of his warm, hard body crushed against hers, but she fought strenuously against it, seeking furiously to avoid being engulfed by the carnal delight his kiss promised.

Ignoring her frantic attempts to escape, his mouth locked fiercely on hers, Adam swept her up into his arms and strode into the bedchamber. Reaching the gold, silk-covered expanse of the bed, he carelessly tumbled Savanna onto the feather-filled mattress.

She landed in a sprawled heap, the peignoir flying

open to reveal the clinging fabric beneath, and Adam stared at her lush curves as if he had never seen a woman before in his life. She was incredibly lovely as she lay there before him, her red-gold hair wildly cascading down her shoulders, her bosom heaving from her exertions, her pink nipples straining against the filmy lace. His body coiled with increasingly hungry desire and a hard smile curved his mouth. Escape him? *Never!* he thought savagely. She was his! His wife, and before this night was through, he would show her just how thoroughly she was indeed his!

This wasn't how he had planned to take her, but all his good intentions had vanished the instant she had hurled that "not a normal marriage" nonsense in his face. She was his *wife* and he would not be denied the pleasures he had dreamed of these past weeks!

Reading the openly licentious expression on his dark face, Savanna glared at him and scrambled clumsily to the middle of the bed just as he caught one slender ankle in a firm grip. "Let me go!" she cried, kicking viciously in his direction, trying vainly to free her ankle from his unyielding grasp—until she realized that her gown was slipping ever upward and that he was frankly enjoying the nakedness that was being revealed with every move she made. Her teeth clenched together, her aquamarine eyes turbulent with despair and fury, she ground out, "I hate you! Let me *go!"*

There was an oddly dazed look on Adam's face and with an effort he tore his gaze away from the long lengths of silken legs that her struggles had exposed. "Let you go?" he repeated thickly. He shook his dark head slowly. "No. Never!"

They stared at each other, their eyes locked in a silent battle of wills, and with every passing moment Savanna's heart beat faster, a languorous heat spreading steadily through her body, the unwanted fascination he held for her increasing. She was shamefully aware of how she must look, sprawled in erotic disarray on the bed, her gown angling up across her thighs, one hip half exposed, her nipples pushing against the blond lace, and yet it occurred painfully to her that a part of her was glad he found her attractive.

Her eyes fell first and she cried unhappily, "Oh, let me go! I didn't want this marriage and I don't want you!"

A muscle in Adam's jaw leapt and his hand tightened around her ankle. "You will," he said huskily as he began inexorably to drag her toward him. "Believe me, sweetheart, this time, you will."

She glanced at him as he stood there, tall and disturbing in the flickering candlelight, his thick blue-black hair attractively tousled from their struggle, the fine black silk dressing gown he had put on after his bath revealing the width of his broad shoulders. With his handsome features and powerful body, few women would have resisted his advances, and Savanna didn't doubt that he could indeed make her want him. But then she had never doubted his ability to make her forget everything but the dizzying intoxication of his possession; it was the knowledge that there were no deeper, finer feelings involved in his lovemaking that made her fight so strongly against his seductive lure. It was a bitter struggle she waged, not only against him but against herself as well, her own flesh betraying her, her very skin seeming to tingle with hunger for his caress. As she stared at him, to her intense mortification, she was angrily aware of the changes taking place within her, of the liquid fire pooling in her belly, of the throbbing of her nipples and the craving of her lips for more of his demanding kisses.

Inch by inch, Adam pulled her to him, his eyes locked on hers, daring her to deny the attraction that lay between them, daring her to deny him the pleasures he could give them both. It was the movement

of the silken gown that finally broke their silent battle of wills, Adam unable to keep his gaze from the
pale limbs that had haunted his dreams. With a sensuous appreciation, his eyes roamed over the voluptuous charms that lay before him, the sweet ache
between his legs becoming more urgent and pronounced with every passing second.

Savanna was utter masculine temptation as she lay
there on the gold coverlet, the curling mane of fire-
kissed hair spread out like a river of flame, the aquamarine gown bright against the alabaster smoothness
of her skin. Her eyes were brilliant, with all the conflicting emotions that raged inside her, her cheeks
flushed, her mouth a half-parted rosy invitation, and
Adam's eyes rested a long time on those unknowingly provocative lips before his gaze slid compulsively down the wondrous charms of her tall shape.
The gown had slipped upward at an angle, baring
just enough of her flesh to tease him with images of
the soft curves that still lay hidden. One full breast
was partially uncovered, the nipple hidden beneath
the silky fabric; half her rib cage and part of her
stomach and hip were bare, and at the junction of her
naked thighs, a few light red-gold curls were tantalizingly revealed before his eyes traveled down the
long, lovely length of her legs.

Savanna knew she should do something, that she
should not simply lie here so complaisantly and allow him to look his fill, but a strange languor seemed
to hold her motionless on the bed. She felt weak, unable to move, as if she were melting under Adam's
look, and desire, insidious and irresistible, spiraled
slowly through her body. The knowledge that he was
her husband, that together they had made a child,
that, willingly or not, she loved him, mingled with
that wanton, perfidious desire and she was unhappily aware that she was struggling against forces far
stronger than she was . . . or than he was. She wanted
him, every nerve and fiber of her being calling out to

him, and suddenly the urge to fight against the fundamental demands of her own flesh vanished and she was left helplessly adrift in a sea of hungry yearning.

The sensuous drift of Adam's fingers up her leg sent a shiver of delight through her body and she glanced downward, his hand appearing very dark against the whiteness of her skin. Mesmerized, she watched as his head appeared and he pressed a shockingly ardent kiss near the top of one thigh. She jumped, startled by the frankly erotic feelings that coursed through her at his actions, and Adam looked up at her, the wicked gleam in his sapphire-blue eyes making her pulse leap.

"We have," he said thickly, "a long night ahead of us, with much to learn . . . and enjoy."

She wanted passionately to refute his words, but she could not, and while she made no move to escape him, she had to offer one last protest. Bleakly, she muttered, "I don't want . . ."

"Don't want me to do this?" he asked mockingly, his mouth sliding seductively across her skin. Dropping hot, stinging little kisses on her soft body, his lips traveled ever upward, following the line of the fabric across her trembling thighs, making her jerk when his questing mouth brushed faintly against the tight curls at the V of her thighs before continuing across her stomach and rib cage. Gently nuzzling her breast, he murmured indistinctly, "Or this?" Through the fabric his teeth found her swollen nipple and teasingly he toyed with it, his ministrations making Savanna arch up, burning for him to take it fully into his mouth.

He deliberately denied them both what they wanted, but by the time his seeking mouth found hers, Savanna was one long ache of unfulfilled desire. She met his kiss recklessly, the battle against him lost long ago, perhaps from the moment she had first laid eyes on him, and her lips parted easily as his tongue surged into her mouth.

Inflamed by her response, Adam crushed her beneath him, his tall, muscled body joining hers on the bed, his hands holding her face to his as he drank deeply from the honey of her mouth. His robe was half open and their naked legs tangled as they lay there kissing each other with unrestrained passion. The sensation of her soft limbs rubbing against his was unbearably tantalizing, but he was impatient with even the slightest barrier between them, and with a soft curse he left her lips long enough to struggle out of the confines of his robe. Lowering himself once more, he pressed a series of brief kisses along her earlobe and jawline, his hands ruthlessly removing the enticing garments she had put on earlier. It was only when she lay before him in naked splendor, a lushly curved alabaster figure illuminated by the fiery glow of the red-gold hair on her head and between her legs and the swollen rosy nipples of her bosom, that Adam was satisfied. Carelessly tossing the clothing onto the floor to join his robe, he stared reverently at her naked exquisiteness, his gaze lingering on her still-flat belly.

Astonishing both of them, he suddenly dropped a tender kiss where their babe grew within her. "My child," he murmured, an odd note of wonder and awe in his voice, as if the reality had just now dawned on him.

It was that kiss and the undisguised hint of wonder in his voice that were Savanna's final undoing, and when he came down beside her on the bed, she went ardently into his powerful embrace. He might not love her, but he cared about the child and she would try to be content. His hand cupped her breast and Savanna shuddered at the longing that went through her, and as his mouth closed urgently over hers, she reminded herself dizzily that whatever difficulties lay before them, at least they had *this!*

Adam's thoughts, when he could think at all, were remarkably similar to Savanna's, but the heady enchantment of her drove coherent thoughts out of his brain. She was fire and silk in his arms and she smelled deliciously of lavender and tasted of honey and he simply could not get enough of her, his mouth and hands moving feverishly over her supple flesh. She was everything he wanted in a woman, everything, he realized dimly, that he would *ever* want; this knowledge made the aching desire that hummed through his taut body all the more intense because she *was* the only woman for him and he loved her as he had never dreamed to love any woman.

Oblivious of everything but Adam's increasingly arousing lovemaking, Savanna was delightedly learning the contours and planes of his magnificent body. Wonderingly her hands roamed over him, across the broad shoulders, down the steel-hewn sinews of his back and the hard curve of his buttocks. It was exciting to touch him this way, to feel his big body tremble beneath her wandering hands and to know that she was giving him pleasure, that she was wantonly fueling the fire that was already within him, within them both. . . .

His mouth was sweet fire at her breast, the scrape of his teeth across her distended nipples causing her belly to clench in yearning anticipation, and she moved restlessly against him, moaning softly when his hand slid sensually down her body and his knowing fingers sought the red-gold curls between her legs. He toyed with her, lightly rubbing, slowly exploring the soft flesh he found, driving her half mad for him to deepen the movements. Her breathing became labored and she moaned in frustration, but the sensations he aroused by those intensely intimate caresses were still too new, too frighteningly rousing, for her to accept casually, and at the first thrust of his finger inside her, she reared up, both seeking and rejecting his exploration.

"Gently, gently, my sweet," Adam breathed raggedly against her mouth, never stopping the motions that had her nails digging into his shoulders and her body twisting with rising delirium beneath his ministrations. He smiled down into her passion-flushed face and murmured, "Don't fight me, sweetheart. Let me teach you, let me show you just how much pleasure a man can give a woman."

He wasn't asking, he was telling, and Savanna's arms closed tightly around him as his plundering mouth found hers once more. He kissed her with barely leashed violence, the demands of his own body making it increasingly difficult to restrain his instincts. But he denied himself, wanting to please Savanna, wanting her to experience all the erotic delights he had promised himself he would lavish upon her.

Utterly dominated by the pleas of her clamoring flesh, Savanna was his willing captive, his kisses and caresses destroying rational thought and normal inhibitions, and she felt only the frankly lascivious sensations streaking through her agitated body. He kissed her many times, half-savage, demanding kisses that left her yearning for more when his mouth finally left hers and slid like fire down her breast to suckle briefly before continuing ever downward across her belly and lower. . . .

The shifting of his body as he moved between her thighs only slightly disturbed the sensuous trap Adam had created, but when his lips and tongue replaced his hand as he nuzzled the red-gold curls he found there, Savanna gasped with shocked, shameful pleasure and she froze, hardly able to believe what he was doing to her. Her stunned eyes met the hard glitter in his and Adam muttered thickly, "You are very beautiful to me—I want, no, *need*, to taste and explore every inch of you."

Mercilessly gripped by desire, Savanna couldn't have stopped him even if she had wanted to, and when he pushed her legs farther apart and bent his head to flick the tender flesh with his tongue, she shuddered with intense pleasure and went weak at the sensations he was evoking. The sucking and stroking of his mouth was nearly unbearable, the movements making her twist and arch upward, a fierce excitement coiling in her belly. Helplessly, her hands clenched into his dark hair, wanting to touch him, to caress him and share with him the incredible feelings that were racking her body. She was on fire, her breasts aching, her mouth hungry for him, but she was held fiercely enthralled by what he was doing to her, writhing frantically beneath the lash of his tongue.

Savanna's uninhibited response only added to Adam's own growing excitement and he feasted even more hungrily upon her, eager to drive her over the edge and feel her convulse beneath him. He sensed that she was very near, the almost painful ache between his own legs reminding him vividly of how very close he was himself, and the urge to plunge into her welcoming sheath was almost more than he could bear. With desperate vigor his hands cupped her buttocks and he held her thrashing body against the hot questing of his tongue.

Suddenly Savanna stiffened and a soft, choked cry escaped her as wave after wave of exquisite pleasure exploded through her body. One moment she was fiercely buffeted by the sweet violence of her release and the next she was floating, drifting, her limbs weightless, her body sated. The world had spun away and when reality returned, there was only Adam, Adam holding her, Adam gently murmuring shockingly sensuous promises in her ear. . . .

As the minutes passed and she became more and more aware of her surroundings, Savanna's entire body still seemed to tingle with tiny aftershocks of pleasure, and she was both embarrassed and stunned by the force of the ecstasy that had shaken her. She was stingingly aware of Adam's warm body pressed to hers, and her thoughts were filled with the wickedly wondrous things he had done to her. But it gradually dawned on her, once her breathing had returned to normal and the last faint ripple of pleasure had disappeared, that while she had reached the pinnacle, Adam had been denied it. She could hardly ignore proof of that as she lay cradled in his strong arms, his lips caressing her hair, her cheek resting against his hard chest while the rigid length of his swollen manhood lay like a burning brand against her thigh!

She glanced up at him, her gaze noting the hard line of his chin and jaw, and involuntarily she reached up and gently explored the chiseled planes of his face. At her touch, Adam bent his head, and nipping her fingers slightly, he murmured, "Come back down to earth, have we?"

Her eyes met his dark blue ones and, a beguiling blush on her lovely face, she smiled shyly. "I think so . . . but you never left, did you?"

He grinned crookedly. "You *do* intend to let me do something about that, don't you?" he asked softly, his lips brushing her temple.

To her astonishment, Savanna felt a quiver deep inside her at his words. She still wanted him, she realized with amazement, she wanted that hard body of his to possess her fully, and even as she acknowledged that thought, her nipples began to tighten and desire began to rapidly replace her contentment. Stretching languidly, a surprisingly sensual invitation gleaming in the depths of her aquamarine eyes, she looked at him, her smile full of promise. "Oh, I imagine," she said mockingly, "that there is something I could *let* you do!"

With a soft growl, Adam caught her to him, his mouth crushing hers, one hand reaching for her soft breast. Mindlessly she responded to the fierce demands he made upon her, her body flaming into life at his touch.

Despite the almost frantic urge to join their bodies, Adam held back, ensuring that Savanna was once more an untamed wanton before he finally gave them both the relief they sought. With a half-savage groan of entreaty, he buried himself in her silken heat, and, their bodies meeting and parting in a blatantly carnal tempo, together they found paradise.

And during the long night that followed, Savanna learned that there were several things that a woman would let a man do to her—particularly when the man was her husband and she loved him . . . and he very generously invited her to use his own body as she willed. It was a heady experience and Savanna took full advantage of it, her mouth and hands learning every inch of his lean physique, thoroughly entranced that she could make him writhe and tremble beneath her own inexperienced caresses. Adam would bear the torture of her sensual demands of him until, driven beyond control, he would lose himself again and again in her soft heat.

The first pale streaks of dawn were gliding into the room and she was sweetly exhausted when Adam had slaked the worst of his seemingly boundless craving for her and allowed them both to sleep. After all they had shared, it seemed the most natural thing in the world to sleep naked in his strong arms, his powerful body curved protectively next to hers, his lips buried in the red-gold mane of her hair.

She had no idea how long she slept, but when she awoke, Adam was gone and she was alone in the big bed. She lay there for several seconds, gazing blindly at the gold silk bed-curtains, images of the night just passed flickering through her mind. Uneasily she wondered how she was going to face him in the unsparing light of day or try to deny that in his arms she became another person, a wanton, passionate creature who had eagerly followed wherever he had led.

One thing was patently clear, though. Despite last night, nothing had changed between them—the only reason for their hasty marriage was growing in her womb. There had been no word of love between them, and in spite of the pleasure he had given her body, there was a deepening ache in the region of her heart. Burying her head in the pillows, she groaned. Without love, last night suddenly seemed sordid and tawdry and she wondered bleakly how she was going to regain all the ground she had lost by the treachery of her very own flesh. She could not blame him for what had happened last night—after her initial resistance, she had been a willing convert to all the carnal joys he had revealed. If only, she thought grimly, I could hate him! Convince myself that he is totally despicable—convince my body to tremble with disgust, *not* with delight, when he touches me!

Eager to escape the demons in her brain, Savanna sat up quickly and dragged aside the bed hangings. Bright sunlight flooding the room made her blink and realize that the hour was very late. Finding the lovely gold-striped wrapper where Adam had tossed it last night, Savanna draped it around her and scooted gingerly from the bed. The room was empty, but she spied a piece of paper propped conspicuously on her dressing table.

Crossing the room, she lifted it and read Adam's bold scrawl. It seemed that he had some business to see about and would return soon. In the meantime, he had made arrangements for her bath and breakfast. All she had to do was touch the bellpull and her wishes would be immediately gratified.

Half smiling, trying very hard not to be warmed by his thoughtfulness, she did as he had directed and alerted the staff that she was now up and ready for their services. While waiting for the bath to arrive, she walked over to the tall satinwood wardrobe, where she had placed her clothing last night, and opening one of the doors, she gloomily surveyed the contents.

Savanna had never possessed an extensive wardrobe, but then, what she had worn had never mattered very much to her . . . until now. Despite telling herself weakly that last night changed nothing between them, she couldn't deny that she would have liked to have something fashionable and stylish to wear. Viewing with a jaundiced eye the meager selection in front of her, she finally chose a serviceable, full-skirted gown of pale-green-striped gingham, the square neck and bodice trimmed with a dark green ribbon.

She enjoyed her bath thoroughly, just as enthralled this morning with the lavender-scented bubbles as she had been the previous night. Feeling vibrant and stingingly alive, she eventually left her bath and dressed hurriedly in the striped gingham gown before reentering the bedchamber. She barely took a step into the room before the tantalizing aroma of coffee teased her nostrils, and glancing around, she instantly noticed a tray of food and drink that had been placed on one of the marble-topped tables near the bed.

A silver pot of steaming hot café au lait, a small crystal dish of glazed strawberries and beignets, still warm and fragrant, dusted with delicately powdered sugar, lay before her. Breathing in the delicious scents, she took a bite of the square beignet, the yeasty flavor of the fried dough melting on her tongue. Smiling, she took the tray out onto the small balcony of the bedchamber and there in the summer sunlight, seated at the small table and chair she discovered there, enjoyed her breakfast.

With her breakfast finished, Savanna wandered back inside and after sitting down at the dressing table, with nimble fingers she swiftly fashioned her rebellious hair into two braids, which she twisted around her head in a coronet. Standing before the cheval glass, she surveyed herself, her lips twisting. She looked ... presentable, she finally decided with brutal honesty. Her hair was neat, her gown clean and not *un*attractive, and she was just going to have to be content. Besides, she reminded herself miserably, have you forgotten that you're supposed to be angry with Adam? That he forced you into a loveless marriage and that no matter what physical pleasure you shared with him last night, it changes *nothing*? You're merely his broodmare and don't forget it! Be *glad* you have nothing more fetching than this old gown! That the dark green ribbon which trimmed the neckline of her gown formed a charming frame for her vivid loveliness, the severity of her hairstyle only making the sculpted perfection of her features more pronounced, didn't occur to her, nor did the fact that, while her gown was not in the first stare of fashion, it looked *very* attractive on her tall, lush form, the full skirts swinging gently with every step she took.

Uneasy and restless, her emotions veering wildly first one way and then another, Savanna left the bedchamber and walked into the main salon. She was just starting to wonder how long Adam would be gone when he strolled in.

Savanna's heart gave a silly little leap at the sight of him, his handsome face dark and vital above the starched white cravat, the dark blue jacket fitting his broad shoulders so superbly, the long length of his powerful legs outlined by the yellow nankeen pantaloons he was wearing. Oddly shy with him, considering the night that had just passed, she felt her cheeks suddenly burn as *precise* memories of what they had done to each other flooded her brain, and she rushed into speech. "G-g-good morning! D-d-did you complete y-y-your business?"

Adam grinned at her and, sweeping her into his embrace, kissed her soundly. His lips warm against hers, he murmured, "Indeed I did! I can only hope that you will be pleased with the results."

Her mouth throbbing from his kiss, Savanna stared at him. "Me? What do I have to do with your business?"

Adam only smiled and looked mysterious. "Have you eaten?" he asked. When Savanna nodded, he said merrily, "Excellent! Now come with me; there are some places I want to show you."

Reluctantly Savanna allowed him to usher her out of their rooms. She felt oddly ill at ease, thinking she should not be enjoying his company quite so much, nor that she should fall in with his plans so effortlessly; thinking that if she were wise, she should try to explain to him why she didn't want what had happened last night to happen again. . . .

Savanna would have been hard-pressed to explain the turmoil inside her at that moment, but she perceived uneasily that, despite the bitter fact that she loved him, Adam *had* to be made to see reason, had to be forced to realize that while she would bear his child, she couldn't share his bed. Pride would not let her. She couldn't bear to continue to be subjected to those stunning intimacies, knowing that he didn't love her . . . that it was only lust, lust that any woman could satisfy.

The sudden stiffening of Adam's body instantly distracted her and she glanced at him. His expression gave nothing away, but something was wrong. As they reached the bottom of the staircase and stepped onto the tile floor of the cream-and-gold foyer of the hotel, Savanna immediately noticed the couple bearing down on them, but for the life of her couldn't understand why the sight of them had made Adam so tense. Unless he was ashamed of her and didn't want to introduce her to his friends. . . .

The woman was lovely. Garbed in the first rank of fashion, she was small, blond, winsomely curved and with a pouting beauty that turned more than one head. As they approached, it was apparent that the attractive, fair-haired man at her side was a relative, their facial features similar, although the man's handsomeness was not as eye-catching as the woman's beauty. The gentleman, too, was dressed impeccably, his dark green coat as superbly tailored as Adam's, his cravat as blindingly white and his boots as highly polished.

Paying not the least heed to Savanna, the woman drifted up to Adam, and tapping him playfully on the arm with her ivory-and-lace fan, she said gaily, "Oh, Adam! Here you are! Someone said that you were going to be visiting in this area, but I never *dreamed* that we would actually run into you this way! Charles and I have left Natchez and are on our way to stay with the Michauds at their plantation, Oak Shadows, on Bayou Tchoupitoulas." She smiled archly at him. "Perhaps you might come to call. . . ."

Politely, but barely that, Adam replied, "Hello, Miss Asher—what a surprise to see you here in New Orleans." He nodded to the man at her side and added, "And you, Asher."

Charles Asher, apparently no happier to see Adam than Adam was to see them, said stiffly, "Pleasure. Are you here for very long?"

"No. Merely a few days." Manners dictated that he introduce Savanna, and wishing Betsey Asher and her brother to the devil, Adam said coolly, "Allow me to introduce my wife, Savanna St. Clair. Savanna, this is Miss Betsey Asher and her brother, Mr. Charles Asher."

The effect on Betsey was stunning. She went white, her mouth almost falling open, while Charles looked extremely satisfied.

"*Your wife!*" Betsey ejaculated in an ugly, shocked tone. "You must be jesting!"

Adam smiled grimly and fairly dragged Savanna away from them. "No, I assure you, I am not," he said icily. "Excuse us, we have an appointment."

With malevolent, narrowed green eyes, Betsey watched them stride away. It was only Charles's insistent tug on her arm that broke her stare. Under his breath he hissed, "There is nothing you can do. He is married! You will just have to set your cap for someone else."

Betsey's mouth thinned and something dangerous moved in her green eyes. "Don't tell me what to do! Wife or not, I still intend to have Adam St. Clair as *my* husband!" she said in a voice shaking with rage. Full of malice, she stared at Savanna's disappearing form and added viciously, "I don't know where *she* came from or what hold she has on him, but I'll wager this sudden marriage—and it has to have been sudden—is no love match! I want him and *nothing*, not even a *current* wife, is going to stop me!"

Part 4

Treachery and Triumph

*If you remember'st not the slightest
folly
That ever love did make thee run into,
Thou hast not lov'd.*

AS YOU LIKE IT
William Shakespeare

Chapter 18

Charles Asher bit back a furious oath, but mindful where they were, he kept his temper under control. Smiling through gritted teeth, he said, "If you don't mind, sweet sister, I would prefer to discuss this in a much less public place!"

Betsey shrugged her shoulders, but she followed his lead and kept a pleasant expression on her face as they mounted the stairs and made for their rooms in the hotel. They had arrived in the city only two days previously, and since New Orleans at this time of year was notoriously bereft of society, all the planters busy on their estates and everyone else avoiding the city to escape the heat and the seasonal fevers, the Ashers had found themselves somewhat bored. That, of course, would change once they arrived at Oak Shadows, where Charles had high hopes that Betsey could charm a proposal out of the Michaud heir, Pierre. The Ashers had only recently met the Michauds, mother and son, when they had come to visit a distant elderly relative in Natchez, in May. It had been apparent almost immediately that Pierre was greatly smitten with Betsey, and since Pierre so neatly fitted his requirements, Charles had graciously accepted the young man's excited invitation that the Ashers come for an extended visit at his home, Oak Shadows, in the fall.

The door to their connecting rooms had barely shut behind them before Betsey hurled the lovely ivory-and-lace fan onto the floor, and, her beautiful face contorted with rage, she snarled, "*Married!* I cannot believe it! Especially since the bastard wouldn't marry *me!*"

Well used to Betsey's rages and vanity, Charles wisely made no comment, but let her storm around the room, waiting for the worst of her fury to abate. Only after she had hurled a crystal decanter against the wall, kicked over a dainty inlaid mahogany table and viciously flung all the satin pillows from her bed onto the floor did she gain some semblance of control.

Bosom heaving, she faced her brother and snapped, "I know you never wanted me to marry him, and though he may not suit your needs, he suits me just fine. I want *him!* Pierre is just a boy—he doesn't even begin to compare to Adam St. Clair!"

"That may be, but while Adam may satisfy you in bed," Charles said nastily, "I doubt that he would tamely allow you to plant horns on his head or turn a blind eye while I played ducks and drakes with his fortune!"

"Well, it's your own fault! You were the one who gambled away our fortune. I'm just glad Mama and Papa aren't alive to see what straits you have reduced us to!"

There was nothing Charles could say to her angry statement—he *had* done precisely that, gambled away the impressive fortune that had been left to him by his father. No one, not even their sister, Susan, realized just how desperate their situation had been when her invitation had so providentially arrived.

The house, the plantation, Charles's fortune and even Betsey's inheritance, which had been under his control, had gone to pay Charles's enormous gambling debts in Virginia. Susan's invitation had been a godsend; though Betsey had always been courted, once there were whispers about Charles's huge losses, suddenly the majority of Betsey's suitors simply melted away. Of those who were left, few had a fortune large enough to satisfy Charles.

Betsey had been furious when the full extent of the disaster had been borne upon her, but if she loved anyone, other than herself, it was her brother, and eventually he made her see a way out of their dilemma—her marriage to an *indulgent*, wealthy gentleman. And it had to be Betsey who did the marrying—just as her suitors had disappeared as word had gradually spread through their friends and neighbors, so had Charles's prospects for a suitable match disappeared. A gentleman intent upon marrying Betsey wouldn't want to appear overly mercenary by inquiring too deeply about her supposed fortune, and while news of the disaster hadn't traveled beyond their home ground, even if Charles was fortunate enough to find an heiress to accept his hand, it was highly unlikely that the marriage would take place without a close scrutiny of *his* finances. Which would be fatal!

Adam St. Clair had been the perfect match for Betsey in many ways, but though she had clamored to marry him, Charles had been adamantly against it. It hadn't taken him more than one meeting with that young man to make him realize that, while easygoing, St. Clair was not a man who would turn a blind eye to Betsey's philandering, nor would he be willing to saddle himself with an extremely expensive brother-in-law! The two Ashers had fought bitterly over it, and Charles had breathed a sigh of relief when Adam had gone to visit his sister and her family.

That he was now married pleased Charles inordinately, especially since a young man who *did* fit all their requirements had appeared on the scene. The only child of a doting widowed mother, Pierre was a handsome, carefree youth, just twenty-three years old, and more important, he was convinced that Betsey was an angel. Not only was he thoroughly bedazzled by her, but both he and his mother had found Charles utterly engaging. These past weeks, while Betsey had kept Pierre in a state of abject adoration, Charles had easily disarmed Madame Michaud by his charming manner and was already stepping into his role of helpful advisor. It was perfect!

A scowl marred Charles's too-handsome features. Provided Betsey didn't allow her fascination for Adam St. Clair to ruin everything! he added to himself.

"It doesn't matter," Charles said dismissingly, "how we come to be in this situation—we *are* in it and the solution is for you to forget Adam St. Clair and concentrate on Pierre Michaud!"

"I don't want Pierre! He's a mere boy! I *want* Adam!"

Charles slapped her. Hard. His face dark with rage, he promised savagely, "Whistle Pierre down the wind, Betsey, and I'll make life so miserable for you, you'll wish you'd died!"

Nursing her stinging cheek, Betsey threw him a vicious look. "Don't threaten me! There are things I could tell about you, don't forget!"

Controlling himself with an effort, Charles said tightly, "I could say the same, my dear! We can ruin each other . . . or we can, as we have always done, join forces. The choice is up to you."

A beguiling smile on her mouth, she said lightly, "Oh, Charles! We're fighting again! Come, let us talk of something more pleasant. Do we have to leave this afternoon for Oak Shadows?" Tugging on his sleeve like a child, she asked sweetly, "Couldn't we stay just one more night here in New Orleans and leave tomorrow afternoon instead?"

Charles stared at her suspiciously, well aware that Betsey was quite capable of pretending one thing when intent upon another, and while he would have preferred to put as many miles as possible between her and Adam St. Clair, he also saw no reason to cause more dissension between them. Besides, what harm could she possibly cause in twenty-four hours?

Betsey herself didn't quite know what she was going to do; she only knew that she wasn't going to let *any* opportunity pass, and since burying herself at Oak Shadows, for who knew how long, wouldn't allow her to forward her own plans for Adam's future, she was desperate for any chance. One more night just might present her with a heaven-sent opportunity to set the St. Clairs at each other's throats. Betsey smiled.

Her smile might have been even wider if she had known that her mere presence was already causing trouble between Adam and his wife. Convinced that Adam had been ashamed of her, hence his quick departure from the vicinity of his friends, Savanna lost whatever pleasure she might have taken from the day. Adam's actions had only confirmed her worst fears, but she was determined not to let herself be beaten so easily. Pride kept her walking gracefully at his side, her chin lifted regally, her back straight, her shoulders squared. But if she was hurt by his actions, she was also very angry, and there was a decided edge to her voice when she replied to Adam's suggestion that they stroll to the French Market. Keeping her gaze directly in front of her as they stepped onto the banquette, she said tightly, "I'm surprised you chose such a public place. Aren't you afraid that you might run into someone else you know and have to introduce me to them?"

That Savanna might feel uncertain about plunging

into his world had never crossed Adam's mind and it didn't now—he was still angry at Betsey's blatant maneuvers. Even if they weren't just married, and under less than the best circumstances, Betsey Asher was the *last* woman he'd want to introduce Savanna to! Cursing Betsey's presence and concentrating on ways to avoid crossing her path during the remaining hours she would be in New Orleans, Adam didn't pay as close attention to Savanna's words and tone of voice as he might have done normally. Smiling, he replied heartily, "Oh, I don't think we'll meet anyone I know—no one ventures into the city this time of year. We'll have it all to ourselves!"

Unaware that he had inflicted further hurt, Adam hustled her along the banquettes in the direction of the French Market. Usually Savanna would have enjoyed a stroll through the raucous, vivid, bustling market, but not today. Her thoughts were turned inward and she was only vaguely aware of the multitude of languages that assaulted the air. French, Spanish, Indian, English, American and even German could be heard as shopkeepers and customers haggled amiably over the abundant selections for which the market was already famous. Live poultry, tied in threes by the legs, quails, freshly caught fish, shrimp and crabs lined the front of the stalls in one section of the huge market hall; in another, an appetizing selection of produce lay ready for purchase—peas, beetroots, tomatoes, Indian corn, ginger, dewberries and artichokes. It was a colorful, shifting crowd—quadroons garbed in lovely scarlet-and-yellow gowns; slaves in drab clothing; half-naked, filthy Indians. A few gentlemen in dark blue and their ladies in pastel-hued frocks drifted around, and through it all, moving with a quick grace, black women offered bouquets of roses, violets, Spanish jassamine and carnations for sale. But Savanna hardly noticed any of it, and when Adam, with a little frown at her air of distraction, guided her away from the bustle and urged her steps in the direction of a discreet little shop on Chartres Street, she went without demur.

She puzzled him, instinct telling him that something was wrong, but he couldn't figure out what! Hadn't last night proved anything to her? She'd been warm and pliant in his arms and he knew that he had brought her pleasure, just as she had brought him untold ecstasy. So what was wrong? Surely she still wasn't angry with his high-handed actions in forcing her to marry him? His frown increasing, Adam suddenly realized that if their positions had been reversed and *he* had been the one compelled to marry her, perhaps he wouldn't be precisely in a cheery mood either. He'd have been furious! And bitter. And resentful.

Uneasily he eyed Savanna's closed expression. She didn't look furious, or bitter, or resentful, but somehow that didn't make him feel any better, and he realized belatedly that last night hadn't really proved anything—except that he could make her want him and that he could give her pleasure. By the time they entered the little shop of Chartres Street, Adam was scowling blackly, and considering the way he had dragged her away from first the Ashers and then the French Market, Savanna was thoroughly convinced that he did not want to be seen with her. He was, she decided miserably, ashamed of her and already regretting that he had married her. When she discovered the purpose of this visit to Chartres Street, it only confirmed everything that she was feeling.

A breathtaking, dazzling array of beautiful, luxurious materials and patterns were laid out for her inspection by the owner of the shop, Madame Galland, well known for her excellent needlework and flair for color and style. Small and dark, her black hair caught neatly in a chignon at the back of her head, Madame Galland waved Adam and Savanna to the comfortable settee covered in pale rose silk damask. If Madame noticed that her clients seemed unusually dour and silent, she kept it to herself and began to display the nearly finished garments that Adam had ordered from her when he had first arrived in New Orleans.

Smiling, her liquid brown eyes alert and friendly, Madame Galland draped a charming pelisse of Prussian blue silk across Savanna's lap and murmured, "If Madame would like to try it on, I can make any adjustments that might be necessary, *oui?* I have several other garments that are almost ready—they only need your approval and perhaps a petite tuck here and there to make them fit perfectly." Running an expert eye over Savanna's voluptuous curves, she added lightly, "Monsieur was quite specific in his measurements, and except for very minor changes, I believe that you will be pleased with these initial garments."

Savanna remembered little of the visit to Madame Galland's. She knew that Madame had led her to a small fitting room and efficiently whisked on and off her what seemed like innumerable gowns and shifts and various other pieces of feminine apparel. Afterward a grim-faced Adam had helped in the selection of more items and patterns and fabrics and trimmings to go with the fabulous wardrobe Savanna was acquiring, but through it all, she was only half aware of what was going on around her. She was dying inside. Every lovely garment, every wisp of lace, every expensive trifle added to the growing heap before her made Savanna cringe and cruelly emphasized the vast gulf that lay between her pleasant little gingham gown and the fashionable, luxurious garments that Adam was buying for her.

The trip to Madame Galland's seemed to sum up the fathomless chasm that lay between them and intensified all of Savanna's fears. That Adam's good humor had disappeared only added to her despair, and it stiffened her resolve to make him understand that while she would bear his child and try to be a dutiful wife, it would be folly for them to even pretend that theirs would be a normal marriage, and that meant *no* repeats of last night!

After making arrangements for some of the finished garments to be delivered that afternoon, with the air of constraint almost tangible between them, they left Madame Galland's and returned to the hotel. There was little conversation between them, each one busy with his own decidedly unpleasant thoughts, but once they had reached their rooms, Savanna said stiffly, "I suppose I should thank you for all the things you are buying for me."

Angry and baffled by the situation in which he found himself—who would have ever thought that he would fall in love with a woman who didn't care a farthing for him?—Adam stared grimly at her. A mocking twist to his mobile mouth, he murmured, "*Should?* Most women would be over the clouds if their husbands were as generous." His gaze narrowed. "But then you're not like most women, are you?"

"No," Savanna replied sharply, further mortified that he seemed to think he could *buy* her good graces. "And ours is hardly a marriage that *most* people embark upon!" After the humiliating morning she had spent, determined to make the situation clear, she went on bitterly. "I have no choice but to bear your child and carry your name—you made certain of that—but I will not be used simply to satisfy your lusts . . . and from now on, I *insist* upon my own bedchamber and privacy."

Adam's face went white, a muscle jerking in his cheek. For her to dismiss so cavalierly what they had shared last night hurt him more deeply than he had thought anything ever could, and he reacted with Adam-like predictability. Mouth tight, he grasped her arm and gave her an ungentle shake. "Lusts?" he snarled softly. "Is that all it was for you last night? Simply lust?"

Savanna could not meet his furious gaze. Telling

herself this was necessary, she turned her head away from those piercing blue eyes and remained stubbornly silent.

Adam stared at her averted profile for a long minute and then anguished rage got the better of him. "Very well, madame!" he snapped in an icy voice. "You have made your wishes clear! And since I am to be denied my marriage bed, you will excuse me if I go and find some other, more amiable woman with whom to slake my *lusts!*" Contemptuously flinging her aside, he slammed out of the room, the door banging shut behind his tall form with a thunderous crash.

Savanna stared in mute misery at the closed door. It was for the best, she reminded herself valiantly. After all, they came from two different worlds, and it had been obvious this morning that he had been ashamed to publicly acknowledge her as his wife and had even found disfavor with the very clothes she wore. Dispiritedly she wandered over to the sofa, telling herself not to let his actions distress her—it would only have been a matter of time before he sought other women anyway. She was *really* better off that they had gotten things straightened out right at the beginning! Oh, but it hurt, she thought piteously. It hurt almost unbearably.

Sinking down onto the sofa, she stared blindly around the room, tears sliding unheeded down her face as she wondered how she was going to survive the terrible, empty years that stretched out before her. How long she sat there, the tears drying on her cheeks, she had no idea, but suddenly it dawned on her that someone was knocking on the door.

Hastily wiping away any telltale signs of her pain, she hurried to the door and opened it. Betsey Asher, a sweetly anxious smile on her face, stood there staring back at her.

Betsey was a vision. Her gleaming blond curls peeped attractively out from the charming chip straw hat she wore, an enormous bow of deep lavender silk tied beneath her chin. She was wearing a lovely high-waisted gown of finest muslin in a shade of pale lavender with little puff sleeves. Pristine white gloves were on her small hands and she carried a most fashionable reticule. Painfully aware of her height and the shabbiness of her gown, Savanna felt like a huge lump of coal.

"Oh, I know this is *most* forward of me," Betsey cooed with soft sincerity, "but since my time in the city will be *so* limited, I did want to call on you before we left for Oak Shadows and offer my congratulations on your marriage." Beaming up at Savanna's dumbstruck features, she went on gaily. "I saw Adam leave, and knowing you would be here alone, I was wondering if perhaps you might like to join me for a glass of lemonade in that darling little tearoom downstairs."

Stunned by Betsey's presence and invitation, Savanna merely stared at her for a long second, her thoughts churning wildly through her head. Visiting with Miss Asher was the last thing that Savanna wanted to do—Betsey's elegant garb and genteel air painfully driving home to her the great differences that lay between them. And coming as the invitation did on the heels of the morning she had just spent and the ugly exchange with Adam, Savanna was hard-pressed not to have a case of screaming hysterics. But what had happened wasn't Miss Asher's fault, Savanna reminded herself fairly, and it really was very nice of the young lady to be so thoughtful. Forcing herself to put away her misery for the time being, a tentative smile on her lips, Savanna finally said with blunt honesty, "I appreciate your invitation, but unfortunately, Adam didn't leave me any money—I could not pay for my lemonade."

Betsey gave a tinkling laugh. "Oh, don't let that stop you! It will be my treat! Next time you shall pay! Come, now, I do *so* want to talk to you!"

Reluctantly Savanna let herself be charmed by Betsey, and opening the door wider, she said politely, "Won't you come in for a minute? I shall have to leave Adam a note."

Unaware of the hard glitter in the green eyes that watched her so closely, Savanna began to write her note to Adam. While she sat at a delicate cherrywood writing desk, Betsey wandered around the opulent room, enviously comparing its luxurious size and appointments with the smaller, less expensive set of rooms that she and Charles had procured. It wasn't *fair!* she thought furiously. Adam was hers! She should be Adam's wife and staying here with him in these spacious rooms! Not this hulking *nobody!*

A fixed smile on her lips, Betsey said lightly, "I must apologize for my behavior this morning—it was *such* a shock to hear of Adam's marriage! He was always so adamantly opposed to matrimony! Whatever did you *do* to make him change his mind?"

Savanna flushed, wishing desperately that she possessed a glib tongue. Concentrating fiercely on what she was writing, she muttered distractedly, "Um, I don't know. We, we, uh, just d-d-decided that it would be a good thing."

"Do you know, I don't believe I ever heard your name mentioned by any of our friends. 'Savanna' is such an unusual name, isn't it? I'm sure I would have remembered it if someone had said it aloud, and certainly if Adam had!" She sent Savanna a kind glance. "Do not feel uncomfortable—Adam and I are such very good friends—he tells me everything! Have you known him long?"

"N-n-no. Not long," Savanna mumbled, feeling slightly winded.

"Your marriage . . . it was rather *sudden*, wasn't it?"

Savanna's flush increased. Uncertain in her new role as Adam's wife, feeling just a little in awe of and inferior to this beautiful young woman who had obviously been on close terms with Adam and who moved in the highest society, Savanna was at a loss. Despite everything, she didn't want to embarrass Adam by being rude to one of his friends and she certainly didn't want to offend Miss Asher—the notion having innocently occurred to her at first that perhaps she and Miss Asher could become allies. With Miss Asher's help, with someone more worldly and sophisticated than she to show her the way, the transition from Savanna O'Rourke, backwoods tavern owner, to Mrs. Savanna St. Clair, wife of a wealthy, aristocratic gentleman like Adam, might be less arduous. But as the minutes passed, she did wonder if Miss Asher wasn't just a little too nosy and if there wasn't some other reason for her seemingly kind invitation. Rapidly Savanna began to revise her initial favorable thoughts about the young lady.

Stiffly she replied, "If our marriage was sudden, I think that's our business, don't you?"

"Oh, my! I've offended you, haven't I?" Betsey said with some distress. "Forgive me! I didn't mean to! It is just that Adam and I have *always* been so close, and to suddenly have an utter stranger presented as his wife ..." Betsey laughed ruefully. "My wretched tongue! Do forgive me!"

What could Savanna do? Graciously she pushed aside Betsey's polite apologies, but any enthusiasm she might have had for her company had vanished, and she wished she had immediately declined the invitation. Savanna might not, until now, have moved in the highest circles, but instinct told her that Miss Asher was up to no good. . . .

The limited conversation with Savanna had answered several questions that had been burning in Betsey's breast all morning, and she had been able to deduce much more from what Savanna *hadn't* said than from what she had said. It was apparent that the marriage had not been a love match; it had been sudden, and from her reading of Savanna's apparel, it was also apparent that money, at least money coming from Savanna, had not been an issue. The planter aristocracy in the southern United States was small and virtually everyone knew everyone else and in most cases was related, even if only distantly. The fact that Betsey had never heard *any*one mention the name Savanna was telling and she drew the obvious conclusion—Adam's wife was not someone who moved in the upper reaches of society; worse, she probably wasn't even some poor little cousin twice removed of a wealthier, more powerfully connected relative! She was a *nobody!* And this incensed Betsey almost as much as the fact that Savanna was married to Adam. But having drawn her own conclusions, Betsey was still puzzled as to why Adam should have married a provincial miss with no pretension to wealth or power. Oh, there was no doubt that Savanna was a striking creature and that most men would find her attractive, but *marriage?*

Betsey was still mulling this over as the two women left the room and began walking sedately in the direction of the long, curving staircase which led to the foyer of the hotel. What possible reason could Adam have had for having married her? Betsey wondered viciously—not that it made any difference to *her* plans! She just hadn't quite figured out precisely how she was going to dispose of his present wife. She would have to move swiftly, though, she realized—Adam was a virile, demanding lover and she certainly didn't want to get saddled with another woman's brat!

Betsey stopped as if she had walked into a brick wall. Of course! she thought with a narrowed cruel gaze on Savanna. The stupid bitch was pregnant! *That* was how she had trapped Adam! The oldest trick in the world!

Oblivious of Betsey standing transfixed behind her, Savanna reached the top of the stairs. Betsey didn't plan what came next—it just happened, rage and fury making her react without thought. An opportunity suddenly presented itself and she took it; from the foyer below, no one would see what had happened, and up here there was no one nearby. The sight of Savanna, a *pregnant* Savanna, Savanna, Adam's *wife*, standing there with one foot outstretched as she prepared to begin her descent down the stairs was simply more than Betsey could bear. Her lovely features twisted horribly by the ugly emotions that racked her, she rushed forward and gave Savanna a swift, powerful shove.

Caught totally without warning, Savanna could not save herself, and a soft, frightened gasp came from her as she was pitched violently forward. Frantically she tried to right herself and grabbed at the wooden railing, but her hand missed its mark and sheer momentum sent her crashing uncontrollably down the long staircase. Jolting pain exploded through her body as she tumbled and bounced downward to land in a silent, rumpled heap at the bottom of the stairs.

Appalled and excited at the same time, Betsey stared down at Savanna's still form from the top of the stairs. She had done it! Killed the silly bitch! she thought elatedly, her eyes glittering with satisfaction. As the horrified onlookers in the foyer rushed forward to lend aid, her elation faded just a bit and a strong sense of self-preservation quickly asserted itself. Fixing a becomingly distressed expression on her beautiful face, Betsey floated gracefully down the steps, crying out in a pitiful voice, "Oh! Oh! What can have happened? I saw her start to fall and tried to grab her! Oh! Oh! This is *dreadful!* The poor, *dear* girl! Tell me she is not dead!"

As several people rushed to comfort Betsey, who was sobbing prettily, the gentleman who had first reached Savanna's side glanced up at her. "She is not dead yet," he said soberly, "but she is bleeding and I fear the worst."

Not dead? Betsey could have stamped her little
feet with vexation, but lifting her face from where
she had so affectingly buried it in her hands, she
stared in riveted fascination at the crimson stain that
inexorably seeped out from the lower half of Savanna's body.

Chapter 19

S<small>AVANNA</small> DRIFTED HAZILY INTO AWARENESS OF HER SUR-
roundings and in the dim light she stared, puzzled,
at the satin hangings of the bed. As she regained her
senses more fully, she recognized where she was—in
the bed that she and Adam shared at the hotel. But
why was she in bed? Surely it was not still nighttime?
And where was Adam? She frowned, trying to remember. The events of the day suddenly flashed
through her mind . . . except that once she had left
her rooms with Betsey Asher, her memory dimmed.
Vaguely she recalled that they had walked down the
hall together and she could faintly remember standing at the top of the stairs preparing to descend, but
after that there was a terrifying blank.

Filled with an odd foreboding, she jerked upright,
only to gasp and fall backward as pain erupted
through her body. She ached in every bone and muscle, and for one terrible moment she feared that she
would faint. What had happened to her? What was
wrong with her?

There was a curious emptiness within her and her

breath caught painfully in her throat as she became aware of the thick padding between her legs . . . as if someone had tried to stanch the flow of blood. . . . Her baby! Comprehension exploded in her brain— she had lost her baby!

Savanna had always viewed her pregnancy with mixed emotions, and her life had been in such turmoil since before even its conception that, beyond a fierce protectiveness toward her unborn child, she had never been able to experience the more tender emotions that most expectant mothers did. But the knowledge that the child was no more sent a shaft of agony through her entire body. A tiny broken cry came from her and she began to sob quietly, the tears streaming down her cheeks as the full enormity of it hit her. She would never hold this child in her arms, never hear its first cries or touch the downy softness of its head. . . .

The silk bed-curtains were suddenly thrust open and faint morning light spilled into the widening gap as Adam, his face haggard and drawn, stared down at her. "You're awake," he said thickly and with such heartfelt relief and great satisfaction that Savanna could only look at him in astonishment.

Her lovely blue-green eyes drenched in tears, she stared at his strained features. He looked terrible. His lean face was shadowed with a bearded stubble, his cravat crumpled and his hair mussed and untidy. But it was the agonized expression in his dark blue eyes that made Savanna look at him in growing confusion. Had the baby meant that much to him? The memory of the way he had kissed her abdomen and of the wonder and awe in his voice when he had said, "My child!" suddenly swept over her, and she knew that for whatever reasons, he, too, mourned the loss of their child.

In a small, pitiful voice she asked, "What happened? How did I come to lose the baby?"

Adam's heart twisted painfully in his chest as he

relived those first terrible moments when he had returned to the hotel and found the foyer in an uproar and a crowd gathered around the fallen body of his wife. He closed his eyes in anguish. He should never have left her! If he hadn't let his damnable, *damnable* temper rule him, this would never have happened! It was *all* his fault! And it didn't lessen his pain any to know that he had already realized that stalking off in a flaming rage was no answer to their problems. He had stormed but a short distance away from the hotel before the worst of his hurt fury had dissipated, and once cooler reasoning had taken over, he could see that finding solace in the arms of another woman was *not* the way to handle the situation! Savanna was his wife! She had to be made to understand that their lives were inalterably linked and that they *were* going to make this marriage work! He had spun around on his heels and walked rapidly back in the direction of the hotel, his mind busy on ways to woo his intractable bride, thinking of all manner of schemes to win her love. . . .

The devastation he had first felt when he had stared down at Savanna's crumpled, bleeding form suddenly swept over him again, and dropping down gently on the bed beside her, mindful of her injuries, he very carefully folded her into his arms. His mouth against her temple, he confessed baldly, "I thought you were dead! I have never been so frightened in my entire life!"

It was wonderful to have his strong arms around her, and leaning confidently against him, her hand lightly caressing his chest, she asked softly, "But what happened? I can remember nothing beyond starting down the stairs to have lemonade with Miss Asher."

Adam's mouth thinned. He would have liked to wring Betsey's neck! If she hadn't meddled, hadn't been trying to worm her way into Savanna's good graces, none of this would have happened! She'd been like a little bee buzzing around him as she, and the physician who had been instantly summoned, had bent over Savanna where she'd still lain at the base of the stairs. "Oh, Adam!" Betsey had exclaimed. "It was terrible! I was just being nice to her—we were going to have a lemonade and she fell down the stairs! We were standing there and then all of a sudden she just *fell!* It was horrible for me! Just horrible! I'm sure I don't know how I've kept from fainting from the shock of it all."

Adam had brutally ignored her prattling, and once it had been determined that it was safe to move Savanna and she had been solicitously transported to their rooms, it had given him great pleasure to shut the door on Betsey's incessant chatter. He had barely understood a word she had said anyway, all his attention being on Savanna. He never again wanted to experience anything remotely like the night that had just passed. The loss of the baby hadn't really impinged upon him in the beginning. He'd been too terrified of losing Savanna to fully understand what had happened. The physician had been grave as he had worked over Savanna, but after an anguished, interminable length of time to Adam, the physician had nodded and said, "She should recover without any lasting harm. She is sleeping now—she must have taken a hard knock on the head on the stairs, but I believe that by morning she will come to her senses. There are no broken bones, and though she has bled heavily, she is young and healthy and should, within a few weeks, be her old self."

All through that seemingly endless night, Adam had sat at Savanna's bedside, sometimes wiping her brow with a damp cloth, other times just helplessly holding her limp hand, willing her to wake and look at him. He had thought a lot about the baby during those long, black, lonely hours, and the heaviness in his spirit had grown. The baby hadn't even been real to him until last night, it had merely been the means to make Savanna marry him, but the knowledge that the child was dead had made him feel as if his living heart had been ripped out of his chest. It hurt him deeply to know that there was nothing he could do, nothing he could do for either his lost child or Savanna, but wait here and pray that when morning came, Savanna would indeed wake. He had been in the other roon ordering a pot of coffee when Savanna had awakened, and upon returning to the bedchamber, he had heard her soft sob.

That sound had rent his very heart and as he gathered her closer, he kissed her cheek and murmured, "Don't talk now, darling. The physician said you were to rest."

"But how can I rest if my mind is going to be full of questions?" Savanna asked softly. "Please, Adam, tell me what happened."

Reluctantly he told her what he knew: she and Betsey Asher had been on their way for some lemonade, and she had somehow missed her step and fallen down the stairs.

Looking down into her pale face, he inquired gently, "Do you remember any of it?"

Savanna shook her head, wincing as her bruised muscles protested. "Only that we were going for the lemonade and that I was standing at the top of the stairs . . . after that it is all a total blank, until I woke up here."

"The physician believes that you might have suffered a fainting spell and that's what caused you to fall. It sounds reasonable. Betsey says that one minute you were there at the top of the stairs and the next you were tumbling downward."

"Oh," Savanna said blankly, something niggling at the back of her mind. She frowned. She had never fainted before in her life, and somehow that explanation didn't satisfy her. There was something . . .

"About the baby," Adam began tentatively. "Do you want to talk about it?"

A smothered sob came from her and she nodded. "I wanted it, Adam. Despite everything."

"I know, sweetheart," he replied softly. "I know. I did, too."

There was silence between them for a long time, each lost in their thoughts about the child who had died, but eventually they began to talk of their loss, sharing the sorrow only those who have suffered the same devastating experience can understand.

Adam watched Savanna's expressive features closely, and after the first outpouring of grief had subsided and he saw that she was tiring, he carefully guided the conversation away from the child and convinced her to rest. She slept nearly the entire day, waking in the early evening to the aroma of chicken soup and freshly baked bread.

She lay there for a moment, her first waking thoughts of the child she had lost. Her eyes clouded and she knew that the pain would never truly go away. It might lessen, but the memory would always be there within her.

With an effort she tore her melancholy thoughts away from the loss and tried to concentrate on more practical things. To her surprise, she discovered she was ravenously hungry and she started to sit up, only to give a soft moan as wrenched muscles made themselves felt.

Once again the bed-curtains were jerked aside and Adam stared in at her. He looked much better this time, his jaw clean-shaven and a warm expression glinting in those sapphire-blue eyes. Sending her a smile that turned her heart right over in her breast, he murmured, "I thought the smell of food would waken you! How are you feeling? Well enough to eat?"

Savanna nodded, and felt much improved after she had hungrily consumed two bowls of the soup and half a loaf of still-warm-from-the-oven bread. When Adam tenderly escorted her back to the bed, she eyed it with loathing. With a look of entreaty at him, she said, "Please! I am not an invalid! *Must* I go back to bed? I'm sure I would feel much better if I could change my clothes and sit up for a while."

Adam eyed her keenly. Her color was good and she did not seem unsteady on her feet. He shrugged. "I don't think there can be any objection to your resting on the sofa in the other room."

Shortly thereafter, feeling refreshed from the sponge bath she had taken, with her hair falling in a glorious red-gold cloud about her shoulders and wearing one of the becoming gowns that had arrived from Madame Galland's, Savanna was regally ensconced in the sitting room, pillows behind her back and a soft blanket across her lap. She wasn't about to admit it, but the effort had tired her slightly and she was very glad to do nothing more than sink down onto the sofa and allow Adam to drape a lovely paisley shawl, also from Madame Galland's, around her shoulders. Having seen to all her needs, he took a seat in a high-backed chair directly across from her.

There was an awkward silence between them and Savanna's fingers nervously plucked at the gown of delicate fawn cambric that she was wearing. With nothing better to talk about, she said softly, "Thank you for the beautiful clothes. There seem so many of them! I can't imagine that I shall be able to wear them all!"

There were many other things that Adam would have preferred to talk about, but if she wanted to exchange polite nonsense, he could see no harm in it. A sardonic smile on his lips, he replied, "You're welcome. As for not being able to wear all of them—believe me, from what I know of your sex, before very long you shall be telling me that you haven't a thing to wear and that we must repair immediately to Madame Galland's in order for you to select some other outrageous, expensive bit of feminine apparel!"

At the stricken expression that crossed Savanna's

face, Adam could have torn out his tongue. Flying from his chair, he knelt beside her, one knee on the floor, and grasping her hand, he said urgently, "Oh, sweetheart! Don't look so! I only meant to tease you!"

Her face averted, in a constricted tone Savanna mumbled, "If you are so ashamed of me and my clothes, I don't see why you went ahead and married me!"

A ludicrous expression on his handsome features, Adam stared at her. "Ashamed of you?" he exclaimed in shocked, angry accents. "Good God! How could you think I am ashamed of you?"

Savanna risked a glance at him. He looked totally at sea. Just as if he had no idea what she was talking about. Baffled, she stared at him. "But that's why you took me to Madame Galland's, isn't it?" she demanded huskily. "Because you were ashamed of my old gowns and didn't want to be seen in public with me?"

"Of all the nonsensical notions!" Adam growled disgustedly. Springing up to sit on the sofa beside her, he took both of her hands in his. "Sweetheart," he began passionately, "the only reason I took you to Madame Galland's is because I thought you would *like* some new gowns! Not to wrap it up in clean linen—I'm a rich man and it gave me pleasure to buy things for you. It had nothing to do with being ashamed of you! Good Lord! What sort of coxcomb do you take me for?" His blue eyes almost black with emotion, he said deliberately, "You are the most exciting woman I have ever met, whether you are garbed in that frightful brown, er, frock you wore when we first met or wearing the most fashionable clothes money can buy. Wear what you damn well please! It makes no difference to me!"

There was such vehement sincerity in his words, such heartwarming candor in his eyes, that Savanna had no choice but to believe him . . . and to feel slightly foolish for having doubted his motives. Her cheeks flushed, she lowered her eyes to their clasped hands and muttered, "I'm sorry! I should have realized that!" She swallowed and met his gaze. "I apologize."

"Well, I should hope so!" Adam returned smartly, a teasing twinkle in the depths of his eyes. As he stared intently at her, the twinkle faded and he said softly, "You can't have thought I was ashamed of you, sweetheart! You silly goose! Whatever gave you that idea?"

Her cheeks blazing with embarrassment, Savanna wanted to look anywhere but into those mesmerizing sapphire-blue eyes. Nervously she cleared her throat and confessed, "When we met your friends, the Ashers, you seemed in a hurry to get away from them—as if you didn't really want to introduce me to them."

"I didn't," Adam admitted frankly, and when Savanna's outraged gaze swung back to him, he smiled. "But not because I was ashamed of you!" A scowl darkened his brow and his mouth twisted wryly. "Sweetheart, it wasn't *you* I was ashamed of, but that I found myself in an, er, embarrassing situation. I was once, er—" Adam stopped, and to Savanna's astonishment, she distinctly saw a flush mount his lean cheeks. Adam, that cool, uncaring sophisticate, actually blushed. "You see," he finally said lamely, "I was once, ah, *friendly* with Miss Asher—before I ever knew you!"

"Oh," said Savanna hollowly, her aquamarine gaze fixed accusingly on her husband.

"Savanna! I didn't even know you existed. Surely you cannot hold past peccadilloes against me?"

"Probably not," she admitted primly, "but it does explain a lot." She frowned. "Except her excessive friendliness with me. I'd want to scratch her eyes out if our situations were reversed!"

Adam grinned with such masculine satisfaction

that Savanna wished the floor would open up and swallow her. The heat in her cheeks became an inferno, but lifting her chin pugnaciously, she said with suspect airiness, "Of course, that's only the way I would feel if we had married under *normal* circumstances!"

"Oh, absolutely!" Adam returned, an unholy gleam of amusement dancing in his eyes, his heart rejoicing at this first sign that Savanna cared for him. "Only under normal circumstances, of course!"

Savanna sent him a quelling look. "Are you teasing me?"

Adam flashed her one of those knee-weakening smiles and slowly pulled her toward him. "Definitely! But I'd much rather kiss you!" And suiting words to action, he pressed his warm mouth to hers.

It was a tender kiss, a wealth of never-spoken emotion behind it, and Savanna's defenses crumbled, her arms creeping around his neck. He kissed her for a long, dreamy time, his firm lips moving in gentle eroticism against hers, but never plunging them into wild passion.

When his head finally lifted, Savanna was still flushed, but for far different reasons, and there was a soft, bemused expression on her features. His hands cupped her face and locking his gaze with hers, he said clearly, "I could *never* be ashamed of you! You are my wife! And if there is any shame between us, it is because I did not come to you as innocent as you came to me. And if I hurried you away from the Ashers, it was more because they are not very nice people and because I did not like the notion of my wife consorting with a former mistress than because of any shame for having married you." He stared at her keenly. "Understand?"

Dazedly Savanna nodded, her heart suddenly light and filled with hope. He had not said the words aloud she yearned to hear, but she would have had to be a silly goose indeed not to have concluded that his emotions for her ran very deep. She smiled at him, a dazzling smile of such warmth and brilliance that Adam nearly blinked at the sheer wonder of it. "I *am* a silly goose!" she admitted. "I should have known better."

Adam knew he was grinning idiotically, but he suddenly felt drunk, and striving to regain command of the situation, he said gruffly, "Yes, you should! And because you must be punished for thinking so ill of me, I shall insist that Madame Galland come to call here at the hotel and you shall be forced to select at least three more gowns!" An enchanting gurgle of laughter came from Savanna, and Adam tried to look stern. "Now, don't trifle with me! Or you'll see what a really clutch-fisted husband you've married—I'll increase the number to five!"

They sat there on the sofa grinning at each other, but as the minutes passed, their amusement fled. His face suddenly intent, Adam leaned forward and with fingers that trembled slightly he touched her cheek. "Oh, Savanna," he breathed passionately, "I do lov—!"

There was a sharp rap on the door, which shattered the mood and interrupted Adam's words. A vexed expression on his face, he sprang up from the sofa, smothered a curse under his breath and walked to the door.

Flinging open the door, he didn't change his expression; if anything, it increased. And as soon as Savanna recognized the voice of their unexpected and decidedly unwanted visitor, she knew the reason for his darkening scowl.

"Oh, Adam! I just *had* to see you before we leave," Betsey began in a breathless tone. "Charles just insists that we leave tomorrow morning and this is the only moment I shall have to see you." Peeping up at Adam's unrelenting expression, she asked concernedly, "How is Savanna? Has there been any improvement?"

"See for yourself," Adam said ungraciously, reluctantly allowing Betsey to enter the room.

If Betsey was disappointed to see Savanna sitting up and looking, if not in blooming health, certainly enchantingly attractive, with her aquamarine eyes appearing enormous in her pale face, the fiery glow of her hair intensifying the alabaster purity of her skin, no sign of this showed outwardly. There wasn't even a sign of the trepidation Betsey must have felt, wondering if Savanna had remembered her part in the fall. Rushing to Savanna's side, she gushed, "Oh, my dear! How well you look! My goodness, but you gave me *such* a scare yesterday! I swear I didn't sleep a wink last night worrying about you!"

Savanna made a polite rejoinder, but her thoughts weren't on Betsey—at least not on Betsey's words. At the sound of the young woman's voice, she had received an unpleasant jolt, and in her memory something vaguely stirred, a flashing fragment that was gone as soon as it had appeared. Only half listening to Betsey's conversation, Savanna frowned. Now, what was it? Why couldn't she remember?

Betsey kept her visit short. She had come mainly to spy out the territory, and on the one hand she was pleased that Savanna's memory seemed to be faulty, but on the other, she was furious to see how little damage the fall had caused. Of course, the fact that Savanna had lost the baby was wonderful, but still!

Drifting away from Savanna, her stylish gown of pale green jaconet muslin floating daintily above the floor, Betsey reached out and laid her slim white hand on Adam's arm, where he still stood by the door. The sight of that little hand reaching out had a startling effect on Savanna. Memory, sharp and vivid, erupted in her brain, and as if it had just happened, she could feel the savage impact of those two little hands on her back.

Savanna jerked upright and in tones of incredulous

fury she exclaimed, "You pushed me! I didn't fall.
You *pushed* me!"

Betsey stiffened, her green eyes meeting Adam's
kindling blue gaze for a split second. Spinning
around to look at Savanna, she asked with credible
innocence, "Whatever are you talking about, my
dear?"

Her voice shaking with suppressed rage, Savanna
snarled, "I'm talking about yesterday afternoon,
when you pushed me down the stairs. I remember it
all. I didn't faint and I didn't fall—you came up and
pushed me!"

Betsey flashed a sorrowful look at Adam's suddenly rigid face. "Oh, my dear, I am *so* sorry! You
didn't tell me that she was not in her right mind.
How sad for you!"

"I'm not crazy!" Savanna said, struggling to stand
upright. "I just didn't remember until I heard your
voice and saw your hand on Adam's arm, and then
it all came rushing back to me. You deliberately
pushed me down the stairs—you killed my baby and
tried to kill me!"

A swift glance at Adam's white-lipped, frozen face
told Betsey that she would find no help from that
quarter, and giving a nervous titter, she edged closer
to the door. "Well, I won't argue with you, my dear,
but I'm afraid that your memory is faulty. What possible reason could *I* have for doing such a horrid
thing?"

In a cold, inimical tone, Adam said slowly, "I think
I can answer that—you hoped that with Savanna out
of the way I would return to you."

"My dear, *dear* Adam," Betsey said lightly, "aren't
you being just the tiniest bit conceited? As if I would
do such a thing merely to fix a man's interest! Have
you forgotten that I am on my way to visit with a
gentleman I will very likely marry? Believe me, I
found you very attractive, but—" She laughed depre-
catingly. "Darling, our time together was heavenly,

but it is over and no one is happier than I that it is so. How can you even *conceive* that I would do such a dreadful thing?" An ominous silence greeted her words. "Well!" she uttered in an offended accent. "I can see that you don't believe me! And to think I only came to call out of kindness! It's obvious that there is no talking to either of you! If you will excuse me, I will be on my way!"

"Not so fast," Adam snapped, catching her arm in a brutal grip. "Do you really believe that I shall allow you to harm my wife and child and escape unscathed?"

Nothing had gone precisely as she had planned, and Betsey lost her temper. "How dare you!" she exclaimed furiously. "I don't give a damn what you believe!" From the icily wrathful expression on Adam's face, it was obvious that she had lost the gamble. "You can't *prove* anything!" she hissed. "It's my word against hers, and everybody knows that she suffered a knock on the head. Are you so certain that she is telling the truth?" Adam's features remained implacable and Betsey could have screamed with frustration. A sneer on her lovely face, she added, "How I ever thought that I wanted to marry such an overbearing brute like you is beyond me! Let me go!"

Adam's hand tightened savagely on Betsey's arm, a fierce desire for revenge clawing through him. "I ought to break your neck," he snarled softly, the look on his handsome face murderous, and for one dangerous moment the outcome hung in the balance. With a tremendous effort of will, Adam reined in his blazing fury. Killing Betsey wasn't the answer. It would give him great satisfaction to strangle her with his bare hands, but his pleasure would be over in an instant. No. She had to pay for what she had done, in such a way that she would live and go on paying for years to come. Taking a deep breath, he contemptuously flung her arm aside. "You're not worth it! I'll not hang for your death! But hear me well, Betsey, for I'm not through with you." He smiled, a terrifyingly cruel smile, and murmured almost gently, "No, I'm not through with you yet, my dear, but when I am, perhaps you'll wish I *had* broken your neck!"

Betsey grasped the crystal knob, and opening the door, her green eyes flashing with hatred, she glared at him and spat venomously, "I'll make you sorry for this, Adam St. Clair! You see if I don't!"

The door slammed shut behind her and Adam turned to Savanna, who was standing, strained and pale, next to the sofa. "*Dios!* What an *awful* woman!" Savanna said with loathing. "I should like nothing better than to drop her in an alligator hole, but I am very glad that you did not strangle her." She sent him a shaky smile. "I would not like for you to hang either!"

With swift strides Adam crossed the room to fold her into his arms. "Sweetheart! I'm sorry that you had to endure that ugly scene." His mouth twisted. "Sorrier than you know that it was because of me that you had to suffer."

Her head pressed against his shoulder, she murmured, "It wasn't your fault, Adam. You could not have known. She must be mad!"

"Mad and vicious!" Adam said grimly. Aware that the scene had taken more out of Savanna than she had realized, he picked her up and carried her to the bedchamber. Smiling down at her, he said lightly, "The physician said that you were to rest, and I think that whether you like it or not, the best place for you right now is bed."

Savanna didn't argue. She was suddenly shockingly tired, and while she had wanted to be up such a short while ago, the thought of her bed didn't seem as undesirable as it had previously.

Adam made an excellent ladies' maid, deftly whisking the gown from her body and instantly sliding a soft, delicately embroidered shift of finest lawn over her. He settled her into the bed and after plumping the pillows behind her back, he surveyed her closely. There were purple circles beneath her eyes and a hollowness about her cheeks that he did not like, but considering the narrowness of her escape, he was not displeased.

Lounging at the side of the bed, he took one of her hands in his and murmured, "As soon as we can, I think we should return to Campo de Verde. You will feel better in your old home with your mother nearby." His face twisted. "I should never have brought you to New Orleans—not only is it the worst time of year, but our paths would not have crossed with the Ashers!"

There was a heavy silence, the terrible loss Betsey had caused them in both of their minds. Adam roused himself first and forced a light note into his voice. "I waited until you had awakened this morning before I wrote to your mother. While you slept today, I sent off a message to her, explaining everything, and though I reassured her that you were recovering, she will be anxiously awaiting our arrival."

Savanna smiled faintly. "She will cosset me to death!"

"Naturally!" He cast her a considering look. "I think it is just what you need right now. Go to sleep, sweetheart. I shall just be in the other room, so call out if there is anything that you need."

With a docility which would normally have been foreign to her, Savanna nodded, and before Adam had even reached the doorway that separated the two rooms, her eyes had closed and she was sleeping dreamlessly.

For Adam there was no such escape, and he spent the next several hours restlessly pacing the confines of the sitting room, his mind tortured by how easily he could have lost Savanna. It did not help his frame of mind, either, to know that he had been, albeit unknowingly, the direct cause of what had happened. Because of his meaningless affair with Betsey, his wife had nearly died and their child had been destroyed. His fists clenched impotently at his sides. The cost be damned! He *should* have broken Betsey's neck when he'd had the chance!

But despite his black, bitter mood, despite even the hungry desire for revenge that clawed and twisted in his gut, there were more mundane things to distract him, and eventually, a snifter of brandy in front of him, he sat down and began composing the various letters necessary to inform his family of not only his marriage but also the tragedy that had struck. In the letter to his parents, he stated only the bald facts, promising to write more soon. The letter to Jason and Catherine, however, revealed not only how desperately he loved Savanna, but also his terrible guilt and grief over the loss of the child. In neither letter did he mention Betsey's part in the tragedy—he wanted no sane counsel, no coolly reasoned arguments, no interference when the time came to take his revenge. . . .

Chapter 20

INTENT ON HIS OWN PLANS FOR VENGEANCE, THE ONE thing that never occurred to Adam was that *Betsey* would strike out at him! Hurrying along the corridor to her own rooms, green eyes glittering with rage, Betsey had her head full of decidedly nefarious plans for revenge against Adam. *How dare he!* she thought furiously as she stormed into her room, slamming the door shut behind her. The very idea! It was bad enough that he'd married that common little slut, but to have believed Savanna's story over hers and to have actually *threatened* her! *Well!*

Having heard her angry return, Charles wandered into Betsey's room through their connecting doorway, and surveying the damage she was wreaking upon anything that crossed her path, he saw that his sister was thoroughly enraged. He had been highly annoyed yesterday when she confessed to what she had done, but he hadn't been surprised—Betsey could never bear to be thwarted. His main worry was that there might be unpleasant repercussions, and when Betsey had insisted upon visiting the St.

Clairs this afternoon to survey the situation, he had been adamantly against it. They'd had a terrible argument, but he had been unable to sway her from her decision and, short of locking her in her room until they left tomorrow morning, there was nothing he could do. Many times, Charles found it easier to let Betsey have her way, and this had been one of them. The fact that she had returned so furious meant that her winning little ploys hadn't fooled anyone, or something infinitely worse—exposure. Betsey's exposure was the last thing he wanted. Charles wasn't overly worried; it would be Betsey's word against Savanna's in any case, and he very much doubted that Adam or Savanna was going to wash their linen in public.

Lifting a haughtily sculpted brow, Charles drawled, "What's the matter? Adam put a flea in your ear?"

Flashing him a wrathful glance, Betsey snarled, "Don't be vulgar, Charles!" And while normally she would have been perfectly content to turn her rage on Charles, or anyone else unfortunate enough to cross her path, she was too angry to bother with such satisfaction now. She wanted revenge. She wanted Adam to be punished, and Charles could help her. . . .

An ugly expression on her lovely face, and her limpid green eyes narrowed and hard, she walked over to him and said fiercely, "I want him dead! He insulted me!"

"I do hope you don't expect me to challenge him to a duel?" Charles responded dryly. "He's reputed to be an excellent shot and pure grace with a sword."

"Don't be silly! I don't want *you* to get hurt—only him!" She frowned, thinking furiously. A gleam of excitement suddenly leaped into her eyes. Almost gleefully, she suggested, "We could hire someone! Maybe not to kill him, but some thugs to beat him! Couldn't we?"

Charles gave her a thoughtful look. "Are you serious?" he asked carefully. "You want me to arrange to harm your wonderful Adam?"

Betsey's mouth tightened in an ugly line. "Yes! I want him to learn that no one discards *me!*"

Charles gave an ironic little laugh. "I wish you'd felt this way earlier—hiring someone to beat him would have been much less expensive!" When Betsey looked puzzled, he seated himself casually on a small chair and admitted coolly, "When you seemed determined to marry him in Natchez, I took matters into my own hands and spent a great deal of the capital that we managed to salvage from Virginia on hiring a thug to kill him." Charles's face twisted. "Unfortunately, the bastard took my money and didn't hold up his end of the bargain, and now I'm afraid that with our funds so low, I dare not lay out the amount of money needed to hire someone else."

Betsey looked outraged at Charles's confession, and stepping near him, she slapped him viciously. He flinched from the force of the blow, but deftly catching her wrist in a crushing hold, he twisted her arm until she cried out in great pain. "Don't *ever*," he said glacially, "do that again. I've warned you for the last time."

Betsey began to cry pitifully. "Oh, Charles, you know I don't mean to hurt you, but what are we going to do? I want him punished! It's just not fair!"

He knew how she could work herself up into a frenzy, culminating in tears, tantrums and sulks, making his life and everyone else's around her miserable; and with the possibility of a proposal of marriage from Pierre Michaud in the offing, it was imperative to restore Betsey's spirits immediately. His irritation showing on his handsome features, Charles released her arm and said, "I'll see what I can do. I can't promise you anything, but perhaps I can arrange something. . . ."

Betsey was instantly all smiles. "Oh, *could* you?"

She lowered her lashes. "It would make me so much more agreeable to tying myself to that mere boy!"

Charles snorted. "I'm sure it would!" He caught her chin in a painful grasp. "But you're going to tie yourself to that mere, *rich* boy, aren't you? Whether I can concoct something unpleasant for St. Clair or not!"

A sullen droop to her mouth, Betsey nodded. "I hate being poor! It's, it's so uncivilized!"

"Well, just keep in mind that it is that mere boy, Pierre Michaud, who can keep you in a *very* civilized state!" Charles reported brutally. Seeing that Betsey understood, he relaxed slightly and continued in a kinder tone. "And you should know that while you were attempting to charm your way into St. Clair's good graces, I received a message from Pierre. He is so eager to see you that he has made plans to meet us here tomorrow morning and intends to escort us to his home." Charles sent his sister a stern glance. "Whatever your personal feelings, tomorrow morning I want you looking your best and I want a beguiling smile on your lips when you see him."

Betsey pulled a face. Sullenly she muttered, "I could probably be more resigned to Pierre if I knew that you would see to it that Adam was beaten . . . and made arrangements so that I could watch it being done. Oh, *please*, Charles!"

Charles sighed. Once Betsey got an idea in her head, there was no swaying her, and unless he was prepared to watch her whistle the Michaud fortune down the wind, which he wasn't, it was clear that he was going to have to placate her. "Very well, little sister," Charles said grimly. "If I can have your word that you will behave yourself with Pierre, you may watch and I shall find the wherewithal to hire someone to administer a sound thrashing to Mr. Adam St. Clair!"

It was late when Charles returned to their rooms,

and from the expression on his face when he entered, it was obvious that his errand had been successful.

"You found someone!" Betsey squealed with pleasure.

"Yes, I found someone—a pair of river rats who would no doubt slit their own mother's throat if the price was right!" Charles frowned. "We do have a major problem, though—getting Adam to the riverfront where those two will be waiting for him! I cannot conceive of a reason *why* he would go there—and late tonight at that!"

Betsey looked thoughtful. "What about a message concerning that brother-in-law of his? You know, Jason Savage. Everyone in Natchez talked about how close the two men are, almost like brothers. If Adam received a note implying that Savage was in grave danger and that only Adam's presence could save him, wouldn't that bring him?"

"Very good!" Charles said admiringly. "Since the message wouldn't be directly from Savage, we wouldn't have to worry about him recognizing that the handwriting is not his brother-in-law's either."

When the dirty, crumpled note that the Ashers had gleefully concocted was delivered to Adam later that evening, he stood staring thoughtfully at it for a long time. Savanna was still asleep in their bedchamber and Adam had been alone in the salon when the message had arrived.

He didn't believe the contents for a moment. Even if Micajah had somehow managed to kidnap Jason, which was highly unlikely, it was even more unlikely that he would bring him to New Orleans, or that, having done such an inane thing, he would now want to speak with Jason's brother-in-law! The note didn't make sense at all, but because of all that had gone on previously, and knowing that Micajah and Jeremy could still be in a position to cause trouble, Adam didn't see that he had any choice but to follow the note's instructions and go to the Broken Sword

Tavern just off Girod Street near the waterfront at midnight.

But there were a few things he could do in the meantime. A hasty visit with the hotel's night clerk confirmed his opinion that the Broken Sword was *not* a tavern patronized by genteel society—far from it! A messenger sent to the Savage town house returned shortly with news that came as no surprise to Adam: neither Monsieur Savage nor his wife had been in residence lately, nor were they expected to be at any time soon.

That the note was a trap was becoming clearer by the moment, but there was still a niggle of worry for Adam. Just because the meeting was at a tawdry waterfront tavern and Jason hadn't been in New Orleans recently didn't mean that the note *wasn't* genuine, and therefore, he dared not ignore it.

Briefly Adam cursed the fact that Bodene was at Campo de Verde. He would have felt a lot easier about the whole situation if he had Bodene at his side. But since he didn't have him . . .

Not wasting a moment, Adam immediately dispatched an urgent message to Bodene's henchman, Jake, at The Golden Lady. Bodene trusted Jake implicitly and had informed Adam that if ever he needed someone to rely on, Jake was his man. While he waited for an answer, he swiftly changed into the plainest clothing he possessed, and when Jake arrived a short while later, Adam quickly explained the situation.

Jake didn't like it any better than Adam. "I still think you're wrong," Jake growled when he heard what Adam planned to do. "You're a damn fool for not letting me and Dooley follow you down to that place."

Adam smiled faintly. "I need you and Dooley here to watch over my wife . . . and I need you and Dooley to rouse the alarm if I don't come back from the Broken Sword."

"Don't think Bodene is going to like me letting you risk your neck this way."

"I don't see that I have any choice!" Adam replied sharply. "If the note *is* genuine, I don't want Jason's life put in further danger, and while I'm sure that you and Dooley are the souls of discretion, I don't want to do anything that might make our quarry nervous or suspicious. It's possible, though unlikely, that the author of the note might recognize you as Bodene's man and realize that I'm not following the instructions ... and *if* Jason's life is at stake ..."

Jake grunted. "I see your point, but I still don't like it one bit."

"That may be, but I'm confident that I can handle the situation. Besides, as I said, I want you and Dooley here to protect my wife, just in case the note is merely a ruse to get me away from her."

For a moment, his face softened as he thought of Savanna. A dozen times this evening he had very nearly blurted out his feelings for her, but seeing the signs of fatigue, and aware of her pain and exhaustion, he had ruthlessly tamped down his powerful emotions and exerted himself to be a charming, undemanding companion.

His eyes fell on the note in his hand. He sighed. Well, there was nothing for it—he would have to go to the Broken Sword at midnight and hope to God that he could keep his wits about him and avoid whatever trap he felt confident had been laid for him.

When Jake left to go get Dooley from The Golden Lady, Adam checked on the sleeping Savanna several times while he awaited their return. Standing there at her bedside and staring down at her face in gentle repose, her flame-red hair flowing over the plump white pillows, he felt his chest tighten painfully. If anything had happened to her!

In the salon, he swiftly wrote her a note, explaining where he had gone and why, and when Jake and Dooley returned a few minutes later, he handed Jake the note. With that done, he had no more reason to procrastinate, and having already concealed a small pistol in his waistcoat and a knife down the inside of one polished boot, he felt that he was as prepared as he ever would be to meet the author of the mysterious note.

Adam arrived several minutes before midnight, not at all surprised that the Broken Sword turned out to be a rough-and-tumble sort of place, the ceaselessly churning Mississippi River fairly lapping at its sagging foundation. The small tavern was dimly lit and the air was full of the sour scent of unwashed bodies, liquor and several other offensive odors that Adam didn't want to identify. As he had been instructed, he selected an empty table near the door and after taking a careful glance around, he sat down and ordered a whiskey from the slatternly tavern maid who approached him.

Having no intention of being drugged, Adam deliberately left the drink untouched when it arrived and coolly lit a long black cheroot. A thin line of blue smoke drifting upward near his dark head, he smoked his cheroot and continued to watch the inhabitants. They were just what one would have expected to find in a low place like this—an obvious whore or two, a few trappers, some riverfront bullies and several raucous members of a flatboat crew. His arrival had caused a stir, but after a moment everyone had gone back to what he had been doing in the first place. No one seemed the least interested in Adam and as the minutes passed and he remained alone at his table, he began to grow uneasy. Surreptitiously, he glanced at his pocket watch. It was by now over a half hour past midnight and there seemed to be no sign of the person who had written the note. Continuing to leisurely smoke his cheroot, every nerve braced for danger, Adam took another long survey of the room.

There were a few candles guttering here and there, and though his gaze tried to pierce the dark shadows of the corners, he could see nothing to alarm him. Growing annoyed and a trifle concerned at the absence of the note writer, he eyed the untouched pale amber glass of whiskey. Was it drugged? Was that why nothing had happened? They wanted him groggy or senseless before they made their move? He smiled grimly. Too bloody bad! He had absolutely no intention of accommodating them. The minutes continued to spin out and slowly, like a snake oozing into view, another possibility occurred to him: had the note just been some sort of vicious prank? Perhaps he hadn't been wrong when he had considered the note to be a ruse to get him away from Savanna.

Adam was on his feet in an instant. Carelessly tossing down some coins on the battered table, he spun on his heels and barged out the door. If anything had happened to her! If the entire point of the note had been to get him away from her so that she could be kidnapped or harmed . . .

It didn't bear thinking about, but he couldn't shake the notion from his mind, Micajah's gloating features suddenly floating menacingly in front of him. Heedless of anything but the frantic urge to see his wife, Adam bolted down the uneven street, hardly aware of his surroundings, and because he was distracted by thoughts of Savanna's peril, he was not mindful of his own very real danger. . . .

The first blow caught him totally by surprise, the viciously swung cudgel striking him fully on his left side, the heavy club savagely crashing against his head and shoulder. The impact nearly drove Adam to his knees, and as the pain surged through him, he fought desperately to clear the dancing black mist that seemed to explode before his eyes.

Adam's attacker had chosen his site well and had been waiting for him in a dark, rank alley, revealing his presence only when the trap was sprung. Fight-

ing to stay on his feet, Adam suddenly became aware
that there were two men, their voices echoing painfully inside his head.

"Goddammit! Don't kill him! We're just supposed
to beat him up! We ain't being paid enough to *kill!*"

"I ain't taking no chances. He's a damned big
bloke and I wants him softened up afore I lays my
weapon down and see how handy he is with his
fives!"

"Never mind that! Grab him! Grab him! Quick,
drag him back here, where they're waiting!"

Adam felt rough hands lay hold of him and hustle
him swiftly down the alley. It was to his advantage
to appear stunned, and since he wasn't far from that
state, it seemed simpler to go along with them rather
than fight. But he used the time it took them to drag
and push him down the twisting alley to gather his
senses and prepare himself for the battle that was to
come.

The note had been a bait for him after all, and like
a green boy, he'd let his fear for Savanna blind him
to dangers outside the tavern. Furious with himself,
he ignored his aching head and vowed fiercely that
someone was going to be in for a very big surprise.
It was obvious that the men who held him prisoner
were only hired bullies, and from their conversation
it was also apparent that the beating for which these
fellows had been hired wouldn't be administered until the three of them had reached wherever "they"
were waiting.

Adam became aware of the faint glow of lantern
light and almost immediately he was flung violently
forward and landed painfully on the filthy floor of
the alley. He started to spring to his feet, but a boot
connected brutally with his ribs before glancing off
his head, nearly knocking him out. Trying desperately to clear his head, Adam only barely heard the
exchange going on over his prostrate body.

"Is this the fellow?" one of his captors growled.

In the faint light of the lantern set on a low post, Adam risked a look, but could only make out two heavily cloaked shapes. They remained in the shadowy darkness out of reach of the lantern's light, and beyond the fact that there were two of them, he could tell little about them, until he heard Betsey's breathless "Oh, yes! That's him! Now *beat* him!"

The two men instantly set to work with a will, and, caught at a distinct disadvantage on the ground, too busy trying to protect himself to take offensive action, Adam suffered several vicious blows and kicks to his head and ribs. Dimly he was aware of Betsey's delighted laughter in the background. "Yes! Yes! Kick him again! *Again!* Make him bleed! I want him to bleed."

Her voice a cruel litany in his head, eventually Adam managed to roll away and stagger upright to his feet. Groggy and in severe pain, he stood there swaying in the flickering glow of the lantern. Icily furious and so filled with a fierce need to give as good as he had got, he forgot the weapons he had brought with him.

With a snarl he charged the two men, his powerful fists violently pummeling indiscriminately left and right. His charge surprised them, and in the scramble to avoid those lethal fists, one of his assailants fell down. Despite his pain, Adam grinned and aimed a savage kick at the fellow's head even as he continued to rain blow after telling blow upon the other man.

This was not what the two assailants had been led to expect and they were utterly undone. They were bullies and jackals, not fighters, and had not planned on their prey inflicting any hurt on them. Filled with sullen resentment at the way things were turning out, they began to retreat, but Adam would have none of it.

Not allowing them any room to escape, he sent a fist flying into the nose of the upright man, another into his mouth, and as that fellow yowled and, holding his face, stumbled backward, Adam turned his savage attention to the man on the ground, who was attempting to rise. Calmly he sent a boot smashing into the creature's belly. When the man groaned and doubled over clutching his belly, Adam said impersonally, "Doesn't feel very good, does it, my good man?"

There was silence, except for the faint groans of the beaten men, as Adam stood there swaying slightly from his battering, but his fists were clenched and ready. His two assailants were clearly no longer a threat, and it was then that Charles rushed him, his malacca cane upraised to strike. Unfortunately, Charles was no fighter, and Adam deftly avoided the cane and contemptuously knocked him out with one brutal punch.

As Adam's fist connected with Charles's handsome chin, Charles gave a funny little sigh and collapsed onto the floor of the filthy alley, his black cloak billowing out around him. Dispassionately, Adam stared down at his fallen enemy, disgust and a deep weariness that went beyond pain washing over him.

He glanced over to where he knew Betsey still lurked in the darkness. "Happy, my dear?" he asked with deceptive lightness.

Betsey remained mute, but one of his original assailants whined, "Well, I sure ain't! You was supposed to be a dandy, a way to earn some easy money, and now all I've got to show for it is a busted nose and an aching lip. Don't seem fair."

Adam cocked an eyebrow. "Oh, I'm sure that if you check your, er, patron's pockets you will probably find enough to satisfy you. In his present condition, I doubt he will object."

The two men looked at each other and grinned. "Why, that's right generous of you!" Like the scavengers they were, ignoring Adam, they fell upon Charles and proceeded to strip him of anything valuable.

Betsey could stand it no longer, and stepping out into the glow of the lantern, she cried, "Stop it, you monsters! Leave him alone! Stop it this instant!"

It proved to be a horrible mistake on her part. The hood of her cloak had fallen back and the lantern light fell full on her gleaming blond hair and lovely face. The two men, who had been busily lifting Charles of anything of value, turned to stare at her, their mouths going slack at the sight of this vision of loveliness here in this sordid, wretched little alley. Avarice faded from their eyes as they stared at her, lust clearly overtaking them.

One of them rose to his feet and murmured, "Well, well, what have we here? As plump and pretty a little dove as I have ever seen."

Betsey realized her error and shrank back, but it was too late. The other man stood, too, and began to advance upon her. "Now, I think that a piece of this little dolly would go a *long* way to making me resigned to what happened." He stopped uncertainly and glanced back at Adam. "That's if you don't have any objections?"

Adam looked at Betsey coldly, the knowledge that this woman had murdered his child burning hotly, brightly, in his mind. The memory of Savanna's white face as he had sat by her bed last night fearing that she would die was also in his thoughts, and he said disinterestedly, "No, I have no objections."

The two thugs snickered lewdly. One of them reached out with a grimy paw and touched Betsey's breast. "Not here," the other said roughly. "Let's take her where we can enjoy her all night."

Betsey gasped, her eyes wide with outrage.

"And where would that be?" Adam asked, only faintly curious.

"We have a boat, the *Merry Madam*, docked not far from the Broken Sword."

Looking at the brutish, grimy faces of his onetime assailants, Adam could imagine just what sort of squalid vessel they owned. Somehow, after all she had done to those he loved most, it seemed a fitting place for Betsey Asher. Sending Betsey one last cold, detached glance, Adam shrugged and, turning on his heel, began to walk away. "Just don't kill her," he said calmly. "I want her to live a long time."

A ludicrous expression on her face, Betsey stared after his departing figure. Impatiently slapping away the hands that reached for her, she stamped her foot and cried angrily, "Adam! You can't possibly leave me here with these filthy oafs!"

Adam stopped and turned around. The brilliant blue eyes surveyed her coldly. He smiled suddenly, a tiger's deadly smile. "Oh, but I can, sweetheart," he said softly. He bowed with insulting disdain and began once more to walk away. Ignoring Betsey's outraged shriek, his mind full of thoughts of his wife and his dead child, he never faltered in his steps or slowed as he left the alley.

It was only when he had reached the safety of his rooms that the iron hold he had kept on himself was allowed to crack, and ignoring Jake's and Dooley's horrified exclamations, he collapsed with a groan on the sofa, every bone and muscle in his body screaming with pain. Briefly he explained what had happened, and after assuring them he would live, he dismissed them. Not wanting Savanna to find him in this condition, he staggered upright and slowly walked into the dressing room. It was too late to order a bath, but wincing from the effort, he stripped off his fouled and filthy clothing, and after pouring some tepid water from the china ewer into a matching bowl, he began to gingerly clean his many cuts and bruises.

Savanna found him thus and her heart contracted painfully as she caught sight of his poor, ruined face and the ugly black-and-blue bruises that were springing up all over his body. Fear in her lovely eyes, she rushed to him. "Jake gave me your note—it was a trap, wasn't it?" she demanded anxiously. Taking the cloth from his limp hand, she tenderly took over the job that he had abandoned.

Sinking down onto a stool nearby, Adam said wearily, "Oh, yes, it was a trap—sprung by our dear friends, Charles and Betsey Asher!"

Savanna's lips thinned and in a low, vicious voice she said, "I think I shall pay a call on Miss Asher tomorrow and tear every hair from her head—and then throw *her* down the stairs!"

Adam smiled faintly. "After tonight, I doubt that Miss Asher will want to come within a hundred miles of either one of us. Put her from your mind."

Though she was full of curiosity, it was only when he was lying beside her in the soothing darkness that Savanna ventured to question him further. "What happened, Adam? Tell me. Everything."

Adam sighed and succinctly he told her what had transpired. She was silent for a long minute when he finished speaking. Then she touched him lightly, a butterfly's caress on his battered cheek. "I'm glad you left her. It's what she deserved."

Adam yawned, flinching from the pain of his split lip. Drowsily he murmured, "My thoughts precisely."

The next morning Adam's face was enough to make strong men shudder, and viewing his still-swollen eye, puffed upper lip and scraped cheekbone, he grimaced. Sourly he viewed the many bruises on his body. Not even a hot bath had lessened his many aches, but he wanted to leave for Campo de Verde as soon as possible and, wincing painfully, he struggled manfully into his clothes.

Concern on her face, Savanna stared at him as he walked into the sitting room. Despite his elegant clothes and powerful body, he looked terrible, but he smiled when he saw her and Savanna felt a glowing warmth spread through her.

She was wearing a most becoming gown of pale yellow muslin, the lace-trimmed, fashionably low neckline revealing a tempting amount of her magnificent bosom. There was more lace on the puffed sleeves and she had woven a yellow silk ribbon amongst the fiery strands of her glorious hair. She looked adorable.

Despite his many aches, Adam caught himself wishing that her condition would allow him to make love to her, but sighing regretfully, he pushed the thought away, saying instead, "I'm going to arrange to hire a comfortable carriage for us, and if all goes well, perhaps we can depart in the morning for Campo de Verde. Any objections?"

Savanna had none and Adam left on his errand. After he accomplished his task, he returned to the hotel, and it was there that he once again laid eyes on Charles Asher.

Charles, looking none the worse for his activities last night, was talking earnestly to a handsome young man when Adam entered the lobby. Blue eyes grim, Adam stalked over to the two men.

"Good morning, Charles," he said easily. "I trust that you are feeling well after last night's escapade?"

Glancing up impatiently, Charles blanched when he caught sight of Adam, and with satisfaction Adam noticed the faint bruise on his chin. A sickly expression on his handsome face, Charles swallowed painfully and, having no other choice, said nervously, "Yes. It was most pleasant."

"And did the fair Betsey also enjoy herself last night?" Adam asked silkily.

The young man beside Charles frowned. "Monsieur," he said, looking at Charles, "I thought you said that Mademoiselle Betsey has been most grievously ill and could not see me this morning."

Before Charles could answer, Adam broke in lightly. "Oh, but that could not be! Why, I saw her just last night and she appeared to be enjoying herself hugely. Wouldn't you say so, Charles?"

Paralyzed with rage and fear, Charles could only

stare helplessly at Adam's battered features. Contemptuously turning his back on Charles, Adam said to the young man, "I am Adam St. Clair, and you must be Pierre Michaud?"

Pierre smiled politely and nodded, clearly puzzled by the situation. Glancing from one man to the other, he returned to the topic that interested him most. "Mademoiselle Betsey is *not* ill?" he asked anxiously. "She will see me?"

Again it was Adam who spoke first. He had no desire to hurt Pierre, but he also wasn't about to let Charles and Betsey regain any lost ground. Pity in his blue eyes, he said softly, "Yes, she'll see you. I believe that you will find her with her two, er, companions on the *Merry Madame*, docked not far from the Broken Sword Tavern near Girod Street."

There was a strangled croak from Charles, and Adam turned to smile at him, that same tiger's smile that Betsey had seen last night. "I'm sure," he added dulcetly, "that she will be most eager to see you."

As Adam walked away he felt regretful for the pain and disillusionment that Pierre would suffer, but also confident that when Betsey's disgrace was known, as it surely would be, she and Charles would never again be able to show their faces in decent society, and consequently, another young man like Pierre would not fall into their unscrupulous hands. Socially, the Ashers were ruined; they would be viewed as pariahs. And thinking again of his wife's brush with death and his dead child, Adam was not really bothered very much at all by the fate awaiting the Ashers. . . .

Chapter 21

$\mathbb{A}$DAM'S LETTER CHRONICLING THE RECENT TUMULTUOUS events in his life reached Jason Savage at Terre du Coeur near the end of September. The fact that Adam had married Savanna O'Rourke came as no very great surprise to Jason, nor did the pregnancy, but the news that Savanna had lost the child greatly disturbed him. Too well did he remember the pain he and Catherine had suffered when she lost their second child just after she had escaped from Davalos.

Meditatively, Jason stared at Adam's letter as he sat in his study, late afternoon sunlight filtering through the long windows of the house. So. Adam was married, was he? A rueful smile curved Jason's full mouth. And like the scamp he was, Adam had left *him* with the delicate task of informing Catherine of the news!

Catherine did not take it well. Her amethyst eyes burned with indignation after she had read Adam's letter, and since the object of her wrath was safely situated at Campo de Verde, she glared impotently at

Jason. *"Married!"* she exclaimed fumingly. "How *could* he! And to that, that *creature's* daughter!"

She took an agitated turn around Jason's study and he eyed her slender form appreciatively. Despite more than twelve years of marriage and five children, Catherine Savage was still the most bewitching woman he had ever laid eyes on, and when she was in a temper, as she was now, her cheeks becomingly flushed, her eyes flashing with purple lights, the heavy black silk hair tumbling in ringlets over her shoulders, she reminded him vividly of the little gypsy wench with whom he had first fallen in love all the years before.

Smiling imperturbably, Jason drawled, "Kitten, he didn't do it to hurt you or to make you angry. He simply fell in love and couldn't help himself. You aren't going to hold that against him, are you?"

Catherine stopped her angry perambulations and those beautiful eyes of hers suddenly filled with tears. "Oh, Jason! You know I don't begrudge him any happiness—it is just that Mama and I have so looked forward to the day he would be respectably married to some *decent* young woman, and what does he do but leg-shackle himself in some hole-in-the-corner affair to *Davalos's daughter!*"

Getting up from his position behind the massive oak desk, Jason strolled around to the front of it, and resting one hip on the corner, he pulled a rigid Catherine into his arms. Amusement flickering in his emerald eyes, he stared down into her unhappy face. "It isn't," he began deliberately, "the marriage that either one of us would have wished for him, but unless you want to be estranged from him, I think you had better prepare yourself to be, if not enthusiastic about his choice, at least cordial when you meet her. He loves her, kitten! And knowing Adam—he'll not take kindly to any slight shown his bride."

Catherine snorted and Jason said coaxingly, "Sweetheart, I know it will be hard for you, but Savanna is nothing like her father. She bears no resemblance to him in face or form and she has inherited none of his ugliness of spirit."

When Catherine looked skeptical, Jason gave her a little shake, saying persuasively, "Blood Drinker approves of her. On our way back to Terre du Coeur, he said that she was precisely what Adam needed, a beautiful, spirited woman who could match him for stubbornness and temper!" A reminiscent grin split his mouth. "And if you could have seen them together, the news of their marriage would not come as any great shock. It was inevitable!"

Catherine remained unconvinced, but she did pick up the letter again and reread it, this time her eyes filling with tears when she came to the part about the child. "They must be shattered," she said in a soft voice. A look of determination crossed her face. "We shall go to them! Perhaps, because of the loss of our own child, we can help them deal with this tragedy."

Jason relaxed, a warm light in his eyes as he gazed at his wife. He had known that Catherine would take the news of Adam's marriage to Davalos's daughter hard, but it said much of her character that she was willing to put aside her own feelings and want to help Adam's wife.

Dropping a kiss on her nose, he got up from his perch and murmured, "I shall leave the packing to you."

The Savages were not the only ones planning on traveling to the New Orleans area. At the same time that Catherine began her packing, Micajah Yates was also considering a sojourn in that fair city.

Micajah and Jeremy had lurked about Natchez for a while, hoping to get word of the mysterious stranger who had originally wanted Adam St. Clair killed. Their efforts, as well as those of Jem, came to naught, but they did pick up an interesting tidbit: it appeared that Adam St. Clair himself was currently in the New Orleans area.

The Aztec gold was still uppermost in Micajah's mind, but at the moment, he had been brought to a standstill. Without his having either the knowledge which Jason Savage possessed or the information Savanna claimed *not* to possess, his only link to the gold was Jeremy, and Micajah still wasn't precisely enamored of the idea of putting all his trust in Jeremy's abilities. It might come to that, but not before he'd given it considerably more thought—or figured out a way to once again be in a position to torture the knowledge he wanted out of Jason Savage. In the meantime, there was the matter of St. Clair. . . .

Determined for pride's sake alone to dispatch the elusive Mr. St. Clair, Micajah and Jeremy left immediately for New Orleans. Micajah had another reason for wanting to go to New Orleans as well—he figured that if anyone knew anything about Savanna's fate, it would be Bodene Sullivan. Once they had reached New Orleans, deliberately leaving Jeremy to his own devices, Micajah wasted little time in making his way to Bodene's gaming establishment.

Micajah found The Golden Lady with ease, but having reached his destination, he did not enter the handsome building. Instead he prowled around in the darkness, familiarizing himself with the place. There were only two ways into The Golden Lady, a front exit and a rear one, and Micajah immediately dismissed them as ways of access for himself. As far as he knew, there hadn't been any *recent* warrants sworn out against him, and since few of his victims ever lived to tell of his atrocities, he wasn't very concerned about being recognized as a notorious killer, but the idea of boldly confronting Bodene made him distinctly uneasy. Bodene was likely to be mighty angry about Savanna's kidnapping, and now that the moment was upon him, Micajah was more than a little worried about facing Bodene's probable wrath.

He scouted out the building again, this time looking specifically for a way to break in undetected. There were few windows on the bottom floor and most seemed to be occupied by gamblers intent upon private games, from what he could hear with his ear pressed against the heavily draped glass. Becoming slightly dejected, he approached the last window at the back of the building and, placing his ear once more to the warm glass, nearly jumped out of his skin when Bodene's voice said silkily from behind him, "You know, one of my men thought it was you lurking about out here. What were you hoping to do—hear something interesting, my friend—like where Savanna is?"

"God*dammit*, Bodene! Don't go sneaking up on a man that way!" Micajah yelped, jerking away from the window. Chagrined and uneasy, he waited for Bodene's next move, becoming even more uneasy when he became aware of the pistol that was poking him in the spine.

"Well, if you wouldn't go sneaking around my place, I wouldn't *have* to go, er, sneaking up on you. And since that little bit of business has been settled, why don't you join me in my office, where we can have a nice, quiet, *private* conversation, hmm?" Bodene murmured.

The pistol barrel left his spine and Micajah breathed a trifle easier until Bodene said softly, "I have the pistol on you—make one move that I don't like and I'll be happy to put a hole through the middle of your back. Right in front of a dozen witnesses, if need be. Understand?"

Micajah swallowed painfully and nodded vigorously.

"Very well, then," Bodene went on quietly. "We will now walk into The Golden Lady. Don't stop to talk to anyone and walk directly to my office, which is the second door from the left as we enter. Try anything at all, and it will be my pleasure, my very great pleasure, I might add, to end your villainous days. Have I made myself clear?"

Micajah nodded unhappily, wondering miserably why with Bodene he always seemed to end up in this invidious position. Once they were in Bodene's office, however, some of his bravado came back and he attempted a bluff. Turning to look at his captor, he blustered, "What the hell's going on? Can't a man have a drink of whiskey without you breathing down his neck?"

Bodene smiled coldly. "Considering what you did to Savanna, you're damned lucky that I don't kill you! And the *only* thing that is stopping me from doing just that is the fact that I don't want to dirty my hands with you—and that Savanna is safely at Campo de Verde."

Micajah felt a wave of elation surge through him at Bodene's words. It would appear that Savanna had survived her kidnapping by Jason Savage and had somehow managed to come back home again. Uneasily aware that Bodene was still looking at him with daggers in his eyes, Micajah whined, "Now, don't take on that way! I didn't mean her no harm! You know that I've always had an eye for Savanna, and I swear to you that I would have married her in the end, after I'd, um, softened her up some."

"You mean raped and beaten her into submission, don't you?" Bodene snarled softly, and the expression on his face made Micajah step backward, his shoulders bumping into the wall.

Micajah swallowed. "Well, if she wouldn't listen to reason, what else could I do?" he asked with paralyzing candor.

Bodene's fine lips curled scornfully, but the urge to throttle Micajah had left him. From days of old, he knew that there was no reasoning with a man of Micajah's caliber and he was disgustedly aware that no amount of argument could ever make Micajah see that there was anything wrong in what he had done.

Not bothering to hide his contempt, Bodene said coolly, "Forget about Savanna—she's a married woman now."

Micajah's eyes nearly started from his head and he stared back at Bodene's hard features in slack-jawed astonishment. "*Married!*" he ejaculated in a stunned voice. "But she couldn't be! No one but me would be foolhardy enough to marry such a hellcat!"

Bodene seated himself on a corner of his desk, still watching Micajah with open contempt. "I'm sorry you view the news with disfavor—especially when I have even more unpleasant news for you."

"What do you mean by that?" Micajah demanded warily.

"I mean, my craven friend, that I'm afraid you have finally run your length. You made a fatal error when you kidnapped, or *thought* you kidnapped, Jason Savage."

Micajah's eyes narrowed. "Thought?"

Bodene smiled grimly. "It wasn't Jason Savage you kidnapped that night, it was his brother-in-law—and it is his brother-in-law, who is, I might mention, a wealthy planter from Natchez, who married Savanna. You could say you even introduced Savanna to her husband—Adam St. Clair."

If Micajah had resembled a fish gasping for water at the news that Savanna was married, this new broadside had him purpling with rage, his narrowed eyes nearly disappearing inside his skull as he glared at Bodene, his fists clenched menacingly at his side. "*St. Clair!*" he said with such loathing, in such explosive accents, that Bodene was startled.

"Do you *know* Adam St. Clair?"

"No, I don't know the bastard!" Micajah bit out harshly and he was on the point of furiously spitting out his whole sorry tale when he suddenly closed his mouth with a snap. Besides the money, he now had another reason for wanting to end Mr. St. Clair's days and he sure as hell wasn't so stupid as to blurt out his plans to Bodene Sullivan!

A frown on his face, Bodene questioned bluntly, "If you don't know St. Clair, why does his very name provoke you so?"

Thinking rapidly of a way to divert any suspicions Bodene might have, Micajah forced a weak smile onto his lips. "Oh, it ain't *him* in particular," he explained carelessly. "It's just that it don't seem right that some rich dandy should come along and snatch Savanna right out from underneath my nose! I always figured that someday Savanna and me would settle down together." He sighed heavily. "Now that she's married to this here St. Clair, reckon I'll just have to put aside that idea and shake Mr. St. Clair's hand."

"I doubt Mr. St. Clair will want to shake your hand. In fact, I'm damned sure that he has every intention of putting a bullet between your eyes! Something I should have done years ago!"

"Since it would appear I'm not very welcome around here, reckon I'll just be on my way," Micajah replied testily, not liking the look in Bodene's eyes.

"Unfortunately, you won't be able to do that either," Bodene snapped coldly. "I told you—this time you've run your length. I intend to hold you prisoner, and you're not going anywhere until Savage and St. Clair decide what *they* want to do with you!"

There was suddenly a deadly, threatening silence in the room as the two men stared at each other, their bodies tense and ready to spring. For a fraction of a second they were frozen like an ancient tableau of good confronting evil, and then with a muffled oath Micajah sprang at Bodene. Even though he'd expected it, Micajah's powerful charge milled Bodene over, Micajah's massive limbs closing crushingly around him, pinning his arms to his sides, effectively stopping him from reaching for his pistol.

Swaying in a violent embrace, they fell to the floor,

Bodene's pistol flying from his pocket in the struggle. Micajah grunted with satisfaction, but he didn't lessen his hold and over and over they rolled, chairs flying and crashing against the wall as Bodene fought maniacally to escape the paralyzing force of Micajah's rib-cracking imprisonment. By sheer blunt strength, Bodene finally managed to break Micajah's hold on him, but as they fought, each to overpower the other, one of Micajah's fists struck him viciously on the chin. Dazed by the powerful blow, Bodene went weak for a mere second and by then it was too late. Micajah leapt to his feet and pulled his own pistol.

The weapon pointed at Bodene's heart, Micajah smiled toothily down at him. "Well, well, ain't this a pleasant change of events! I'll wager you never thought this would ever happen!" There was no time to gloat, however. It was obvious that the sounds of their fight had not been heard above the noise of the gaming rooms, but that didn't mean that one of Bodene's men wouldn't be knocking on the door at any second. Micajah's smile faded and, his blue eyes icy, he growled, "On your feet! Get over there and sit behind your fancy desk."

Seething with impotence, Bodene did as directed. In seconds he was tightly bound and expertly gagged.

Certain that Bodene was not going anywhere soon, Micajah put his pistol away and said, "Reckon I'll be going now. Can't say I liked your hospitality."

He sidled out the door and hurried from The Golden Lady, his thoughts bitter indeed as he realized that the man he had been hired to kill, the man he had wasted days—nay, weeks—trying to find, had actually been right under his very nose! A cold fury grew in his chest when he understood just how duped he had been, the depth of his rage growing when he realized that *everything* he had done since he had first heard that blue-eyed devil's name in

Natchez had been for naught! In Micajah's mind the list of crimes committed by Adam St. Clair against him were endless and unforgivable! Every ill, every setback, every misfortune he had suffered since the night he had been hired to kill him could be laid directly at Adam St. Clair's feet! Micajah's massive fists opened and closed impotently when he considered how differently things would have turned out if only he could have found the bastard and murdered him in the beginning. Not only would he have been many dollars richer, but his reputation as a fellow who could be counted on to accomplish the dirtiest deeds would still be intact. Adam St. Clair, simply by living, had tarnished Micajah's standing and damaged a lucrative trade for him. Not content with doing that to him, Adam St. Clair, by being mistaken for Jason Savage, had destroyed the initial plan to find the gold, and—far worse—had made a fool of Micajah Yates. Heaping further indignities on him, he had boldly stolen and married the one woman Micajah had always figured to make his own. It was downright insulting what that man had done to him and it certainly wasn't to be tolerated! A cold smile crossed Micajah's face as he went in search of Jeremy. A plan was forming in his brain and in the *very* near future Adam St. Clair was going to learn precisely why he was called *Murdering* Micajah!

The door had hardly shut behind Micajah's retreating figure when Bodene began to struggle violently against the bonds that held him captive, and though he was an unusually powerful man, Micajah had known what he was about and Bodene's actions came to naught. Thoroughly infuriated, Bodene continued to fight and twist at his bonds and when they remained tight, he tried time and again to spit out or loosen the gag, but even that proved futile. In frustration he tipped over the chair to which he was bound, crashing to the floor, he wiggled and squirmed his way over to the door. It was an awkward business, but he was finally in a position to pound against the door to his office with his feet and he could only hope that someone would eventually hear the thudding sounds above the noise of the gamblers.

While it seemed like an interminable time, it was only some minutes later when the door to his office was cautiously pushed open, and Jack Mooney, one of his most trusted men, peered inside the room. His craggy features congealed into shock when he viewed Bodene still trussed and tied like a chicken on the floor.

Leaping into action, Jack swiftly undid the gag. Heedless of anything else, Bodene said urgently, "Never mind me! Get some of the men and start searching for Micajah Yates—we've got to find him and hold him before he causes any more trouble. On your way out, send in one of the girls to set me free. Go!"

Jack didn't hesitate, and whirling away, he rushed out of the room. When he returned an hour later, it was to find Bodene impatiently pacing the confines of the restored order to the office. As Jack opened the door, Bodene's hopeful gaze swung to him.

Jack shook his head. "Nowhere. We checked every place we could think of, chased down several of his cronies and questioned them, but it's as if he's disappeared. No one has seen him, either in the city or leaving it."

Bodene cursed virulently under his breath, his uneasiness growing with every moment. "He's going after Adam, I just know it!" Seating himself behind the desk, he searched for a quill and paper and began to write, saying to Jack as he did so, "I want you to deliver this message to Adam St. Clair or Savanna, at Campo de Verde, *immediately!* Take Toby Willis with you—use a pair of my best horses—not the black—I'll need him myself later—and ride as if the devil were on your heels. Stay at Campo de Verde until I arrive—I shall be following shortly behind you, once I've made another sweep of the city. There may be someplace you've overlooked, and I want to satisfy myself that Micajah *really* has left the city and not just gone to earth." He looked up at Jack's rough-visaged features. "Adam is his main goal, but watch out yourself and remember he has Jeremy Childers with him. Leave the back way—and for God's sake, be alert for treachery!"

Jack nodded and turned on his heel and departed. Moodily Bodene stared at the closed door. He had done what he could to protect Adam and Savanna for the moment, but a deep sense of guilt filled him. If only he hadn't relaxed his guard and allowed Micajah to overpower him, then none of this had to happen! Furious with himself, he rose to his feet. He wasn't going to do anyone any good brooding here in silence. He needed to find Micajah. Thoughtfully he took out the small pistol he usually kept in his desk and carefully placed it inside his waistcoat. "Always knew I'd have to kill the bastard someday. . . ."

Late the next afternoon, Adam read Bodene's note with his features becoming increasingly grim. No more than Bodene did he trust Micajah, and he cursed himself for not having realized that Micajah could *not* allow him to live with impunity. Being the creature he was, Micajah *had* to kill him! Sitting in the back room that Elizabeth had turned over to him to use as a private study when he had offered to help her with some of the plantation's accounts, Adam frowned blackly. Having Micajah lurking about with who knew what sort of murderous vengeance burning in his heart was not precisely what Adam needed to worry about right now. At the moment, he thought bitterly, he needed to concentrate on his deteriorating relationship with his wife!

Adam poured himself a tumbler of whiskey and stared broodingly out of the window that overlooked the home garden. When he and Savanna had returned to Campo de Verde, he'd had such hopes that, despite a bad beginning and the loss of their child, they had begun to grow closer and that the day he could openly declare his love for her and have her reciprocate his feelings could not be far away. But ironically, the nearer they had come to Campo de Verde, the farther Savanna had seemed to slip from him, and the closeness they had shared in New Orleans just seemed to vanish.

There was not open hostility between them, at least not yet, Adam admitted with a scowl, but there *was* a distance in her manner, an aloofness in her attitude, a cool politeness that he was powerless to shatter. He was furiously aware of the barriers she was flinging up between them, of the way she was retreating from him, seeking some private place where he could not reach her.

Increasingly Savanna treated him like a damned visitor, he decided angrily—like some bloody *stranger!* There were times, when she would give him one of those detached little smiles and offer some polite reply or comment, that Adam came near to violence. He wanted to hit someone or smash something, to bellow aloud his baffled frustration, and yet at the same time he desperately wanted to snatch her into his arms and kiss her passionately and demand that she tell him what was wrong, what was going on in that beautiful head of hers ... but he did nothing, mindful of the traumas that she had suffered, mindful of his own part in them.

Adam had noticed that she was quiet during the ride to Campo de Verde, but he had assumed that she was still suffering from her recent tragic ordeal. He'd even used that excuse when they had arrived at the plantation and she had fallen, weeping, into her mother's arms and Elizabeth had tenderly wafted her away to the master bedchamber, which had been prepared for their arrival. It was natural that a woman would want her mother at a time like this and he had discreetly made himself scarce. Even when it was suggested oh-so-delicately to him by a stammering Elizabeth that first night that he sleep in the adjoining chamber, he had not demurred or considered it unreasonable, although he had been disappointed not to be able to share the comfort of each other's nearness as he and Savanna had in New Orleans. What he hadn't expected was that weeks later, when Savanna was in obviously blooming health, the connecting door to their bedchambers would remain staunchly locked.

His scowl deepened, his dark blue eyes icy. What sort of animal does she think I am? he wondered furiously. I'm not going to fall upon her and demand my conjugal rights the first moment that presents itself! A twisted smile curved his mobile mouth. I might *want* to, he admitted ruefully, picturing all the silken, voluptuous flesh he knew lay beneath the lovely gowns she was wearing these days. Yet just thinking about making love to his wife had its usual effect upon him, and irritably ignoring the heat pooling in his belly, he turned impatiently away from the uninspiring view of the vegetable garden. The ache to feel his wife in his arms once more didn't go away and he wondered bleakly if perhaps she wasn't wise to keep the damned door locked!

But it wasn't just the wretched locked door, although it seemed to symbolize the current situation; it was also Savanna herself and the way she deftly avoided him—or any talk of the future! Just the slightest mention of leaving for Belle Vista and Natchez, and she would smile blandly and gently change the subject. It was clear that not only was she keeping a cool distance between them, but that she also had no intention of leaving Campo de Verde any time soon! And short of kicking down the door between them and subjecting her to his obviously unwanted caresses, or tying her on the back of a horse and forcefully dragging her from her mother's home,

Adam saw no way out of his present circumstances. Worse, in his estimation, however, was the fact that Savanna never seemed to wander more than two feet away from her mother. Elizabeth *always* seemed to be underfoot! He liked his mother-in-law, but he would have happily consigned her to Hades if that would have given him a few minutes alone with Savanna.

During the time they'd been staying at Campo de Verde, he had been hard-pressed to have even *one* private word with his wife, let alone anything else! He'd patiently borne with Savanna for weeks now, reminding himself of all that she had gone through, but of late, his temper, never very good at best, was fraying badly. What the hell sort of game was Savanna playing?

Savanna wasn't playing any game at all—she was suffering more than she had ever thought possible, and she had painfully come to the conclusion that she had but one choice to make. That it was going to come at a high cost to herself, she didn't doubt, but during her restless, sleepless nights, as she had miserably viewed the situation, it had become clear that if she was ever to find any peace again, it must be done—no matter how much her heart might ache.

While Adam raged around in his study, Savanna was upstairs in her bedroom, lying on the plump, feather-filled mattress and staring blindly at the ceiling. She was steeling herself to confront Adam and tell him what she had decided.

He will probably be relieved, she told herself bitterly. After all, he had never *wanted* to marry her—it was only because of the baby that he had married her in the first place, and with the baby gone ... with the baby gone, their marriage was over. Done with. Finished.

Drearily her eyes closed, but she couldn't shut out the images that danced beneath her lids. Adam laughing at her, his blue eyes sparkling mischief; the sensual curve of his wicked mouth just before his lips would find hers; the frown he wore when he was troubled or puzzled; the crisp curl of that thick black hair across his forehead and that heart-thumping, dazzling smile of his—she had a million memories of him and they would have to last her a lifetime.

In those first terrible moments when she had awakened after Betsey had pushed her down the stairs, she had been too taken up with mourning the loss of their child to really understand precisely what it had meant, and it wasn't until she and Adam were actually on their way to Campo de Verde that the horrible truth had struck her: with no baby in the future, *there was absolutely no reason for them to remain married!* There was now nothing tangible to bind them together—no matter how kind he had been, no matter how close they had been during their joint mourning of the infant. The situation was appallingly clear to Savanna: Adam might indeed derive enjoyment from her company, he might also have, at the moment, a great passion for her body, but he did not *love* her, and since the baby had been, as far as she knew, his main impetus for taking the drastic step of marriage to someone of her background, she was positive that only too soon he would take action to free himself from a marriage he had not *truly* wanted. When Savanna had fallen into her mother's arms weeping, the tears had flowed as much because of the lost child as because of the knowledge that a life with Adam was also lost to her.

Savanna had tried to hide from it, but like a starving wolf slinking near a cabin door, those unpleasant thoughts kept creeping around the edges of her mind, sometimes darting fully into view, other times almost forgotten, but always there. . . . She knew what she had to do, if only to save her own sanity, but she shrank from taking the final step, and in her pain and confusion she kept herself aloof from Adam, not allowing herself to respond to any of the

solicitous lures he sent her way, not allowing herself
to believe that he felt anything but kindness and perhaps pity for her.... It was a horrible thought and
suddenly she could bear the situation no longer.

Savanna sat up abruptly. Rising hurriedly from the
bed, she spared a moment to glance into the cheval
glass in the corner of the large room, her mouth
twisting wryly at the elegant reflection that stared
back at her. Even Savanna would have to admit that
she was looking uncommonly attractive today—not
at all like a woman whose heart was breaking! Her
red-gold hair curled in a becomingly tumbled mass
around her shoulders, and the gown she wore, a
lovely confection of delicate lace and finest muslin in
a shade of glowing amethyst, deepened the aquamarine hue of her eyes and imparted a pearly sheen to
her skin. The signs of her recent suffering had only
highlighted the fine structure of her face, her eyes
with their long black lashes appearing larger, more
luminous, and the soft hollows in her cheeks increasing rather than diminishing her haunting beauty.

Her lips thinned and her shoulders stiffened. It
must be done. Like a warrior queen, head held high,
she strode from the room, never slacking or faltering
in her stride until she reached the door to Adam's
study. There she stopped for a long moment, breathing deeply, cursing the tears that suddenly flooded
her eyes.

Smothering back a curse that would have done a
flatboat captain proud, she flung back her head and,
without knocking, stalked into the room. "Adam!"
she said imperiously as she closed the door behind
her, "I must talk to you!"

If her husband was startled at her sudden advent
into his sanctuary, he gave no sign of it. Carefully
setting down his tumbler of whiskey, he glanced
courteously across the small room at her.

Savanna's resolve almost melted when he turned
those brilliant sapphire eyes upon her, and her heart

began to beat thunderously as she stared at his tall, magnificent form. He was undoubtedly the embodiment of a maiden's dream, his face rising darkly handsome above the starched white cravat, the Prussian blue coat fitting his wide shoulders admirably and the long, hard-muscled legs clearly revealed by the tight-fitting breeches. Her gaze clung compulsively to his chiseled features and a pang shot through her. Oh, God! I love him! she thought piteously. How can I do this?

Hideously the answer slid through her mind: But *he* doesn't love you! Her chin lifted. Of course. How could she have been so stupid as to forget?

Unaware of just how tempting, just how lovely she looked as she stood there facing him, unaware of Adam's aching need to touch her, to drag her into his arms and swear aloud his love for her, Savanna forced herself to coolly meet his eyes. Shoulders squared, body stiff, she said with outward calm, "I think this has gone on long enough—we cannot continue this way—I want a divorce!"

Chapter 22

At HER WORDS, ADAM PALED AND VISIBLY FLINCHED. HE looked away for a moment, trying to hide the furious anguish her demand had caused. Nearly reeling from the bitter knowledge that, despite all that had passed between them, she still wanted to be free of him, he stared blindly at the shabby carpet on the floor. Unrequited love, he decided, torn between fury and pain, was not something that he had ever expected to face, and the anguish of knowing that Savanna was *never* going to love him hurt him unbearably.

Every instinct Adam possessed raged against simple acceptance of her demand, and he felt an almost overpowering impulse to stride across the room and drag her into his arms and force her to take back her words. Force her to admit, once and for all, to the potent attraction that lay between them. But he could not. He was cruelly aware that compelling Savanna to give in to him would accomplish nothing—he'd been ruthlessly bending her to his will practically from the moment they had met, and it had, he conceded grimly, gained him nothing.

Adam was an intelligent man, a determined man, even a stubborn man, but he was not a foolish man, and only a foolish man would persevere in the face of such clear rejection. He took a deep, shuddering breath. Perhaps she was the wise one after all. Perhaps it would be best if they did divorce. Free of each other, they could then pick up the threads of their previous lives. A bleak smile touched his lips. Somehow he could not imagine a life without Savanna, but it appeared that he was going to have to face that particularly barren existence. Not one to linger over painful decisions, he lifted his head, and levelly meeting her gaze, he said in a voice devoid of any emotion, "Very well, my dear. If a divorce is what you want, I will not stand in your way."

Savanna had been prepared to do battle; she had been certain that he would furiously refuse to countenance such an action. Feeling very much as if the wind had been knocked right out of her, she stared numbly at him. It had never really occurred to her that Adam would submit so tamely, give into her demands without a fierce struggle, and she was left floundering helplessly in the wake of her startling victory. She also realized rather sickly that a divorce was the *last* thing she wanted, that in some twisted, *foolish* way she had hoped that she could force him to reveal his emotions. She choked back a hysterical laugh. What had she expected? That, faced with her demand for a divorce, he would fall on his knees and declare his love for her? Beg her to stay with him?

She had, Savanna admitted wretchedly, made a miserable mess of the situation and had put herself in an untenable position. But at least I know, she thought bitterly. At least I know that he doesn't give a damn about me! Why else would he have agreed so readily to a divorce? Her chin lifted proudly. The aquamarine eyes dark like the sea before a storm, she muttered, "How do we go about it?"

In that same unnervingly lifeless voice, Adam re-

plied, "I'm not really certain. I shall write to the at-
torney I use in Natchez and have him advise us." He
suddenly shot her a keen look. "Do you wish me to
leave Campo de Verde immediately?"

The question caught her off guard and she nearly
blurted out that she *never* wanted him to leave, but
holding back those betraying words, she shook her
head, stammering, "I—I didn't m-m-mean ... I d-d-
didn't believe ..." She stopped and, taking a deep
breath, continued more coherently. "It's not necessary
for you to leave this very instant! I just wanted
things to be clear between us and—and I see no reason why we cannot part, er, friends."

His blue eyes glittering dangerously, Adam crossed
the room in two swift strides and jerking her next to
his hard warmth, he crushed her lips under his. Savanna shuddered at the savagery of his kiss, her
body surging into life, her blood singing in her veins,
and hungrily she met his plundering mouth, the long
weeks since they had last made love intensifying her
craving for his touch.

She was melting into him, her fingers already
reaching to caress the dark head bent to hers, when,
just as unexpectedly as he had pulled her into his
arms, Adam tore his lips from hers and set her
roughly from him. His expression shuttered, he
growled, "From the moment I laid eyes on you,
friendship never entered my head! For such as you
and I, we can either be enemies or lovers, but never
something as tame as friends!"

He spat out the last word as if it fouled his mouth
and Savanna stared dazedly at him, her body still
tingling and clamoring for his touch even as she
sought to clear her befuddled senses. She took a step
away and with her back to him, she confessed unhappily, "Adam, I don't want to fight with you! I
cannot be your lover, and we have shared too much
to be enemies. Friendship is the only thing I can offer
you. Please take it."

Quietly Adam said, "I'm afraid that I don't understand why you think you cannot be my lover. We *are* lovers—we have been almost from the second we met. I know that the marriage was not what you wanted, but do not insult me by trying to end it because you claim that you cannot be my lover."

Oh, God, he was making it so difficult for her! How to put in words all the insecurities that ate at her, how to tell him how vulnerable she felt, how to explain how *very* uncertain she was in her position as his wife—his *un*loved wife? It was an impossible situation.

Thickly she said, "Very well, then—even you will admit that ours was *not* a love match! The b-b-baby forced the situation upon us and without the baby . . ." The pain of her recent loss swept over her and she added dully, "Without the baby there is no reason for us to remain married. Please do not make this any harder for me—divorce is the only option open to us. I *beg* you to allow us to end this unfortunate affair with dignity."

Adam stared impotently at her rigid shoulders, his emotions torn and raw, and yet . . . and yet underneath all the hurt and fury, he was aware of the faintest flicker of hope. He had felt her warm response when he had kissed her, and only a blind man could not see that she was obviously suffering— she was finding this conversation no less painful than he, and if he meant absolutely nothing to her, such would not be the case. . . . He realized suddenly that while he might have agreed to the divorce, he was not going to let Savanna go without a fight. He loved her! And he was going to make her love him!

Gently he spun her around to face him and looking down into those lovely aquamarine eyes, he felt his heart knot in his chest. He could not give her up! But too often he had brutally overridden her objections, arrogantly brushed aside her wishes, and he wasn't, if he could help it, going to do that again. But he also wasn't just going to tamely admit defeat either!

Softly he said, "Savanna, if you want a divorce, I swear I'll give you one . . . but—" He hesitated, not certain of his way. He cursed under his breath and muttered angrily, "We have done everything wrong! The baby, the marriage! Everything!" He took a deep breath, and staring intently at her upturned face, he said quietly, "Perhaps you're right. Perhaps we *should* attempt to become friends." He smiled twistedly. "I've never been a woman's *friend* before—I don't know how well the role of gelding will suit me—I have been a stallion too long!"

It wasn't precisely what Savanna wanted to hear, but she was so grateful that he wasn't making immediate plans to implement her muddleheaded demand for a divorce that she was more than happy to accept the opportunity presented. Hiding the turbulent emotions that churned in her breast, she fixed a smile on her lips and said with a lame attempt at gaiety, "I'm positive that you will make a magnificent gelding!"

He shot her a dark look. "I've said I will try to be your friend—just don't test my patience—some geldings never lose their stallionlike tendencies!"

Savanna smiled wryly. "It's difficult for me, too, Adam. I did not mean to be insulting."

Adam grimaced, his withers still badly wrung from the entire situation. Determined to change the painful subject, he walked over to his desk, picked up Bodene's note and handed it to her. "Bodene sent this to me. It would seem that our old friend Micajah has been in New Orleans, asking questions about you. He also apparently is not best pleased to discover my real identity or the fact that I am married to you."

Savanna fairly snatched the letter from Adam's grasp, their present difficulties fading in the face of a possible threat from Micajah. She read Bodene's

words swiftly, an unaccountable dread spreading
through her. She knew Micajah too well, knew how
he would feel at being made a fool of—even if it was
his own fault! And Bodene's scrawl only confirmed
her worst suspicions. She glanced across at Adam, an
anxious expression on her face. "It's clear that
Bodene feels that Micajah means you harm. What are
we going to do?"

Adam shrugged. "Until Micajah makes his presence known, I'm afraid that there is very little that
we can do! As his letter states, Bodene sent two of
his best men with this message and will soon be here
himself, for which I am grateful. The more eyes we
have, the better chance we stand of not being surprised. Other than being on our guard and keeping
our wits about us, there really *is* nothing we can do!
The next move is up to Micajah." He sent her a
thoughtful look. "You know him—what is he likely
to do?"

Agitated, Savanna took a step forward. "From Bodene's description of his reaction to learning your
name, I fear that he will try to kill you!" She came up
to him, her hands beseechingly clasping the crisp la-
pels of his jacket. Her eyes bright with fear, she said
huskily, "Bodene and I grew up around him—he is a
deadly, unpredictable man. He *likes* to hurt people.
He always has, and his reputation as a killer is well
deserved. When I was a small girl I once saw him
shoot a man simply because he did not like the poor
fellow's hat!" When Adam appeared unmoved by
her words, she shook him slightly. "You must believe
me! You were inordinately lucky that he didn't kill
you when you were his captive—and the only reason
that prevented him from doing such a thing was because he thought you were Jason Savage and that
you had information that he wanted. It was *conve-
nient* for him to keep you alive ... and it isn't anymore." Her expression of anxiety increasing with
every word she spoke, Savanna took a deep breath

and said harshly, "You must leave! He knows where you are and it isn't safe for you here now. You are too vulnerable here—we are too isolated and there's no use making it easy for him!"

Adam shook his dark head. "No, I'm not leaving you! And I have no intention of running like a dog with my tail between my legs! Besides, have you forgotten that he also has a very definite interest in *you?*" His face hardened. "I'll not leave you to face him alone!"

"Oh, Adam, don't be a fool! I have been fending off Micajah's persistent attentions for years, but I swear he means to *kill* you!"

"And do you think that I could live with myself if he were to *succeed* in his attempts to possess you?" Adam demanded angrily. "Do you think that I could ever be at peace with myself if I let him harm you?"

Savanna silently cursed Adam's misplaced concern. It was true that Micajah had managed to kidnap her, but that had been because she had, for once, underestimated him—and she wasn't likely to do so again! While she could not totally dismiss the prospect of further attempts on her person by Micajah, she was so confident of her ability to thwart him that she viewed her own peril as negligible, whereas the danger to Adam was enormous. His life was at stake!

A steely glint in her eyes, she said coolly, "At least I would still be alive. *You* would be dead!"

Adam smiled crookedly. "Then you wouldn't have to worry about a divorce, would you, my dear?"

Pain and fear and fury twined in Savanna's breast at his words, and before she could stop herself, her temper erupted and she stuck him across the face with all her strength. "Don't mock me!" she spat, an angry flush staining her cheeks as she glared at him.

She had lashed out at him too swiftly for Adam to react, and almost with astonishment he touched his stinging face where the imprint of her hand was clearly delineated. He had been like a wounded, caged tiger for weeks now, and Savanna's slap suddenly was like the cage door bursting open and all the hurt, frustration and violence within him boiled to the surface. Dangerous emotions darkened his blue eyes, and with a menacing silkiness he drawled, "I believe I warned you about that nasty habit of yours once before...."

Fear and excitement nearly choked Savanna as she stared at Adam, watching the fiercely carnal expression that crossed his handsome face, knowing that whatever restraints he had placed on himself had been unleashed by her violent action. Had she done it deliberately? she wondered, horrified. She didn't like the answer that occurred to her, especially not when he jerked her into his arms, and with a moan of half entreaty, half delight, she met his plundering mouth.

It was madness! Sheer insanity! This was the very thing that she had sworn she didn't want! To escape from his loveless power over her own treacherous flesh had been the reason behind today's confrontation, and yet, when his lips crushed against hers and his hands tightened on her arms and he held her pressed closely to his long length, coherent thought, logic, sane reasoning fled and Savanna was left with only the hungry clamoring of her own yearning body.

Hating herself, she tried not to respond, tried desperately to remember all the reasons why this shouldn't happen, tried despairingly to remember that he was only using her ... but *she loved him* and the instinctive craving for his touch was too powerful, too strong, to be overcome. Her senses reeling, every nerve in her body suddenly, gloriously alive, with a shiver of anticipation, she parted her lips for him. Right or wrong, sane or mad, as he deepened the kiss, his tongue boldly taking what she offered, Savanna knew that she was not going to deny him ... that she *could* not deny him. All that mattered was his warm mouth upon hers, his strong arms around her and his hard body pressed demandingly next to hers.

Adam had made her love him, but he had also awakened her to desire, her young, vibrant body discovering in his arms its own sensuality. And now, having been denied the sweet succor that only he could give, at the first touch of his mouth on hers, Savanna gave up fighting against the elemental needs that racked her. United together, her love for him and the natural demands of her own flesh ultimately defeated her and helplessly she moved deeper into his embrace, her arms closing impetuously around his neck.

Locked passionately together, they kissed each other with a feverish intensity for several long, mindless moments, all the love suppressed deep inside them only deepening their need for closer contact. Not even the sound of her gown tearing as Adam's impatient hands ripped it open, baring her body to the waist, impeded the frantic desire that scalded through each of them. His buttocks braced against the front of his desk, Adam pulled her between his legs, his ravenous mouth finding her hard-peaked, aching breasts, his teeth and tongue wreaking havoc wherever they touched. Savanna gasped with pleasure as his dark head moved against her breasts, the aching fire centered deep in her belly flaring higher and hotter with every kiss, every wicked flick of his knowing tongue.

Adam might have been furious and retribution might have been in his mind when he had first reached for her, but the moment his hands had closed around her arms, the instant his mouth had found hers, he had forgotten everything but the infinite pleasure of having his wife in his arms once more. Drowning in his need for her, a need that had been suppressed for so long, he was powerless to stop himself, powerless to step aside, to put her from him, all the love he felt, all his despair and anguish, his fear and fury, destroying his fine intentions, obliterating everything but his fierce need to possess her one more time. He loved her! And if he could not say the words aloud, his body would say it for him!

He never remembered ripping her gown, he only knew that the fabric was an impediment that could not be borne, and at the sight of the full, milky-white breasts and the stiff coral nipples as they sprang free of the gown, a shudder of pure animal hunger had gone through him. Blindly his lips had sought those tempting peaks, and as the taste and scent of her soft flesh filled his nostrils and mouth, the driving urge to bind them together, to bury himself deeply within her, became almost unbearable.

Trapped in his arms, her lower body held tautly against the hard promise of his manhood, her lips and breasts at the sweet mercy of his marauding lips, Savanna arched up against him, dizzy with the desire that spun out of control within her. His clothing prevented her from touching him the way she wanted to, and moaning aloud her frustration, she plucked and tore at the offending garments, wanting to feel his warm, naked skin against her hands.

Vaguely aware of what she was doing, Adam smothered a curse and in between stinging little kisses on her mouth and chin managed to remove his upper clothing—cravat, shirt, vest, jacket flying wildly in all directions. Parting from her only long enough to get rid of his boots, he jerked her back into his embrace and kissed her with a carnal explicitness that had them both trembling with the need for even more of the same. He could not get enough of her, could not hold her close enough, and, his hands on her hips, he slid her sensuously against the tightly swollen length of his bulging shaft, groaning aloud at the pleasure it gave him. There was a feral, hasty madness about all of his actions, almost as if he feared that she would be torn out of his arms at any moment—or that sanity would return to one of them.

Naked except for his breeches, with a growl of satisfaction he felt her hands moving across his bare shoulders and broad back, her nails scraping his flesh tantalizingly whenever his teeth erotically grazed her nipples. He wanted his hands everywhere on her, and heedless of the damage he was causing to her expensive gown, he roughly stripped her out of it, the garment pooling in a pastel hue around their feet.

Savanna naked in his arms was the most intoxicatingly erotic sensation he had never experienced in his life. The feel of her soft, supple flesh under his roaming hands was such an earthy delight that he was nearly shaking from the powerful force of emotions she aroused. He ached for her, ached for her as he had for no other woman. The passionate kisses, the sweetness of her flesh under his lips, the shape and texture of her lovely body beneath his exploring fingers, weren't enough anymore; the demand to sheathe himself, to feel the silken heat of her body close around him, was driving him to reckless heights.

Only half aware of what he was doing, he turned their bodies until it was Savanna's hips that rested against the desk. His hands on her shoulders, he gently guided her down onto the smooth surface, her long legs dangling over the edge of the desk, her bright hair spread out like a fiery mantle around her shoulders. Poised between her thighs, her soft, lovely body laid out before him, Adam greedily drank in her charms. From the passion-bright gleam of her eyes to the enticing thrust of her bosom and the lush flare of her hips to the tight fiery curls between her legs, she was blatant carnal temptation. Had he ever even dreamed such an arousing sight? Unable to help himself, he bent over her, his lips closing urgently over her breasts, his knowing hands stroking her belly and thighs.

Burning for him, every fiber of her being aching and eager for his caress, beneath his ravening mouth and searching hands Savanna twisted wantonly on the cool surface of the desk, her fingers eagerly finding and rubbing the pebble hardness of Adam's own nipples. He groaned with obvious delight, but, intent on further exploration, her hands slipped lower, following the dark arrow of hair as it flowed down his body until she encountered his breeches. Gently she traced the shape of his manhood beneath the fabric, her fingers sliding and caressing the hard length of him, her wandering hands inflaming them both.

It was a remarkably sensual sensation for Savanna to be lying there on the top of his desk, her legs splayed on either side of Adam's hips, the wood smooth and cool against her back and buttocks and the velvety heat of his body burning against her breasts and stomach as he half leaned, half lay, upon her. The insistent tug of his mouth on her nipples was an erotic pleasure all its own, but the trembling awareness of his hands sliding slowly up her legs to the curls between her thighs, the feel of her flesh parting as he deepened the deliberate exploration of his fingers, had Savanna thrashing uncontrollably from the hungry excitement that welled up within her. Again and again she surged up against his invading fingers, soft mewling sounds coming from her mouth, her head moving wildly from side to side as Adam stroked her to the brink of ecstasy.

Already consumed by the needs of his own body, Savanna's sweet abandonment overpowered Adam. Smothering an impatient curse, he raised himself upright and tugged open his breeches. His dark blue eyes glittering brightly from the storm of emotion which propelled him, he lifted her hips slightly and, head thrown back, eyes closing in exultation, he drove his throbbing shaft deeply within her eager body.

The intoxicating sensation of her silken flesh closing hotly around him made Adam sway drunkenly and mutter, like a joyous litany, "Oh, God! Oh, God! Sweetheart, sweetheart, sweetheart. . . ."

It was savage, primitive joining. There was no finesse about their actions—it was raw, primeval man with his woman, and both of them were too snared by the shudders of lusty delight that coursed wildly through them to wonder at this fierce mating. His hands gripped her hips, holding her firmly in place as again and again he plunged rampantly into her tight slick channel, the blind, unbridled pleasure she gave him only increasing his frantic movements.

As trapped as he, Savanna was utterly dominated by her erotic senses, thrilled by the power of Adam's lovemaking, shaken by the depth of the emotions that spiraled out of control through her. As heedlessly as he, she met every thrust of his big body, soft moans of intense pleasure coming from deep in her throat every time his shaft drove into her. Eyes closed, body straining to meet his, hands reaching wildly for him, she whirled faster and faster toward completion with every powerful thrust he made. Ecstasy, when it came, stunned her—pleasure suddenly spiraling explosively through her, startling a small, shocked scream of delight from her.

Even lost in his own carnal world, Adam heard her scream and his dark blue eyes snapped open and intently he watched her features, exulting in the myriad expressions of astonished pleasure that were revealed. The look of wonder on her beloved face pushed him to the pinnacle, and bending over her, he roughly caught her mouth with his and kissed her frantically, and pounded urgently into her, discovering for himself almost immediately that same fierce ecstasy that had overtaken Savanna. . . .

Passion spent, their bodies still joined, he collapsed

gently onto her soft flesh. Giddily savoring the tiny aftershocks of pleasure that trembled through her, Savanna welcomed the warm, heavy weight of Adam's body as he lay half slumped over her, his mouth now gently nuzzling her neck and collarbone, his hands still holding her hips tightly to him as he continued to move lazily against her. It was a wonderful sensation, but as her own labored breathing lessened, reality began to creep into her sated senses. All too soon she became mortifyingly aware of her undeniably lewd position on his desk, aware, too of how wantonly she had responded to his drugging lovemaking, and a wave of embarrassment swept over her.

Shame clawed its way up through her and she was suddenly desperate to get away from him and the memory of this savage, tempestuous mating. Her cheeks flaming with mortification, she shoved insistently against his shoulders and wiggled forcefully, her one thought to flee.

Her increasingly violent struggles brought Adam sharply back from the soft, dreamy haven in which he floated to ugly reality. Instantly, bitterly, realizing that he had done his suit no good by his reckless actions, he immediately levered himself away from her. In one swift movement he refastened his breeches and turned to help Savanna, but she would have none of him.

The moment she was free, Savanna had scrambled off the desk and grabbed up her torn and ruined gown. Not risking a glance in his direction, she clasped the gown to her, her movements jerky and frantic as she tried to put it on. Her thoughts were jumbled, embarrassment and shame making her clumsy as the fabric seemed to have a life of its own, refusing to go where she wanted it to. She wasn't even aware of Adam attempting to help her; like a wounded animal, she simply wanted to escape, and that need was so strong that with a frustrated half curse, half sob, she finally dragged the ill-used gown over her head and, not caring that it gaped open here and there, bolted from the room.

His eyes bleak, Adam stared at the doorway through which she had disappeared. The urge to go after her was strong, and he had hastily donned his discarded clothing intending to do just that when the unpleasant thought occurred to him that perhaps *now* wasn't precisely the best time to confront her with what had happened. She had been wild to escape from him, her embarrassment a palpable thing. Should he give her a chance to recover her obviously ragged composure? Yet did he dare to wait until she'd had time to think about what had happened between them? Time to erect more barriers between them?

A rap on the door interrupted his considerations and, torn between the fierce hope that it was Savanna and the cold certainty that she would be the last person looking for him at this moment, he flung open the door. Jack Mooney stood there, his rough-hewn features wearing a slightly worried expression.

"Have you noticed," Jack began immediately, "that there is a storm brewing up outside?"

Adam hadn't, and waving Jack inside the room, he shut the door behind them. Walking over to the window, he noticed that the sunlight had disappeared and that there were ominous dark gray clouds flying across the previously blue sky. A storm! Adam thought viciously. How appropriate!

Glancing back at Jack, he said, "I don't think it should trouble us too much. Have you and Toby settled in?"

Jack nodded. "Yeah. The horses are stabled and"— Jack suddenly grinned—"we just got through sampling your dinner!"

Despite his grim mood, Adam smiled faintly. "I trust you enjoyed it?"

"Right tasty," Jack confessed, his grin vanishing as he continued in a more serious tone. "Storm bothers me. I'd figured originally that me and Toby could conceal ourselves a little distance from the house— just far enough away so that, between us, we'd be able to watch the entire house, yet close enough that if Micajah or Jeremy did slip past us, a shout would bring us running. Storm'll make it difficult. Didn't want to alert that bastard Micajah that we're here, but, considering the storm and the lack of visibility it'll cause, think I'd feel better if one of us openly patrolled the house. Might make him think twice about doing anything and we'd still have the surprise of one of us inside the house. Or if you'd rather, both of us inside—whichever you'd prefer."

A crack of thunder suddenly broke the quiet and a moment later the black sky was lit by a jagged streak of lightning. As if the lightning had been a signal, the heavens opened up and heavy rains lashed against the earth. Hoping that the storm wouldn't last more than a few hours and doubting that Micajah would have formulated definite plans already, Adam said calmly, "Why don't you two familiarize yourself with the house until the rain lets up, and then we can decide our strategy for the night. If the weather is a factor for us, I'm sure that even if Micajah were lurking about, which I doubt, the rain would affect his plans also."

Jack nodded agreeably. "I'll get Toby."

Midnight came and went and still the storm raged. If anything, it had increased in violence and power, and the strong wind that accompanied the driving rain and flashes of lightning made the house creak with odd noises. The whine and snarl of the blowing shrubbery against the roof and the sides of the building only intensified the cacophony of sound, making it impossible to hear anything but the noise of the storm itself.

Jack and Toby were busy making their rounds of the house, continually, discreetly checking doors and windows. Savanna was no doubt asleep in her room, and having dined earlier with Adam, Elizabeth was at present contentedly knitting a shawl out of fine cashmere thread. Adam, feeling like a chained tiger, was locked in his study, glaring murderously at the snifter of brandy in front of him.

The savage emotions inside him matched the fury of the storm roaring outside, and taking a long gulp of his brandy, Adam was undecided whether to blow out his brains or strangle Savanna. Maybe both, he thought with a savage smile.

He was already half drunk, and while he had no real intention of harming either himself or Savanna, he was fighting against the urge to bound up the stairs and smash his way into her room. She had to be made to understand the situation, he decided blearily. She *must* realize that he loved her and that there was no way in hell that he would ever allow her to divorce him! Did she think that it was just any woman he threw on his desk and made such frantic love to? She was his wife, goddammit! He took another long gulp of his brandy. She was going to *stay* his wife and she was also, he vowed with a black scowl, going to stay in his bed!

Brandy fumes deadening his senses, intent on his own grim thoughts, the racket of the storm drowning out any warning, Adam wasn't even aware of the stealthy opening of the window behind him. Didn't hear the muffled sound as a dark figure climbed swiftly into the room and crept slowly up on him.

At the last moment, though, some sixth sense must have warned Adam and he suddenly spun around, staring half surprised, half resigned, into Micajah's contorted features, a stout club held menacingly in one beefy fist. A powerful sensation of déjà vu swept over Adam and the blind instinct for survival made him lunge at his enemy, but the brandy had dulled his reflexes and Micajah's club was already descending. . . .

Chapter 23

WHEN ADAM REGAINED HIS SENSES THE NEXT morning—at least he assumed it was the next morning, since the sun was shining—it was to find himself once again in the ignominious position of being tied across the back of a horse. The brandy he had drunk last night, coupled with the less-than-gentle kiss of Micajah's club, had given him a damned devilish headache. Gritting his teeth against the pounding ache in his temples, he tried to take his bearings.

It proved an impossibility, his view of the world being predominantly the ground alongside the horse and a slight forward and rear angle. It was apparent, however, that he was Micajah's *only* prisoner, and the blind terror that Savanna might also have met with a similar fate lessened.

He was, he guessed, in one of the many swampy areas which abounded in lower Louisiana and he caught occasional glimpses of palmetto leaves and the knobby knees of bald cypress. He also, with even less enthusiasm, caught sight of several alligators sunning themselves along the edges of the murky bayou Micajah seemed to be following and he shuddered, hoping Micajah didn't plan to feed him to one of those snapping-jawed giants.

That Micajah intended to kill him was a foregone conclusion. Adam's only confusion was the fact that he wasn't dead yet. Why was Micajah keeping him alive?

He found out several hours later when Micajah finally halted their horses where Jeremy was waiting for him. While Jeremy tied the horses, Micajah loosened the bonds that held Adam to the horse and threw him brutally on the ground. With his hands and feet still tightly roped together, there was little Adam could do but attempt to struggle into a sitting position.

Catching sight of Adam on the ground, Jeremy smiled nastily and, leaving off his chore, promptly came over and gave Adam a swift, vicious kick in the ribs.

"Seen any more snakes around, mister?" he demanded sourly, the expression in his eyes making it clear that he hadn't forgotten Adam's earlier ruse. Giving Adam another brutal kick, this one at the side of his head, he muttered, "Why, I think I saw one just now!"

Coldly Adam regarded his tormentor. "You could be right, but then again, could be *I'm* looking at a two-legged snake myself."

Jeremy started to kick him again, but Micajah growled, "Leave him be and help me get these horses unsaddled. We'll have time enough for him later."

Grumbling, after shooting a sullen look at Adam, Jeremy followed Micajah's orders and began to take care of the horses.

Propping himself up against a tree, Adam looked around, but beyond confirming that he was deep in a swamp, he had no idea where he was. He and his captors were on a narrow spit of land surrounded on three sides by a seemingly endless body of brackish water, the surface covered with scummy green growth. Tall, gnarled cypress draped with ghostly gray-green Spanish moss loomed up intermittently from the murky depths as far as the eye could see. Behind him there was nothing but the junglelike growth of the swampy forest, and he wondered grimly if this was to be his last resting place.

A fire was burning merrily in the center of the camp, and from the confident air about Micajah and Jeremy, Adam easily surmised that this was a place they were very familiar with and that they didn't expect any retaliation, either. His mouth twisted. Micajah seemed to have planned well.

Sipping a cup of coffee, Micajah walked over to Adam just then. Smiling down at him, the pale blue eyes gleaming with satisfaction, he asked genially, "Want to know why you're still alive?"

Adam shrugged. "You'll tell me when you're good and ready."

Micajah grinned, nodding his shaggy head. "Think you're a smart fellow, don't you? Tricking ole Micajah that way. Making a fool out of me. Making me believe that you were really Jason Savage when you're only his brother-in-law, Adam St. Clair." Squatting down beside Adam, Micajah took another drink of his coffee. "Can't blame you much for pretending to be Savage—I'd have done the same thing—but as for marrying Savanna ..."

His amiable mood vanished and something ugly flickered behind his blue eyes. "Now, I just can't have that! I alwus figured that me and Savanna would pair up—once she got used to the idea." He shot Adam a sly look. "Still figure it that way."

"So why am I still alive?" Adam asked coolly.

"Ah! Now that's a good question," Micajah responded evenly. "You see, you're my bait ... it was too risky to search the house for Savanna last night, but I left her a little note...."

Adam stiffened. "A note?" he said with commendable composure in spite of the fear and rage that was rioting through his deceptively lax body.

"Yeah! A note." Taking another sip of coffee, Micajah glanced around. "This here place is known as Gatorhead." He pointed to a half-rotted stump at the edge of the swamp. "Used to be a great big ole gator head nailed to that stump. Only one way into this place, and that's the way we came in. Lot of us fellows from Crow's Nest used to hide out here— Savanna came with Bodene once or twice when he'd bring in supplies. Of course, that was a long time ago, before he got all respectable and when Savanna was just a child, but she won't have no trouble finding her way."

His dark blue eyes mocking, Adam asked interestedly, "And why would Savanna want to come to Gatorhead?"

Micajah smiled odiously. "Why, to rescue you, of course!"

Adam's heart sank. But it wasn't because Savanna *wouldn't* come after him that had caused his heart to sink and a feeling of helpless anger to surge in his veins; what he feared was that she *would* come after him! She might very well want to skewer him herself, but she'd never allow even her worst enemy to remain in Micajah's cruel hands. Keeping his features bland, he replied calmly, "Which still doesn't explain why I'm still alive. You could have killed me at any time, but you didn't. Why?"

"Well, now, you see, Savanna don't exactly trust me," Micajah said in all seriousness. "She wouldn't jest take my word for it that I'd release you once she came to me—she'd want to see you, to convince herself you really were alive." He smiled happily at Adam. "She thinks I'm going to do a trade—you for her!"

"But you're not going to, are you?" Adam murmured softly, his mouth curved in a humorless smile.

"The instant you get your hands on her, you're going to kill me."

Micajah nodded, pleased that Adam grasped the situation. "Yep! I surely am! Got it all figured out."

This time it was Adam's turn to nod his head. "Seems that way."

Enjoying himself hugely, Micajah said with obvious relish, "I've been looking to kill you for a long time . . . even before you played that trick on me, pretending to be Jason Savage."

Adam's brows snapped together in a frown. "Before? But you didn't know me before then!"

"Knew *of* you!" Micajah replied smugly. "Met a fellow in a tavern on Silver Street in the spring—blond, fancy-faced dandy—and he paid me good money to kill you. Half then and half when the job was done. Thing is, you had already left Natchez to go visit your brother-in-law." Micajah beamed at him. "When you're dead I'll not only have Savanna, but I'll get the rest of my money!"

Adam had no trouble identifying the man who had paid to have him killed—Charles Asher. He took small comfort from the fact that Micajah was not likely to collect the rest of his money; Asher was, no doubt, as good at double-crossing as Micajah. His lips quirked in a wry smile. "Like you said, you've got it all figured out."

Annoyed by Adam's unruffled demeanor, Micajah scowled and, his eyes hard, he muttered darkly, "And don't forget it! Savanna'll be along directly and then you're going to be gator bait!"

Lying there bound on the ground, helpless to protect himself or the woman he loved, Adam could only pray that Savanna would discard Micajah's note . . . that she'd still be so outraged from his reckless lovemaking that she wouldn't risk her life in a fruitless bargain. . . .

It wasn't until nearly noon the next day that Adam's disappearance was discovered. No one had seriously thought that Micajah would strike so swiftly, and the assumption had been made by the others that Adam had simply gone to bed late the previous evening without seeing anyone. Even his absence the next morning was not remarkable—either he was sleeping late or he was probably busy in his study. No one even considered that he had already been kidnapped by Micajah. Bodene's arrival just before noon changed all that.

After greeting Savanna and her mother and exchanging a few hurried words with Jack and Toby, Bodene, his brow furrowed with worry, immediately went in search of Adam. Uneasy when he could find no trace of Micajah and Jeremy in New Orleans, he had ridden to Campo de Verde with a strong sense of urgency. The fact that no one had seen Adam since last night gave him a distinctly ominous sensation in the pit of his belly.

He found the note that Micajah had left in Adam's study just a few minutes later. He would have hidden it and taken matters into his own hands, but Savanna had been right on his heels, and he had barely read the message himself before she had snatched it from him.

From the moment they had entered the study, Savanna had known Micajah had already struck. Even without the note she had instantly guessed the significance of the shattered brandy snifter on the carpet by Adam's desk, and of the open window, the floor wet from the rain that had blown in by the storm. Her heart a leaden weight in her breast, she read Micajah's untidy scrawl.

In a dull voice, she muttered, "Have someone get me a horse. I'll have to change into riding gear, but I should be able to leave within the hour."

Bodene's mouth tightened. "Don't be a fool, Savanna! It's a trap and you know it!" Taking a deep breath, he said as gently as possible, "He's probably already dead, my dear. Micajah is unlikely to have kept him alive."

Savanna's bright head jerked up at that and, her aquamarine eyes blazing, she spat, *"Don't say that!* I'll not listen. Adam is alive! *He has to be!"*

"All right," Bodene said harshly, "perhaps he is, but do you really think that Micajah is going to keep his word?" He grabbed her shoulders and shook her roughly. "It's a trap, Savanna! You cannot ride coolly into Micajah's camp!"

Savanna's chin jutted at a stubborn angle, causing Bodene to swear and desperately try another tactic. "If Adam is still alive," he said sharply, "the only thing that is *keeping* him alive is the fact that Micajah doesn't have you! You give yourself to Micajah, and your husband is going to be dead within seconds. Think about that!"

Everything Bodene said made sense; she'd already come to those same terrifying conclusions herself, but she also knew that she had to take the risk: she *had* to try to save the man she loved! If Adam was alive. In order to preserve her own sanity, she had to believe that he was; she didn't let Bodene sway her. Bodene was motivated as much by cool logic as by a powerful instinct to protect her and Savanna knew that he would never let her follow Micajah's instructions. He would unwittingly further endanger Adam's life by coming up with another plan, one that would involve her remaining safely here at Campo de Verde while he rode off to save Adam. She smiled bitterly. The only problem with that plan was that Bodene had forgotten just how vicious and devious Micajah could be. Micajah would have figured on that eventuality and taken precautions, and Bodene and Adam would *both* die! The *only* chance Adam had was for her to go to Micajah! But first she had to prevent Bodene from stopping her. . . .

Her gaze fell on the heavy crystal decanter on the corner of Adam's desk. Grimly she knew what she had to do at the first opportunity. Playing for time, she said reasonably, "Very well. What do you suggest?"

Bodene stared at her suspiciously. Savanna stared serenely back.

"If you're serious," he began slowly, "you can tell Jack and Toby to saddle up the horses and see that we have the necessary supplies."

She nodded docilely. "Of course. Anything else?"

Still suspicious, but distracted by thoughts of how he was going to save Adam, Bodene glanced away. Bending over Adam's desk, he started to rummage around for some paper. "While you're doing that, I'll—"

Having given herself no time to think, Savanna had snatched up the decanter and brought it down squarely on Bodene's head. He dropped like a stone, his big body sprawling on the floor in front of the desk.

"Oh, God, Bodene," she uttered miserably as she stared down at his limp body. "I'm sorry. I'm so sorry, but I can't let you stop me. Forgive me!"

Hoping fervently that he would suffer nothing worse than a slight headache when he awoke, Savanna glanced around desperately for something with which to tie him up. Spying several pieces of tack lying near the door of the study, she pounced upon a pair of reins in the pile, then quickly tied Bodene's feet and hands. His cravat made an excellent gag.

Wasting not a second more, she hurried from the room, stopping abruptly when she almost ran full tilt into Jack Mooney coming down the hall. Smiling artlessly, she inquired breathlessly, "Did you want to see Bodene or Adam?"

Jack nodded.

Her expression regretful, she murmured, "Oh, I'm sorry. I hope it's not important, but they asked me specifically to tell everyone that they don't want to be disturbed for a few hours. Could it wait?"

Jack shrugged. "Whatever Bodene says. Guess we'll just continue to patrol outside the house."

Savanna flashed him a dazzling smile. "Yes. That's an excellent idea!"

Within minutes she had gathered up what she needed from her room and was on her way out of the house. Smiling charmingly at Toby, she walked down the broad steps and headed sedately to the barn, an innocuous basket under her arm. Once she was inside the building, her movements became frenetic as she saddled a horse and changed into the masculine clothing which she had concealed in the basket. Mindful of the patrolling men, she eased the horse out the back of the barn and stealthily led the animal into the encroaching wilderness. Nearly bursting with impatience, she mounted the horse the moment she felt safe, and together they plunged into the concealing undergrowth.

It was miles before she really believed that she had managed to escape without an alarm being sounded. If she was lucky she would have a good two- to three-hour head start over Bodene, and if she was very lucky, he wouldn't kill her when he caught up with her!

She put Bodene's eventual wrath out of her mind, and for the first time since she had walked into Adam's study today and realized that Micajah had captured him, she gave the anguished fear that filled her very soul free rein. Oh, God! she prayed fervently as her horse careened through the wilderness, please don't let Adam be dead! *Please!* It doesn't matter what happens to me. *Let me save him!*

The thought of Adam dead by Micajah's hand was nearly unbearable, and Savanna was filled with bitter, acid regret for every misunderstanding, every harsh word they had ever exchanged. If only she could have a second chance! She'd do it differently.

Pride be damned! If she got him away from Micajah alive, she'd tell him *immediately* that she loved him!

Savanna tried not to think of their parting yesterday, tried not to think that her last memory of him would be that savage, primitive mating. A tear trickled down her cheek. Would she ever know his touch again? Sweet or feral? Her heart twisted with anguish. He *had* to be alive! Knowing that if she was to rescue her husband she couldn't let terror rule her, after that one brief moment she shoved aside her fears and began concentrating on ways to outwit Micajah. There was only one way into Gatorhead and there would be no element of surprise for her to use. She never doubted that Jeremy was in on this with Micajah, and she was certain that Jeremy would be positioned somewhere along the trail, ready with the cry of some wild bird or animal to warn Micajah of her approach to Gatorhead. Once she was past him, Jeremy would then close the trap behind her. . . .

But what if she found Jeremy first? A decidedly ruthless expression crossed her lovely face. If she managed to disable Jeremy, and if part of Jeremy's purpose was also to alert Micajah of her presence, she would gain a small amount of surprise. Which left only Micajah. . . . She bit back a sob. And, pray God, Adam alive!

Heedless of the twisted vines and low-hanging tree limbs that clawed and slapped at her as her horse galloped pell-mell through the tangled wilderness, Savanna tore her thoughts away from any notion of Adam *not* being alive and focused once more on how she was going to rescue him. It wasn't likely, she admitted bleakly, that Micajah was just going to let her ride up to him—he'd know she would try to kill him. He'd also know that she would not surrender tamely to him unless she saw Adam . . . alive.

A tremulous smile suddenly curved her mouth. Adam *was* alive! Micajah would keep him so, she realized jubilantly, until he was certain she had fallen into his trap. She almost laughed out loud. *Adam was alive!*

But her joy faded when she acknowledged the nearly insurmountable task before her. She had to get Micajah off guard and kill him before he could kill Adam.

No real plan occurred to her as her mount continued its frenetic pace along the barely discernible trail, but just believing that Adam was still alive gave her a feeling of intense confidence. She'd find a way!

Dusk was beginning to fall as she approached the area near Gatorhead. Halting her horse, she stared speculatively about her. There was no sign of any human passing, no sound to guide her, merely the silent, almost suffocating press of the swampy forest. She sat there for several long minutes, trying to remember all she could of the way in to Gatorhead, trying to remember where the lookouts had been stationed when she had come with Bodene. It was an eerie place where she had stopped, the waiting silence and a green, seemingly impenetrable wall of trees and foliage greeting her, the rapidly increasing shadows giving the area an ominous air.

She took a deep, steadying breath. She had to go on afoot. She had to find Jeremy. Her face set, she dismounted and tied her horse to a small sapling.

Thoughtfully she examined the only weapon that in her haste she'd been able to bring with her: the stiletto Bodene had given her when she was ten years old. The dagger was small, the blade slender and tapering, but she knew of old the damage it could cause, and without further thought, she gripped it expertly. Pausing a moment longer to undo some rawhide straps from her saddle to take with her, she melted into the wilderness.

As silent as a stalking tigress, Savanna glided back and forth across the faint animal trail that would end at Gatorhead, every sense alert for danger. She moved with extraordinary stealth, but Jeremy was so well hidden in a thicket of young willows and wild vines that she almost stumbled across him.

Heart slamming into her ribs, she froze, the murky mauve shadows of impending nightfall making her task even harder. But as she half crouched behind a big water oak, her eyes straining to pierce the shadows, she realized that the hump some three feet before her had a distinctly human shape. Jeremy!

She swallowed. The palms of her hands were suddenly damp and sweaty. Though she had been prepared to, she had never killed a man before, and she wasn't certain she could do it now. She swallowed again, the taste of bile rising in her throat. Jeremy had to be silenced; she could not let him cry out and warn Micajah! She glanced around, searching for anything that could be used for a club, anything that would knock him out and allow her to gag and tie him up, but in the gloom she could find nothing. Jeremy would have to die, yet she quailed at the thought.

Somberly she reminded herself that Adam's life depended upon her. She had to do it! She closed her eyes, took a deep breath, and before she could think twice about it, was upon Jeremy. Her knife flashed once, and with a soft groan, he slumped to the ground.

In horrified fascination, she stared at his still body, nausea roiling in her stomach. Gagging, she stumbled away, intent on getting her horse. A few minutes later she rode past the willow thicket, her eyes averted.

Not allowing herself to think about Jeremy, she halted her horse some ten yards farther along the trail, her entire focus on a way to outwit Micajah and free her husband. Micajah was not likely to let her ride right up to him, and she remembered enough about Gatorhead to realize that there was no way for her to sneak up on him as she had done with Jeremy. She couldn't surprise Micajah. Nor could she trick him. The instant she appeared, not having heard any warning from Jeremy, he'd know that she had eliminated his partner and that she was not going to let him win without a fight. She bit her lip. So how was she going to get close enough to him to kill him?

Savanna sat there as the night deepened and the moon rose bright and full in the black sky, her thoughts racing around like a rat in a trap, trying to anticipate just what Micajah would do. He would, she deduced, make her dismount and get away from her horse. He'd also want to make certain that she carried no weapons before he let her get near him. But how would he do that? Make her strip at gunpoint?

She grimaced. It was possible. So, if she was standing there naked as the day she was born, where was she going to hide a weapon?

Unwittingly she toyed with her hair, which was fastened in a thick braid across her shoulder. A second or two passed before she became aware of the silky strands beneath her fingers, and when she did, she sucked in her breath in excitement.

A feral grin slanted across her lips. Swiftly she undid the fiery braid and spread her hair out across her shoulder. Taking the stiletto, she wiped it clean of Jeremy's blood and carefully fastened it beneath the tumbling, wavy mass with six strands of hair. It was going to hurt when she jerked the knife free, but that pain would be negligible, and if it would save Adam, she'd allow herself to be scalped!

Certain the stiletto was well hidden, yet accessible in an instant, she slowly urged her horse toward the rendezvous with Micajah. In a moment she would know if she had read the situation right, and she offered up a deeply passionate prayer that she would find the man she loved alive.

A few minutes later, the glow of firelight alerted her to the fact that she had finally arrived at Gatorhead. Her heart in her stomach, she checked the dagger once more and then calmly guided her horse forward.

She'd traveled only a short distance when Micajah said, "You can stop right there."

Savanna did so, sitting regally in the saddle, her gaze deceptively cool as she glanced around. The fire was burning cheerfully, but it was the sight of Adam, Adam *alive*, standing on a three-foot-high block of wood, that sent a flood of joy rushing through her. *He was alive!*

He was more than a hundred feet in front of her, the base of the block of wood actually resting in a couple of inches of the swampy water near the shore, but hungrily her eyes ran over him, noting with a pang the dark, haggard look on his beloved face, the wild disarray of his thick black hair. He was also, she realized with a painful thump of her heart, in immediate danger of becoming alligator bait, the significance of the placement of the block of wood and the several pairs of fire-red eyes in the water just behind it dawning on her. Even without Jeremy to warn him, Micajah must have sensed her approach and set the horrifying scene before her.

Adam, looking so worn and dear, was bound hand and foot, totally defenseless as he stood there on that narrow block of wood, staring back at her through the flickering light of the fire. A rope had been tied around the block, near the base, the remainder of the rope snaking along the ground until it disappeared into the shadows beyond the fire. Micajah was not in sight, but Savanna had no doubt that he was holding the end of the rope, and that if she made one false move, the rope would be jerked and Adam would go tumbling into the water and the gaping maw of one of the alligators whose eyes gleamed in the darkness.

Hiding the fear that clutched at her, she tried to pierce the darkness where she knew Micajah waited. Frantically she debated several courses of action, but none of her inward turbulence was apparent as she said coolly, "Get him off there, Micajah! I'm not coming any closer unless I know you're not going to feed him to the gators."

Aided by the light of the full moon, Adam watched her closely, memorizing her lovely face, his heart aching in his chest. He had hoped and prayed that she would not come, but he couldn't deny that if he was to die, he was inordinately grateful for one last sight of her. She looked magnificent as she sat there on her horse, ramrod-straight, her chin held proudly and the firelight turning her hair into a blazing mass of fiery waves. His own fate was sealed, and while he didn't fear dying, the ugly knowledge that she would end up in Micajah's hands made him strain mightily once more against his bonds, heedless of the fact that the block rocked perilously with every desperate move he made. Savanna had to be saved! He had to make her leave him before it was too late!

Never ceasing his struggles, his sapphire-blue eyes glittering fiercely in the firelight, Adam said grimly, "You've wasted your time, sweetheart. He means to kill me, no matter what you do! Get the hell out of here!"

The rope suddenly snaked taut, the stump tottering dangerously as Adam fought wildly to keep his balance.

"No!" Savanna screamed. "*NO!*"

Chapter 24

HEART IN HER THROAT, HEELS DIGGING INTO THE SIDES of her horse, Savanna was intent upon one thing: reaching her husband before he tipped over and stumbled into the water . . . and into the maw of one of the alligators half circled behind him.

Her horse had even started to leap forward when Micajah's voice rang out across the firelit darkness. *"You stop right there,* missy, if you don't want me to finish the job!" Micajah growled from the darkness beyond the fire.

Instantly Savanna brought her horse to a rearing stop. A tremor in her voice, she said again, "Get him off there! Drop the rope!"

The tautness of the rope lessened slightly, the block no longer teetering dangerously, and Micajah stepped out of the shadows. He still held the rope in one hand, and even though he was staring at Savanna, there was a pistol aimed at Adam in his other hand. A leer on his face, he murmured, "If you ask me real sweet-like, I might. Then again . . ."

Her hands clenched into fists on the reins, she said

through gritted teeth, "Micajah, drop the rope and lower the pistol, *please!*"

Micajah glanced from one strained face to the other. Smiling, he asked, "And if I don't?"

"If you don't," she said levelly, "I ride away." It was a flagrant bluff, but she had to try to gain some leverage—Micajah held all the cards.

A tight, uneasy silence spun out and then Micajah said thoughtfully, "You get off the horse, I drop the rope. The pistol stays."

It was, she realized helplessly, as much as he was going to give her. Wordlessly, she slid to the ground. Her heart racing painfully, she waited anxiously, and a second later, the rope dropped from Micajah's hand. The pistol was still pointed at Adam's head, but at least one form of danger had lessened.

Micajah, other than keeping the pistol generally aimed in his direction, wasn't paying much attention to Adam anymore; instead, his lustful gaze was traveling hotly over Savanna's body. Adam took advantage of the other man's distraction, increasing his frantic struggles to break free of the bonds that held him. If he didn't get free of the rawhide in mere minutes, he'd be dead and Savanna would be left totally at the mercy of Micajah. The image of her struggling in Micajah's arms, the thought of Micajah tasting those charms that had been for him and him alone, nearly drove Adam insane, and it was with the strength of a madman that he fought against his bonds. His wrists were slippery with blood from his desperate struggles, and with a sudden jolt of excitement he felt the faintest, nearly imperceptible give in the narrow strip of rawhide that kept his hands secured behind his back.

Micajah was smiling as he stared at Savanna, a smug, lewd smile that made Savanna shiver with revulsion. Her eyes were locked with his—she dared not risk a glance in Adam's direction. To save her husband, she needed to get within knife-range of

Micajah and, equally important, she needed to keep his attention focused on her and away from Adam. As clearly as if she were privy to his thoughts, Savanna knew that Micajah had no intention of keeping his word to free Adam. The instant he felt confident that she couldn't escape from him, right before her eyes he'd shoot her husband in cold blood ... and laugh about it. Her lips tightened and one hand strayed to the knife tied beneath her hair. Just let me get close enough, she prayed silently. Let me have a chance. Just one!

"Step away from the horse," Micajah said, the smirk on his coarse face plainly revealing how *very* much he was enjoying himself. When Savanna had done as he requested, he added, "Lift your arms and turn around."

Again Savanna did as he had ordered, her thoughts churning wildly in her mind. Would he let her get close enough to him *before* he killed Adam?

Micajah glanced again in Adam's direction and Adam froze, not moving a muscle, hoping desperately that his face did not reveal his savage elation— behind him, *his hands were free!* Micajah looked back at Savanna. "Strapping fellow you married," he commented casually. "'Course, I would've made you a better husband."

"I don't think so," Savanna said softly, and looking at Adam, her heart in her eyes, she added clearly, "You see, I love my husband very much."

Suddenly heedless of the circumstances, Adam stared at her, thunderstruck. "You love *me?*" he said hardly daring to believe his ears, the sapphire eyes darkening with some deep emotion.

This was hardly the way she had envisioned telling him, but the knowledge that she might fail, that Adam might die not knowing how she felt about him, had driven her to speak of what was in her heart. "Only you," she said passionately. "Only *you!*"

"That's *enough!*" Micajah ground out furiously. "I

didn't set this up to listen to your mawkish sentiment." As if becoming aware of something for the first time, he narrowed his eyes and, staring hard at Savanna, demanded, "Where's Jeremy? He was supposed to warn me when you showed up."

With an effort, Savanna brought her gaze from Adam's lean face and looked contemptuously at Micajah. Almost with relish, she said, "Jeremy's dead. I killed him."

To her astonishment, instead of angering Micajah, her words seemed to please him.

"Well, well," he murmured. "So you finally got your gumption up, did you? I alwus knew you had it in you, girl." He smiled hugely. "Glad you took care of that little chore for me."

Savanna's face showed her shock. "You were going to kill Jeremy?"

Micajah nodded, his earlier jovial mood apparently restored. "Surely was. You saved me the trouble."

"But what about the gold?" she demanded. "Without him, you'll never find it!"

Micajah looked sly. "Well, you see, I figure different. *You're* going to lead me to it!"

"*Me!*" Savanna burst out, plainly confused by this turn of events. "I don't know where the gold is. I never even knew about it until you and Jeremy told me! How can I lead you to it?"

Keeping a wary eye on Micajah while he was intent on his conversation with Savanna, Adam carefully hunkered down until his fingers could touch the knots that kept his feet bound. The knots seemed to be hopelessly snarled together, and no matter how nimbly Adam's fingers tugged and scrabbled about, the knots refused to budge. Fearful that Micajah would notice his actions, he gave up after a few seconds and very slowly assumed his original position, holding his hands behind his back to continue the illusion that he was still completely bound.

One of the alligators suddenly let out an angry

roar, startling the three people. The fire had begun to die down, and with the lessening of the flickering light, a huge male had become bolder and had approached within a few feet of where Adam was perched on the block of wood.

It wasn't in Micajah's plans for Adam to die just yet, and with a curse, he quickly threw several more pieces of wood on the fire, the sudden blaze of light driving the alligator back to join its mates. The night air was filled with the sound of churning water and the furious bellows of the reptiles as they fought among themselves before breaking ranks and allowing the big bull to assume his previous position in their midst. It was only when a relative silence had fallen and Micajah was confident the fire would keep the alligators a safe distance away that he returned to the matter at hand.

"I think you know more about that gold than you ever let on," he told Savanna. "Yore daddy told Jeremy that you had the golden armband. I figure if he left you the armband, he probably left you some instructions on how to find the place where the gold is hidden."

Her face white and strained, Savanna snapped angrily, "Micajah! I've told you, I *don't have any damned golden armband!* Jeremy *had* to misunderstand Davalos—or he made up the entire thing!"

Micajah rubbed his chin thoughtfully. "Nope. Talked a lot to Jeremy these past months, questioned him real close-like. Davalos told him that you had the golden armband." He grinned at her. "You and me are going to be partners."

His eyes and ears trained on Micajah, Adam still fought to free himself. Since undoing the knots that kept his feet tied together was not feasible, he was attempting to wiggle out of his boots. If he could get just one foot free ....

But Micajah was growing impatient with the situation. Savanna was so close, almost within his reach, and his entire body had responded to her nearness, his swollen shaft nearly bursting from his breeches as he stared at her. Soon he'd have all that soft white flesh beneath him. He'd teach her to forget that husband of hers. He'd show her what a *real* man was like! His breathing deepened just at the thought of what he was going to do to her, and for the moment, he had forgotten Adam, all his attention focused on Savanna and the charms that had been so long denied him. But he wasn't so far gone with lust that he had forgotten that Savanna could prove deadly to him, and, his voice thick, Micajah muttered, "Take off your clothes." A noxious grin on his face, he added, "Got to make sure you don't have any weapons. So take 'em off—all of them. Real slow. And don't try any tricks, or I'll shoot him."

Bile rose in Savanna's throat, and though she'd expected this, the thought of Micajah staring at her naked body was revolting. But Adam's life depended upon it and so, with fingers that trembled, she reached for the fastening of her breeches.

Every muscle in Adam's body clenched in furious denial. Harshly, he cried out, "No! For God's sake, Savanna, don't do it. I'm not worth it! He's only playing with you!"

Micajah laughed. "Well, now, maybe I am and maybe I ain't, but I don't think she has any choice." He looked at Savanna and licked his lips. "Either you take them off or I'll shoot him between the eyes right now. And don't think I don't know that you'd like to kill me—that's why you're not getting any closer to me until I know you don't have a weapon on you. Now get busy!"

For one wild moment Adam even considered lunging at Micajah, envisioning the feel of the man's neck beneath his choking hands, but he knew that with his feet still bound together he'd never reach him in time and that all he would accomplish would be to betray the fact that his hands were free and get himself killed, without doing Savanna any good at all. Unhappily he was aware that their only hope lay in his being able to free his feet. Adam knew that his task was incredibly difficult, almost impossible, but, outwardly stoic, he continued his struggle, the occasional bellow of the alligators keeping him chillingly aware of what even the tiniest slip would mean, aware that he must remain as still as possible to avoid falling—or worse, alerting Micajah to what he was trying to do. With grim concentration, he renewed his delicate maneuvers to get his foot free of his boot. His heart nearly stopped a second later when he actually felt his foot begin to slide ever so slowly upward.

Savanna never looked at Adam. She dared not. All her attention was centered on the leering man in front of her. A man she intended to kill. Not bothering to hide the hatred she felt for Micajah, Savanna kicked off her boots and gracefully stepped free of her breeches, the firelight flickering sensuously on her long, beautiful legs. Mindful of the need to get nearer to Micajah while he was distracted by staring lasciviously at her naked flesh, she casually took several steps in his direction.

His jaw slack, Micajah continued to gape greedily at her legs, imagining them locked around him, imagining what it was going to feel like when he was buried deep within her. He was so lost in his erotic imaginings that he was hardly aware of Savanna's actions, and she had closed half the distance that separated them before he realized what she was up to. Grinning maliciously, he drawled, "Hold it right there! I think you've forgotten something . . . like taking off the rest of your clothing."

The pistol was still on Adam, and trying desperately to even the odds, Savanna halted and pleaded, "Lower the pistol."

Again Micajah looked from one to the other, nearly laughing out loud at the expression on Adam's face.

Despite his best efforts, Adam's features were contorted by the tortured rage that filled him, and his blue eyes were flashing with a savage wrath. His big body was tensed as if for a blow, the powerful bunching of the muscles of his shoulders and arms clearly revealing how very much he would like to hurl himself upon his tormentor.

Micajah smiled at him. "Think I'll let you watch us before . . ." He glanced back at Savanna and, smirking, said, "Why not?"

He kept the pistol in his hand, but he did lower it, and Savanna felt a surge of elation course through her body. Now to get close enough to him . . .

For a moment Savanna considered rushing him, but she was too far away, and though the pistol was no longer aimed at Adam, one false move on her part would have Micajah shoot Adam before her very eyes. She had no choice.

She took a deep breath and, suddenly eager to get it over with, with one rapid motion she flung aside her shirt, standing tall and proud in the firelight, seemingly indifferent to Micajah's stare. In a sense, she *was* indifferent to her nakedness, a curiously dreamlike state having overtaken her, all her emotions and energies, every fiber of her being, tightly focused on the dangerous, deadly task before her.

Micajah was nearly shaking with excitement as he stared at Savanna. One of her breasts was totally vulnerable to his hot gaze, only the nipple of the other one peeking through the thick, nearly waist-length hair that spilled over her shoulder. His mouth was dry, his entire body quivering at the notion that she was his for the taking, and his salacious gaze traveled possessively down to the narrow waist and the seductive flare of her hips. When his eyes reached the triangle of red-gold hair at the junction of her thighs, his breathing increased dramatically and he seemed mesmerized by those luxurious curls burning against the whiteness of her skin.

Her mind curiously blank, Savanna glided forward.

Breaking his absorption, he glanced up as she came toward him and in a movement Micajah mistakenly attributed to shyness one of her hands reached up to touch the fire-bright waves that cascaded over her breast. He was enthralled by her, Adam forgotten, everything forgotten but the vision of loveliness that was approaching him. The pistol slipped from his slackened grasp and, dazed by the knowledge that he had won at last, that in seconds he'd ease the ache of his body with hers, he stumbled forward, clasping Savanna in his arms, his mouth brutally closing over hers.

Hardly aware of Micajah's fumbling movements, barely aware of his hand seeking her breast, of his rapacious tongue plundering her mouth, almost dreamily Savanna closed her fingers around the dagger. As if from a great distance, she heard Adam's cry of tormented rage, and in that same instant, the knife came free in her hand.

Micajah was not so overpowered with lust that he didn't realize that there was something strange about Savanna's easy surrender, and uneasily he lifted his mouth from her bruised lips. Eyes narrowed, he stared down at her, trying to gauge her mood.

A sudden fierce smile on her lips, Savanna met his gaze squarely and in one lightning movement plunged her dagger deep into his breast. An expression of utter astonishment crossed Micajah's features and with a soft, half-surprised sigh, he sank to the ground beside the pistol.

Even as Savanna stabbed Micajah, Adam's foot came free of the boot, and with a bellow of rage he charged awkwardly across the space that separated him from the other two. He'd crossed only half the distance when Micajah had slumped to the ground, and wearing an expression almost as astonished as Micajah's had been, Adam came to a sudden halt. It took him a split second longer to realize what had happened, and, his face blazing with frank admiration and all the love he felt for her, Adam closed the distance between him and Savanna and jerked her into his arms.

Oblivious of their surroundings, of Micajah's body on the ground, of the occasional roar of the alligators, of Savanna's nakedness, they kissed each other with a desperate, grateful abandon, their bodies melding together to form one telling silhouette against the fire. Frantic kisses were rained on faces and lips, hands urgently explored as if reassuring themselves that it was true—they were safe and in each other's arms.

It was several moments later, his breathing ragged, that Adam finally raised his head and gazed intently into Savanna's lovely face. "Oh, Jesus, sweetheart! I do love you!" he said thickly. "I've wanted to tell you for weeks, but somehow the time was never right." He kissed her again, the fiercely tender kiss of one lover to another. Reluctantly ending the kiss, blue eyes nearly black with emotion, he uttered with passionate intensity, "Before anything else happens, I want you to know that I've loved you practically from the moment I laid eyes on you—only like a damned fool, I didn't realize it."

A tremulous smile curved Savanna's mouth. His words were everything she had ever wanted to hear, a sweet flood of delight coursing through her body. He loved her! She smiled shyly up at him, her aquamarine eyes soft and glowing. "We were both fools. I've loved you for almost as long, and when I read Micajah's note, I was so afraid that I'd never get to tell you."

Unable to help himself, Adam kissed her again, hardly daring to believe that he could be so happy. She loved him!

But despite Savanna's burgeoning joy, there was still one tiny niggle of doubt, and a shadow flitted across her face. Hesitancy in her voice, she asked, "When you married me, it wasn't *just* because of the baby?"

His hand caressing her fiery hair, Adam smiled gently and murmured, "If you'll remember, I asked you to marry me *before* I even knew of the baby's existence."

"But I thought that was just because you felt you should offer it—not because you cared anything for me."

Adam's lips twisted. "I cared for you—I might not have admitted to myself that I loved you, I only knew that the thought of never seeing you again was tearing me apart." Looking wry, he added, "When I got Bodene's letter telling me of your pregnancy, I was overjoyed! Not, I'm ashamed to admit, because of my impending fatherhood, but because I was so certain that since there was to be a child, you would be more agreeable to the idea of marrying me. I was positive that when I arrived in New Orleans I could woo you, exert my reputed charm and convince you to marry me—if only for the child's sake." His lips twisted again. "You gave my pride a thorough battering, sweetheart, and when nothing I could say would convince you, I'm afraid that I let my hurt and anger prompt me into forcing you to marry me. I didn't plan it—I was just so blasted furious at you that the words popped out before I even had time to think about it."

A glint appeared in Savanna's eyes. "Well! I'm pleased to hear that you don't normally go around blackmailing people to get your way. Even though I forgive you for it, it was a dastardly thing to do, Adam."

Reaching down and handing her the shirt she had discarded earlier, he helped her into it, his expression rueful. "I can't deny it. My only excuse is that I was a driven man!" He looked at her, a look that nearly

made Savanna's knees buckle. One lean finger sliding tenderly down her cheek, he said huskily, "The
only woman I loved, will *ever* love, would have nothing to do with me. What else could I do?"

It was an odd place to be sharing these most intimate exchanges, but both of them had hidden what
was in their hearts for too long and this frightening
brush with death had made them, each in his own
way, determined that not another moment would
pass without the truth being told. Nothing mattered
to either one of them at the moment but that they declare their love for each other, and if it was done
with a dead man lying on the ground and alligators hissing and roaring just beyond the firelight, so
be it.

Half-annoyed, half-teasing, Savanna pulled her
breeches on and, giving him a dark look, muttered,
"You could have told me that you loved me!"

"Would you have believed me?" he asked steadily,
the sapphire-blue eyes boring into hers.

Savanna started to answer with a vehement affir-
mation, but she stopped abruptly, thinking back to all
the uncertainties that had beset her then. Would she
have believed him? Probably not, she admitted with
painful honesty. Confused as she had been, she'd
have viewed his confession of love as just another
ploy to convince her to marry him.

She smiled wryly. "Feeling as I did then, I'd no
doubt have called you a liar and tried to put a knife
in you!"

Adam smiled faintly, nodding his head in agreement as he helped her finish putting her clothing to
rights. "I almost told you the day I confronted you
about the baby," he admitted suddenly. "You were
sitting under that oak tree and I thought you had
never looked lovelier . . . it was right at that precise
moment that I realized what was wrong with me—I
loved you!"

"Oh, Adam!" Savanna exclaimed breathlessly. "That's when I realized that I loved *you!*"

After that, what could he do but kiss her? Lost in the world that only lovers can enter, they were completely unaware of two things: the slight, stealthy slide of Micajah's hand toward the pistol that lay next to him on the ground, and the soft thud of approaching horsemen.

Savanna's wound, while deadly, had not been instantly fatal to Micajah, and she and Adam had made the mistake of not making sure that he was really and truly dead. Micajah's face was twisted in a horrible grimace and his hard blue eyes were fixed in deadly concentration on the two lovers as his hand inched nearer the pistol. He knew he was dying, but before he succumbed, he was viciously determined to kill the man who had upset all his plans—the desire to kill Adam St. Clair the only thing that was keeping him alive. His fingers closed unsteadily about the pistol and with a last, tremendous surge of power, Micajah lurched upright and aimed the pistol at Adam.

Micajah's dreadful chuckle was the first and only clue Adam and Savanna had that he was not dead. In dawning horror Savanna stared at the man she thought she had killed. Frozen in terrifying disbelief, she watched hypnotized as Micajah slowly began to pull back on the trigger. An anguished scream of denial was already rising in her throat when a shot rang out through the night.

Incredibly, Adam was alive, his arms still locked tightly around her, and dazedly she stared at Micajah as a bloody hole suddenly erupted in the middle of his forehead and the pistol slipped for the last time from his nerveless fingers. A sound behind her made her whirl around, and in stunned comprehension she watched as Bodene calmly put away his own smoking pistol and, followed by Jack and Toby, slowly urged his horse into the firelight.

Tall and dark in the saddle, Bodene stared down a long while at Micajah's corpse. Glancing across at the two lovers, he finally said dispassionately, "Always knew I'd have to kill that bastard someday."

Epilogue

The Golden Armband

The wine of Love is music,
And the feast of Love is song:
And when Love sits down to the banquet,
Love sits long.

"The Vine"
From Sunday Up the River
James Thomson

Chapter 25

P ALE NOVEMBER MOONLIGHT FILTERED SOFTLY INTO THE
bedroom that Adam and Savanna shared at Campo
de Verde. Upon their return to the plantation nearly
two months ago, considering all the events that had
transpired, they had put off leaving for Natchez and
Belle Vista until after the first of the year. After all,
this would be a holiday season to celebrate, and
Adam had seen no reason that it shouldn't be spent
at Campo de Verde. They had done enough racketing
around this past half year, and it would be *most*
pleasant to remain in one spot for a while before em-
barking upon another journey! And while Adam was
eager for Savanna to see her new home, she would
see Belle Vista soon enough.

The decision to remain at Campo de Verde had
proved to be a wise one. Ensconced in familiar surroundings, with a doting mother and an equally doting husband to cosset her, Savanna blossomed as
never before in her life. There was a soft, contented
radiance about her these days, and if she had been a
striking woman before, she was a breathtaking one

now. Her red-gold hair seemed to shine and curl with a life all its own; the beautiful color of her aquamarine eyes seemed to deepen and intensify in brilliance, and there was a luminous glow to her skin that reminded Adam vividly of the rich sheen of a perfect pearl. Garbed these days in an expensive and fashionable wardrobe from New Orleans, the glorious hair tamed into a neat chignon at the base of her neck, Savanna hardly resembled the disheveled virago who had faced Bodene over the barrel of a long black rifle that spring day, nor the flashing-eyed vixen that had been Adam's first sight of her. And yet, despite the outward changes, Savanna was still both of those creatures and none knew better than she that there would come a day when she would need to embark upon some wild adventure with her husband.

Snuggling deeper into his embrace this particular night, she smiled as she thought about the places he had promised to take her—the wilderness trails they would travel together, the awe-inspiring sights never seen by a white woman that would be hers. She was looking forward to those days, but she was also looking forward to her first sight of Belle Vista and making the acquaintance of the rest of the family.

Within a month of Micajah's death, Jason and Catherine had come to visit them at Campo de Verde. Leaving their children with their nanny at the town house in New Orleans, Catherine and Jason had stayed with Jason's grandfather, Armand, who lived on the plantation adjacent to Campo de Verde, but they had spent most of their waking moments at Campo de Verde.

Savanna grimaced as she remembered her first uneasy meeting with Adam's sister. Catherine Savage, though slight in build, had been as regal as an empress when she had been introduced to Savanna, and though Catherine had tried very hard to overcome it, it had been obvious that only the great love she bore her brother had allowed her to speak with anything approaching civility to Savanna. It had begun as a very stiff, uncomfortable meeting and Savanna's heart had sunk. Because it would please Adam, she had so wanted for his family to accept her as his wife.

Adam had already explained his relationship to Jason, and Savanna had been fascinated to hear the tale of Guy and Rachel, and eager to renew her acquaintance with the man she now knew was Adam's half brother. She had already formed a favorable opinion of Jason Savage, and Jason, greeting her affably and with great warmth when he and Catherine had come to call that first day, had confirmed her earlier good impression of him. That Jason had seemed to unconditionally accept her marriage to Adam had made Catherine's less-than-enthusiastic greeting not as painful. But if Catherine had been politely aloof in the beginning, it hadn't taken very long for her to thaw. That same afternoon, after having been regaled with the story of Adam's kidnapping by Micajah and Savanna's daring quest to save him, Catherine had immediately unbent. Obviously any woman, heedless of her own danger, who would undertake such a perilous scheme to try to save Adam was without question *precisely* the sort of wife Catherine would have wished for him! As Jason had said, there was nothing about Savanna to remind her of Davalos, and Catherine's manner, as the day progressed, had become warmer and more friendly. It wasn't until several days later, however, when the two women had been talking quietly about the loss of a child that they both had suffered, that the real bond had been forged between them, and when it became time for the Savages to leave for New Orleans, it was with real regret that Savanna and Catherine had said good-bye to each other.

It hadn't been a very long parting, however. Since the Savages would be spending the majority of the winter months in the city, like most of New Orleans society, Elizabeth and Savanna had invited the family to join them for a celebration dinner. With gratifying promptness Jason and Catherine had accepted. Swelled by the influx of the active Savage brood as well as their parents and Jason's grandfather, the house at Campo de Verde had been overflowing.

The Savage children had returned to New Orleans with their grandfather and several servants only yesterday, Jason and Catherine having decided to remain for a longer visit with the newlyweds. Fascinated by the stories of the time Adam and Catherine had spent with gypsies and by Jason's riveting tales of his early adventures with Blood Drinker, Savanna was especially glad that they were staying longer. Two nights ago, Jason had, at Savanna's request, again told the story of the Aztec gold and, after much prompting by the others, had reluctantly stripped off his upper clothing to reveal once more the emerald-and-gold armband that he always wore on his arm. It was such a beautiful object to have wreaked such violence and bloodshed, and Savanna had stared at it utterly mesmerized. For a long time after Jason had shrugged back into his clothing, she had been very quiet, realizing that it had been the discovery of the twin of that band that had started her father down the tragic path that had led to his death. Then she had smiled at Adam. If it had been Nolan's golden armband that had brought her father death, it had been that same armband that had brought her Adam. For if Jeremy had not heard the tale from the dying Davalos, she and Adam would never have met. . . .

While Jason had dark, bitter memories of her father, he also had some good ones, memories of when they had been boys together, memories of a different Davalos, of a lighthearted young man who had been a boon companion. After the tale of the golden armband, as if aware of Savanna's brooding thoughts

about her father, Jason had made a point of recounting some of the pleasant times he had shared
with Davalos before events had twisted the Spaniard
into a vicious, soulless man, and Savanna had been
grateful to him for it. It comforted her to know that
there had been a time when her father had been a
good man, and watching the soft glow on her mother's face as Jason talked of those days, Savanna had
been deeply moved.

The slight coolness of the room made her snuggle
closer to her husband's warm body and she was wig-
gling about, trying to get comfortable, when Adam, a
teasing note in his voice, said somewhere above her
head, "Are you attempting to tell me that I did not
satisfy you earlier? That I'm already failing in my du-
ties as a loving husband?"

Her cheek resting sweetly on his broad naked
chest, Savanna smiled. Oh, he had satisfied her, all
right. He always did. During these past months Savanna had learned a great deal about the pleasures of
the marriage bed—that and the fact that her desire
for her husband was nearly as insatiable as his
seemed to be for her. She moved experimentally
against him, somehow not surprised to find that in
spite of having made thoroughly passionate love to
her less than an hour ago, he seemed to be more than
willing to do so again—if the size and hardness of
his manhood pressing urgently against her hip was
anything to go by!

She angled her head upward and dropped a swift
kiss on his chin. "Why do I have the feeling," she
asked demurely, "that *you* are the one who is unsat-
isfied?"

Adam shifted slightly, pushing her down into the
softness of the feather bed as he loomed over her. In
the faint moonlight, the sensuous glitter of his dark
blue eyes was apparent, and kissing her lazily, he
muttered, "You satisfy me in all ways, my love. . . ."

When he finally lifted his head, Savanna was

breathless and her body was suddenly thrumming
with sexual anticipation.

"The problem," Adam went on in a thickened
voice, just as if a long, carnally explicit kiss had not
interrupted them, "is that I never *stay* satisfied!
You're a damned seductive baggage and I can't seem
to get enough of you."

Savanna stretched slightly, deliberately letting her
tingling nipples rub against the thick black hair on
his chest. "And what," she asked huskily, "do you
expect me to do about it?"

"Oh, God, nothing!" Adam growled. "Just be the
woman you are and let me love you!"

He proceeded to do just that, and it was quite
some time later before Savanna drifted back to the
present. Her head was on his shoulder and Adam
had one arm wrapped possessively around her, their
legs tangled beneath the sheet, when she became
aware of her surroundings. In the glowing aftermath
of their joining, they lay there together, murmuring
the tender words that lovers have always shared.

Eventually talk of the future drifted in and Adam
said casually, "After the spring planting, how would
you like to retrace our path through Texas?" Raising
himself to stare down at her bemused features, he
said mockingly, "I have several, ah, fond memories of
that trip and would like to see if my memory com-
pares with reality." He brushed his mouth against
hers. "One place in particular appeals to me . . . the
place where I first discovered just how sweet and exciting making love to you could be. . . ."

Recalling that tear-shaped pond, the sparkling blue
clarity of the water and Adam's passionate lovemaking, Savanna was not adverse to the idea, but not this
spring. . . . A soft, mysterious smile on her mouth,
she stared up at him. "Not this spring, my dear," she
said lightly. "This spring, I expect that I shall be too
clumsy to ride all day in the saddle."

Adam frowned. "Savanna, you're the least clumsy

woman I know! Why will you be clumsy this spring?"

Gently her hand reached up to caress his lean, handsome face. "Because," she said softly, "I shall be *very* pregnant!"

Adam froze. The blue eyes suddenly blazed with delight and in a voice of awe, he asked huskily, "Are you certain? We're to have a child?"

Savanna nodded, and a quiver of laughter in her voice, she confessed, "I believe that our child will have had the dubious honor of having been conceived on the top of its father's desk!"

"Oh, sweetheart," Adam breathed, raining sweet, soft kisses over her face, "I love you more than life!"

Naturally such good news could not be kept a secret, and that morning as they joined the others for breakfast, Adam proudly made the announcement of their impending parenthood. The reaction of the family was eminently gratifying and most the remainder of the morning was spent in talking about the baby.

It was only later in the day, when, taking advantage of a particularly fine afternoon for this time of year, the two couples were strolling around the grounds of the plantation, that the subject strayed to the golden armband. A thoughtful expression on her lovely face, Savanna mused slowly, "It's strange isn't it? The way that Nolan's golden armband was the beginning of so many tragedies and yet, in the end, it was the catalyst that brought us all together?"

In varying degrees the others all nodded in agreement, and Adam's arm, which had been resting casually about her waist, suddenly tightened and he pulled her nearer to him. Dropping a kiss on her cheek, he said bluntly, "I'm not sorry that they are dead, but I can't deny that I have every reason to be grateful to Micajah and Jeremy."

A slight frown on his face, Jason glanced at Savanna and asked, "Once you had learned of its existence from Micajah and Jeremy, did you ever look for

Nolan's band? After all, Davalos did say that you
would have it."

Savanna smiled wryly. "I have to believe that those
words were simply the ravings of a dying man. Over
the years since I inherited Campo de Verde, we've
been over the house from top to bottom. Of course,
in the beginning we didn't even know of the armband's existence, so we weren't looking specifically
for it, but if he had hidden it in the house, we would
have found it. The place was practically falling down
about our ears when I first inherited it, and since
then, during renovations and what not, either my
mother or Bodene or I have discovered every nook
and cranny in the house." She smiled up at Adam.
"And during the past couple of months, Adam has
poked and prodded and tested every brick, panel
and step to see if he could discover a secret hiding
place within the building."

Looking rueful, Adam admitted, "Jason, there isn't
any place that it could be—I know, believe me!
Davalos must have been out of his head, or Jeremy
misunderstood him."

Jason's frown didn't abate. "No. Davalos wasn't
out of his head, and the one thing we all have to remember is that Davalos *did* have Nolan's band! It
was *because* he had Nolan's armband that he knew of
the gold's existence."

Savanna was frowning now, too. "But if he had the
band, where is it? Where would he have hidden it?
And why did he say I would have it?"

"Because," Jason said slowly, obviously thinking
out loud, "you have Campo de Verde. You were his
heiress and the only thing you inherited from him
was a run-down plantation. . . ." A gleam in his emerald eyes, Jason looked impatiently at the other
three as they viewed him skeptically. "Don't you see,
he said Savanna will have it—the plantation . . . the
golden armband!"

"But where is it?" Savanna demanded, puzzled. "If

it is hidden here, he didn't leave me any instructions or clues, or anything! And it's not in the house." She swung her arm wide, encompassing the oak-dotted area some distance from the house where they were walking. "And if it's hidden out here or in the cane fields, we'll never find it!"

Suddenly there was an arrested expression on Jason's handsome face. The emerald eyes narrowed. "I could be dead wrong, but it's worth a try. . . ."

"What the devil do you mean?" Adam asked, aware of Jason's rising excitement.

"I mean," Jason admitted slowly, "that when we were boys, Davalos and I roamed over these lands together—we knew every tree, every bush, every bayou. We had our secret places and we had places where we would hide our private treasures—and it just occurred to me that I might have known all these years where Davalos put Nolan's armband!"

Startling them all, he suddenly set off at a brisk pace, the others following quickly behind him. He hadn't gone far before he stopped in front of a massive oak, its thick, heavy branches liberally strewn with gray-green Spanish moss. At first glance, it didn't look any different from a dozen other oaks in the same vicinity, but when one looked closely, there was something that differentiated it from its neighbors. A few feet above the ground, in the trunk of the tree, there was a small, irregular-shaped hole where a branch had rotted off years ago.

While the others crowded around, Jason picked up a fallen limb from the ground and rather cautiously probed around inside the hole. At first there was nothing, and as he gradually dragged out half-rotted matter and the signs that at some time various animals had used the hole for nesting, his certainty faded slightly. He was on the point of giving up when from deep inside the trunk came the unmistakable clink of metal.

Everyone was instantly electrified and with bated

breath watched a few minutes later as Jason, almost reverently, pulled a tin box from the bowels of the tree. Despite its weight, there was a note of caution in his voice as he handed it to Savanna. "There may be nothing in it, you know." He pulled a wry face. "Or just some boy's memento."

Savanna smiled at him. "I know, but still it's exciting, isn't it? To think that we may have found it?"

The box felt heavy in her hands and with fingers that trembled slightly, she fumbled at the catch. Adam's hands were resting warmly on her shoulders and when the rusty metal suddenly gave, she glanced back him. It was, in many ways, a precious moment to them, not because of the wealth the golden armband represented, but because, in some odd way, it had become a symbol of their love for each other.

The lid flipped open and Savanna sucked in her breath as she stared at the contents. There was only one object in the tin box, an object that had been carefully wrapped in oilskin. She lifted it out, the box falling to the ground. From the shape and weight of it, they all knew that it had to be Nolan's armband, and yet, when the oilskin fell away and the late afternoon sunlight caressed the bright golden band, the emeralds twinkling in the golden rays, there was a moment of stunned silence as they stared at the exact twin to the band Jason always wore.

It was Catherine who spoke first. "I'm afraid that over the years I have grown so used to seeing the one on Jason's arm that I've forgotten what a glorious object it is!" Her face twisted slightly and her eyes clung to Jason's. "Or what," she said huskily, "its mere existence has cost us."

They were both thinking of the child Catherine had lost all the years before, and gently Jason drew her into his arms. Softly he murmured against her hair, "Don't grieve. It's in the past." He looked at

Adam and Savanna. "I think we'll leave you two alone for a while."

Silently Adam, his hands still on Savanna's shoulders, and Savanna, the golden armband resting in the palms of her hands, watched them walk away. It was only when the other couple had disappeared from view that Savanna turned to Adam. Her heart in her eyes, she offered the golden armband to him.

He shook his head. "I think," he said thickly, "that it rightfully belongs to our firstborn son." He pulled her into his arms, the golden armband crushed between them as he kissed her deeply. Lifting his head, he stared down into her bemused face and murmured, "What need have I of gold and emeralds, when I have you?"

Choked with emotion, Savanna couldn't speak; she could only smile tremulously up into his beloved face. He kissed her again and it was several long moments later before they became aware of where they were. Ruffling her hair, Adam admitted bluntly, "Unless you want to shock everyone by having me make love to you in plain sight of the house, in broad daylight, I think we had better rejoin the others."

Her mouth still tingling from his passionate kisses, Savanna moved reluctantly out of his embrace. Looking down at the golden armband clasped tightly in her hand, she murmured, "It's strange, isn't it? How one simple object could cause such misery and violence?"

His fingers lightly tracing its rim, Adam said, "It wasn't the object that set those terrible events in motion, sweetheart, but the *lust* for it."

Together they stared at it, the emeralds gleaming darkly in the bright gold of the band, both of them thinking of all the savage and ugly deeds that had been wrought because of it. And yet, in the end, the golden armband had been the catalyst that had united them, the catalyst that had allowed them to find each other and, having found each other, to find love.

Secure in her husband's love, their child growing strong beneath her breast, Savanna felt her eyes fill with tears of happiness as she traced the beauty of the golden armband. How odd, she thought, that in the end, the golden armband which had been the cause of so much wretchedness had ultimately given her the greatest gift of all—love.

Savanna glanced up once more into Adam's face, her gaze moving over those dearly loved features, the love that was in her eyes reflecting back from his. Yes, the golden armband had brought her love, she thought dizzily, a love as rich and precious, as enduring and lasting as the gold and emeralds themselves. . . .